PLAGUE OF MEMORY

A StarDoc Novel

S. L. Viehl

A ROC BOOK

For Frank and Gretchen Andrew,
gone but not forgotten.
Thank you for being my friend, Frank.

"We make war that we may live in peace."
—Aristotle

The Stardoc Novels

by
S.L. Viehl

STARDOC
0-451-45773-0

BEYOND VARALLAN
0-451-45793-5

SHOCKBALL
0-451-45855-9

ETERNITY ROW
0-451-45891-5

ENDURANCE
0-451-45814-1

REBEL ICE
0-451-45946-6

Available wherever books are sold or at
penguin.com

Roc Science Fiction & Fantasy

Available January 2007

TRAITOR TO THE BLOOD:
A Novel of the Noble Dead
by Barb & J.C. Hendee
0-451-46090-1

The adventures of Magiere and Leesil continue as
they journey into Leesil's savage homeland
seeking the family—and secret burden—he
abandoned long ago.

Available February 2007

PROVEN GUILTY:
A Novel of the Dresden Files
by Jim Butcher
0-451-46103-2

The White Council of Wizards has drafted
Harry Dresden as a Warden and assigned him to
look into rumors of black magic in Chicago.
Malevolent entities that feed on fear are loose
in the Windy City, but it's all in a day's work
for a wizard, his faithful dog, and a talking
skull named Bob...

**Available wherever books are sold or at
penguin.com**

ROC
Published by New American Library, a division of
Penguin Group (USA) Inc., 375 Hudson Street,
New York, New York 10014, USA
Penguin Group (Canada), 90 Eglinton Avenue East, Suite 700, Toronto,
Ontario M4P 2Y3, Canada (a division of Pearson Penguin Canada Inc.)
Penguin Books Ltd., 80 Strand, London WC2R 0RL, England
Penguin Ireland, 25 St. Stephen's Green, Dublin 2,
Ireland (a division of Penguin Books Ltd.)
Penguin Group (Australia), 250 Camberwell Road, Camberwell, Victoria 3124,
Australia (a division of Pearson Australia Group Pty. Ltd.)
Penguin Books India Pvt. Ltd., 11 Community Centre, Panchsheel Park,
New Delhi - 110 017, India
Penguin Group (NZ), cnr Airborne and Rosedale Roads, Albany,
Auckland 1310, New Zealand (a division of Pearson New Zealand Ltd.)
Penguin Books (South Africa) (Pty.) Ltd., 24 Sturdee Avenue,
Rosebank, Johannesburg 2196, South Africa

Penguin Books Ltd., Registered Offices:
80 Strand, London WC2R 0RL, England

First published by Roc, an imprint of New American Library,
a division of Penguin Group (USA) Inc.

First Printing, January 2007
10 9 8 7 6 5 4 3 2 1

Copyright © S. L. Viehl, 2007
All rights reserved

 REGISTERED TRADEMARK—MARCA REGISTRADA

Printed in the United States of America

Without limiting the rights under copyright reserved above, no part of this
publication may be reproduced, stored in or introduced into a retrieval system, or transmitted, in any form, or by any means (electronic, mechanical,
photocopying, recording, or otherwise), without the prior written permission
of both the copyright owner and the above publisher of this book.

PUBLISHER'S NOTE
This is a work of fiction. Names, characters, places, and incidents either are the
product of the author's imagination or are used fictitiously, and any resemblance to actual persons, living or dead, business establishments, events, or lo-
cales is entirely coincidental.
    The publisher does not have any control over and does not assume any re-
sponsibility for author or third-party Web sites or their content.

If you purchased this book without a cover you should be aware that this book
is stolen property. It was reported as "unsold and destroyed" to the publisher
and neither the author nor the publisher has received any payment for this
"stripped book."

The scanning, uploading, and distribution of this book via the Internet or via
any other means without the permission of the publisher is illegal and pun-
ishable by law. Please purchase only authorized electronic editions, and do
not participate in or encourage electronic piracy of copyrighted materials.
Your support of the author's rights is appreciated.

ONE

I did not often think of abducting my daughter, stealing a launch and leaving the *Sunlace*, the ensleg ship upon which we presently lived. Perhaps two or three times during my waking hours did I consider how it could be done, and only when there were no ensleg near me.

The other people on the ship never left me alone for very long.

I woke up one morning, several weeks after joining the crew, and thought myself alone until I saw the beast. It sat only a few inches from my face. It stared at me, its eyes the color of old ice, its thick pelt in the gray shades of storm-brewing skies. The beast was, like the crew, ensleg—not from my homeworld of Akkabarr—but I knew it did not like me. As I sat up, it hunkered down and made a low, rumbling sound like that of a jlorra prepared to make a kill.

"Try," I told him, showing him my blade as I did every time he came to threaten me. "I will wear your fur."

The beast rose on all fours, the hair around his neck bristling before he backed slowly away. His mate, a black-furred, smaller feline, stood watch by the door panel. The two touched noses and padded out of my daughter's room.

I rose with care from the place on the floor where I slept, and in silence scanned the area. Sounds told me that the child was taking care of her needs in the privy room. I went to check anyway. In this place, I could not take anything for granted.

Once I assured that my daughter was reasonably safe, I left her room and went to the metal box where I stored the garments the ensleg had given me to wear. I took out the blue-and-white uniform that I was obliged to wear while working as a healer, and the strap-sheaths and blades I had carried during the rebellion. Here on the ship I did not have to hide my features behind a head wrap, as was proper for women on Akkabarr, or under a mask formed by the sentient mold my husband called Lok-teel, as I had when I was vral. These ensleg thought nothing of looking upon a woman's face. I had never shown mine to so many; it made me feel naked.

"Cherijo."

I fastened the front of my tunic and clipped on my belt before I turned to face my husband.

Duncan Reever, the Terran linguist who had taken me to wife, stood a short distance away. Tall, lean, and very fit, my husband had the same golden hair and curious, color-changing eyes as Marel, our daughter.

He held out his hand. "Please give me the blades."

I curled my fingers around the hilts of the two I wore on either side of my belt. My daggers had been gifts from various Iisleg warriors grateful for my healing. I was very fond of them. Although my impulse was to immediately obey him—among my people, a woman did not argue with a man's orders—Reever had made it clear that it was acceptable among his kind for me and every other woman to question any such command.

So I did. "Why?"

"You are making the cats and the Jorenians nervous," he told me. "None of the other crew members report for duty armed with six different weapons, and I have told you before that Jenner and Juliet will not harm you."

I usually carried eight blades, not that I would volunteer such information. Reever knew enough about me.

"The ensleg will grow accustomed to my ways," I suggested, although I only meant the Jorenians. The small, sharp-toothed beasts perpetually stalked me. Them I thought I might have to kill.

He frowned. "You are ensleg, too."

My body might be ensleg, but my soul had been born on the ice-bound slave world of Akkabarr. Whatever Reever wished to think of me, I was Iisleg, one of the people of the ice.

"Weapons are not necessary here," my husband said. "We are no longer at war."

He wasn't. Each day for me was a battle against the strange, unfamiliar, and disturbing newness of my life. I also suspected it would be a very long time before the fight ended, if it ever did.

"War is like death," I said. "It comes regardless of invitation."

"It came, and it left." A faint edge colored his

tone. "You refused to touch weapons in the past. You hated them."

There, the first shot in the day's battle: Another reminder of a past that did not belong to me, a life I had not lived. It gave me another reason to dislike the female who had once inhabited my mind and body. Cherijo had been trusting and foolish enough to walk about unarmed. I carried daggers.

Why could he not see that my way was better? After all that had happened, we owed it to ourselves and our child to be on our guard. It was not as if *she* had ever given any thought to our personal safety.

I must not despise her, I thought. If not for Cherijo, I would not exist. I could not fight a memory.

Still, they were *my* blades, not hers. "My former self hated weapons. I do not. This ship is strange to me, as are you and all who serve on it." I would not plead—it was beneath my dignity to behave like some frightened tribeswoman—but I had learned to use his odd concern for me to obtain what I wished. "The blades give me comfort."

Reever's face never showed any emotion, but he would look away whenever I spoke of anything he disliked, as if he could not bear the sight of me. "Would you conceal them in your garments, so they are not where they can be seen?"

"If they are not seen, I will be viewed as defenseless," I pointed out. He was ensleg; it was not his fault that he did not understand how wisely the Iisleg lived. "A show of weapons is as much a deterrent as the use of them. These ensleg on the ship—"

"Jorenians."

"These *Jorenians* are ruthless fighters." This I knew from firsthand experience serving Teulon Jado, an enslaved Jorenian who had become the Raktar of the Iisleg rebellion. "I would earn their respect by demonstrating that I am not helpless."

"I understand your logic," Reever assured me, "but by wearing them so openly you are also frightening some of the children."

I frowned. "I am?" He nodded. "Why? They are the children of warriors, are they not?"

"They remember you as you were." He touched my face. "Please, Joey."

Joey was his pet name for my former self. He had others as well: *beloved, wife,* Waenara. I did not understand his need for so many. Had not one been enough?

I would have to consult Cherijo's journal files again.

Each day I put aside my plans to escape to learn more about the woman who had lived in my body before me. Dr. Cherijo Torin had been a Terran surgeon who left her homeworld to be a healer to other ensleg beings. From the files Cherijo had written about her life, she had also cured a plague that thought, stopped a disturbed killer, saved this ship upon which we traveled, allowed the Jorenians to adopt her, become enslaved, led a revolt and destroyed a slave depot, returned to Terra to confront her father, and cured another plague on her homeworld and two more on other worlds, before witnessing the Jado Massacre and being captured by the League and taken to Akkabarr to be sold as a slave.

Simply reading about all the woman had done made me feel weary.

If the journals were true, disaster, heartbreak, and death had chased my former self as fervently as the mercenaries wishing to collect the various bounties on her head. I felt I would be very happy not remembering a single moment of Cherijo's life. It had not been a pleasant one.

"I will wear my daggers beneath my garments." I watched the fine tension lines around Reever's mouth relax. "Someday, will these people accept me for what I am?"

"It will not be necessary." Reever sounded more confident now. "It is only a matter of time before you remember who you are."

My own past was brief and uncomplicated in comparison. I had been born in Cherijo's body after her ship crashed on Akkabarr and her mind had been erased. For more than two years I had lived as Jarn, a handler of the dead and later a vral battlefield healer among the Iisleg, the natives who inhabited the surface of the ice world. I had borrowed the name from the true Jarn, who had also lost her identity on the day my mind had been wiped clean of Cherijo's memories.

Reever and the others on this ship were waiting for me to revert back to the woman for whom they cared.

I did not believe it would happen. My friend, the true Jarn, had eventually regained her memories, but I never had. Inside my head, there was only me; my personality, my memories. I suspected that all Cherijo Torin had been had died on Akkabarr, and her passing had left behind only an empty shell for my use. That was why it was so difficult to make myself answer to her name.

I was not Cherijo Torin. I had never been.

The real Jarn had also acquired a new name for herself—Resa—by the time we met again on Akkabarr, more than two years after the crash that had so altered both of us. We became friends and joined the native rebellion, serving Raktar Teulon together. The war on Akkabarr had been long, bloody, and, at times, terrifying. It had ended only when Teulon used it to stop another, intergalactic war between the reptilian slaver Hsktskt Faction and the space-colonizing Allied League of Worlds.

Resa was with Teulon now, helping to negotiate peace between the League and the Faction. That my friends had found happiness together pleased me, but too often I missed them. They had never known me as Cherijo. They had been the most important people in my life as Jarn.

Reever had come closer, and his expression was so fierce that I abandoned my brief defiance and dropped without thinking to a respectful crouch.

He will beat me this time, I thought, closing my eyes and bowing my head to the inevitable. Daneeb, the headwoman of the skela, had warned me it would be so, and while I despised the thought of again being treated like a woman of the tribe, which was little better than a life slave, a tiny part of me felt almost relieved to see my husband act in a manner I understood.

"No." He took my hands and drew me up, handling me as he might an infant. "I will not strike you. I will *never* strike you. I am not angry with you for thinking of Teulon and Resa. The men here do not beat women."

Because Reever was a telepath, and shared a bond with my mind and body that I had yet to understand, he always knew precisely what I thought.

"I am scheduled to report for duty in ten minutes. Before this, I must take the child to where she is educated." I stared at his boots, which were black, like his garments. Reever did not wear uniforms. I would not think of my life on Akkabarr. Reever did not like it. "May I do so now?"

"I have told you, you need not ask my permission to attend to any task." He bent forward and pressed his mouth to my forehead. "I will pick up Marel after school and prepare the evening meal. Signal me if you need me."

It all sounded so bizarre. On Akkabarr men were not obliged to care for children, prepare food, or wait on signals from women. They would whip any woman who dared imagine such things, much less suggest them. Sometimes Reever's behavior made me wonder if he truly was a man.

I turned my head and smiled at the small girl who had emerged from her bedchamber. The sight of our daughter calmed me as nothing else could. "You are ready to go, little one?"

"Yes, Mama." Marel walked over to kiss her father—another morning ritual—and then took my hand.

My daughter had a curious dignity for one so small. She preferred not to be carried by me unless she was extremely weary, so we left together walking hand in hand. As soon as we were outside Reever's quarters, I released her hand, drew a dagger, and tucked the blade under the edge of my sleeve.

Marel moved to my other side and took my free hand. "Daddy didn't take away your blades?"

"He has said that I am to wear them under my garments when I am near the crew. I see no crew yet. It is mostly under my garment." I thought of what my husband had told me and glanced down at her. "Do my daggers frighten you, child?"

Her small blond head tilted to one side. "I think they're pretty and I know you feel better having them. But they scare Daddy and Uncle Squilyp and ClanUncle Xonea. A lot."

"I will never understand the ensleg." I accessed a lift and followed her inside. The lifts whirled around the outside of the ship, which was shaped like the curl of a ptar's tongue. I did not enjoy being whirled, even if I could not feel the motion, but Reever said walking through the corridors required too much time. Ensleg were very much concerned with time efficiency, yet I still did not know what they did with all the time they saved by doing things so quickly. "What are you to do at the place of learning on this day?"

"Reading, mathematics, sonic sculpture, and a biology experiment." Marel drew a child's datapad out of her satchel and handed it to me. "We're pruning the Jorenian *p'naloit* fruit clusters that we grew in the hydroponics lab."

But for the food cultivation, none of it seemed

very practical. Although Iisleg had no formal education for children, they began teaching them how to survive as soon as they were weaned. It seemed excessive to make the girl go to this school for many hours each day as well. We only had her to ourselves every sixth and seventh day.

"What about hunting, catching, and butchering game?" I asked her. "When do they teach you this?"

My daughter peered up at me. "We don't kill our food, Mama. We eat—"

My vocollar, which translated everything the child said into Iisleg, buzzed on the last word. I touched the mute switch and tried to repeat it. "Syn-the-tics?"

"Food made from organic material," Marel reminded me. "Do you remember where we get it?"

"The wall machines." Reever had one in his quarters, and there was another, larger area where many more machines were made available to the crew. "I do not much like the taste of what comes out of them." They reminded me too much of what we had been forced to live on in the last days of the rebellion.

"It's okay, Mama." My daughter grinned up at me as if I were the child and she the mother. "You'll get used to it."

"What of when we land on a world?" I asked her as we stepped out of the lift. "We will hunt then, yes?" I had so much I wished to teach her.

Golden curls bounced as she shook her head. "We do not use living things for food, Mama, and we never hunt them. Many living things are our friends."

"Friends." Another difficult concept for me to grasp. How could one be a friend to one's future meal? Still, I did not like to admit my confusion in front of Marel. She needed a strong mother to protect and guide her. "I thank you for explaining this to me."

Outside the entrance to the education facility, Marel stopped and tugged on my arm. I dropped into a crouch before her. She pressed her small hands against my cheeks before she touched her forehead to mine. I was not alarmed; Reever had told me that among Jorenians such was a show of deep affection. Sometimes my daughter did this thing; sometimes she pressed her mouth to some part of my face. Any touch from her made my heart swell with affection.

"Mama, Daddy loves you. I love you." Her eyes, so close to mine, changed from blue to a clear gray. "Please don't go away again."

"They will have to kill me to separate us," I promised, holding her in a loose but secure embrace. I saw her mouth curl down, and touched my forehead to hers. "Akkabarr did not kill me. Nor did the rebellion, or our enemies." So that she did not worry, I added, "Your father will protect us."

She nodded and buried her face against my neck.

How much I loved this little female child who I had known for so short a time. It did not matter that I could not remember her, and she had only a few memories of me. The moment they had told me that she had been born of my body, my heart had been lost to her. I did not fully understand it myself. I had never considered having a child when I lived among the Iisleg. Perhaps there was a bond between mother and child that did not require memories or explanation; a bond that no misfortune could touch or destroy.

In the oldest dialect of my people, I said, "Wherever you walk, child, shall I follow."

Someone made an uncertain sound in their throat, and I glanced up to see a seven-foot-tall blue-skinned female hovering behind us. Like the other Jorenians on board the ship, she had long, thick black hair, and solid white eyes, like one who had been blast-blinded. She could see, of course; her people's strange eyes worked perfectly.

"Healer Cheri—uh, Jarn," she said. "It is a pleasure to see you."

"Is it?" I had never met the woman in my life, so what pleasure was it of hers to lay eyes on me? I tightened my fingers around the hilt of the blade tucked under my sleeve. "What do you want?"

"Mama, this is my new teacher," Marel said.

"Thalia Adan," the woman said, flapping her hands in the complicated greeting gesture of a Jorenian. "I saw you from the view panel and thought I would come out to greet Marel." Thalia looked upon my daughter. "We are preparing to begin our morning meditation." She held out her hand. "What say we join the others?"

This Adan female was an educator. She would not hurt Marel. If she tried to, I would gut her.

You must not say such things, Reever had told me, over and over. *No one on this ship wishes to harm you.*

Perhaps it was true, but many moments in this place did me harm. Placing my daughter into the care of a stranger terrified me. I knew I could put my trust in Reever, for he had demonstrated that he would face death rather than relinquish his claim on Marel. No one else had yet proven to be worthy of my confidence.

There were also the duties to which I had been assigned. My supervisor would not schedule my shifts so that I could remain outside the education facility while Marel was being taught. Even when my off-duty time coincided with her hours of attendance, Reever would not permit me to stand watch.

My daughter squeezed my hand. "I'll be all right, Mama."

I took in a deep breath, bent, and rubbed my cheek against her soft one in the brief Iisleg gesture for affection. "If your father does not come for you, signal me at once."

She would not signal, I thought as I watched her take the female's large blue hand and walk with her into the entrance. Reever was never late.

Once the door panel closed, I made myself return to the lift and take it to the seventh level, where Medical Bay was located. Reever had told me that the *Sunlace* had been badly damaged during the Jado Massacre and that much renovation had been done to repair as well as improve the ship. He had warned me that Medical, which had been expanded, upgraded, and retrofitted with all manner of ensleg technology, might appear strange to me.

Nothing on this ship seemed familiar, new or old. Some areas of the ship, like Medical, were now restricted or duty-access-only areas. I walked up to the access panel and stood before the scanner.

"Healer Jarn, reporting for duty," I said as it swept a greenish-blue light over my face.

"Repeat ID," a drone voice asked from the panel.

"Healer J—" I stopped and sighed. No one had yet reprogrammed the database to accept my name. "Healer Cherijo, reporting for duty."

"Welcome, Dr. Torin," the panel said as it opened for me.

"I am *not* Dr. Torin," I muttered as I strode past it.

Coming here to work with the ill and injured was another in my many daily skirmishes with my former self's life. My expertise lay in treating patients on the field of battle, where they had fallen, or in our field hospital at battalion command, where those who could be safely transported were evacuated. Providing first aid while pulse fire screamed over my head had been nothing unusual for me, nor had performing emergency surgery behind a line of rebels as they held back the advancing Toskald infantry.

Here the cleanliness was blinding, and the silence deafening. Everyone wore the same type of uniform, so I could not tell who was friend or enemy.

"Good morning, Healer." A Jorenian nurse whose name I could not remember stopped and, as Thalia had, made hand motions at me. Reever said it was part of their language.

"Nurse." I did not respond in kind, for Iisleg only made such hand and finger gestures as obscenities or to mark a death curse on an enemy. Also, I felt certain that my hands would not move in such ways. "Will you aid me with rounds?"

The nurse's smile faded. "Senior Healer Squilyp wishes to speak with you before you begin your shift. He is waiting for you in his office."

I went to the Senior Healer's private chamber and buzzed the panel chime. It opened and I walked in.

"Good morning, Doctor." Squilyp did not call me Jarn or Cherijo. He appeared to be entering information on his console and did not look up at me. "I'll be with you in a moment. Sit down, please."

Sitting was another thing these people did; so frequently that I often wondered why they did not have calluses on their buttocks. Iisleg women did not sit; they crouched or stood. I lowered myself into the only comfortable chair in his office, a rigid-backed curl of alloy with little cushioning.

Senior Healer Squilyp was an Omorr, not a Jorenian, so he appeared radically different compared to most of the crew. He was a little taller than Reever, and humanoid, with a dark pink dermis and bald cranial case. He had four limbs like a Terran, but the three that had very dexterous, sensitive membranes on the ends were used as hands. The fourth had a much broader base and served as the Omorr's only leg.

I liked the Omorr's dark eyes, which like his manner were sharp and direct. I did not have to interpret any shifting gazes or surreptitious looks from this male. I also found the long, thin white appendages that formed a beard around his oral cavity and on the lower half of his face rather mesmerizing. Called gildrells, they each measured a meter long, were prehensile, and were used mainly as extra "fingers." It was by close observation of these gildrells that I had learned to read Squilyp's moods. When he was busy, they were busy. When he was feeling pleasant, they were relaxed. When he was unhappy or angry, they turned stiff and straight.

This morning Squilyp's gildrells were as icicles. *I did something wrong again.*

During my time working in Medical Bay I had learned that the Omorr disliked being interrupted with a lot of unsolicited questions, so I held my tongue and waited in silence for him to complete his data entry and address me.

"Stop doing that," he said as his membranes sped across the console keypad.

I looked down at myself. "What am I doing?"

"Behaving as if I mean to—"

My vocollar did not translate the final words he used. "I do not understand your meaning. Please restate in terms that can be translated by the device around my neck."

"Never mind." Squilyp shut off his console and at last looked at me. "Have you considered relearning Jorenian? It would make communicating with you easier for the rest of us."

I did not wish to learn the language of the large blue people. The vocollar functioned adequately, and I had too many other things to learn.

"I speak Terran," I said in the same language. "I will use it instead of Iisleg." I often did while in Medical, for there were not many Iisleg words for matters and materials involved in healing.

He shook his head. "The Terran you speak is corrupted by Toskaldi and outdated. It will not suffice. You should relearn Jorenian."

"I never learned Jorenian, Senior Healer." Dr. Cherijo Torin had, and I was so sick of hearing about her many perfections that I could happily thrust a dagger into my own chest to prevent her from ever returning and seizing control of my body. I rose from the chair. "I will speak to Reever about teaching me." My husband was the ship's linguist; it was his job to ensure everyone understood each other. "I may attend to the patients now?"

"No, that is not all I have to say." He stood and handed me a chart. "Please explain this entry you made during your last shift."

I scanned the contents of the chart display. "I examined Dapvea Adan and checked his stumps. I explained to him why his crushed limbs could not be regenerated by your machines. The male was adamant in his refusal of prosthetic replacements. Everything is as I noted it here."

"You recommended killing the patient," Squilyp said through stiff gildrells.

"I made no such recommendation." I had killed for food, of course, and once to prevent a Toskald from assassinating Teulon, but I did not kill people or advise anyone else do so. Before and during the war I had disguised myself and pretended to be a creature of Iisleg divine myth called a vral in order to deliver men from death.

The color of the Omorr's facial skin darkened. "Consult your end notes again, please."

I consulted them. "I wrote that the patient made a request for his Speaker, whatever that is, and the means with which to self-terminate. This is simply a record of his requests." I handed the chart back to him. "I do not see the problem."

He took the chart. "You would permit Dapvea Adan to commit suicide because he is now a paraplegic?"

"It is my understanding that the right to self-terminate is protected and enforced by Jorenian custom, whatever the condition of the body," I said. "Was I instructed incorrectly on this subject by the ship's protocol officer?"

"No, you were not." Squilyp sat down and looked through the viewer panel at the patients in the surgical ward. "Suicide was an accepted practice among the Iisleg, I take it?"

"There were circumstances when it was deemed appropriate to give oneself to the ice." I had never agreed with it, as I had not agreed with the Jorenian amputee's request, but it was not my place to question a male's resolution. It was not something a woman of the tribe did.

His gildrells snarled for a moment. "Life is precious, Doctor. Never more so than after so many lives were wasted by war."

Akkabarr's rebellion had ended the war between the League and the Hsktskt Faction, and I was proud that I had, in my small way, contributed to resolution. Reever had told me that most of the inhabited worlds supporting both sides of the galactic war were pleased to see an end to the aggressions. I also understood that this initial peace effort was a fragile thing. One error might destroy it.

"There has to be a way," he was saying.

I did not wish to interrupt his conversation with himself, but I wanted to go to work. "Senior Healer, I will gladly correct the mistake I made with this patient's chart, but you must be more detailed as to how I should do that."

"Once I saw you threaten to kill yourself along with a suicidal patient," Squilyp said. "You did it to make him realize what an enormous waste it was, to discard his life so readily." He moved things on the top of his console, aligning their edges. "It was a moment in which my admiration for you went from grudging to monumental."

He was speaking of her, not me. He admired her, not me. *He does not know me.* "I regret that I am not that person, Senior Healer." Cherijo was dead. When would they accept this and permit me to be Jarn?

"I try to remember that, Doctor, but it is difficult. When I look at you, I . . ." He would not finish the sentence.

I had hoped that our mutual skills would form the basis of some alliance. I had no true friends on this ship. But just like the others, Squilyp was so enamored of my former self that he was not interested in befriending me.

Suddenly I was tired of it. "If my presence is proving this painful, perhaps I should request reassignment. You have adequate medical staff, and there are other things I may do." Things like adequately guard my child.

He sat straight up and gave me an outraged look. "You will request no such thing."

I had no desire to challenge his authority. At the same time, I could not work for the man if he could not accept who I was. It was difficult to know what to say. "Senior Healer, I know there are nuances to customs and practices among you ensleg, but obviously I do not know them. I am not a telepath, as my husband is. If I am in need of remedial instruction or special guidance, I ask that you provide it so that I may better serve." There, that sounded almost humble.

"You were never like this," he muttered. "Never. You were brilliant and headstrong and so quick to act I thought you might someday drive me insane." At my blank look, he added, "Forgive me. I speak of your former self. In all the years that I knew her, I followed her lead. *She* taught *me*. Now . . ."

"You might repay her by providing some guidance for me," I suggested.

He seemed surprised, and then nodded slowly. "In the future, if Dapvea or any patient expresses a desire to self-terminate, please do not note it on the chart, but relay it to me privately. It is an old Jorenian custom, one that we are obliged to honor, but I wish to discourage it. I know this is a confusing request, but life is a finite resource. We cannot squander it."

I did not have to understand the reasons he had for giving me an order. I only had to know precisely that which he wanted me to do. "It will be as you wish."

"Excellent." He picked up a medical scanner and

came from behind the desk. Due to their singular lower limb, Omorr hopped rather than walked, but he had a very graceful bounce. "We shall conduct rounds together this morning, and then convince Dapvea Adan that wearing prostheses is more desirable than killing himself."

TWO

Rounds in the *Sunlace*'s Medical Bay were not very different from those I had performed in the battlefield hospitals on Akkabarr. It was true that the patients were kept much cleaner, and their surroundings even more so. Ensleg technology and medicines proved much better than what we had been able to salvage from the wreck stores, and the nursing staff worked without fear of male retribution. No one on the ship suffered from malnutrition, snowbite, or fleshrot, as so many of my people had during the rebellion. Still, the sick and injured here were not healed by any magic means. Here as on Akkabarr they needed constant monitoring and evaluation of their conditions, which required Squilyp and me to examine them daily.

Our inpatient ward held four patients, and we went to evaluate the youngest first.

"Knofki Adan," I read from his chart before I looked at his smiling face. "How do you feel this morning?"

"I am well, Healer Cherijo." Like Marel's teacher Thalia, Knofki was not a Torin, but one of House-Clan Adan, which had sent several of its people to serve as crew for the *Sunlace*. The Adan were allying themselves with the Torin for some reason too complicated and Jorenian for me to fathom.

The boy fidgeted too much for my liking. "Why do you squirm like that?"

Knofki went still and grimaced. "My new toes itch."

Our youngest patient had been involved in an engineering accident that had also injured our other three patients. The young male had been visiting his father, one of the ship's senior engineers, to watch him at work. This was some sort of thing the Jorenians did to expose their young ones to various occupations. A work crew had been refitting the shell on a large piece of equipment and had not judged the weight correctly. The hoisting equipment had failed, causing the shell to fall atop those observing from the deck.

The edge of the shell hitting the deck had neatly amputated five of the six toes on Knofki's right foot, which had been directly under it. Fortunately the boy's sire had jerked him back at the last moment, or he might have been cut in two.

"Nurse, please remove the dressing," Squilyp said to the Jorenian female attending to the boy. I gave the Senior Healer the chart and took Knofki's vitals, which were at acceptable levels. "Have you tried to move your toes, ClanSon Adan?"

Knofki nodded. "That makes the itching stop."

I examined the foot when the nurse clipped away the last of the gauze strips covering it. The boy's severed toes had been crushed by the falling shell, too badly to consider reattachment and regeneration therapy. Instead, we had used bone, nerve, ligament, muscle, and dermal grafts grown from Knofki's own cells to fashion him five new toes. I had offered to perform the delicate surgery to attach the new toes, but the Senior Healer had elected to do it himself. I had the impression that he didn't yet trust me enough to let me use the equipment in the surgical suite.

"Have you felt any pain or lack of sensation?" Squilyp asked the boy as he inspected the foot.

"No, Senior Healer." Knofki tried to remain still. "It only itches."

"Bring some dermal emollient," I told the nurse. I took the boy's foot in my hand and tested each toe. "He heals well. We should splint the foot and permit him to try walking on it." I noted the boy's delighted grin. More was itching than his foot, I imagined. Had I been ten years old, I would not have wished to spend every waking hour in a berth and endure being prodded and poked by healers and nurses.

"I disagree," the Omorr said. "It has only been two weeks since the attachment surgery. Too much weight on the foot could cause the internal tissues to tear."

"Not if it is properly bandaged and supported," I said. "His circulation will not further improve without proper exercise."

Squilyp appeared ready to argue the point, and then he looked down at the boy. "If I permit you to walk about, will you promise to restrain your exuberance and follow instructions on how you are to distribute your weight and use the walking supports?"

Knofki's grin only widened. "Yes, I vow I will, Senior Healer."

"Very well, then." He patted the child's shoulder. "We will have you up and about after your morning meal."

The next two patients had also improved; one enough to be discharged and returned to limited duty. Squilyp hopped over to Dapvea Adan's empty berth and glared back at me. "You provided the means for him to self-terminate? Without my permission?"

"I relocated his berth." I indicated a room, which was generally used for those requiring very close monitoring. "I had thought he might need the space and time to be private and make peace with his deity." Dævena knew these people never gave anyone much solitude.

"Has a nurse been monitoring him?" Squilyp hopped past me and quickly entered the room. I followed, and found him hovering next to Dapvea Adan's berth, checking his vitals.

"Greetings, ClanSon Adan," I said.

The Jorenian opened his white eyes and nodded. "Has my Speaker arrived?"

I still did not know what a Speaker was, but no one new was present in Medical, so I assumed not and shook my head.

"It is time," he said, closing his eyes. "Summon her."

"I must first compose the signal to send to your HouseClan on Joren," Squilyp said. "It is difficult to find words to describe your condition. Were I to call you a coward, they might declare me ClanKill on the spot."

ClanKill? These ensleg actually killed something other than the taste of food? I looked at the Omorr with new interest.

"My Speaker shall inform my ClanUncle of my decision," Dapvea told him. "I am not a coward."

"Surely no," I said, stepping up to the other side of the berth. "It takes great courage to face one's death. I should know. I am told that I have died at least four or five times."

Squilyp glared at me. "Your sixth may arrive sooner than you think."

I thought of flashing a dagger. "Death never forgets a promise." I glanced down at Dapvea, who watched us with an appalled fascination. "Jorenian, if you wish to end your life, so be it. As you have no mate—"

"I have a bondmate. She is on Joren," he said, his expression turning sad. "My Speaker will relay my wishes to her."

"I see. Well, then, it is not as if you have children—" I stopped when I saw his black eyebrows draw together in the center. "Forgive me. You also have children?"

"Five." He gestured toward the empty half of the berth. "I will not have my ClanSons and Clan-Daughters seeing me reduced to this—this half of what I was."

"Ah, so you wish to die rather than shame your children and mate," I said, nodding. "I did not know of their existence, or that they held you in such low regard. You should have said so, Jorenian. My sympathies."

"My embrace of the stars will be celebrated," Dapvea snapped. "They honor me."

"But they would wish you to live only if you have four limbs? A strange sort of honor you people have for each other. I was told your kind were most affectionate, particularly toward kin. Ah, well." I sighed and made a notation on his chart. "Senior Healer, under the circumstances, perhaps we should persuade Knofki Adan to self-terminate as well."

Squilyp caught my eye and nodded. "Yes, I see the wisdom in that, Doctor."

"Knofki is a child who lost some toes," the Jorenian shouted. "I have no legs."

"Toes, arms, legs—does it matter?" I shrugged. "A flaw is a flaw. One does not wish the boy to suffer the pain and humiliation of being outcast on the homeworld when we could have attended to his proper disposal here." I gazed at Squilyp. "How, exactly, do you help boy children take their lives? This custom is strange to me."

"I know what you are doing," Dapvea said, and fell back against the pillows to stare at the ceiling. "I would not have them see me a cripple. I have always been the strongest of my ClanFather's children."

"To lose two legs, learn to use prosthetics, and walk again requires great strength of body and will. I saw much of that during the rebellion." I measured him with a glance. "You reminded me of those fighters, until this talk of death. To die is to lose. Everything."

Dapvea fell silent, and the Omorr and I used the interval to examine his stumps and update his chart. It was difficult not to say more, but I sensed that to do so would push the Jorenian too far. The Senior Healer seemed also aware of this.

At last he struggled to sit up and gestured to the berth linens. "I want to see them."

Squilyp appeared ready to refuse, but I pulled away the sheet and showed him the neatly bandaged stumps.

"Your thighs are mostly intact," I told him, speaking quickly as the skin of his face turned a chalky color. "The prosthetic limbs can be fitted to the stumps when they heal, and work off the nerve and muscle tissue we were able to salvage. In time, you will walk and perhaps even run, as any strong man does."

"Or woman," Squilyp said briskly. "ClanLeader Sajora Kalea lost most of her leg during the siege of Reytalon. Do you know of her?"

"Know? I celebrated her return to the homeworld, when she and the Blade Dancers were made ClanJoren and named the House Kalea." Dapvea reached down to gingerly touch one of the dressings. "Do you know that she had one of her kin weld her shattered leg together before it was removed, so that she could fight to avenge herself and her Chosen?"

I would have to ask Reever about her. "She sounds like a brave woman."

His white eyes lifted to mine. "Indeed." He took

one last look at his stumps before he reclined. "I revoke my request for my Speaker. I would know more about these prosthetics, and how it will be for me."

Squilyp summoned the resident responsible for fitting amputees with artificial limbs, and we left him discussing the details with Dapvea. I walked out into the ward and looked down the row of berths. A nurse was clearing Knofki's morning meal, which he had apparently wolfed down, while another was measuring him for support braces. He was trying very hard not to squirm. I would have to keep a close eye on the boy, or he would be racing through the corridors on them.

"We have time to perform a halo-stim," the Senior Healer said as he joined me.

I stiffened. "I had one only yesterday."

"The stimulation is necessary if we are to make any progress with recovering your memories."

"Her memories," I said, wishing an emergency appendectomy would walk in at that very moment. "Not mine."

"When we achieve a successful recovery," the Omorr said with the deliberation of a tested patience, "they will be yours. Come now."

I did not wish to go with him into the neurological treatment room, but Reever had directed me to allow the Omorr to continue his attempts to revive my former self's memories. Thus I went, although slowly and without a great deal of enthusiasm, and sat in the padded patient's seat.

The room contained the latest technology being used to treat patients with brain injury, disorder, or disease. A long bank of consoles measured brain activity, performed continuous neurological scans, and applied finely controlled doses of medications, sonics, energy, and other stimulants to the patients.

"Try not to wriggle this time," Squilyp said as he lowered a bowl-shaped web of alloy bands studded with stim ports and sensor pads over the top of my head.

The feel of the cold metal on my skin made my nose wrinkle. "Would you sit still if you felt as if lice were crawling in and out of your ears?"

"If I knew the lice were going to give me back my life, yes." The Senior Healer hopped over to the console and initiated the treatment program. "Sit back, close your eyes, and relax."

Relax, when my life might be eradicated in favor of hers. Impossible. Only his past failures reassured me enough to do as he told me. "When will I have had enough treatment?"

"When I see some positive results from the stim," Squilyp said, and switched on something that made the short hairs on my neck rise. "Cognitive impairment from trauma-induced amnesia is not always permanent. A substantial amount of memory loss is to be expected, but over time that should reduce until your memories are intact up to the time of your injury."

No sensation of lice in my ear canals, but I resisted a sudden, terrible urge to squash what felt like invisible worms inching under my hair. "Which time? When the prisoner shuttle crashed, or when Daneeb shot Cherijo in the head?"

"Don't fidget," the Omorr said. "When the native

woman shot you, obviously. The crash landing only fractured your skull."

"I reviewed the last set of brain scans you performed," I said over the faint buzzing in my ears. I did not like it any more than the lice-infested sensation. "You noted that the bilateral lesions to the hippocampus were severe."

He nodded in an absent fashion. "They should be. You were shot twice at point-blank range. That it did not destroy your hippocampus is a miracle."

"You agree that such would be enough to inflict irreversible retrograde amnesia," I suggested, cringing a little as I felt the energy of the first round of stim come through the bands. I opened my eyes and saw white spots. "As would damage to the entorhinal, perirhinal, and parahippocampal nodes. Judging by the age of the tissue in those cortical areas, all three were virtually destroyed by the head injuries Daneeb inflicted."

"I disagree." The Omorr left the console and came over to adjust the halo device. "Your semantic memory is largely intact. You recalled words spoken to you just before the head injury. You even remember specific medical skills and how to function as an adult in society, limited as yours was."

"After two years of wandering about and behaving like a mute madwoman," I reminded him. The outrage in his eyes made my heart constrict. "Senior Healer, I do not mean to offend, or show disrespect, but all you do with this"—I tapped the halo—"is disrupt my brain waves, make my skin crawl, and give me a headache."

The door panel opened abruptly, and Xonea Torin, captain of the *Sunlace*, strode in.

I waited in silence for Cherijo's adopted brother to speak to Squilyp. He was almost as tall as Teulon had been, but much broader through the shoulders and chest. When I had first come on board the ship, the crew's blue skin, black hair, and white eyes reminded me so much of the Raktar that it had been a comfort. Only in time did I learn how different the Torins were, collectively as friendly as children who had never left their shelter.

They were nothing like Teulon.

These people might all have eyes the color of new snow, but the subtlety of emotion in them ran the spectrum from soft powder to sharp ice. Xonea's gaze most often relayed the cool, watchful attention of a battle-seasoned warrior, but presently something much fiercer blazed in his eyes. Xonea turned his attention, but he did not smile, and he did not bother to address the Senior Healer at all.

"Cherijo," he said. "You are to come with me to the command center at once."

After the damage inflicted on the *Sunlace* during the Jado Massacre, the ensleg had retrofitted the vessel, and constructed not one but two command centers within the ship. The first was located in the customary position, near the primary helm and navigational array, where most of the ship's flight officers performed their duties.

That was not the command center to which Xonea Torin escorted me.

In the heavily shielded and reinforced engineering section, located in the heart of the vessel, a second command center had been added. From this secondary flight deck, the *Sunlace*'s crew could perform the same functions that they would on the primary with far more protection and safety. Reever had told me that the second command center was only used while the ship was under attack or engaging in the field of battle.

We were doing neither, so I was somewhat confused as to why I had been brought here. Still, the captain was the highest-ranking male on the ship, the equivalent of a rasakt among the Iisleg, and a female did not speak to such a man unless commanded by him to do so.

Xonea and I submitted to a DNA test before we were permitted access to the command center. He led me past the consoles and equipment, which were not in use, and into a room with a large table, many chairs, and a sophisticated computer array with multiple terminals and access consoles. Waiting for us were Reever and eleven Jorenian officers who supervised various operations on board the ship.

There were more men than women here, and all of them were staring at me. This promised to be unpleasant. Hopefully I would not be stripped and beaten here. I saw no discipline posts or whips.

"Sit down, Healer," the captain said.

I sat down in the chair Xonea indicated, to the right of his own and directly across from my husband's, and waited. My face felt as immobile as a Lok-teel mask in a blast of ice wind.

"We have received an urgent relay from the

Hsktskt Faction homeworld of Vtaga," Xonea said, activating the central console. A data copy of the relay appeared on the screens set into the table before us. It was shown in a language I could not read, so it meant nothing to me. "As you can see, it came from SubAkade TssVar, the former general of the Faction armies, and currently the chief Hsktskt negotiator at the Jado peace talks. He has personally requested our immediate assistance. Specifically, he asks that Cherijo come to Vtaga."

The other men were reading the relay. Their reactions appeared to be a blend of surprise, disbelief, and, oddly, anger. I recalled TssVar as the big reptilian who had been present when Raktar Teulon delivered his ultimatum after the rebels had taken control of Akkabarr. TssVar had not struck me as a being who would casually ask for anything—and how was it that he knew Cherijo?

Reever finished reading the relay. "No," he said to Xonea.

"This is not a matter of simply refusing their request, Duncan." The captain looked distressed, as if he did not wish to say those words. "There is precedence."

"Not this time." Reever looked at me. "Jarn, leave us."

Surprised that my husband had called me by my name in front of so many who did not, I rose to my feet.

"Sit down, Cherijo," Xonea said.

I sat down.

Reever folded his arms. "She is my wife. Jarn, leave."

I stood.

"She is a member of my crew," Xonea shot back. "Healer, you will remain."

Bobbing up and down seemed ridiculous, so I stood and silently waited for them to sort it out. I belonged to Reever, but Xonea was the leader of the Torin and captain of the ship. Iisleg custom would have placed Xonea as the ranking male, but we were not on Akkabarr. The protocol officer's briefing had not covered what to do when caught between two men issuing conflicting orders, or to whom I owed obedience under such unusual circumstances.

Someone would simply have to tell me which order to obey.

Reever noticed my expression and turned to Xonea. "She does not understand. I will speak for her here. Go back to Medical, Jarn."

"You may not speak for her, Linguist. She is yet a member of the Ruling Council, and as such outranks both of us." The captain eyed me. "You will stay here, Cherijo."

This Ruling Council business was something else new to me; no one had mentioned it. Why would anyone elect a physician to rule them? Why had Cherijo not written about any of this in her journals? I did not wish to leave now, but I did not want to defy Reever.

"I have an objection." Salo, the head of the communications department, stood up. A stern-looking Jorenian with many battle scars, he commanded instant attention. His daughter often came to visit Marel and had proved to be a cheerful, polite child.

"One cannot follow two guides, or walk two paths." He gave me a bleak smile. "Jarn, wish you to stay or go?"

I felt a small twinge of pleasure at being addressed by my true name by one of the crew. "Am I permitted to answer that?" I asked, keeping my voice carefully neutral. Tension made the air thick; I did not wish to be the cause of a fight between these men.

My husband came to me and rested his hands on my shoulders. "What will be said here will be confusing to you. Without knowledge of what has happened in the past, you cannot make this decision. You can trust me to decide this for you."

Could trust, or *had* to trust? I did not know, but his logic seemed reasonable. If only I trusted him.

"I do not wish to make uninformed decisions." I glanced at Xonea. "Is it permitted for me to stay so that I may know what is decided for me?"

One side of the captain's mouth curled. "You can have no objection to that, Reever."

My husband released me. "As long as it is understood that I serve as my wife's proxy." When Xonea nodded, he gave me a long, piercing look before he returned to his seat.

I sat down and released the breath I had been holding. I had traversed ice fields pocked with unexploded ordnance with less worry.

Naln Torin, the chief of engineering, occupied the seat next to mine. Another blue-skinned giant of a female, she had a gentle manner and had come to Medical each day since the accident in her section to visit Knofki and the others who had been injured.

She bent her head so she could speak softly to me. "Need you explanation of anything said here, Healer, you have but to ask me."

"I thank you." I picked up a datapad to take notes, and to give my hands something more to do than clench with nerves.

"Very well, let us examine what details we have," Xonea said, removing the relay transcript from the screens and replacing it with a star chart. "Here you see the Faction homeworld of Vtaga, where the unidentified plague has emerged. We have no live or recorded transmissions from the planet—the Hsktskt have never permitted such—but TssVar claims this disease is killing everyone who contracts it."

"The plague itself is not lethal," Reever countered. "He stated that in his relay."

"True, but the symptoms induced by the contagion are driving the infected to extreme violence. More than two-thirds of the victims have committed suicide." Xonea paused to reference another file. "The medical data provided show victims suffer from progressive psychotic delusions and brain dysfunction. TssVar assures us that these symptoms are not being experienced by the non-Hsktskt portion of their population—"

"Their slaves," Reever said. "No humanoid is permitted to set foot on Vtaga unless they are in a collar and chains."

"As you say, Duncan." Xonea displayed current world population figures for the Hsktskt homeworld. "TssVar's physicians are unable to account for the spread of the plague, the source, or the means of transmission. That is all the information we have."

"During the war, whole companies of Hsktskt chose to cut their own throats when defeated rather than be captured and taken prisoner by the League," Salo said. "Is it possible this plague is more a form of mass hysterical response to the peace talks?"

"It seems unlikely." Xonea frowned at my husband. "Duncan, you know these people better than any of us. What say you of Salo's theory?"

"Some conservative Hsktskt might protest the end of the war and having equal dealings with the warm-blooded, but they would not be driven to violence and suicide by them." Reever sounded slightly impatient. "It does not matter. After the liberation of Catopsa, the Faction levied a blood bounty on my wife's head. Whatever TssVar may say, that bounty cannot be lifted by anything but her death or execution at the hands of the Hsktskt. She cannot go to Vtaga."

"But I *have* died," I said, drawing everyone's attention. Moments such as these were why I wished I could wear a head wrap. "The death of my former self—her mind, her memories—occurred on Akkabarr, when the slave ship transporting her crashed on the surface."

"That may serve as justification to lift the blood bounty," Xonea said. "What other objection have you, Duncan?"

"Have you forgotten what happened the last time she went to stop a plague, Captain?" my husband asked, his voice soft and low. "They took her from us. Took her as if she were nothing but an exotic animal to be chained and caged and sold to the highest bidder."

Another good reason not to recover Cherijo's memories, I thought. I did not wish to relive any of what she had suffered at the hands of the League.

The captain's skin darkened. "We will take measures to protect her."

"As the Jado did? Every member of their House-Clan save Teulon and his son died on that day. Our daughter and I nearly joined them in death." Reever spoke without emotion coloring his words, which gave them a ghastly, appropriate emptiness. "From that day it took us almost three years to find her, only to discover that she had been attacked while wounded by primitives. Their brutality caused the brain damage that destroyed her memory."

The captain sighed. "I understand this better than you think, Duncan."

"If what you say is true, then you would not ask this of her." My husband looked at all the other men in the room. "Forget that this woman is my wife, and your kin. Look upon her as a sum of her experiences. How much more must she suffer? When will she have sacrificed enough to have earned her freedom?"

No one seemed to know what to say.

Reever came from his place and drew me up from mine. "I made a promise to someone after I first met you," he said to me. "I vowed that no matter what happened I would keep you safe. I have done a poor job of that in the past, but I am determined, if nothing else, to keep my promise now.

That is why I must say no to this scheme. If you go to Vtaga, you will die there."

This was the reason I had given myself to Reever. He had sworn to care for me and Marel, and protect us with his life. How could I undermine that by providing aid to a species that had wanted me hunted down and killed? "It will be as you say, Husband."

Reever kept my hands in his as he addressed the captain. "You will signal SubAkade TssVar and refuse his request."

Xonea looked angry—and a little relieved—before he replied with, "Yes. I will do so at once."

Reever did not permit me to return to Medical Bay. Instead he signaled Squilyp from one of the command center terminals and informed him that I would be unavailable for the remainder of my shift. The Omorr must have heard about TssVar's request, for he only asked if we were going to Vtaga, and seemed quite happy to learn that we were not.

I followed my husband to a lift, but instead of taking me to his quarters, he sent it spiraling to the very bottom level, an area the protocol officer had told me was used mainly for star-viewing through its transparent walls.

The entire level appeared to be a squared-off bubble. Not only were the walls transparent, but so was the lower deck. Only the strips of alloy between the fitted sonic buffer panels and the exit from the lift seemed solid; the rest made it seem as if we walked through space itself.

I kept thinking of this, to prevent my mind from traveling in other directions.

"You have not spoken much since the meeting," Reever said.

Now he wishes me to speak. I turned away from him, and saw what appeared to be a crumpled, threadbare veil of red, yellow, and purple color pocked with tiny stars. Marel had once pointed it out to me from the viewport in Reever's quarters and called it a nebula. It looked like the sun shining through one of the clear ice pillars near a vent shaft, and made me long again for the clean, spare beauty of Akkabarr.

"Jarn?"

Why was he using *my* name so much? I was not his beloved. "Yes?"

"Tell me what you are feeling."

"Content. This is a pretty place. I like looking at the stars." I dismissed all of the unhappy emotions from my mind and moved to stand in front of one deck-to-ceiling panel. "Will I have to report for an additional shift in Medical, to make up for the time I spent at the briefing?"

"No." He came up behind me, but he did not touch me. "Why don't you trust me?"

"I do trust you. You vowed to protect our child, and me, and I believed you." Would he put his hands on me now? He had tried to do so once, the first week I had been with him, but I had avoided the contact. Now that I was more accustomed to his presence, and his touch, I thought I might tolerate more of it—but not in this open space, where anyone could walk in on us. "How long are we to stay here? If I am not to work a shift, I would return to your quarters."

"Our quarters." He turned me to face him. "They are yours as much as mine."

They had been Cherijo's; I was only a guest in them. I shrugged instead of saying this.

"We need time alone." He moved his fingers over my cheek in a gentle manner; a caress like those an Iisleg man bestowed on a woman he wanted or who had especially pleased him. "I want you to stop sleeping in Marel's room."

That confused me. "Why? You never said I could not."

"I wished you to have enough time to adjust." He traced the lines of my mouth, his gaze intent.

"To adjust what?" I felt his body tighten and change, and then it became clear to me. When we had made this agreement, Reever had promised he would take no other women. To my knowledge, he had kept that promise. "You mean coupling with you? I do not have to sleep with you for that. I can go to sleep in the child's room after it is done."

His hand fell away. "You don't want me."

Want him? I hardly knew him.

"I am your wife. I know my duty. You had only to say." We were talking too much; a male was supposed to take, not ask. I disliked this area, but the door could be locked, and one of the benches would serve. "If you will secure the entry, we can begin now." I started unfastening the front of my tunic. "Should I take off everything? Is there something specific that you wish me to do?" What knowledge I had of coupling was very limited, and of ensleg ways I knew nothing, so I was sure I would need a certain amount of instruction.

"Stop it." He caught my hands. "I am not going to take you on the observation deck."

"Very well." I waited, and then asked, "Where should we do this?" For all I knew, the ensleg had some special department on the ship for it. They had them for everything else.

"I will wait until it is something that you desire," he said slowly.

He would wait a long time, then. "I may still sleep with the child?"

"No. Yes. I don't care." He turned his back on me. "Stop asking my permission for everything."

"That is how it is done among my people, Reever," I reminded him. When he did not reply, I added, "I do not wish to displease you."

"You are not here to humor me." Reever made a swift, cutting gesture. "You are no longer on Akkabarr. You're free now. Stop acting like you're still a slave to men."

How easily he said that. So easily it made my blood run hot and my tongue grow reckless.

"Indeed. I did not wish to leave my Raktar or our people, but to be a mother to the child of my body, you said that I must come with you and be wife. Thus I am here, following your wishes, not my own. I do not know these Jorenians, but they say that I am their sister and must treat them as family. It makes me uncomfortable, and it is not my wish to be a part of their HouseClan, yet I have also tried to do this. Each day more than one of you put a mask on me—the mask of a dead woman—and call me her name, so that you may pretend she yet lives. I am not her, yet I again tolerate it and say nothing. Now I am prevented from attending to those who are in need on Vtaga, and you would tell me where I can sleep but that I may not attend to your needs as a woman should until it is something I wish." I gazed up at him. "Tell me, how is any of this free, exactly?"

"This is your life, Jarn. One day, you will remember it—"

"No." I stepped back, away from his hands. "I will not remember. I did not live her life. I was born when it was over. I am a woman of the Iisleg, a skela, a healer, and a rebel fighter. I killed a man during the war, to save the life of my Raktar. If not for the child, I would still be with Teulon and Resa. I would have gladly become his second woman to remain at his side." I saw the pain in his eyes, but he needed to face my truth. "I am not Cherijo Torin, Linguist. Your wife is dead. She died when her ship crashed on Akkabarr, and nothing you say or do to me will ever bring her back."

He stared at me in silence for a very long time. "I will not let you go."

I knew that. "I am not asking you to."

"Very well." He turned to face the emptiness beyond the ship. "Go back to work, Wife."

THREE

The Senior Healer showed surprise when I returned to duty, but asked no questions and permitted me to finish my shift as scheduled. Perhaps he sensed how uneasy I felt, for he did not force me to complete the disrupted halo-stim treatment, either.

Before I left, we spent a few moments in his office reviewing charts. The Omorr consulted with me on the various types of prosthetics made for paraplegics that the resident had recommended as suitable for Dapvea Adan, and we agreed that those made with reconstructed technology would be the most resilient and restore the widest range of function.

"Jorenians heal very quickly," I mentioned as I made the final notes on Dapvea's chart.

"Is there something bothering you?" Squilyp asked. "You seemed quieter than usual today."

So he had noticed. "I do not understand some of your ensleg ways," I admitted. "I will use the database later to find out what I do not know."

His brow furrowed. "What don't you know?"

"The ways of coupling. I do not know how it is done among your kind." I checked my notes to ensure I had recorded the necessary details. "Reever wishes to make use of me, but I am not doing something right. He will not tell me what it is, and so we do not couple."

The Senior Healer cleared his throat. "We do not, ah, discuss such matters openly."

I looked up. "Speaking of coupling is taboo?" The protocol officer had not included it on his list of things I was forbidden to do on the ship.

"No, but it is . . . a private concern between the partners involved." His hide turned dark pink. "You should ask Reever to explain such things to you."

"I have already angered him by doing so, and he will not tell me." I gave him a speculative look. "You know how it is done by Terrans, do you not? Is there some ritual involved? Some thing that must be said? You ensleg seem very fond of saying many words before you actually do something."

"Wait." He turned to his console, downloaded several files, extracted a disk, and handed it to me. "This contains all the data you need on Terran sexuality. Study it, and then ask Reever whatever questions you have that it does not answer."

He behaved as though shy and confused and embarrassed, as a girl coming into her bleeding time would. Perhaps it was something inherent to his species.

"I thank you." I took the disk and tucked it into my tunic pocket. "Dapvea's stumps should be ready for fitting preparations in five to seven days. Shall I have the lab begin manufacturing the necessary components?"

"We will see what his state of mind is next week,"

Squilyp said, his disapproval quite visible now. "I don't want him discouraged."

"It is discouraging to lie in that berth and stare at the upper deck all day and night." I switched off the chart. "We should encourage him toward recovery, not shield him from it."

"That is a militant attitude, Doctor." The Senior Healer made a sniffing sound. "Our patients are not soldiers being sent back to battle."

"This *is* battle; a very personal one. Every day Dapvea will fight enemies he has never before faced: pain and physical limitation." I placed the chart on the Senior Healer's desk. "Sympathy cannot help him with these things. If that is all we offer him, he will lose heart again. I do not think we can shame him out of a *second* decision to end his life."

Squilyp's gildrells became spokes, but he kept whatever he was feeling out of his voice. "We will discuss this again another time. Good night, Doctor."

I went to the lift that would take me to Reever's quarters, nodding to crew members who greeted me as we passed each other. Everyone had to say something to me; one could not traverse a meter of space on this ship without someone offering some form of useless greeting.

Today I felt tempted to linger and speak with them.

For the first time since I had left Akkabarr, I did not look forward to returning to my husband's quarters. What had been said between us on the observation deck had left me feeling unsettled. Reever did not behave like an Iisleg male. Sometimes he reminded me of Teulon, especially when he didn't talk, for they shared that eerie ability for absolute stillness and silence. Yet when he did speak, Reever confused me. His continuing refusal to relieve his needs with me only made matters more puzzling.

Why had he insisted on taking me to wife if he had no desire to use me as one?

"Healer?"

I looked up into a scarred Terran male face and saw my reflection in his mild brown eyes. It was the one with wings . . . Hawk, they called him.

Beside him stood what appeared to be a larger version of Reever's small feline. This beast walked upright, as a person would. It, too, only had four limbs, which seemed abnormal to me, as the jlorra, the only feline species on Akkabarr, had six. The feline's scrawny body did not appear to be the result of abuse or starvation; its musculature looked normal for its lean body frame and its pelt had a healthy sleekness. That its fur was the color of shadows on ice and its eyes had no color at all was also no indication that it was ill-treated.

Perhaps it was, like Reever's beasts, a domesticated companion. It did not wear a collar, but the Terran had dressed it in a strappy, gem-studded garment. "Yes?"

"You are standing in front of an open lift," Hawk said, gesturing behind me. As he spoke, the dark-feathered wings growing from his upper back spread slightly.

I felt embarrassed to be found idle and lost in thought when I could have been working. "I think I will walk instead." I moved to walk around him.

"Is the lift malfunctioning?" the feline said to me in a perfectly articulate voice. "Should I signal . . . ?"

I backed away from it so quickly that my shoulder blades slammed into a corridor panel. I had never heard an animal speak.

Hawk looked at the freakish thing. "She does not remember you." To me, he said, "Healer, this is Alunthri, from planet Chakara."

The talking cat bared its teeth. "We are old friends, Cherijo."

"We were?" Now I understood what my daughter had said about not killing things. You could not very well butcher and skin something that could have a conversation with you. "Why?"

"You helped me when we lived together on K-2. We were both classified as nonsentient." Alunthri's pointed ears flicked back and forth. "I am distressing you, forgive me. I have stayed away so that I would not." It made as if to move closer, but stopped as I flinched. "Fare you well, Cherijo."

I watched the talking cat stride off. "I had a relationship with that creature?"

He nodded. "You were Alunthri's friend and mentor."

I knew Hawk to be the only other Terran on board the ship beside me, Reever, and Marel. Even so, Reever had explained to me that he was not fully human, but a hybrid, the child of a Terran female and a Taercal male. Hawk had been a special friend of Cherijo's, but then the woman had dozens of those.

I was beginning to wonder if anyone besides me had ever dared dislike her. Maybe she surrounded herself with beasts for reasons other than companionship. Certainly no one had ever told Teulon they disliked him; his pet jlorra Bsak would have ripped off their heads.

Hawk was watching me. "Duncan said that you have no memory of anything that happened before Akkabarr. You don't remember me from our time together on Terra."

"I know *of* you." I had read a little about him from the journal files. "You sing. You cared for Cherijo's brother. You saved her and Reever. She thought well of you."

"You speak of yourself as a stranger." Like the others on the ship, he seemed appalled and fascinated. "I did not simply care for Jericho. I loved him."

Judging by his tone, he was expecting me to react negatively to this declaration. There were some Iisleg men who desired other men instead of women, and the women of the skela had only each other, so his preference did not offend me. One found comfort where one could.

Or perhaps I was reading him wrong; it could be that he regretted how his relationship with Jericho had ended. "I am sorry that Cherijo killed him."

"She did not. After he went completely mad, our tribe did." He frowned. "Healer, has no one told you of who you were? I could—"

"Please." I lifted one hand. "I mean no disrespect, but I have heard enough of what happened in her life." I looked around. "Are there any other talking animals on the ship?"

"Alunthri is not—" He paused and grimaced. "It may seem like an animal to you, but it is not."

I moved my shoulders. "If you say so, Kheder."

"I also apologize for prying," he said. "You must think us all rather obsessed with your past."

"Cherijo had great value among this tribe. I understand that. I hope I will prove of equal worth someday." I felt a little impatient. "Is there anything else you wish from me?"

"I had thought I would tell you . . . but no, it is not important." He lifted his hand and touched my arm without warning, and then dropped it when I flinched away. "I won't hurt you." His facial skin darkened and his eyes became angry slits. "What did they do to you on that world?"

Hawk was not as big as the Jorenian males, but he was still larger and more muscular than me.

"Men only touch women who do not belong to them to use them or beat them. You have no desire for women." Recalling how Cherijo had written of the man's gentle nature, I felt ashamed of my reaction. "I mean, that is how it was on Akkabarr. Reever has said you ensleg are different, but it is hard to forget such things. Forgive me."

"Don't apologize." The lines around his mouth disappeared, and he held out his hand. "Come, share a meal with me. I would like to know more about who you are, and what life on Akkabarr is like."

My eyes stung. It was the kindest thing that had been asked of me since I left my homeworld. "I thank you but I cannot. Reever is expecting me to return to his quarters. He will grow concerned if I do not." I hesitated. "Could we do so another time, perhaps?"

"Of course." He smiled. "Signal me. I share my quarters with Qonja Adan. We would welcome you to join us whenever you wish."

I did not recall the one called Qonja Adan—all these blue-skinned ensleg looked so much alike—but I nodded and thanked him again before I moved into the lift.

Reever had a meal prepared and waiting for me when I came in, and only offered a terse greeting. Marel came rushing out of her bedchamber to hug and kiss me before she launched into a description of her day at the educational facility. I ate sparingly—Reever always made too much food—and listened to our child's bright chatter. After the meal, I cleared and sat with Marel while she read a story from her datapad and then played with the beasts. They seemed fond of her and the games she invented for them with bits of string, but I still kept a sharp eye on both cats. They might be tiny compared to Alunthri, but they had sharp teeth and claws. If they used them on my daughter, they would quickly meet one of my blades. So would that Chakacat.

The evening rituals continued. Reever insisted the child use the cleansing unit before she went to sleep (he made the same demand of me; never had I been so continuously clean in my short life.) It was my habit to go to sleep with her on the pallet I had made in her room, but tonight I rolled up the linens and removed them. Reever had made me aware of his needs; I could no longer attend only to the child.

"Are you sleeping somewhere else tonight, Mama?" she asked.

I saw Reever standing in the doorway. "Yes. I will sleep in your father's chamber now." My revelation produced no distress in her expression. "You will come to me at once if you need me."

"I will, Mama."

"At any hour." I brushed the golden curls back from her face. "Or call. You have only to say my name and you know that I will wake."

"I'll be fine, Mama." She put her small arms around my neck and squeezed, and I breathed in her sweet scent before I left her with Reever.

I used the cleansing unit to wash myself, and changed into the soft, loose garments Reever told me were customary for one to wear for sleeping. Had the ship been as cold as Akkabarr, I could have understood the necessity. The interior temperature was kept at a comfortable level, though, so I could have slept naked like a proper Iisleg female and saved the clothing for when I left his quarters.

Perhaps that was contributing to our problem. Reever always kept me covered up, even at those times when I should not have been.

The sight of my body was not the only thing he denied himself. It was unhealthy for a man to go so long without fulfilling his needs with a woman. It would probably make things simpler if I feigned the desire Reever wanted me to feel for him. I disliked pretense, but the situation between us would not improve if I did not do something. Such seductions were not something a woman did, but these ensleg

men would not talk about it. They were all polite-
ness and disapproval.

What else was I to do but take the initiative?

Reever was not in his bedchamber or in the front
room, and when I looked in on Marel I found her
alone and sleeping. Since I doubted that my husband had hidden himself in one of the storage containers, I assumed he had left and went to the
console where Cherijo had stored her journal files.

Reever had adapted the console to display both
in Iisleg and a form of Terran I could understand. I
chose the latter for the files' display, as there were
words she had used that did not exist in Iisleg. I
went to the place where I had stopped reading—an
entry she had made after a brief battle between
wounded League and Hsktskt soldiers being
treated for their injuries on the *Sunlace*.

*Marel is asleep, and unharmed, thank God. I'm so
angry with Reever I could dismember him with an
Omorr challenge blade. Angry with myself, too. Why
can't I think straight when my child is in danger? Why
do I still want to go down there and kill every one of those
soldiers who put her in the middle of their stupid fight?
I'm a doctor, I shouldn't feel this way.*

There was a gap in the data, an odd space that
showed something had been erased. I had seen others like it scattered through the files, especially the
earliest ones. She must have regretted what she had
written and deleted it out of the permanent memory.

I wished she had not erased part of it, for this
entry, like many others, confused me. Why did she
hate herself for wishing to protect her Marel and
avenge herself on those who would have harmed

her? A mother did not ask for her sheltering in-
stincts; she was given them for the benefit of her
child. Under the same circumstances, I would not
have sat and written about my feelings. I would
have drugged or knocked out Reever, taken Marel,
and left the ship.

*I told him that if he ever did this again, I would take
Marel and leave him, and he would never see either of us
again. I meant it. He'll be a proper father to our child, or
no father at all, damn him.*

I sat back. It was almost as if Cherijo had read
my thoughts. *All this time I thought her to be nothing
like me.*

"You have a great deal in common with her,"
Reever said from behind me, making me jump.
"However much you resent or dislike her."

I looked up at him. "I did not hear you come in."
I switched off the display. "I do not really like or dislike Cherijo. To do so properly, you must know the
person."

"You don't know me."

The words hung between us. What was I to say
that would not offend or anger him? "It is enough
that I belong to you. With time, I will come to
know you."

"*Is* that enough, Jarn?" The words came slowly,
painfully.

For me, it had to be. For him, I could not say.
"Among the Iisleg, a man takes two women. I do
not resent sharing you with the memory of another." I rose and went to him. "Reever, we are not
children. I wish to make the best of this. You have

said the same. We cannot do that if you live in a past that is lost to me."

"We can't be together if you go to bed with me merely to placate me." He glanced at Marel's room. "That was what you were thinking when you told her that you would be sleeping with me."

"I did not think of how my place is with you, but it is. I did not think of how I wish to please you, but I do. It is selfish to think I might gain some pleasure from it for myself, but that thought, too, appeals to me." I shrugged. "If you would rather just sleep—"

He made an odd sound and pulled me into his arms. "No." A moment later he was carrying me into his bedchamber.

Once there, he enabled all of the light emitters. There would be no shadows in which to hide, so I kept my expression calm and resisted the urge to cover myself as he undressed me. Seeing my body seemed important to him, for he looked all over me.

I did not know why. I was small and healthy, but hardly a beauty. Men enjoyed plump, well-endowed women; there was not enough of me to be appealing.

After Reever pulled off his own garments, we stood naked before each other. His long, pale-skinned body was quite attractive, if a little too lean yet from many months of fighting during the rebellion. I touched a scar on his shoulder, and saw another further down, on his side. There were others; scars he had carried for many years—too many for a man who used words instead of weapons.

Scars were a sign of courage and masculinity among the Iisleg. They reassured me as well, for a man who could survive so many injuries possessed strength and luck. What did the ensleg think of them?

I stopped counting at fifteen and covered the scar on his shoulder with my palm. "You have endured much." I moved my hand over to stroke his shoulder blade and felt ridged flesh. A strange rage began to burn inside me. Who had whipped him? "So much I do not know."

"While you have not?" He covered my hand with his, and I felt it shaking. "I live for you and Marel."

Unwilling to begin this in anger, I gentled my thoughts. "That is enough for any woman."

Coupling with an ensleg proved an awkward business at first. There was the kissing to start with, of which I had no experience, and no small amount of apprehension. My fears turned out to be needless; it felt far more pleasant in reality than it had sounded in theory. Had he not been in such need, I could have spent several hours exploring what we could do with our mouths together.

That Reever wanted me was, as with Iisleg men, something impossible for him to hide. An aroused Terran male's body changed from a bow to an arrow, and yet from the sweat on his skin and the bunching of his muscles, I sensed he was attempting to control himself. Teulon had done the same thing during the night that Resa and I spent together with him. I appreciated the concern, but I was not interested in Reever holding back with me, not when we were here and together alone.

I pulled him down to the floor, and straddled him, holding his hands against my breasts as I opened myself to him. There was a brief interval of discomfort—Reever's shaft was very hard and swollen—and then I adjusted to the unfamiliar penetration.

"Wait." He clasped my hips, and held me still when I would have shifted. "Let me feel you like this for a moment."

"Wait. Yes." I took several deep breaths, trying to be patient, but he was hard and deep inside me, and I wanted to move. The moment he wanted was taking too long. "Reever—"

He rolled with me, putting me under him, pinning my wrists to the floor when I would have embraced him. His eyes had turned to a bright, brilliant blue.

"You're my wife," he said, punctuating his words with deep thrusts into my body. "My woman. My love. Mine."

I could not think what I was. He was all over me, inside me, and the thing I had expected to be pleasant had grown enormous and hot and streaming through me like pulse fire, until everything was gone and there was only us and what we were doing to each other.

He bent his head to say my name against my mouth. My name, not hers. It snatched me out of the delicious torment and flung me helpless into a dark place. He didn't come after me. He was waiting for me there.

In that moment, at last, we belonged to each other.

Someone must have reprogrammed the morning alarm chime, for it began to make noise only two heartbeats after I closed my eyes that night. I groaned and rolled over, groping for the panel switch, only to find another hand there before mine. Reever sat fully dressed beside me.

I wanted to pull him down beside me; I wanted to hide beneath the linens. How long had he been watching me sleep?

"Not long. I have an early meeting this morning," he said. He sounded much more relaxed than he had since claiming me from Teulon. "I signaled Squilyp and told him you would not be in to work today."

"Why did you do that?" Rather alarmed, I sat up. "I am not ill."

His hand stroked my arm. "I didn't let you sleep much last night."

No, he had not, but I would gladly remain awake for more of the same. Last night had been a revelation, and not just of the ways of intimacy among the ensleg.

Stop thinking about coupling. "I will take Marel to the learning facility," I said, trying to rise.

He did not permit me to do so. "She has already gone. Fasala came to walk her to school. I will meet her when her classes are over."

Fasala was Salo Torin's daughter, and a trustworthy child, but having her look after Marel did not sit well with me.

"She will be fine," Reever assured me.

He kept reading my thoughts before I could speak them. *That* was still annoying. "If I am not to look after the child, or report for duty," I countered, "then what am I to do?"

"Go back to sleep," he suggested. "Later you can read or listen to music. Rest, Jarn."

I could rest when I was dead. Feeling bold, I tugged on his hand. "Stay with me."

"Then there would be no rest for either of us." He pressed his mouth to the top of my head. "Don't kill the cats while I'm gone."

I could see the gray-furred one lurking near the storage container. "As you say, Husband."

I did not go back to sleep, however, and as soon as Reever left I got up to dress and arm myself. On Akkabarr I had been an outcast, but I had never been permitted to spend much time alone. Daneeb had rightly feared that my ignorance would kill me. The skela who had taken me in also lived as a tribe unto themselves, and they believed the tribe should remain together. Daneeb had repeatedly told me that it was not good to become lonely and depressed on a world that could kill you ten paces from your shelter.

Even with a protector like Reever to guard me, someone or something on this ship could do that quite easily. I needed to learn more about these people and their technology, and quickly, or I would not be able to keep myself or my daughter safe when Reever was not with us.

The beasts trailed after me as if watching me, but both kept a respectable distance between us, so I ignored them. I ate a small meal of synthetic meat from the wall machine. It was plain fare, but better than the strange dishes Reever kept preparing for me. Perhaps now that we were closer as husband

and wife I could persuade him to allow me to program some meals.

One of the small banes of my existence was that nearly everyone on the ship, including my former self, did not eat meat. We Iisleg had relied heavily on synthetics toward the end of the rebellion, but before that I had lived mostly on the meat of the animals we killed, or a portion of what we butchered for the iiskar.

Pretend meat was not very appetizing, but I was sick unto death of eating pretend plants.

Once I had cleared up after my meal, there was nothing left for me to do. I only listened to Cherijo's music when Reever insisted; the strange sounds of it did not move or intrigue me. I had grown weary of reading her journals. There were no hides for me to scrape, stretch, or cut; no furs to be cleaned. The wall machines prepared the food we ate. The three of us were tidy, and even so there were small drones that Reever had programmed to clean the surfaces and furnishings once a week. The beasts had gone off into Marel's room, and now slept huddled together in the center of her bed. I would have gone to work, but for Reever's orders.

I stood by the viewport and looked out at the stars, feeling utterly useless. Despite Daneeb's efforts, I had been a lonely creature among the skela, bound only to the work, but no more. Reever and the child had already made a place inside me, and I found myself empty without them.

Empty, useless Jarn. A pretend Cherijo who wanted to be anything else.

The door chime sounded, startling me so much

that I jumped and drew a blade. I went to the panel and enabled the screen to show a view of the outer corridor.

At first I thought it was Squilyp, but the Omorr outside the door bore only a rudimentary resemblance to him. She was female, to begin with, and had a thicker torso. She also wore very elegant, colorful garments with so many baubles that she practically glittered.

I had never seen her before now, so I kept the panel secured and enabled the audio panel. "Yes?"

"I am Garphawayn, the Lady Maftuda," the Omorr female said. "Squilyp's mate. I would speak to you, Terran."

She didn't sound angry or disturbed, but her posture and tone indicated what I interpreted to be determination and resolve. I didn't see any weapons on her, but that meant nothing. I rather doubted the Senior Healer had sent his wife to assassinate me, not when he could have done it himself in Medical and made it look like an accident.

I released the security mechanism on the panel, opened it, and stood back.

"Thank you." The female Omorr jingled as she hopped in. Little gem-encrusted rings around some of her gildrells sparkled, and four circular strands of matching gems swung from her throat. "Where is your lavatory?"

It took a moment for me to realize she referred to the privy. I pointed to it.

"Excuse me." She bounced quickly over to the unit and shut herself inside. A few minutes later, she emerged. Her hide seemed a little pale compared to

Squilyp's, but that might have been a normal gender difference among the Omorr. "Thank you. I nearly had an accident."

It took a moment to realize she meant her body functions. "Do you not have your own privy?" I had thought sanitary facilities standard in all the quarters.

She stared at me, and then sniffed. "Of course I do. I could not make it there in time." She rested the membranes of one arm against the straining bulge of her belly. "Not when he kicks like this."

"A son?" I smiled and went over to her so I could admire the fertile curve. "When is your birthing moon?"

"My . . . the child is due to be born soon. Among my kind, each mother's time is slightly different." She sounded stiff but appeared slightly bemused by my question. "It is my first, too, so we cannot judge by past deliveries."

"Come, sit." I took one of her arms and guided her over to the front room's furnishings, offering her the most comfortable place. "Are you thirsty, or hungry? I can procure something for you from the wall machine. Do you enjoy pretend plants?"

"Pretend plants?"

Wall food might not be good enough for her. Fertile females needed the best, freshest nourishment. I eyed the entry to Marel's room, but remembered that I had promised Reever I would not kill the beasts. "There is no fresh food to be had."

"It is not necessary for you to feed me. Please, sit down." She studied me as I sat across from her. "I apologize for not calling upon you sooner. I thought you might need time to . . . adjust."

"Adjust what?" I scanned the room, but all the lights and equipment seemed to be working properly. The female Omorr did not answer, so I added, "If you people do not tell me what you want adjusted, I will never find it on my own. Do you know how many things there are on this ship? They are as crystals in a frost storm."

"We—I—meant adjust as in grow accustomed to your surroundings," she said. "Our environment on board the ship must seem very strange to you."

"It is warm, there is food and water, and no one is trying to shoot me," I told her. "I do not need to adjust to that. I am grateful for it."

"Yes. Well. You seem very different." Garphawayn gestured toward my head. "I have never seen you wear your hair loose in such a fashion. I had not realized you possessed such a large quantity of it."

The female Omorr had no hair, but there were some long, feathery-looking growths on the very top of her scalp. They were red and purple and blue, and quite striking against her pink skin.

I must look like a beast to her.

"If I had belonged to a tribe, I would have had to cut it off. Only outcast females among the Iisleg grow their hair long." I ran a hand over the unruly mass that I kept forgetting to groom. "I plait or roll it up and clip it for work. It requires much care, but Reever forbade me to cut it."

Her gildrell rings tinkled as she sat up. "He did *what*?"

"I do not mind," I said quickly, worried that I had given her the wrong impression. "The length of my hair pleases him." In that moment I realized that Cherijo must have worn it long. "I will, ah, adjust to it."

Garphawayn muttered something under her breath before she asked, "What would please *you*, Terran?"

I did not understand the question. "You should not call me that. I speak Terran, and my body belongs to their species, but in all other things I am Iisleg."

"Well, I will not call you Iisleg; it is considered rude by my kind. Your name is Jarn?" When I nodded, she asked, "Then what would you do with your hair to please yourself, Jarn?"

"Among my people, a woman's greatest pleasure is to serve." When her expression remained blank, I added, "It pleases me to satisfy Reever's desires." After last night, a great deal.

"Indeed." She thought for a moment. "I would know more about these Iisleg women. Would you be so kind as to tell me of their lives?"

I told her what I knew, making it clear from the beginning that I had never been permitted to live among the tribes, and what I knew had been gained through stories told by my sisters and my own infrequent observations. I added a little about my life among the skela, the outcast Iisleg females who recovered ensleg corpses from surface shipwrecks and butchered game for the tribal hunters so they would not have to sully their hands with the taint of the dead. She seemed interested in how hard my sisters had worked to ensure their survival away from the protection and safety of the iiskars.

"When the rebellion came, and so many were lost fighting the Toskald, things changed for the women of the tribes," I said. "Part of that was because our Raktar made the skela into vral."

"Vral?"

I explained the old Iisleg legend of the vral, the dead whose spirits returned as faceless healers to judge and restore to health those who were sick or injured, and how we pretended to be the vral by concealing our faces behind Lok-teel masks. "We became vral to save fighters who had fallen during battle, and our men did believe we were gifts from the Gods, sent to those worthy of saving. But Toskald survivors and reinforcements did not know our legends, and often forced us to defend ourselves."

Garphawayn *hmph*ed. "You should not have had to resort to such a ruse."

"We eventually exposed ourselves." I thought of Resa, and how much I missed her fearless presence. "That we had deceived them angered our men, but by then we had healed so many of them that they forgave us for our deception."

"How generous." Garphawayn rose on her one leg. "I have but one question for you, Jarn. Why do you continue to behave as an Iisleg female would among us? You must know by now that we are not like the people of Akkabarr."

I wondered why her skin had flushed. "Daneeb, our headwoman, advised me do so. I do not know ensleg ways so it seemed sensible. You females have much more freedom, but your males are not so different from the kheder I knew. Are you feeling ill?"

She ignored my question. "Has my mate been ordering you about, as Reever has?"

"Squilyp is my superior," I reminded her. "He

guides me and prevents me from making mistakes. I am grateful for his direction."

"Cherijo was once Squilyp's superior. He has spoken of those years often, and credits her with teaching him to be a better physician." She hopped over to me. "You did not lose any of your healing skills on Akkabarr, did you?"

"No, but—"

"You are superior in authority to everyone on this vessel. Did no one tell you this?" she continued, her voice growing louder. "I imagine they would not. Always believing they know best."

Now I felt confused. "Something was said about Cherijo's position on some council, but I was told I would not understand—"

"Pah." She made a dismissive gesture. "The males on this ship have gone too far this time. They treat you like a sick child but make use of you as a woman grown. They conceal vital information from you on the pretext of protecting you. This cannot be permitted to continue. You are functioning in a coherent manner. I will not have it."

She had completely lost me. "This is not the way of the women of the tribe."

"In this tribe, Jarn, men and women are equals. Power commands respect. The key to power is knowledge, and it cannot be withheld from you simply because you are ignorant of it. So." Garphawayn's expression turned grim. "I will tell you everything they have not."

FOUR

It took Garphawayn some time to relate the many
facts that she felt were imperative for me to know.
Most had to do with the reasons why my former self
had fled Terra. I was shocked to learn of the bioengi-
neering her creator, a Terran named Joseph Grey
Veil, had used to transform his own cells into a female, altered version of himself. His experiment
had made Cherijo into something more than
human, the female Omorr told me, and discovering
her uniqueness had shaped her and her life.

I could not believe that my body had been copied
from that of a male. What did that make me? Were
there others? "Is it customary to create genetic
copies of other ensleg and then change them so?"

"No," Garphawayn assured me. "You are the
only one that we know of, but there may be others.
Cherijo's creator told her that she had 'brothers.'"

The female Omorr also repeated what her mate
had told her of my former self, Reever, and a Jorenian named Kao Torin, and how the three had contributed to the long, troubled relationship between
Cherijo and my husband. None of these things had
been detailed in the journals, but Garphawayn assured me that Squilyp would attest to the facts.

It seemed that there was much I had not been told.

Squilyp's mate then detailed how it was with ensleg females, and permitted me to ask anything about ensleg ways, no matter how embarrassing. She remained patient with my ignorance, tolerated my many questions, and when something made no sense, she took me to the console and used the database to illustrate the point. She dismissed the laws of the Iisleg as gender bias born of ignorance-riddled custom and superstition. When I refused to believe her, she showed me examples of other species that had developed similar and opposing cultures, as well as the doctrines agreed upon by the Allied League.

She did not argue with my beliefs. She destroyed them.

By the time Garphawayn had finished my world had turned upside down and inside out. I could no longer look upon myself or Cherijo as the same person. All I could think was that I inhabited a body more valuable than anyone suspected, and the danger to me and Marel seemed to loom higher and colder than anything I knew, even an ice cliff ready to collapse.

Why had Reever kept such things from me?

I felt so many emotions that I could not untangle them: confusion, bitterness, anger—and an overwhelming sense of outrage. I only had one last question for Garphawayn. "What am I going to do, now that I know all of this?"

"Jarn, you said that when you were among the skela, you did not act like a woman of the tribe or follow the skela ways," the female Omorr said. "You saved lives."

I gave her a blank look. "It was my work. I knew the work had to be more important than anything the skela did. Besides that, the Iisleg would never have accepted the survivor of a crashed ship into an iiskar; I could never live among them as a proper woman."

"Your work is the same here. Even if the men do not agree with it, you must do what *you* feel is right." Garphawayn rose. "Now I must go and have harsh words with my mate. Signal me if you again need to speak of this or anything we have discussed."

She left me in that muddle of emotions and thoughts. Some time later the console blipped, indicating a priority relay was waiting, and I answered it. It came from the ship's communication center.

"ClanLeader Teulon Jado is signaling from the peace summit," Salo Torin told me. He did not seem to want to meet my gaze directly. "He insists on speaking with you, Healer."

"Permit him to do so, please," I said.

Salo forwarded the signal, which made Teulon's image appear on the console screen. The distance between us caused some slight distortion, but his familiar features loosened the knot inside my chest.

"Jarn." He lifted his hand and touched the screen.

I did the same. "Raktar." He looked tired and worried. "You and Resa are well?"

"Yes." He smiled a little. "My Chosen asks the same of you."

"I miss you both, but I am making a place here

for myself." A place that I was no longer convinced I wished to occupy, but Teulon had not signaled me to listen to my woes. I also needed to check further into Garphawayn's claim that Cherijo had been grown from her creator's own cells to be the perfect, immortal physician. It was not something I entirely believed possible. I had been a man? "What is the matter?"

"HouseClan Torin has refused to permit you travel to Vtaga, to aid the Faction with this sickness on their world. Is this so?" When I nodded, he said, "SubAkade TssVar has just presented an ultimatum to the mediators here. If you will go to Vtaga, the Faction will voluntarily abandon their slaver operations and free Hsktskt-held slaves."

"They will? All of them?" I was stunned.

The Hsktskt Faction administered the most extensive network of slaver operations, depots, and transport routes in the territories bordering League-explored space. It had been the collision of Faction slavery and League colonization that had created the tensions that eventually built up to outright war. No one knew how many slaves were held by the Faction, but conservative estimates were in the tens of millions.

"There is more," Teulon said. "TssVar stated that if you do not go to Vtaga, the Hsktskt will cease negotiations and resume hostilities with League forces at once. As a SubAkade and the only supporter among Faction leaders for the peace talks, we believe he can make this come about."

"Have you reminded the Hsktskt of the crystals?" I asked.

During the rebellion on Akkabarr, Teulon had acquired the Toskald's greatest treasure: crystals permanently etched with command codes that controlled the militaries of ten thousand worlds. The crystals had ended the war between the League and Hsktskt. No one knew that the Raktar had since placed them beyond the reach of himself or any being.

"SubAkade TssVar believes that if you do not go to Vtaga, the Hsktskt will perish. By plague or by crystal, it matters not to them." Teulon sounded as tired as he looked. "I have used every argument I can. He will not listen to me."

I felt cold. "What are your orders, Raktar?"

"No orders, my friend." Another smile, this one sad and resigned. "Your life is your own now, Jarn. You are slave to no one."

Except to Cherijo's past. I thought of all Garphawayn had told me, and something clenched inside me. "Reever and the Torin will not allow me to go."

"I anticipated as much. Use this." He displayed a signal code sequence on the screen. "It cannot be blocked or monitored. Should anyone interfere, they will help you."

I memorized the sequence. "I thank you for it. Teulon . . ." There was so much I wished to say to him. "I am sorry. Peace should not rest on the will of one person."

"As I know from experience." He touched the screen again. "If you have need of me, signal. I will come to you." His face vanished from the screen.

With it, a remote-connection light flickered off. I

knew enough about the console equipment to real-ize what they were doing. *I should have expected this.* I could not use the equipment for what I needed, and if I did not hurry even that avenue of appeal might be denied me, so I left Reever's quarters to go directly to communications.

"Healer." Salo Torin met me at the entry. "Is something—"

"From the light on my panel, I know that you recorded my exchange just now with Raktar Teu-lon," I said, noting the immediate guilt that crossed his features. "Which one of them told you to moni-tor my relays? The captain, or my husband?"

"Both. Your pardon, Healer, but I must follow my orders, even when I do not agree with them." His dark brows drew together. "You wish to dispute this? I will happily add my objections to yours."

"Another time, perhaps. At the moment, I need to send a relay to the code the Raktar gave to me." I did not recite it, for he already had a copy of the signal.

"You might have done that from your quarters."

"I should like to send it without being monitored or recorded." I gestured toward his station. "May I do so, and use one of your terminals?" I needed to offer something in return. "I would provide ease for you, if you wish."

"We do not . . . ah, no, I cannot permit either." He hesitated, and then checked the deck above us. "I must perform a routine diagnostic scan on the en-cryption hardware in the transponder control cen-ter. It will keep me occupied for the next hour. During that time, I would not see anyone who made use of the equipment here."

"So you would not." We understood each other perfectly. "I thank you."

I waited until Salo had disappeared before I went to an open terminal and input the relay sequence. The code opened a priority crisis relay channel between the *Sunlace* and the planet Joren. There was no display this time, only a male Jorenian voice identifying himself as adjunct to the Ruling Council, and requesting a statement of the emergency.

"This is Cherijo Torin," I said, glad for once to use her name. "I have been told that I am a member of this council, and I would speak on a matter of great importance."

"Healer Torin, the council is present and monitoring your relay," a female voice said. "Tell us how we may be of aid."

I related the details of my conversation with Teulon, and the decisions being made for me by the Torin and Reever. "Under the present circumstances, I would know what I am permitted to do of my own accord."

"As a member of the Ruling Council, you have absolute sovereignty over HouseClan Torin," the female told me. "You have but to issue the order to take you to Vtaga, and the captain will obey you. Should he not, he will be removed from command by our authority."

So the female Omorr had been correct in her assessment of my rights. "The ensleg—the men on the ship—they question my ability to make informed decisions. They feel that with my memory loss I am incapable of such."

"We see no evidence of this from the medical reports issued by Senior Healer Squilyp," the female said. "ClanLeader Jado has communicated the gravity of the situation to us. Know you what will happen should SubAkade TssVar follow through on the ultimatum he has offered?"

An end to slavery, or more war. "I understand the consequences, Council Member."

"We cannot compel you to go to Vtaga, Healer Torin. We can only urge you to do so." The female made a soft sound like a sigh. "It is our hope that you will."

There was more I had to ask, and the answers were immediate and positive. When I was satisfied that I had enough information, I thanked the council, terminated the relay, and went to speak to Salo. After discontinuing his pretend inspection and listening to what I had to say, he insisted on accompanying me to the command center. I paused only long enough to signal Reever and ask him to meet me there.

"You are certain this is what you wish to do, Healer?" he asked me just before we went into the lift.

"I am not certain of anything." How bitter that was, now that I knew why my former self had been created, and how hard she had fought that fate. I was a woman made from a man—how did I cope with that? "One cannot walk two paths, is that not what you said?"

"Perhaps I have said too much," he said as we went in to see the captain.

Reever was with Xonea, and looked rather

agitated. "You were not in our quarters. I was concerned—"

"I am well." I turned to face Xonea. I had been made from a man, thus I would assert my authority as a man would. "Captain Torin, you must alter the ship's course and take me to Vtaga."

Impatience filled his eyes. "You cannot go there. It is too dangerous." He looked at Duncan. "Did you not explain this to her?"

"Raktar Teulon signaled me about a serious development at the peace talks." I quickly explained TssVar's ultimatum, and added, "If I do not go, the Hsktskt will go back to warring with the League. Thus, I must go."

"Teulon does not comprehend what he asks of you," Reever said. "I will signal him and explain the blood bounty. He will make no more demands."

"No, you will not signal the Raktar." I ignored the impulse to drop to the floor and kept my spine straight, the same way a man would. "This demand is made of me, not you. *I* have the skill to accomplish this task. *I* decide whether to go or not. *I* say that I will go."

A muscle ticked on the side of Reever's jaw. "They will execute you, Jarn."

"They are dying. This is my work. Why should they murder the one who may help them live? I am told that I cannot be killed so easily, should they try." I addressed Xonea again. "You will take me to Vtaga now."

"I cannot do this, Cherijo," he told me. "You do not appreciate the—"

I looked at Salo. "How do I remove him from

command? Do I simply say the words?" Salo nodded. To Xonea, I said, "You will take me to Vtaga or I will remove you from command and make another serve in your place." I was not sure who I would make captain, but surely Salo would advise me.

Xonea's hands curled. "You do not have command of this ship."

"As a member of the Ruling Council, she does, Captain." Salo made a very formal-looking gesture. "She has the full support of the rest of the council."

"She has never spoken to . . ." Xonea gave Salo a furious glare. "You permitted her to send an unmonitored signal?"

"I did so without his aid or his permission." I regarded the captain steadily. "Will you take me to Vtaga or not?"

Xonea glanced from me to my husband, and then gave me a very reluctant nod.

"No. I won't let you." Reever latched onto me with a hard grip. "You've wasted enough of your life. You don't have to go. You no longer serve Teulon."

"As you have said, Husband, I no longer serve *anyone*." I glanced down at his hand, and he released me. To the captain, I said, "How long will it take for the ship to make the journey there?"

"If we use transition," Xonea said, "three days."

"Use transition." I walked out of the command center.

I knew Reever had every reason to be furious with me, so I did not return to his—our—quarters. Instead, I went to the deck where a great many members of the crew gathered to obtain wall food and share their meal intervals. I looked around, but I did not see the talking cat. The beast might be considered a person, but I was not going to eat near it. It might favor a bite of me over those pretend vegetables. I selected something my former self had kept programmed on the wall machine, and carried it to an empty table.

A big, muscular Jorenian female came over to me before I sat down. Like me, she held a tray of the wall food. "My name is Darea Torin. I am Salo's bondmate."

Fasala's ClanMother, I thought as I looked up at her. Like all the other females on the *Sunlace*, she was black-haired and blue-skinned, but she had the same direct, piercing gaze as an experienced hunter. She also wore her hair coiled and knotted in what Reever called a warrior's knot. "I am Jarn."

She knew me—Cherijo had written several times of her friendship with this woman—but she showed no surprise at the name I offered. "May I share my meal with you, Healer Jarn?"

Fasala had told me that her ClanMother and ClanFather preferred to eat in their quarters, which made Darea's presence and request a little suspicious. Still, the woman seemed not as joyously friendly as some of the other females on this ship, and I had no reason to dine alone.

"Yes." I sat down and regarded my selections. Broth, bread, and some chopped, cooked pretend vegetables. I knew from past experience that I could not stomach anything from the submenu Cherijo had designated "dessert" as the dishes were all too sweet for my palate. Beverages had also been tricky in the beginning, but through trial and error I had learned which teas would not turn my stomach.

Darea ignored her own selections to watch me tear the bread into chunks.

"You wish to speak with me about something?" I had not bothered with utensils; I always spilled and dropped things when I tried to use them. If my eating with my hands and fingers offended her, she could move to sit with someone else.

Her shoulders lifted slightly. "You do not seem very interested in having conversations."

"My people—the Iisleg—do not indulge in much casual talk. Here on the ship I have had more practice with listening." I tried to think of an interesting topic. "Your mate did a favor for me but refused my offer to couple with him. Did you know that I was made from a man?"

Darea blinked. "We are all made from men and women," she said, very matter-of-fact. "Why would you wish my mate to couple with you?"

"I did not wish it; it was to return the favor. It is the way of my people. I am not like you, though. I came from a man and machines." I dipped a chunk of bread in the broth and sampled it. The unfamiliar taste and spices made me grimace. "Dævena yepa, this is disgusting. Do you care for something called minestrone soup?"

"I do not think so." Darea wrinkled her nose. "It smells odd, and it looks too red and wet."

I liked her better for that. "Excuse me." I went to dispose of the soup and returned. "What is that?" I asked, nodding toward what appeared to be a small pile of white and blue flower petals and dark brown shoots on her dish.

"*C'nabba* and *gnika-la*. They are fresh, not synthetic." She offered me a sample, which tasted a little like the ice plants that grew around the edges of vent shafts. "We grow some foods on the ship, on the hydroponics deck."

"My daughter has spoken of it." I made a mental note of the names, and then something occurred to me. "You do not grow children in machines there, do you?"

"No." Darea smiled. "We reproduce by natural means. What you call coupling. It is our custom to be exclusive to each other as well, so you need not offer to couple with any other crew member who does a favor for you."

I felt as if a huge weight lifted from my neck. "I begin to like your customs, Jorenian."

We continued our meals in silence, but as others came into the galley we became the subject of many speculative looks. No one approached, but many held murmured conversations after spotting us.

"Where do you serve on the ship?" I asked her, mainly to block out the attention being given to us.

"I was a data archivist when I first came to the HouseClan, but now I supervise central processing and technical support." She sipped tea from her server. "It is my responsibility to ensure data and archival integrity at all levels."

Everything on the *Sunlace* depended on data systems, computers, and other related technology. It amazed me that the ensleg would permit a mere woman to oversee it, but this was what Garphawayn had insisted they did. "Do you like what you do?"

"It is challenging, but I would not be content with anything else." She met my gaze. "What of your work? My bondmate tells me that you were a battle-field surgeon during the rebellion on Akkabarr."

"I was." She was speaking to me, not Cherijo. She saw me as a real person, not the flesh left behind by the spirit of one she had known. My pleasure at that warmed away some of the coldness in my heart. "Without healers, people die. With healers, some yet die. It is a struggle to be content with such work."

"I doubt you will find any contentment among the Hsktskt." She gazed around us and frowned twice at particular individuals. "Or, soon, my bond-mate's HouseClan. Word of what you mean to do has spread quickly."

It was then that I saw her motive for coming to me. Darea was not simply sharing a meal. She was keeping the others away from me.

Salo was fortunate in his choice of women. I was glad he had not pressed me to couple with him.

"I will not endanger the people on this ship," I said. "If need be, I will take a launch and go to Vtaga alone." Given Reever's attitude, that might be the wisest course of action.

"You have become a telepath?" She tried to sound amused, but there was too much worry in her eyes. "Your pardon, Healer. When Salo spoke of your decision, I could only think of Fasala and the other children on board the ship."

"I, too, am tempted to think only of them, as well

as my own child. Yet if there is war, then the Hsktskt will kill many more daughters and sons." All the talk around us had ceased, and the others were listening. I did not bother to murmur as they had. "I saw too much of death during the rebellion on Akkabarr. If I can do nothing else with this life, I will use it to stop another war."

Her white eyes softened. "Then your House will stand with you."

All around us expressions changed, and heads nodded before people went back to eating and conversing in a normal fashion.

"I would ask two favors of you," I said to Salo's mate. "Would you look after my child while I am on Vtaga?"

Darea finally smiled. "Of course I will. Salo and I honor Marel as if she were our own ClanDaughter. How else may I help you?"

My cheeks grew hot and I lowered my voice. "Will you tell me what, exactly, transition is?"

I knew that Reever would become impatient if he were waiting for me, so after Darea explained how transition used different dimensions to move the ship over great distances, I went to confront him. Neither he nor Marel were in our quarters when I arrived, which made my heart grow cold.

He has taken her from me.

I hurried over to the console to make a computer inquiry as to their location, but before I could finish inputting the request, Reever entered and secured the door.

I saw no anger in his expression, but that meant

nothing. Reever did not show his emotions on his face. He came toward me, but as I braced myself he walked past and went to the wall machine. "Marel is spending the night with Garphawayn and Squilyp."

"There is no need." Although I was relieved to know Darea would look after Marel while I was on Vtaga, I disliked having others care for my child when I could. "I will go and fetch her."

"She is asleep by now. You were out all day. You must be tired." He began using the machine to prepare a meal. "Would you prefer hot or cold tea?"

"I am not thirsty." Why was he behaving like this? Why was he not shouting at me? Did the man truly have ice for blood? "I ate in the place where all the crew gathers to share food and conversation."

"It's called the galley." He reprogrammed his selections and filled a server with a murky-looking liquid. That was all he brought from the machine to the table where we ate our meals. "You should go to bed."

"I am not interested in sleeping. Darea said she would care for Marel when we go to Vtaga." I sat across from him. "Did you know there is a giant cat on this ship that walks on two legs and talks?"

"Alunthri." He nodded, but kept his head down, so I couldn't see his expression.

"That beast scared the wits from me when I met it today. I thought I might jump through a wall panel. Reever, I know you are angry with me. I also think you will not beat me for what I have done. We should"—what was the way he always said it?—"discuss this."

"You never liked talking to me," he told the server in his hand, not me. "You always thought I said too much. We shared few interests. You often became bored or impatient with me."

"I have never said or felt such things," I was happy to tell him. Whatever that stupid female had felt, I could not call Reever tedious or dull. "You speak of my former self."

"Yes. Your *former* self." He lifted the server and drank from it. "However much I despise what you have done, Jarn, it gives me hope. Cherijo would have made the same choice to go to Vtaga."

He said the last with such venom that I flinched. Not because he despised me, but . . . "Did you love her, or hate her?"

"I hated myself for not being the man she wanted. For not inspiring enough love in her." Now he looked at me, and there was so much pain in his eyes that a sound escaped me. He ignored it. "She chose another man over me."

"Another?" I felt alarmed.

"He is dead."

Why had Cherijo not written about this? "You are not," I pointed out. "She remained with you, did she not?"

"It doesn't matter. Even dead, he always took first place in her heart."

I would have to discover who this dead man was. "A woman would not love a memory more than a real man."

"I thought what happened to you would at last give me some advantage." He looked at the server as if he couldn't quite recognize what it was. "You have no memories of him, only me. I took the first place in your heart . . . or perhaps I have not." He rested his forehead against his fist. "I did not want you to know of him, so I erased everything she wrote about him in her journal files."

That explained the periodic gaps in the data. I couldn't understand why he would do such a thing, but I saw no shame in it. Indeed, I thought his end-less obsession with my former self unhealthy. Such fixations had nearly driven Teulon insane, although it had been more understandable in his case. He had lost his bondmate and every member of his House-Clan except his young son.

Discovering Xan had survived the Jado Massacre had given Teulon hope and renewed interest in life. Could not Marel do the same for Reever?

"I am not interested in the dead," I said. "We are together, and even when we do not agree, we suit each other." I glanced at the bedchamber. "If last night did not convince you of this, remember that we also share a daughter. She needs both of us. Can that not be enough for you?"

"For me?" His head came up. "You don't care that I destroyed some of your past?"

It is not my past. I shook my head. "I might erase the rest of it myself; it would save me much confusion."

He seemed shocked by my words. "You should know how you came to be."

"I know I was made from a man and grown inside a machine instead of a woman's belly. I cannot get sick and I may never die. If there are more unnatural things involved, please, do not tell me of them." He did not respond. "You understand the Hsktskt better than I, Husband. I will need your wisdom when we reach Vtaga. And I . . . care for you. Do not let this become another wall between us."

He was silent for a long time. "If I agree, you must also make a concession."

"Anything."

"When we are among the Hsktskt, you must listen to me and do as I say." Before I could speak, he put his hand over mine. "I know this species intimately. I served as a member of the Faction for years. Your death on Akkabarr may have lifted the blood bounty, but there are other dangers. You cannot recognize them, but I will."

I hardly heard the last of what he said, so busy was I trying to absorb the fact that Reever had once belonged to the Hsktskt. Cherijo had said much about him in her journals, but never this. That he had once been a slaver changed everything. "Perhaps it will be better if I summon Teulon."

"No." His hand tightened. "I did not join them. I made a pretense of it. I never enslaved anyone." When I jerked at his hold, his mouth became a thin line. "You will listen to me this time."

I felt a curious paralysis move up my arm. Before I could react, some unseen force rendered my body immobile. I tried to cry out, but something besides myself filled my mind.

I can do more than read your thoughts, Jarn, Reever's voice said inside my head. *I can use your mind to control your body.*

My heartbeat raced as I tried to escape the invisible force he used to hold me in place. At the same time, I felt Reever's own cool, focused thoughts enclose me as he somehow slowed my pulse and relaxed my knotted muscles.

I had never felt such an invasion, not even when we had coupled. I should have been terrified, or outraged, but his thoughts held me as gently as his arms. *How can you do this?*

I don't know. I have never been capable of such a link with anyone else but you. Reever spoke as if my thoughts were my voice. *It is the bond we have shared since the moment we first saw each other. Kiss me.*

The paralysis lifted, and I shifted forward, leaning across the table to press my mouth against his.

He took his time enjoying the kiss before immobilizing me again. *I can make you say or do anything I wish.*

My lips tingled. *Why have you never done this to me before now?*

It is wrong to control another person. His fingers threaded through my hair. *I'm only demonstrating what I can do. I will not lose you again. It nearly drove me mad when they took you from me the last time.*

The mild affection I felt for Reever tightened inside me. I had respected him before this, but now I understood many things about his relationship with my former self that had not made sense. *You might have said something about this when we made our agreement. You hide too much from me. How can I trust someone as dangerous as you are?*

"Not dangerous." He sat back. "Devoted."

The paralysis vanished, as did his presence in my mind. I lifted my hand to touch my mouth, and then looked down at myself. "This is why she worried about giving herself to you. Because you could do this thing to her. Because you *did* it to her without her say. She knew."

He nodded. He did not seem ashamed of it.

"Do you understand *nothing* about women?" I demanded. When he didn't answer, I got to my feet. Perhaps I had been made from a man, but I felt wholly female now. "You wish me to give you my trust, and then you do things like this as if you would destroy it. You wish me to desire you, and then show me that you do not even need my cooperation to have me whenever you wish."

"I demonstrated the power of our link so that you would know that I love you," he countered. "If I did not, I would use it to take what I want."

"What is it that you want from me?" I shouted.

Reever did not move. "You. All of you, mind, body, and soul. You are all I have ever wanted."

"Are you insane? Blind?" I threw my arms out. "You *have* me."

"I can never have you, just as I could never have her." His thoughts filled my mind again, but this time with an aching longing. *Only you can choose to give yourself to me. Not as repayment of a favor, or in fear of me because I am male. Your choice must be made because you love me as I love you.*

I knew Reever had loved Cherijo. No man would have searched as long and as hard as he had for a woman unless she meant everything to him. He had joined the rebellion on Akkabarr and fought a war not his own rather than abandon his quest for my former self.

For a moment, I felt unworthy of this man and his

love. I was not the woman for whom he had sacrificed so much, and yet he wanted me, and was apparently willing to settle for me—and love me in her place.

Could I be happy with that? "Iisleg men and women do not love each other. Love cannot . . . is not . . ." My vision blurred and the room began to whirl. "Stop doing that, or I will puke."

"It isn't me. The ship is making an interdimensional transition," Reever said, his voice drawing near. "Close your eyes."

Darea had warned me that it would be disorienting, and I squeezed my eyes shut as I felt arms come around me.

Joey.

"Jarn. I am Jarn. I will never be anyone but Jarn." My skin crawled as I realized it was not Reever who had called to me. "Who . . ."

Joey.

"Jarn?"

The two voices blended together, confusing me, and then they were lost in the darkness, as I was.

FIVE

I emerged from the oblivion, but not to myself or even my own body. I had arrived somewhere completely different, and I was not myself.

"Okay, Chief Linguist, I can give you exactly one minute." A woman who looked remarkably like me picked up a stack of charts from the desk. *"What do you want?"*

I heard myself answer her with Reever's voice. *"We must confirm tomorrow's agenda."*

I glanced down at my hands, and saw that they were my husband's. My body had grown taller, leaner, and was no longer female. I felt the absence of my breasts, and the new and rather alarming weight of testicles between my legs.

Somehow I had become Reever, and I was speaking to myself when my body had been occupied by the mind and heart of Cherijo Grey Veil.

Her expression blanked. "Tomorrow's agenda for what?"

"Your community-service quota." When that didn't register, I added, *"You are scheduled to work in botanical fields."*

"What has that got to do with you?" Before I could an-

swer, she closed her eyes briefly. "Let me guess. You're scheduled to supervise me."

"That is correct."

"Okay, Chief Linguist." She glanced at her wristcom. "What do you need to confirm?"

"A time and place to meet in the morning."

"I'm pulling a double shift, and I need five hours of sleep to be human." She expelled a breath. "Meet me at my quarters, main housing building, west wing, at alpha shift commencement." She moved toward the exam rooms, her shoulders hunched—as if she carried a heavy weight on her back.

Did she consider me her burden? Forcing the issue would not instill trust. "I can request another supervisor for you," I called after her.

"Don't bother." She sounded resigned. "Someone obviously thinks I deserve this."

I arrived at Cherijo's quarters the following morning at the time she had specified. She did not answer the door chime until I enabled it for the third time.

"Wait a minute," I heard her call out over the com panel. She mumbled something else before she opened the door. "Come in, Reever. I'm almost ready."

She had dressed appropriately in old, shabby garments, but was still consuming her morning beverage. A small, four-legged, silver-furred mammal approached me. It was something like a feral Vukta from Carsca VII, but smaller and without the venom-filled spine frills.

I had fought a number of felines in the arena, and they were efficient killers. "A domesticated animal?"

"Uh-huh." She finished her drink.

The creature was quite bold—it sniffed my footgear, then began rubbing itself against my calves and ankles.

The odd sounds it produced from its throat were quite plaintive—but so were the Vuktas', just before they pounced and stabbed their prey to death.

If she had domesticated it, she had likely formed an emotional attachment to the creature—so she would not appreciate me shooting it. "What does it want?"

"His name is Jenner," she told me. "He wants you to pet him."

"Why?"

"Didn't you ever—" She halted, then began securing her hair. "That's why they're called pets, Reever. You pet them." She bound the end of her braid. "Most alien cultures have domesticated animals, don't they?"

"No." I thought of my former owner, who had kept me naked, collared, and chained to her side whenever she traveled. "However, there are several species that consume such small mammals as their primary dietary—"

"Never mind. Forget I asked." She crouched down and stroked the animal with her hands. The cat didn't appear to want her attention, and continued to entreat me with its menacing yowls. It had blue eyes, like her—perhaps it was controlled by a mind-eating, sadistic parasite. "Come on. Let's go."

She seemed impressed with my glidecar. "Who did you bribe to get this?" she asked as she entered the passenger side.

"No one." I wondered if she truly cared to hear the tale, or if she was merely making what humans called polite conversation. "It was a gift."

"I see."

"I doubt it."

"Okay, who gave it to you?"

"A grateful Furinac who had been unable to communicate with colonial militia during an unauthorized transport."

"He must have been really grateful." She trailed her fingers over the soft seat covering. "What exactly did you do for him?"

"That requires a rather lengthy explanation." Her moods were erratic and unpredictable, and that annoyed me. That she would have any interest in my activities seemed unlikely—or was she at last taking an interest in me? "Have you toured the Botanical Project Area yet?"

"Some of it." Her interest, and some of her color, abruptly disappeared.

"You're disturbed. What is it?"

She closed her eyes and leaned back against the seat cushions. The way she sat made her look very young and defeated. "I lost a patient last night."

Surely a physician grew accustomed to watching a percentage of patients die—it was only logical that some would. Yet she seemed genuinely distraught. Terrans often avoided discussing painful topics, although I never quite understood why. Suppressing emotions appeared to be more damaging than having none at all.

"We will be working in the hybrid cultivation area today," I told her, changing the subject. "There are a number of off-world specimens being crossbred with native plants in production."

She yawned. "Excuse me."

"You did not get your five hours' sleep."

"No."

That Mayer would verbally abuse her when she devoted so much of her time to his FreeClinic made my thoughts darken. "Charge Nurse T'Nliqinara told me you've worked four extra shifts this week."

"Uh-huh." She avoided my gaze.

"Is Dr. Mayer aware of your extended work hours?" If he was not, perhaps I should inform him. Among other things.

She snorted. "Dr. Mayer probably spits whenever he hears my name. Drop it, all right?"

Another painful topic. I would need help determining what to make the next. "What would you care to talk about?"

"Nothing, Chief Linguist." She made a negligent gesture with her hand. "You can be the conversational navigator."

"Very well." I halted the glidecar near our assigned work area. "Tell me what you know about agricultural cultivation."

"Absolutely nothing outside of a few required botany courses during secondary school." She produced another yawn. "All of which I gave little or no attention to."

"We'll begin with something basic." I thought of the various projects requiring immediate attention. Hydroponics required too much explanation, and grafting—something that, as a surgeon, she would likely be very good at—was restricted to experienced cultivators only. "Perhaps planting some seedlings."

I retrieved several flats of seedlings already removed from their hydroponics pods and prepared for transfer to the soil. The hybrids were particularly valuable, and the senior site botanist expressed his concern, but I felt the doctor could perform the simple task without difficulty. I set her to work on one side of the hybrid field and went to work on the other myself.

I discovered how much I had misjudged Cherijo when the senior botanist stopped at her row an hour later and *began shouting at her. I went over to find that she had placed the seedlings exactly where I had indicated. And every single specimen was planted wrong.*

"Do you see this?" The botanist, a Psyoran, was so agitated that he had turned monochromatic and had distended veins popping from his multiple frill layers. "It took two cycles to germinate these seeds! Two cycles!"

"This is her first assignment." I knelt down and carefully removed one specimen. "She will not make the same mistake again."

"Not as long as I work this field," the botanist promised.

"You know, you should water them more," Cherijo told him. "They might grow a little faster."

"They're grown in water, you—you—" The Psyoran became incoherent.

"Really." She eyed the seedlings. "Then maybe you should stick some labels on them for the rest of us nonplant life-forms. You know, like 'this side up?' "

He stared at her before resorting to language that I had not programmed into the colonial linguistic database, and slighted everything from her mental capacity to her genetic origins.

"Oh, yeah?" She didn't understand the words, but she clearly grasped his meaning. "And what was your mother? A tumbleweed? Poison ivy?"

Before the botanist could say more, I stepped between them. "There appears to be no permanent damage. I will personally correct her error."

"She's not to touch another pod. Keep her black thumb out of my specimens." He flapped as he stalked back to the cultivation center.

"What did I do?" she demanded.

I began digging out the next seedling. "You planted them upside down."

She scowled. "How was I supposed to know the white things are the roots, and the brown part is supposed to be above the ground?"

I could not fathom how someone so intelligent could have done something so ridiculous. "If you had listened when I explained the procedure to you, you would have known."

"Reever, you never once said the roots were the white things."

I paused for a moment, wishing briefly that I could express a few words not contained on the colonial linguistic database. "I was not aware I had to specify that fact."

"Well, I didn't kill any of them." She leaned over me and peered at the row. "Did I?"

"They'll survive."

"Great." She glanced back to where the senior site botanist was still pacing back and forth and complaining to another of his colleagues. "Tell me, what did that raving maniac mean when he said I had a black thumb?"

"He meant you need to be assigned to another project."

"Even better." She sniffed. "What would you recommend that I try next, Chief Linguist?"

I gave the matter some consideration. "Working with something inanimate."

"Very funny."

I brushed the loose soil from my hands as I stood and checked the time. "We're finished."

She eyed the flat of seedlings left to one side. "But I—"

I raised one hand, imitating one of her favorite habitual gestures. "You've done enough."

"Not yet," she said. "Hear me out."

She went on to explain the unusual circumstances regarding Alun Karas, the patient who had died at the FreeClinic the night before. He had evidently aspirated some resin after a collection device exploded, and she thought the sap might be responsible for the infection that had killed him. I agreed that it might help to visit the site where the botanist had been collecting samples.

She seemed to have no recollection of the vision we had shared on the day we met, for she showed no hesitation, even when I indicated she would have to enter the gnorra groves with me.

Her lack of fear would make what I wanted to do easier for both of us.

"I am familiar with his work assignment. He was over in a section adjoining the south range." I kept my voice bland. "We can reach it from here on foot."

Cherijo was quiet as we made our way into the gnorra groves. I opened my mind, gathering in what I could of her thought images and feelings. Her emotions radiated over everything, and I sensed a distinct division in them—she felt despondency over the loss of her patient, and happiness over something completely unrelated and unidentifiable. She demonstrated little pleasure in sharing my company, so what was creating the warmth behind the sadness?

Perhaps she would tell me. "Thinking of pleasant memories?"

"You're certainly interested in what I'm thinking all the time."

"Occupational hazard."

By that time we had left the fields and were walking through some dense growth into the uncultivated areas.

She wasn't paying attention to where she was stepping, however, and I had to catch her as she stumbled over a hidden tangle of roots. I stopped until she regained her balance.

Touching her strengthened the connection between us a hundredfold. I knew what she was thinking, and who had brought her here. Who made her happy and excited. It wasn't me.

It was another man. An alien.

I took hold of her other arm, then brought my hands to her wrists as she raised them in a defensive gesture. Her wrists, in front of my face—it was exactly as it had been in the vision. But I could not think of precognition or the connection we shared, not in that moment.

She had been busy making new friends. Friends who were male, and made her happy, and excited her. Friends who were not human. Friends who were not like me. I increased my grip.

"What are you doing?" she whispered.

I probed her thoughts, determined to know all of it.

"He was here with you."

"What?"

"The pilot, Torin." I saw his face in her mind. "He was here with you, wasn't he?"

I wanted to know what he had done to her, and what she had given him. If she would not tell me, I would locate the memories myself.

"How do you know—" She wrenched away from my hands, breaking the tentative connection between us. "What was that? What did you do to me?"

"I linked with you." And would again, as soon as I could put my hands on her.

Had she been intimate with the Jorenian? How long had this been going on?

"Linked?" She stepped back. "What the hell does that mean?"

"I established a mental link with you, when I touched you. I have tried before, but you did not realize—"

Her chin sagged for a moment. "You did this before?"

"The first time we met, at the trading center." I took hold of her wrists once more and raised them. "This image was one I shared with you." *Before she had met Torin—before she had ever seen him. I had prior claim on her.*

"Reever—you—" Anger reduced her speech capacity significantly. "I never said you could touch me or—or—"

Didn't she understand? Couldn't she feel the connection between us? Did I have to explain everything to her? "I don't have to touch you."

I dropped her wrist, and she swiveled and began to walk away.

No.

What happened next was as much a surprise to me as it was to her. I reached out to her mind to link, but determination to stop her changed the probe and allowed me control over her physical body.

Stop. Her body halted, as if time stood still. She began to cry out, but I stopped that impulse as well. *Quiet.* Then I went after her.

I moved around her, holding her mind with mine as I inspected her. She was trying to speak; I could see her throat moving. But I controlled her speech center, and blocked all sound impulses. I could control everything she did. Her thoughts were frantic—she was wondering how I could be doing this, what type of psychic ability I had.

Even experiencing my linkhold over her, she could not be-
lieve it was possible.

I looked into her eyes, and attempted a direct thought
transfer. Yes, it is.

Reever? *She was even more shocked than before.* Can
you hear me?

Yes. I hear you. *I moved closer, enjoying my power
over her. Who would not wish control such as this over
another being? Especially one I wanted so much?*

*I felt no guilt. She was my balance. She belonged with
me. She belonged to me. And if she did not recognize it
now, in time she would understand.*

You are really doing this. *She didn't want to believe
it, but her mind was logical, and she was not a coward.*
Why? Why are you doing this to me?

*How could I explain the needs surging inside me? She
would not believe them. I did not myself.* You're the
only one I've never had to touch.

*Her mind was a snarl of contradictions and emotions—
curiosity, outrage, fear—and something else, something
she wouldn't reveal to me. She held up barriers there
which I could not penetrate. Beyond her emotions, her
mind was orderly and ruthlessly organized—her cognitive knowledge of medicine alone was astounding—and I
realized that what she had learned during her brief years
would have taken another Terran decades, perhaps even a
lifetime to comprehend.*

*I moved back into what she was unconsciously trying
to conceal—her memory center. Everywhere I saw shadows upon shadows, suppressing and obscuring her life
before she came to K-2. There was only one, very clear
memory I could make out—that of another Terran female,
older than Cherijo, with vivid red hair.*

Lighten up, Joey. You do any more studying and your eyes will fall out of your head. Come on, let's go shopping.

Joey. *Of course, a diminutive of Cherijo. I liked the sound of it very much.*

Jarn.

Images of my own body, injured and in a hospital berth, pushed me back, trying to force me from her mind. Those were coming from the ensleg ship, from the present. Reever was seeing me. My husband was trying to pull me out of this snarl of memories not my own—

Reever could not free me, so he took me back to the grove of purple trees, where he and Cherijo had linked for the first time.

Enough, Reever. *Cherijo's subconscious drew strength from the shadows in her mind, even though I suspected she herself was not aware of them. The combination was quite powerful.* Get out of my head!

My warrior of life. She had yet to recognize that I was her balance.

Wait. *I took her hand in mine, entwined my fingers with hers. I had to make her understand who I was, what I was. She did not understand that she would be safe with me, that I had as many shadows and dark places inside me. She did not know that I would kill anything that harmed her.* There's more.

More what?

I opened my mind to her, sending brief bursts of images from my own past. I had never revealed myself to another with such candor, and I was not sure if she would even comprehend my motive for doing so. I found I did not care—even if it meant nothing to her, I wanted to show her my life, everything about me.

This is who I am. This is what I was.

I thought of the first planet on which my parents had left me. There had been no sapient inhabitants, so I had spent several days alone, acting recklessly, injuring myself as I looked for my mother and father, even though I knew they had taken the ship and left me there. If I kept looking, my younger self reasoned that I would find them, and not have to face the prospect of living and dying alone on that barren world.

My parents had been very disappointed when they returned several days later. I had fallen ill, and nearly died from the fever and an infected wound on my leg. The contempt they had felt as they repaired the damage and brought me back to health had been only too clear.

I had been even more terrified while enduring my trial of discipline on Tarvasc. I made her see that, watch the first time an examiner had slashed the back of my hand with his blade. The many weeks of hunger and punishment that followed had purged me of my youthful insubordination, and tempered me into an obedient child. My parents had never had cause to complain about my behavior again.

I wanted to show her everything I had experienced over my lifetime. I began sending a continuous stream of memory, all the worlds and beings I had encountered until the Hsktskt had taken me from Svcita and enslaved me.

I did not show her everything, however. I kept from her my years in the arena; I did not want her to see that thing that I had become on the killing sands. How I had suffered, and what they had done to me. How it had changed and shaped me into the man I had become. Perhaps some-

day I would tell her, but not now. Not until I was assured of her loyalty to me.

Let—me—go.

She still resisted me, and I could feel something growing inside her mind—she was reaching for her own, unused mental resources. That alarmed me, for if she used them incorrectly, one or both of us could end up with brain damage.

Although it was like tearing a wound in myself, I ended the linkhold.

And I, finally Jarn again, fell into the shadows past all memories.

"She's regaining consciousness. Scanner."

I opened my eyes to be momentarily blinded by a piercing light. The familiar odors of antiseptic and sterile solution told me where I was. I tried to shade my face with my hand to see why, but my arms were restrained. So were my legs.

"Brain wave activity returning to level function," a female said. "Vitals are stabilizing, Senior Healer."

I opened my eyelids to slits until my pupils adjusted to the light. I had been placed on a critical-care berth in the isolation room next to Dapvea Adan's. The Omorr stood over me and moved a scanner over my head.

"Am I injured?" I felt no pain, and no sluggishness from drugs.

"Apparently not." Squilyp lifted the instrument to study its display screen. He did not appear happy with the results.

I turned my head to see two nurses and Reever

standing beyond them. "Was the ship attacked? How did this happen?"

"The ship is safe. You've just come out of a coma," the Senior Healer said, sounding testy. "We don't know why it happened."

I tucked my chin in to look down at myself. I was in a patient garment and full limb restraints. "How long was I in the coma? Why do you have me tied to the berth?"

"You were comatose for approximately seventeen hours. We restrained you . . . for safety reasons." The Omorr released the straps that had immobilized me. "Tell me what you remember."

I easily recalled what had happened between me and Reever, and the unpleasant effects while the ship made the interdimensional jump. The dream of being Reever, and having odd experiences on another world with my former self, also came back to me, so real and vivid that it could not have been a fantasy. Could Reever have made me see those things while I was unconscious? In the midst of it, and immediately after it, came only a jumble of images; too many and too bizarre to make any sense.

I decided to wait until I could talk to my husband about what had happened before confiding the details to anyone else. Knowing now just how much he could control my body and mind, there was much we had to discuss. "I was talking with Reever. The ship transitioned and I blacked out. Did I strike my head?" That, too, might explain the puzzling interval after the dream/memory.

"Duncan said he caught you before you hit the deck." Squilyp looked up and nodded, and my husband came to stand at the side of my berth. "She seems to have recovered, but I want to observe her and perform a full physical exam before discharge," he warned before he and the nurses left us.

Reever appeared pale and tense. "How do you feel?"

"Well. Confused. Ridiculous." I sat up slowly. My body seemed fine and the room did not spin or change form; my head was clear. It felt as if I had only been asleep. I looked around before I lowered my voice and asked, "Did you put me in a coma?"

"No. I would never do such a thing." He took my hand in his. "I may be able to find out why it happened, but I must link with you to do so. May I?"

Now he asked permission? Perhaps it was because we were not alone here. "Be careful."

I experienced the same strange sense of invasion as I had when Reever had taken control of my body, only not as intensely. Feeling my husband's mind inside my head this time was not unpleasant but rather unnerving.

I could feel his regret over what had happened. He had only meant to demonstrate what he would not do to me, so that I could know the depth of his regard. Remorse now colored his thoughts with as much sadness as the longing he always carried inside him.

Since I knew he could hear my thoughts, I directed them at him. *Do you see what happened to me?*

Some of it. He seemed to move to the very center of my mind, which made me shiver. *So much is—*

I didn't understand the word he used, but it sounded angry. Maybe he was still expecting to find

Cherijo somewhere inside my head. Given the love he felt for her, I almost wished he could. *I am sorry.*

Don't apologize to me. Reever left my thoughts and released my hand so quickly that it was as if he had never touched them in the first place. His eyes had changed to the color of new ice at twilight.

Squilyp came over. "What is it?"

"An old problem. It is likely that the stress of being invaded by two telepaths caused the coma." Reever turned away from me and regarded the Senior Healer. "When will you be finished with the examination?"

"I am told I can only keep her for another hour, so I want her to wear a cerebral monitor during the briefing with the Adan," Squilyp said. He gave my husband a hard look. "In the event another telepath attempts to take over her brain."

"What other telepath? What briefing?" I asked, starting to feel as I had when I had woken up on the ice, stripped of all knowledge except being.

"The Ruling Council sent two of HouseClan Adan's ships to escort us to Vtaga," my husband told me. "ClanLeader Adan wishes to coordinate their efforts to safeguard you with ours, so there will be a briefing."

Why had the council sent more ships? How would the Hsktskt react to such a display of force? "Can it not wait?" I asked, feeling overwhelmed now. I had just been in a coma; surely I could be granted more time to prepare for this.

"Not much longer," Squilyp told me. "We will reach Vtaga in three hours."

SIX

Reever returned just after the Senior Healer fitted me with a narrow alloy band that looked like a hair ornament but monitored and transmitted my brain wave activity to a console in Medical.

"You need not wear it when you cleanse or sleep," Squilyp said as he showed me how to switch off and remove the device. "If you feel dizzy or faint, tell Duncan, but don't link with him. If you're alone when something happens, sit quietly. I'll have you on constant monitor."

"I do not think Reever's telepathy caused me to go into a coma," I told him. "It is more likely some remnant reaction from the head injuries I received on Akkabarr."

"I'm not sure." The Omorr looked disgusted and, oddly, a little ashamed. "You were not like other Terrans before this, and none of your readings match the ones I had on file for the various synaptic episodes you suffered in the past that were not attributed to Reever's abilities."

"This happened to Cherijo?" She had never described it in her journals. Did the woman do nothing but write about Reever and herself?

"Something like it, yes, several times. We had

theories, but we never determined exactly what caused the . . . incidents." His dark eyes shifted as he looked over my head at Reever. "They are waiting for you. Go. We will do a follow-up later."

As I walked to the lift with my husband, I silently reviewed everything I had read from my chart. Squilyp's notations were detailed and precise, but my symptoms made little sense. A comatose state was always induced by something; usually an injury or an adverse physical reaction to a drug or chemical. I had experienced neither. The only oddity that had happened before my mishap had been Reever's possession and control of my mind and body, the memories of seeing myself through his eyes, and . . .

Joey.

Someone else had been there. I remembered the voice that had called me by his pet name. A voice that had been, like Reever's thought-link, inside my head. Was it the red-haired woman of Cherijo's memories?

"Did someone enter our quarters just before I became ill?" I asked him. "This other telepath of whom you spoke in Medical, perhaps?"

"There are no other telepaths on the ship." Reever enabled the lift to take us to third level. "We were alone."

"Someone spoke to me through my thoughts. Someone who called me *Joey.*" I frowned, concentrating, trying to recall the voice. "It was not a Jorenian or an Iisleg. The voice was one I have not before heard. Who else uses that name for me?"

"Your—" He used a word my vocollar could not

translate. "She died before you left Terra, but she has used a form of telepathy to contact you—Cherijo—in the past. It always had a severe effect on her." The lift doors opened. "I will tell you what I know about Maggie after the briefing."

"After the briefing we are going to Vtaga." I took hold of his arm. "Who was this Maggie person? Did she have red hair? Use words I can understand. Please."

"Her name was Maggie. She was engaged by your creator to act as a mother to you," Reever said, as if he hated telling me this. "She had red hair when she posed as a human being."

"Posed?"

"Maggie was an alien life-form masquerading as a Terran." His tone chilled with distaste and something uglier; something I almost thought was hatred. "She claimed to have used subliminal implants to enable her to communicate with you."

"So my father made me from his cells and experimented on me, while my *mother* tampered with my brain so she could speak to me from the otherworld." I was suddenly very glad they were both dead.

"Maggie claimed many reasons for helping Joseph Grey Veil to create you, among them to carry on the work of her extinct species, which she claimed founded all of the humanoid races in our galaxy. I do not believe she has ever told you the truth, nor am I convinced that she is dead," Reever said. "I have encountered her more than once in the past, and what she did to your mind required more than subliminal implants."

Another muddle of events from a past not my own: a husband who could but would not control my mind and body, and a dead ensleg intent on possessing me through my own subconscious. "Can no one simply leave me alone?"

"I have never been able to resist you," my husband said as we walked from the lift to an area on the third level.

I looked around but saw only a large, closed entryway. "What is this place?"

"It is the captain's reception room for . . ." He paused, choosing his words. "Important visitors."

I looked down at the simple tunic and trousers I wore. The garments Reever had brought to Medical for me were as modest as any others I was made to wear, but now the ensleg clothing seemed too tight, too revealing. Also I was bareheaded—something an Iisleg woman never was in front of visitors. "It would be better if I covered my face."

"No. They need to see you," he assured me, and guided me into the room.

The important visitors looked exactly like Xonea and the other Jorenians, all blue-skinned and black-haired giants. They wore the Adan garments in the same colors and patterns of muted blue, black, and gray as those who presently served among the crew. These men and women appeared far more heavily armed, however, and their expressions seemed less than welcoming.

"Council Member Cherijo Torin," Xonea said in a loud voice from one side of me, making me jump a little.

The visitors turned toward me and performed

bows accompanied by a terse, swift gesture, all in perfect unison.

Reever gripped my wrist and spoke into my head. *They do this to show that they recognize your authority over them.*

There were more than seventy people in the room, and I was in charge of all? I looked up at the captain. "I should not have threatened to remove you from command. Would you do this?"

Xonea's mouth curled up on one side. "Too late for that, ClanSister."

One of the bigger males, with wide purple streaks in his black hair, approached me. He wore a strip of black-and-silver, metallic, woven cloth across his tunic, upon which were sheathed dozens of small blades that had no hilts. His six-fingered hands moved expressively as he bowed again. "Tlore Adan, ClanLeader of the Adan. My House is yours, ClanJoren."

ClanJoren is a title of honor, given to you for saving their homeworld, my husband explained. *It means you belong to all of their tribes, and they will defend you to the death.*

How do I respond? I thought back.

Offer your hands out, palm up. He will take them and hold them for a moment. Address him as ClanLeader. He hesitated before adding, *Say something pleasant.* He released me.

I did as he said with my hands, and Tlore grasped them gently. "Please call me Healer, Clan-Leader," I said politely. I would never remember to answer to ClanJoren. "Your blades are beautiful. Are they for show, or do you use them?"

Startled, low chuckles erupted around us, and the skin around Tlore's eyes crinkled. "I have had occasion to use them."

I had not meant to say anything funny, but I was not averse to taking advantage of his good humor. "Shall we begin this briefing?"

Tlore offered me his arm, and escorted me to the U-shaped table. I sat between him and Reever, with Xonea taking a place at the console in the middle of the room.

"Council Member Torin has elected to visit Vtaga, the Hsktskt homeworld," the captain said, and touched the console panel before him. A dimensional image of a large, dark-blue-and-orange planet appeared above him and turned slowly. "Atmosphere, gravity, and climate are within our tolerance range, and SubAkade TssVar has guaranteed safe passage for our people. Our probes have picked up no evidence of airborne contaminants."

"The Hsktskt maintain an expansive planetary defense grid," Tlore said, making an elegant, encircling gesture with one hand. "The technology is unknown to us, but they keep it enabled at all times to block access to the surface. The League has studied and attacked the grid for many years, but our sources say they have yet to find any vulnerability. This is a direct threat to the healer's safety and must be deactivated."

"TssVar will not agree to that," Reever said, "but I know how to bypass it."

Xonea gave my husband an astonished look. "How so?"

Reever rose and went to the captain's console,

and used the controls to superimpose a glowing green web of energy around the image of Vtaga. He magnified the image, zeroing in on a small, rust-colored spot at the top of the planet. "The main grid generators are here. They are heavily guarded, but a strike team with the proper ordnance could destroy the station."

"We will be unable to take anything but personal weapons to the surface," Xonea said.

Reever changed the image, magnifying another section of the planet. "You will find all the ordnance you need here, in this dockyard. It is also guarded, but not as heavily as the polar grid station."

Tlore appeared astounded. "How do you know these things?"

My husband straightened. "I was once enslaved by the Hsktskt. I was freed when I saved the life of SubAkade TssVar, who made me his blood brother. As such, I pretended to serve the Faction as a spy while I used my position to free other slaves. I traveled all over Vtaga and gained access to most of their planetary defense intelligence."

Beside me, the Adan ClanLeader stiffened. So did his people, who were all staring at Reever now.

What was he doing, admitting this so openly? The Jorenians had remained neutral during the Hsktskt-League war, but they had no love for the League. Garphawayn seemed to think that was because of its treatment of my former self. Joren had broken off all relations and treaties with the League when it had declared Cherijo to be nothing more than an escaped lab animal.

"What did you intend to do with such treacherous

knowledge?" Tlore asked, his voice deceptively mild.

"Initially I meant to raise an army of mercenaries and return to raid Vtaga," Reever said in his blunt fashion. "I thought I might repay the Hsktskt for their many acts of brutality against the warm-blooded." His gaze shifted to me. "My wife taught me there is no justice in such revenge. So did Teulon Jado."

The Adan seemed to relax, as did Xonea. I saw love and pain in my husband's eyes. Giving such information was perilous, but he was doing so for me, to keep me safe while I was on the planet.

"My ClanSister must be guarded at all times while on the planet," Xonea said. "Reever will serve as her personal escort. Qonja Adan"—he nodded toward a quiet male I had seen around the ship—"will act as bodyguard. ClanLeader Adan, the council suggests a mission team of ten warriors and five specialists."

That meant I would be traveling with seventeen people. "I think that is too many, Captain. We wish to make a show of strength, not create offense."

"I agree," Tlore said before Xonea could argue. "My kin are the best warriors Joren has to offer. Five guards and two specialists will afford the healer the protection she needs without provoking the beasts."

"I hope you are correct, Tlore. The Faction will not allow anything but standard communication devices to be brought to the surface," Xonea warned. "Transponder and locator implants will be considered as surveillance devices and removed upon arrival."

I did not want to think of how the Hsktskt would remove them, not that I would have permitted him to implant anything in me anyway. "There may be treachery involved on the part of SubAkade TssVar, but we cannot go there acting as if we expect it. We only have to be watchful and cautious."

"The Hsktskt do not lie," my husband said. "They consider it beneath them. That is why they use other species to spy for them. They regard such things as too personally demeaning to do them themselves."

"Luckily our kind does not share their distaste." Tlore nodded to one of his men, who began to read from a datapad.

The officer related information gathered by various Adan intelligence officers regarding the present situation on Vtaga. The information, which had been solicited from mercenaries and other frequent visitors to the Hsktskt homeworld, indicated that the native population could be on the verge of civil war.

"Our sources tell us that the present social conflict on Vtaga centers on three concerns: the plague, which has killed hundreds and has created serious tensions among the native population; the older segment of the Hsktskt population, who opposed the peace talks, which they view as cowardice, and consider the plague a punishment for participating in them; and the proposed end to Faction-run slaver operations. Much of the Hsktskt trade system is based on slave revenues, and it is said that the merchant class is extremely unwilling to end its lucrative agreements with outside species."

That seemed far too interconnected to me. "It is as if someone caused this plague in order to harm the Hsktskt no matter what they do."

"That is also a possibility we have considered." Tlore exchanged a look with Xonea. "Whatever we discover about this plague, Healer, we must go carefully."

"As you say, ClanLeader." Hopefully our care wouldn't cost us our lives.

As the *Sunlace* and the Adan ships assumed synchronized orbit above Vtaga, I dressed in my physician's uniform and checked my medical case. The rest of our equipment and supplies were already stowed on board the launch that would take us from the ship to the surface. I had taken Marel to Salo's quarters, where Darea welcomed her and showed her the room she would share with Fasala while Reever and I were on-planet.

Marel did not seem concerned about our jaunt to the surface of Vtaga, but her parting embrace was longer and rather tighter than usual.

"I honor you, Mama," my child whispered. "Be nice to Daddy."

"I will try," I said as I smoothed her golden curls back from her brow. "Why do you say this about your father to me, Marel?"

She frowned. "I don't know. He feels stiff when I hug him. He looks at faraway things. Take care of him, Mama, please."

I promised her that I would, and that we would both return as soon as we could. I knew that we might be walking into a Hsktskt trap. I was relying on Reever and his knowledge of this species to ensure that we could return, but there was this plague, of which I knew nothing but secondhand information.

I told Marel none of this, and it grew inside me as I left her and returned to our own quarters to finish packing.

"Stop worrying," my husband said from behind me. His hands stroked the outsides of my arms. "You will do what you can for them, and we will protect you, and that will be enough."

"I pray SubAkade TssVar agrees with you." I turned to slip my arms around his waist and rest my cheek against his heart. Reever seemed indestructible, but I knew he was not. "He knows you helped Cherijo to destroy the slave depot and free the prisoners held there. Will he seek revenge for that while we are here?"

"TssVar saw me when he came to Akkabarr to negotiate a cease-fire with Teulon," my husband said. "If he had wanted retribution for Catopsa, I would not have left that deck alive."

The thought made me shudder. "Perhaps he was being polite in front of the other leaders."

"Hsktskt are never polite." Reever tilted up my chin and kissed me. "And, like you, I am not that easy to kill."

The jaunt from the *Sunlace* to the planet took a short interval, with Reever serving as pilot. I used the time to check over my medical equipment. The Senior Healer had provided me with a portable diagnostic array, programmed with every bit of knowledge we had on the Hsktskt species and known epidemiology. Reever had fitted the unit with a special interface that would allow it to communicate with similar machines on the planet. No one but my husband could speak Hsktskt, so I and the rest of the team wore League translation devices he had programmed to translate Jorenian, Hsktskt, and Iisleg around our wrists.

When I had finished checking all the medical equipment, I activated my datapad and began reviewing various epidemics experienced by reptilian species on other worlds.

"Healer." Qonja Adan came to sit beside me. "Is something wrong?"

I gave him a quick, wry look. "It takes less time to say what is right, Kheder."

He smiled. "I meant with you. You have not looked once through the view panel since we left the ship."

"I have never been to another world beyond my own," I said. "I am nervous."

"Akkabarr is an ice world. Vtaga is not." Qonja made a fluid gesture. "It may seem extremely hot and humid at first. If you have trouble with the air—"

"I can wear a breather, yes, Reever told me about them." I looked through the clear panel that showed the outside of the launch. We had passed through the thin upper atmosphere and were descending swiftly toward the surface. It seemed bizarre to see the place where the Hsktskt rasakts dwelled on the ground, like some bizarre melding of iiskar and skim city. The constructions appeared squat but immense, stretching out in orderly sections for miles. Beyond the borders of the settlement stretched long, curving, dark sections of blue, green, and yellow.

"What are those?" I pointed to the vivid curves of color.

"Those are the rain forests. One-third of this world is covered with them. Another third is desert, which looks white from orbit." Qonja did something to the panel to alter the view to show a murky brown squiggle beyond the rain forests. "The rest is covered by seas like this one."

Reever had shown me photoscans of the oceans on Kevarzangia Two. "I thought such waters were blue."

"Not on every world. Often the chemical content and evolution of marine life cause . . ." The big Jorenian stopped and chuckled. "Your pardon, Healer. I forgot that you do not care to hear such things."

"I care," I assured him. The more I knew about Vtaga, the better equipped I was to discover a cure. "Please, go on."

Qonja peered at me. "You are serious." Before I could reply, he added, "Your pardon, Healer. I am not used to such . . . polite attention from you."

"Women on my homeworld are polite or they die." I heard the launch's engines transition. "But our discussion must wait. I think we have landed."

The Adan guards removed their harnesses and checked their weapons as they assembled around me. Qonja handed me my medical case and checked my wrist device before joining them. All of the men's movements were as controlled as their expressions.

I had never seen the Jorenians so silent or intent. After weeks of being among them as they smiled and chattered and laughed like boy children preparing for their first hunt, it unnerved me.

Reever came to stand beside me. He had not worn his usual black garments, but was dressed in a fitted tunic and trousers with a mottled pattern of dark green and blue. No one could see the sheaths beneath his clothing, or the access seams that would allow him to draw his blades. For once he was more heavily armed than I was.

"Analysis of air, water, and soil samples shows no dangerous microorganisms," he said quietly. "TssVar has already examined the planetary food supplies, medicines, and indigenous life-forms, and indicates they are also uninfected."

"We will check them again." I slung the strap of my medical case over my shoulder, and saw Reever flinch. "What is it?"

"Nothing." He looked over at Qonja. "She is not to leave our custody at any time for any reason. If I am removed or detained, take her back to the ship at once."

I glared at him—if he thought I would leave him to the mercy of these beasts while I escaped to safety, he was deranged—but said nothing. I was beginning to see how effective a weapon silence could be.

Qonja inclined his head. "I will, Linguist."

The Adan assembled into two lines around me, Reever, and Qonja. The first pair opened the hull access panel and stepped into the air lock, where a bright beam of light passed over them.

"It's a biodecon scanner," Reever told me. "It identifies and neutralizes any exotic microorganisms we carry on our bodies, and provides an internal scan of each passenger so that the natives know we are what we appear to be."

"That sounds prudent." There were people who were not as they appeared to be? "What happens to those who do not, ah, pass this scan?"

"They are arrested and detained until their true form and motives can be identified." Reever moved with me into the air lock, and took my hand in his. "I will explain about the altered life-forms and shape-shifters among other humanoid species another time."

The light felt warm and soft against my face, and then the panel on the other side of the air lock slid open and we stepped out onto the docking ramp. Vtaga's heavy, hot air wafted in my face as if I were standing over a wide vent shaft. The alien dampness and weight of it as I breathed in was very nearly liquid, and vastly unpleasant. I remembered Qonja's warning and struggled to keep my breathing slow and calm.

Vtaga Central Transport appeared empty of ships and people. There were more of the glowing green globes that I had seen from the launch. "What are those things?" I asked, pointing at them.

"Heat reservoirs," my husband said. "Hsktskt cannot naturally regulate their body temperature."

"So they are slaves to warmth, as we were." I filed that away for future reference. It seemed ridiculous now, how unprepared I was for this new place. I spotted a group of towering reptilian beings in metallic silver uniforms waiting at the end of the dock area. They were giants. "You will not leave me alone."

"No." His hand tightened over mine. "Not for a moment."

At the very front of the group of Hsktskt was the tall, brutal figure I remembered from the preliminary negotiations with Teulon at Akkabarr.

"That is TssVar," I said to Reever, who nodded. My voice sounded odd, like I was whispering instead of speaking. "Does the air also make me talk like this?" I was going to have to shout at everyone if so.

"The acoustic dampers do." Reever pointed to what appeared to be a wall of writhing black foam. "They provide a sound barrier for the city and convert captured waves into displacer energy for Transport's operations."

I knew little of such technology, only that League worlds used light-based pulse energy for their needs, while the Hsktskt and their allies used sonic displacer power. Neither was superior to the other, as sound and light were plentiful, often inexhaustible fuel sources.

"It is one of many fundamental differences," my husband murmured as we approached the Hsktskt. He was reading my thoughts again. "Such evolutionary dissimilarities have kept colonial and slaver species at odds with each other for centuries."

"Like shafts, I suppose," I muttered. "Males on Akkabarr are forever bickering about who has the largest and hottest." I realized the ambiguity of my words and glanced at him. "I mean the vent shafts used to provide heat for the iiskars."

He didn't smile, but his eyes warmed. "Males argue about the size and heat-inducing qualities of the other variety of shaft as well."

As our guards stopped moving, so did we. Reever shifted and stepped in front of me at the same time the tallest and broadest of the Hsktskt stepped away from his companions. My husband and the reptilian met in the space between the two groups and, for a long moment, simply looked at each other while I held my breath.

"I should have properly greeted you, Sub-Akade," Reever said, "when last we met."

"When last we met, I should have properly gutted you." TssVar showed every tooth in his jaws.

"When were you elevated to the ruling level?" my husband asked, as if not staring into five rows of razor-sharp teeth.

"When my superiors died in the war, but it came after I had been demoted for my role in the Catopsa incident. I might have been an Akade by now, if not for you." The Hsktskt held up a clawed hand as if he meant to strike my husband, and then brought it down slowly to touch his shoulder. "For the sake of my people and Teulon Jado, I exonerate you of all crimes against the Hsktskt, HalaVar."

I kept my hand on the hilt of the blade at my waist. Diplomatic words and ensleg gestures were not enough to reassure me.

Reever bowed his head in an odd manner and TssVar released him. My husband turned toward me and gestured for me to come forward. I did so, feeling very conscious of Qonja hovering behind me. If I had to stab the Hsktskt, he might interfere.

"My mate has come as you requested," Reever said, taking my hand in his as I came to stand at his side. "She will help the Hsktskt if she can, but she must also be protected while she is on Vtaga. There is the matter of the blood price still on her head."

"Her . . . death . . . on Akkabarr satisfied that debt. I have also persuaded the Hanar to personally guarantee her safety while she is on Vtaga." TssVar's enormous yellow eyes swiveled down as he studied me. "Do you wish additional security, Dr. Torin?"

According to Cherijo's journals, I had delivered this male's five children on K-2. At gunpoint, no less.

"I have brought my own." I nodded toward the Adan surrounding us. "I am told they will kill anyone who presents a threat, verbally or physically, to me or any member of our group." I waited a moment before I added, "So will I."

"You *have* changed," TssVar said. "We shall have to be very careful of what we say and do while you are here."

I studied his expression. Reptilian features appeared harsher than most humanoids', and when he spoke I saw the rows of jagged, sharp teeth that lined his jaws. That, combined with his size, was enough to terrify anyone.

Yet there was something else about this Hsktskt that slipped around my fear. He reminded me of the jlorra: a ruthless and efficient killer, to be sure, but only when necessary. I could see the shrewdness in his eyes and hear the weariness shadowing his voice. He was resolved, but he was also afraid.

As I was. "I am not here to kill, SubAkade TssVar," I told him. "Neither, I think, are you."

"I am happy to agree, Dr. Torin. Come." He inclined his head and gestured toward a waiting land vehicle. "You are first to be presented to the Hanar."

SEVEN

We traveled from Transport to the center of the settlement, Lauc-Hanarat, which Reever told me meant "City of the Hanar." Being presented to the ruler of Vtaga seemed unnecessary—I had journeyed here for the benefit of the sick, not to be paraded like a tithe woman—but it seemed prudent to begin my visit without objecting to the reptilians' customs.

Reever told me of some of them. "Upper houses of lords and lower houses of free citizens contribute to the government, but the Hanar is the empirical ruler. High and low bloodlines serve as soldiers for ten to twenty years. The resident population is merchants, hunters, free raiders, scribes, doctors and architects, masons and carpenters, jewelers, clothiers, and potters. Higher bloodlines own huge family estates away from the city, and keep houses in town only to conduct business. Lower lines still manage to own homes, small gardens, and some animals, kept on leased lands. Products are sold via electronic market and spaceshipment. Economy is free and private property is the rule."

"I understand how a slaver society functions." The Toskald would have enjoyed this world.

"The Hsktskt are not like the windlords, Jarn," my husband said. "The basic unit of the Hsktskt society is family. Love, respect, and mutual obligation bind them together. Marriage is arranged by the parents, who select a bride based on quality of bloodline."

"So the females are repressed, as we were."

"Female Hsktskt have the same rights as males, but choose to remain home as breeders or go into occupations that will not take them away from the planet. Females maintain strong ties to their offspring. As for the juveniles, they live under absolute authority of their parents, but are indulged and even cherished."

I hmphed. "I thought as reptiles they had no feelings."

"They are more like us than they care to admit." He looked through the view panel at a pair of centurons escorting a third male, who wore a curiously marked garment. "There is an obligant."

The male's clothing looked like that of a servant, not a soldier. "What does that mean?"

"There is no word in Terran for it. No Hsktskt can ever be made a slave, but debts can be declared that put them under certain obligation to each other. Those who owe the debt and are compelled to satisfy it are called obligants."

"A fancy word for slave." I looked away from the males and instead studied the buildings that we were passing.

Lauc-Hanarat had appeared large from the launch, but from ground level it might have been a settlement of giants. Structures of stone and alloy had not been built as squat shelters, as I had assumed, but soared hundreds of meters above the wide, smooth vehicle paths. All were fashioned in towers and rectangular shelters that had been grouped together and joined by clear, squared walkway tubes. The effect reminded me of hide-wrapped snow blocks pierced by icicles.

The vehicle, which had comfortably accommodated both parties, stopped before a structure so tall I could not see the top of it.

This Hsktskt-made mountain consisted of eight wide alloy towers ringed at each level with circular transport pads, to which were docked hundreds of scout and raider vessels of various sizes. At its base were many smaller dwellings and more of the green domes I had seen around the city and at Transport. Ornate walls formed an outer barrier around the main structure, and they had been fashioned of smooth stone fused together with alloy seams. Huge columns disguised struts that further reinforced the walls, and formed triangular recesses in which stood armed centurons. The three-sided design was repeated in geometric motifs and depictions of Hsktskt and strange animal figures chiseled into every large stone surface.

This was not a place to be idly admired. Along with the guards stationed in the recesses, dozens of uniformed Hsktskt carrying many weapons patrolled the battlements of the walls. Between the tops of every third and fourth strut were displacer cannons mounted on targeting platforms.

"This is the Palace of the Hanar," TssVar said as

his guards left the vehicle. "The center of our government."

From the manner in which he gazed at me, I guessed he was waiting for me to comment. "It is very . . . tall."

"The Palace is the largest, tallest, and most important building in the city. It rises above all, just as the Hanar does." He turned to gaze down at my husband. "There are other matters troubling him now."

"We are only here for the plague victims," Reever said.

"A band of lineless has been raiding the outer settlements," TssVar told him. "They will be found and executed."

My husband nodded once. "Sooner than later, one hopes."

"Hope is a rare commodity these days. Keep her close to you, HalaVar." The Hsktskt followed his men out.

I looked at Reever. "Close makes it easier for them to shoot us." With the number of centurons and weapons poised around and above us, we would never have a chance to even run away.

"TssVar does not lie," my husband said. "Even if he did, the Hanar does not permit any executions to be carried out in the Palace."

That gave me little comfort. "I hope he does not make another exception."

We did not simply walk into the Hanar's Palace. At the entryway, which was a series of three air locks, we were required to undergo biodecon and surrender all that we carried except our garments,

footgear, and translation devices. The latter were removed and thoroughly scanned, as were we. They
even took from me the headband monitoring device
the Senior Healer had given me to wear. I started to
protest, until I saw that TssVar and his men had to
do the same.

"The Hanar does not permit anyone to bring in
weapons, I suppose," I murmured as one of the reptilian guards returned my headband and waved us
through the last lock and into the courtyard surrounding the Palace.

"This Hanar is very cautious," Reever said. When
a guard made a low growling sound, he added, "Yet
he need not be, for he is most exalted, and receives
the tributary of all the lines. He restored Lauc-
Hanarat to its former glory, and brought back dignity to this world."

The guard stopped looking as if he wanted to
take a bite out of my husband and moved toward
the back of our group.

"One does not criticize the ruler here?" I asked
softly.

"No. This Hanar has little patience and no humor
whatsoever," Reever said. "Stay beside me and
speak only to answer direct questions."

We had to walk across the courtyard, but the first
fifty meters of the Palace had no entryways. Instead,
TssVar directed us to a small vessel, which we
boarded and that rose directly up to the center portion of the main tower, where more armed guards
were waited on the docking pad.

Once we disembarked from the lift-vessel, we
were again made to pass through an air lock, biode-

con, and scan search before we were permitted within the Palace's interior. Once my eyes adjusted to the dimness, I saw smaller versions of the green heat domes set into the smooth stone walls of the round entry chamber. Like giant icicles of stone, tall, narrow pillars had been placed every fifty meters around the circular room, and shed a white mist through their intricate carvings to dampen the hot air. Tiny emitters attached to hover drones floating above our heads provided a scant amount of light.

TssVar and his guards led the way, and we followed. The Jorenians seemed to adjust almost at once to the heat and humidity, as did Reever. After a few moments of uneasiness, so did I, but I hoped we would not spend much time here. The Palace was too dark and sticky and strange for my comfort.

There seemed to be no corridors in the place, only a series of chambers, connected in a straight line, that grew successively larger and warmer as we passed through them. Carvings like those on the mist-shedding pillars began to appear on the walls, as did long, narrow, woven fiber mats arranged to form geometric shapes on the floors.

TssVar came to walk beside me. "This is the Hanar's vestibule. Beyond are—" He said several words that my wrist machine would not translate.

"They are types of shrines to the Hanar of the past, soldiers and important citizens," Reever explained. "SubAkade TssVar's people hold their ancestors in high esteem."

"So I see." I stared at two larger-than-life-size Hsktskt that flanked the doorway to the next chamber. They had been carved from stone, then gilded, painted, and dressed with real garments in such a way as to make them look alive.

They must have appeared very grand to the Hsktskt. To me, they were ten-meter-high monsters from nightmares I never wished to dream.

TssVar stopped before the final entryway. Beyond him I could see more guards than I could count, standing in long rows around a hunched figure perched on some sort of glowing bench.

"After the Tyryr ascended to the stars," TssVar said, "GesVar became Hanar, one above the blood. Line GeVar reigned for twenty-eight thousand eight hundred solars, unto MilulaVar, whose line reigned for thirty-six thousand solars, unto UdireVar, whose line reigned forty-three thousand two hundred years, unto AnallaVar, whose line reigned twenty-eight thousand eight hundred years, unto Izumud-Var, whose line reigned thirty-six thousand years, unto KaralVar, whose line was weakened and then destroyed during the Wars of Tyryr."

Reever's fingers threaded through mine, just as his thoughts did. *What he recites is part of their ritual of presentation. This honors the dead and justifies why the old ways are no longer followed.*

"The loss of KaralVar brought need, and the blood answered." TssVar made a simple, encompassing gesture. "So by free citizens were selected the first Hanar, SubHanar, Akade, SubAkade, Over-Lord, Lord, OverMaster, Master, OverSeer, Seer, OverCenturon, and Centuron to serve the blood. The Rule of Death became law. No one line shall rule the blood, nor shall the blood place the obligation of rule upon one line."

The Rule of Death is the method of advancement in Hsktskt society, my husband thought to me. *One takes the place of another higher in rank who has died.*

Could this rule be involved with the plague? I wondered.

Do not pose such a question to the Hanar or any other Hsktskt. Reever's mind voice changed, becoming urgent and stern. *To imply one of them would kill to attain rank is an unforgivable insult.*

Knowing males, that probably meant a number of them actually *did* kill to acquire more rank and power.

"Wait here," TssVar said, "until I summon you." He walked into the Hanar's inner chamber and halted a long distance from the hunched figure. Four guards encircled him and subjected him to remote scan, and then stepped back. "By the life of Hanar, exalted above all others, as long as days exist and words are spoken, no matter at whose command or at whose request, if I break the vow by which I am sworn, then may the flesh be flayed from my bones and burned while my skeleton is left to crumble to dust atop the nameless sands."

The hunched figure did not move. "I recognize the SubAkade TssVar, blood of the line of OrulVar." The voice was a low, uneven rasp of sound in the otherwise silent chamber.

"Your heart is unfathomable and profound, Supreme One," TssVar responded. "Command me until the fates devour the last of the Tyryr in your midst."

"You have brought the warm-blood?"

"I have, Supreme One." TssVar turned to look

back at us and beckoned with one quick gesture. "I present Dr. Torin and the medical team from the Jorenian vessel *Sunlace*."

Reever and I walked in, stopping when guards immediately surrounded us and subjected us to the same brief scan TssVar had experienced. When they stepped back, we continued until we stood behind the big Hsktskt.

"Bring the warm-blood here so that I may look upon it," the Hanar said.

TssVar put a clawed hand on my shoulder and brought me with him toward the glowing bench.

It was hard to know what to think of the Hanar. Toskald princes kept themselves young and physically beautiful by putting themselves in machines that erased all signs of age from their outsides. The Iisleg rasakt did not, but they too took pains never to display themselves as old and infirm. When an Iisleg became too elderly to perform their function within the tribe, they walked out or were taken out on the ice and left to die. The skela did not sacrifice their older women to the elements, but the hard life did not favor the aged.

All of those reasons made me unable to blink as I beheld the Hanar, who had to be the most ancient living thing I had ever seen.

The Supreme One sat on an open-sided bench of the same glowing green material as the heat domes. Instead of great or ornate garments, the Hanar wore a plain, fitted garment of silvery material. It provided some manner of thermal insulation, I guessed. His head was massive, but the hide covering it seemed riddled with bumps and craters, like the surface of a moon. His scales did not gleam with the deep, vibrant green of the younger males, but had darkened over time to a gray-green black. The yellow of his clouded eyes appeared to have darkened as well. One pair of his eyelids drooped, making him appear as if he were assessing everyone through a suspicious squint.

I took in a quick, deep breath and smelled a powerful astringent odor, like sterilizing solution. It was coming from the area around the throne.

"I am the Hanar," the ancient male said, raising his voice enough that it echoed all around the chamber. "I am one whose command is not questioned; I am the foremost in all things. At my command you have been brought to heal the blood of our lines. I am the father of all and the lines are my children, I am he who directs justice, I am he who decrees the fates. I am he to whom you pay due homage."

TssVar glanced at me. "You may address the Hanar with a response, Terran."

What would be an appropriate greeting? "I am honored to be in your presence, Supreme One. How are you feeling?"

All around us, everyone went still.

The Hanar's broad jaw dropped, showing worn but still lethal-looking teeth, and he made a chuffing sound. "I am weary, but my personal physician assures me that it is age, not plague. She is your doing, I am told." He turned his head. "Come here and greet your namesake, child."

A female Hsktskt dressed in a red-and-silver garment emerged from behind a line of guards. She was as tall as TssVar, but appeared much younger.

Her expression was as blank as the others, but her gaze remained fixed on me.

"My Dominary and Designate, ChrrechoVa," TssVar said. "She serves as personal physician to the Hanar."

The female's name sounded like a reptilian version of Cherijo, a bit corrupted by the Hsktskt's rolled and snapped consonants. I wondered if I should try to pronounce it.

"I am called ChoVa," the female said, relieving me of one burden. "It has been some years. When last we met, I was only a child."

"I regret that I cannot remember that time," I told her. "But I am glad to meet you again, and to know that you are well."

"ChoVa became a physician to honor you." TssVar didn't sound approving or disapproving, but I detected a softer note in his voice as he referred to his daughter. "She brings much distinction to our line."

"She serves adequately." The Hanar looked at ChoVa again, and she stepped back out of sight. "I will forego her attendance so that she may accompany you during your time here and give you what aid you need, Terran."

"I thank you for that, Supreme One." Whatever his reasons for sending her with me, I could use ChoVa's expertise. I had little experience with ensleg, and none treating reptilian life-forms.

"Do not be so eager to offer your gratitude, now that you are here." He almost snarled the words. "I have lost too many of my children. More I will not sacrifice. You shall heal my people, Warm-Blood, and you shall do so quickly."

"I will do everything I can," I promised, choosing my words carefully, "but as the Supreme One must know, I cannot guarantee any results."

"SubAkade TssVar weighed out for me a price for you that was not pleasing to my heart, but I paid it for the blood." The Hanar jerked his lower jaw several times as if agitated—or pretending to chew on something attached to me. "I see it convenient, this plague, to emerge at such a time on our world. Perhaps it was released by our enemies as a coward's weapon, to destroy us when they could not."

"That may be possible," I conceded, "but I think it unlikely. Your planet, like you, is too well protected against such things."

"Your speculations do not interest me," the Hanar said, causing the males around me to tense. "You could be part of a conspiracy to wipe out our kind."

"I am not."

"That you must prove," the old Hsktskt said, baring his teeth in a horrible mimicry of a humanoid smile. "The only proof I shall accept is a cure."

The interview came to an abrupt end as the Hanar's guards surrounded us and led us out of the chamber. On our way out, the female Hsktskt physician joined us.

"It is best if we begin at the quarantine center," ChoVa said as we were escorted to a waiting transport. "We have isolated the active cases there, and perhaps a dozen are still lucid enough to respond to questions."

"How many patients have you quarantined?" I asked.

"Two thousand at last inspection, but the occupancy fluctuates." She opened the access hatch and gestured for me and Reever to enter the transport. "New cases are brought in each morning, and any number of terminal cases is resolved each day."

"Resolved? You mean die?" TssVar had indicated that the plague itself was not fatal.

"We have stabilized the number of deaths by suspending those patients judged terminal in a form of cryopreservation. It is a procedure normally used during certain forms of cardiosurgery on our kind." ChoVa eased down in the seat beside mine and released a very humanoid-sounding sigh. "Cryo does not keep them alive very long. Seven to ten days, at best, and then the blood begins to crystallize."

"But if the plague itself is not terminal, why kill them with cryogenic procedures?" I demanded.

She gave me an enigmatic look. "You must see that for yourself, Healer."

EIGHT

ChoVa questioned me as we rode from the palace to the Hsktskt quarantine facility.

"Conditions on the surface of Akkabarr have been described to me as primitive," she said. "What sort of health care is the native population given?"

Evidently she worried about my ability to provide responsible treatment for her patients. I could not blame her—in her position, I would have done the same—but I was reluctant to talk about Akkabarr. Then I realized that unlike Reever, ChoVa would not care that I longed for my homeworld. She simply wanted to ensure that I would not in ignorance kill anyone on hers.

"Before the war, nothing but what the male tribal healers could provide." I looked through the clear panel to my right and saw two armed centurons patrolling the empty street on foot. "During the rebellion, we skela took over triage and medevac. Skela are outcast females who handle the bodies of the dead for the tribes."

Her tongue flicked rapidly. "I take it they also had no proper medical education."

"I trained them. I do not have Cherijo's personal memories, but her skills are still mine. Once the skela learned how to handle the living, we requisitioned supplies from salvaged crashes and built temporary hospital shelters. Toward the end of the war, we were able to perform almost any surgical procedure." Which had been fortunate, given the number of ruined bodies that we had also carried off the battlefields, but I did not say this. I did not even like to remember the fighting.

"I am astonished that you did so much under such primitive conditions." ChoVa's inner eyelids lowered a notch. "You must have seen to a great many wounded."

"More than any healer would wish." And watched as they were wounded, feeling helpless and terrified, unable to look away. The images in my head made me feel ill, but by that time the transport had stopped in front of an undecorated building of dark stone. I climbed out of the vehicle, glad to escape my thoughts.

"I need a moment with my wife, ChoVa." Reever took my arm and pulled me away from the others. "You are flushed. Are you feeling ill?"

"I am feeling hot." It was not a lie. "This planet could do with an ice age." The worry lines tightened around his mouth, so I added, "A little discomfort will not harm me." Neither would unhappy memories, if I could but discipline myself not to recall them.

My assurances didn't placate him. "If you feel dizzy, tell me."

"If I fall down, assume I cannot." I rejoined ChoVa and we walked to the air lock access panel to the facility. Once there, she hesitated, as if reluctant to go in.

Perhaps she did not believe my assurances to her, either. I needed to work on my powers of persuasion. "Besides what I did during the rebellion, the Senior Healer on the ensleg ship that brought me here made thorough tests. You need not fear that I will harm anyone."

"It is not you. I never want to . . . see them," ChoVa admitted, and then her posture changed, as if she were bracing herself for a blow. "We have so many infected now that we have had to economize on available space." She pressed one hand to a panel that scanned it and identified her. "Our methods may seem unkind to your eyes, but they are efficient, and allow us to treat as many as are brought here."

The reason for her remarks was revealed the instant we entered what must have once been a reception and processing area. The large room was filled with triangular columns of a semitransparent blue color. In each was a Hsktskt, but they were almost too large for the columnar containers, and appeared to be wedged inside, completely suspended in a clear, bubbling gelatinous liquid. Tubes from machines capping the containers snaked around the outside, attached to sensor patches near the necks, chests, arms, groins, and thighs of the patients. Some were apparently to drain urine and waste, others to provide liquids and soluble nourishment. Thick black alloy bands had been applied to each patient's jaw to keep them closed. Oxygen and medicines appeared to be fed through some of the machine tubes directly into the patients' chests.

"You keep them in bottles," I muttered, walking over to the nearest container. I had never seen living beings in such a state. "Is there no other way?"

"No. This is the only form of restraint from which they cannot escape," ChoVar said, and tapped the surface of the clear blue material. A light emitter illuminated the interior, and the patient opened his eyes to glare at me. He must have been making sounds, judging by the pulsing muscles in his throat and the straining of the black band clamping his jaw shut, but I could not hear them.

"Do their cries power the life-support system?" I asked.

"No. Power is provided by the facility's operational grid." ChoVa pointed to several raw-looking wounds on the male patient's face and neck. "This OverCenturon was brought in after he tried to tear out his ears and throat. He regurgitates everything he is fed by chest tube, and is weakening rapidly, so we will place him in cryopreservation tomorrow."

"You might keep him alive longer with intravenous feeding," I suggested as I made a visual assessment.

"As effective as they are, our restraining columns cannot prevent small movements, and regular administration of neuroparalyzer creates a toxin in Hsktskt blood," she said as she adjusted one of the tubes. "Several of the patients we attempted to keep on IV nutrients managed to strangle themselves with the tubing before we could remove it."

I had watched rebels endure varying amounts of

self-hatred from the shock that came after intense battle, but only a few had actually tried to harm themselves. "Surely they are not all suicidal?"

"In the beginning, we thought not," ChoVa said. "The initial symptoms manifested in a wide assortment of bizarre behaviors, and we assumed systemic failure was the cause of death. Only after we performed autopsies on the first victims did we learn that each had in some manner self-terminated. It was then that we interviewed the patients who could still communicate and discovered they all had the same psychotic desire: to die rather than endure."

"Endure what?"

"We do not know," she admitted. "Their vitals only indicate they are under some extreme mental or physical stress. They will not tell us what they endure. When we ask, all they do is scream."

A large, agitated-looking Hsktskt male in a silver-black uniform came to ChoVa. "The Palace signaled of your intention to come here for an inspection." He looked down at me. "I am Dr. IshVar, facility director." He glanced over at the Adan, and Reever, who were staring aghast at the patient tubes. "You may enter, Dr. Torin, but I cannot have armed warm-bloods wandering the facility and agitating the staff and the patients. They must stay here."

"We should perform rounds and then look at the corpses in pathology," ChoVa said to me. "Will your men allow you to accompany me alone?"

"Let me speak to them." I went to Reever, whose face was pale and beaded with sweat. "Are you ill?"

"I never thought to see them like this." He

sounded as if he might empty his stomach on the floor. "It is as if they are cooking them in boiling liquid."

I recalled Cherijo mentioning my husband's dislike for illness and blood in her journals, but she seemed to feel a slight disdain for it. I understood his revulsion better than she had, but I had been through a war. "It is for their safety, so they will not harm themselves. The warmth of the liquid promotes body temperature regulation in the absence of exercise, and the bubbles are oxygen, to keep their derma healthy."

He turned his head to stare at me. "How do you know that?"

"I know what has to be done with such patients." I gestured toward the corridor. "ChoVa and I must walk the wards and examine some cadavers. The male who directs this place will not permit you to accompany me."

His eyes, a pale gray, turned dark. "We will not be separated."

ChoVa came to stand beside me in time to hear this. "HalaVar, you know my obligation under blood law. I am the Designate. I vow to you that I will guard her with my life."

"What if your life is not enough?" my husband demanded.

"It will be." She gave him a rather frightening look that bared many rows of her teeth. "Hsktskt physicians are not only trained to heal."

They stared at each other for a long time before Reever gripped my wrist and did something to the translator I wore. "We will be tracking you by re-

mote signal. Don't leave the facility under any circumstances."

I nodded and went off to the next patient area
with ChoVa.

By the time we reached the patients who had
been frozen, I had examined over fifty patients in
various stages of infection with ChoVa. We had performed all manner of scans and screens and still had
made no progress. ChoVa and I had to don special
insulating garments to enter the cryolab, and we
only stayed long enough for her to show me what
precautions they were taking to preserve the patients in the final phase of treatment.

"One of our chemists has produced a serum
made from a natural anticoagulant that has slowed
the rate of blood crystallization," ChoVa told me as
we quickly walked the silent, chilly ward, "but it
does not eliminate it. Even with the serum, once
frozen, the patient has two to three weeks to be revived before the deterioration of the cells becomes
too extensive."

I had not liked looking upon the patients in the
upright tubes, but seeing the Hsktskt encased like
so many haunches of ptar meat in square, ice-filled
vats was worse. "Have you tried reviving them to
see if the cold affects the pathogen?"

"Yes, but it does not. Even those with significant
cryoexposure revert back to their suicidal behavior.
Any reduction in body temperature only serves to
suspend us, not alter us." ChoVa regarded the tanks
for a moment. "My father discovered that for

himself when he tried to place my mother in cryosuspension."

My nose was freezing, and my breath hung white and heavy on the air, and I felt more relaxed than I had in weeks. It was a pity we could not linger; I felt more at home here than anywhere since I had left Akkabarr. "Your mother has been infected?"

"I meant when TssVar tried to prevent her delivery." ChoVa led me out to the changing area where she enabled a heat emitter and stood before it, warming herself. "You do not remember when you delivered me and my siblings of my mother on Kevarzangia Two?"

"No."

"You were a trauma physician there. My father had to remove my mother from his ship and take her to someplace isolated to deliver, so he chose your world. Hsktskt females are not permitted to reproduce while on active duty, and can be killed for it up until the time they deliver."

I gave her a sour look. "Yours is a compassionate species."

"Newborn Hsktskt are mindless and vicious," ChoVa said. "They are born ravenous, and if not isolated will kill and eat anything except the mother. We practice compassion by protecting their potential victims."

As we walked through corridors crowded with patient tubes, ChoVa told me the story of how Cherijo had delivered her and her four siblings in the FreeClinic on K-2. It was an exciting tale, one filled with the sort of risks and danger upon which my former self had apparently thrived.

"It takes some weeks to tame newborns, but we are conscious from birth," she added. "I never forgot the taste of your scent."

I could not imagine disobeying orders and risking the lives of fragile humanoids to deliver five killers. I would have found a way to remove the mother from the facility first. I saw her tongue flicker out to sample the air between us, and another thought came to me. "Do I smell—or taste—the same?"

She stopped, surprised by the question. "Not precisely. There is enough of the old scent for me to identify you, but there is less of it." She studied my face. "I think you have lost much of yourself, but perhaps your experience purified you."

ChoVa still thought of me as Cherijo, as they all did. "I am not the woman who delivered you. My name is Jarn, and I was born on Akkabarr, in this body. I have some of her abilities, and I wear her face, but her personality—indeed, her soul—is gone."

Her inner eyelids lifted. "You do not resent this loss?"

"Not for myself, but for my husband." Without Reever or the other men near me, I felt free to speak my mind. "I think if Cherijo and I had been born in different bodies, and somehow met in the past, we would probably not have liked each other very much."

ChoVa's facial muscles tightened. "She was a brave and gifted healer."

"Yes, but she could sometimes be thoughtless, even reckless. Some of it was youth and inexperience, but the rest . . ." I shook my head, forcing the displeasure knotting inside me aside. "I should not criticize her. Reever and the others on the ship valued her, and searched so long for her, and fought for her. I am fortunate to have inherited her body, and her skills as a healer."

"You wear another's hide, but it will never be your own," ChoVa said, "as long as others wish to see her in it. Although I wonder if she was so well loved."

"They cannot stop talking about how much she was honored and loved." I made an exasperated sound. "I can recite hundreds of anecdotes. They treasure stories of her as a mother does her son's milk teeth. No woman in existence was ever loved and pampered and spoiled as well as she."

"Yet her transport crashed on your homeworld," ChoVa said. "The League has been hunting Cherijo since she escaped Kevarzangia Two. The Hsktskt would have captured her and brought her back to Vtaga to pay the blood price on her head. How did she—you—end up on Akkabarr?"

"It could not be the Jorenians' doing," I assured her. "They have shown me only kindness. They also consider me kin; they would eviscerate anyone who even hinted at harming me."

She inclined her head. "Then you must ask yourself why such a valuable and beloved being as Cherijo was being transported to an ice world, the surface of which no one can reach, and on which females are raised to be slaves."

I thought of worgald, the face skins the skela had been forced to cut off ensleg cadavers to sell in the Toskald's skim cities. Had someone wished that fate for Cherijo, too? Or was it as ChoVa thought, that my former self had been deliberately marooned on Akkabarr, where she might be treated as poorly as the other females trapped there by Toskald cruelty and Iisleg ignorance?

Yet if these things had not happened to her, I would never have been born.

My head began to ache. "I complain too much. I am alive. I have a child, a husband, and the work. The Jorenians have given me their protection. Despite her unlikable personality, my former self did many wonderful things for others, and will always be remembered for it. That is enough."

Her eyelids lowered a fraction. "Is it?"

A large female garbed in a Hsktskt nursing uniform came around the corner and called to ChoVa. "Doctor, a fatality was brought in, and the administrator thought you and the warm-blood would wish to perform the autopsy." She flicked a slightly disgusted look down toward me.

"The warm-blood's title is Dr. Torin," ChoVa said, her tone suddenly chilled. "Use it." She dismissed the nurse and led me through the corridor toward the facility's forensic department. "We had many more fatalities in the beginning, but the Hanar enacted a law to have anyone showing even mild symptoms brought to the hospital."

"Fear of the contagion would also cause concern." I stopped at a rack of protective garments, made to fit bodies much larger than mine. As I reached for what appeared the smallest size, something rumbled above our heads. I glanced up. "Some of your equipment here is noisy."

"We channel sound into power for the facility."

ChoVa's tongue flickered rapidly. "That noise cannot be coming from our equipment."

A short interval of silence followed, and then a larger roaring sound came through the walls, shaking them and the floor. Lights blinked on and off, and dust showered down on our heads. A second explosion plunged us into darkness until the red gleam from an emergency emitter snapped on.

"Over here." ChoVa seized my arm and guided me through the crimson-tinged haze to a staircase. She wrenched open the door, peered inside, and then pushed me in. "Go, quickly."

I ran up the staircase to the next level, but the door panel was without power and would not open. "How can we get to the patients?" I shouted over the rumbling, which had grown much louder.

"Step back." ChoVa shoved her claws into the center seam of the door and, after several moments of grunting and straining, forced the two sides apart. She had to shove some debris out of the way before we could squeeze through to the other side. An inch of gummy liquid coated the floor.

"The containers have ruptured." ChoVa hurried to a cabinet recessed into the wall and removed two instruments. "These are loaded with neuroparalyzer." She handed one to me.

I squinted at it. "It looks like a pistol."

"It is. Our raiders use them to subdue captives. If a patient charges at you, shoot him in the center of the chest." She turned and sloshed through the spilled suspension gel toward the first row of patient tubes.

I remained at her side, observing how she

checked the first tube before I moved on to do the same on my own. The patients were more agitated than before, their eyes wide and rolling, their muscles bunching as they struggled to free themselves. Beyond the tubes I could see nothing; the emergency lights were few and far between.

"I have a crack in this container," I called to her as I found gel oozing from one damaged tube. "How can we seal it?"

ChoVa did not have time to reply before plas exploded around me, and the patient inside the unit burst free of its confines. He released a terrible screech, and swiped at my head with wet, glistening claws.

I jerked out of reach, raised the infuser weapon, and shot him. A long, narrow dart buried itself in his sternum. I had to move quickly to avoid his body as he tumbled over.

"Never mind," I called to ChoVa.

"Well done." She came and helped me roll the heavy, limp patient over onto his back so he wouldn't aspirate the gel spilling from the tube. Distant, higher-pitched explosions sounded, and she lifted her head and tasted the air. "That is weapons fire."

I thought of my husband and the Adan, and glanced down at the device on my wrist. I could not signal Reever and ask if he was shooting at Hsktskt.

"It is not from your men. Those are Hsktskt thermal weapons firing," ChoVa said. She rose and helped me to my feet. "It is more likely the facility security guards. We must stop them from killing the patients."

We made our way through the debris and darkness out to the ward station, which appeared empty at first. Then I heard low hissing sounds that seemed to be coming out of the walls themselves.

"Jarn." ChoVa put her hand on my shoulder. "Do not move."

I froze, and followed her gaze. A heap of debris near us twitched, and then I saw the blood, and the outlines of bodies and uniforms. They were the ward staff, and they had been torn to pieces. Parts of their bodies were missing, too, as if they had been eaten. Beyond them, dozens of ruptured patient tubes sat empty, and I counted only five that had remained intact and still retained their contents.

The darkness shifted as things moved all around us.

"How many can we sedate before the infusers empty?" I murmured, shifting my grip on the handle and watching the darker shadows creep closer to the pool of light surrounding us.

"If they do not jam, fifty each."

I peered through the darkness. There had to be more than two hundred empty tubes. The hissing sounds closed in around us. "Will the others attack the ones we sedate?"

"No," ChoVa said, "in this state, they pursue only whatever moves. Put your back to mine, Jarn, and try to remain as still as you can."

I moved until my shoulders brushed the center of the back of her jacket. The dark, smoky air and the acrid scent of blood reminded me of the battlefields of Akkabarr. Sweat oozed into my eyes, and I blinked hard to clear them.

I expected the escaped patients to come rushing at us all at once, but a fierce light shot through the corridor wall and whined as it encountered—and quickly melted—an alloy diagnostics cart.

"Rrrrggggrrrr."

Towering figures wrapped in black-and-brown garments and wearing breathers shoved their way through the gap burned in the wall, and began firing at the escaped patients, ChoVa, and me.

I abandoned my efforts to remain motionless and ducked to avoid one wide beam. "Security?"

"Outlaws." ChoVa whirled around, grabbing me by the waist and falling to the floor with me under her. Suspension liquid and rubble covered me, and the impact of her heavy body on mine should have crushed me. But at the last second she rolled to one side instead of landing on me, using two of her upper limbs to cover my face and chest.

I saw the ones she called outlaws firing at the last of the unruptured containers. Plas melted and liquid spilled as the patients inside broke free. A moment later Chova stood and threw me over her shoulder like the strap of a medical case before she ran down the hall.

I had nowhere to look but behind us, and watched as the outlaws shoved the hysterical patients into the stairwell. They weren't killing them, they were herding them out. One of the patients turned around and attacked an outlaw with wild, vicious swipes of her talons. That tore the breather from the outlaw's head, and as he avoided another blow and shot her, the flare of energy from his weapon briefly illuminated his face. A face that was not green and reptilian, but blue and humanoid. His black hair had been pulled back from his face by a knotted thong and tucked beneath his collar to conceal it.

Xonea?

All-white eyes met mine as I stared at the outlaw. He was not Xonea, not with those six diagonal scars slashed across the left side of his face. But he looked enough like the captain to be family. How was this possible? Was he an escaped slave, as Teulon had been?

He did not reveal any indication of his reaction to seeing me except by a slight narrowing of his eyes.

Just before ChoVa carried me around the corner into another corridor, the outlaw turned to retreat into the stairwell. That was when I saw the mark on the side of his throat.

"Jarn." Reever was suddenly there, pulling me down from ChoVa's shoulder. He carried a blade I had never seen before—long, curved, and made of some darkly worked ensleg alloy—and held it ready as he moved his free hand over me.

He was searching me for injuries.

"I am not hurt," I told him, catching his hand in mine. I looked into his eyes, which had changed color again and now were so dark gray they were almost black. "You?"

"Fine." As the whine of weapons fire came from the other side of the ward, he put his arm around me. "We are leaving."

"It is not secure." ChoVa shoved both of us through a panel into another area. Here power and lights had been restored, and the containers lining the walls were intact, yet the patients within them writhed, trying to break free. "Jarn, I need your help with the patients. We must sedate them."

Reever stepped between us. "I did not bring my wife here to play nurse for you."

"This ward's nurses are all dead now. Do as you will." ChoVa went to the first tube to administer the needed tranquilizer.

When I would have followed her, Reever grabbed my arm. "No, Jarn. We will return to the ship now."

"She cannot cope with all the patients by herself." I glanced at ChoVa, who seemed just as furious as my husband. "Stay, guard me if you must, but allow me to help her. The nurses really are dead."

He looked for a moment as if he might beat me. "Who is attacking the facility?"

"I don't know. ChoVa called them outlaws." That one male's face was imprinted on my memory, however, and dread over what I had seen crept deep into my bones. "There was one who might be from our ship."

The lines across his brow deepened. "What?"

"I saw the face of one of the outlaws. He was humanoid, with blue skin and all-white eyes, like the Jorenians," I said, my voice a bare murmur now.

He straightened and scanned the area. "That is not possible. It was a runaway slave, perhaps. One whose species resembles the Jorenians."

I checked the level of tranquilizer in my infuser. "Another species would not possess the mark of HouseClan Torin on his neck."

NINE

As soon as I, ChoVa, and the other Hsktskt physicians who came to assist us had stabilized and secured the patients, Reever and the Adan decided we would return to the ship. Still shaken by the attack, I did not argue. As we left I saw that the streets were no longer empty, and the dwellings surrounding the medical facility were being searched. Everywhere I looked centurons in thick body armor patrolled in pairs and threes. These soldiers had been armed with more weapons than even the guards at the Hanar's Palace had possessed.

"Are the outlaws still in the city?" I asked my husband.

He did not stop scanning the area around us, and only adjusted his hold on his pulse rifle so that he could rest a hand on my neck. "We will not wait to find out."

Qonja, who had stationed himself on my other side, eyed my husband before smiling at me. "All will be well, Healer."

With outlaws attacking the quarantined, the Hsktskt searching their own city, and Reever so agitated that he had to hold me like a wayward jlorra cub, I doubted that.

Back on board the ship, the entire jaunt team was subjected to a thorough biodecon before being immediately escorted to the captain's briefing room. I sat down and sipped a server of something that was supposed to taste like idleberry tea while the men related what had happened to Xonea and the senior members of the crew. Reever asked me to describe what I had seen of the attack and the strange outlaw, and with great reluctance I did so.

As soon as I finished speaking, I glanced at the other men. From their expressions, it seemed that no one believed me.

"There are none of our people on Vtaga save those we sent with you." Xonea turned on the Adan ClanLeader. "Are you missing any men?"

"All of my kin have reported back to the ship." The ClanLeader offered me a reassuring smile. "There is no shame in making such a mistake, Lady. Fear often clouds the mind and, at times, plays tricks on the vision."

"There is a humanoid male among the Hšktskt outlaws. He has dark blue skin, all-white eyes, and the skin mark of HouseClan Torin on his throat," I repeated carefully. "I was not mistaken or hysterical. I saw him clearly. My eyes functioned without impairment."

The men said nothing for a time. Some looked at me, while others looked away.

"I am a battlefield surgeon," I reminded them. "I have done my work under direct enemy fire on the ice for many seasons. I did not panic and I never mistook a Toskald for an Iisleg. I know what I saw. That outlaw was a Jorenian." From their expressions I could tell they still did not believe me. "Why do you doubt what I say?"

"The device on your head," one of the men said, gesturing to the band. "Could it have made you hallucinate?"

"It is simply a monitoring device," I assured him. "It can only record my brain activity, not distort it."

Finally Salo shifted in his seat. "What you saw, Healer, simply could not be. Jorenian HouseClans always know where their kin are. If we did not, we could not protect each other."

"What about the Torin who stayed behind on your homeworld?" Reever asked suddenly. "Could one of them have come to Vtaga for some reason, or been captured and made a slave, without your knowledge?"

The captain shook his head. "All Torin are here on the *Sunlace* or back on the homeworld. We would have been informed if one of our kin chose to travel alone, and alerted if any went missing. HouseClan honor requires us to perform immediate search and rescue."

"Perhaps the outlaw's skin mark was altered to look like that of your clan," Tlore, the Adan Clan-Leader, suggested. "The Torin have taken a prominent part in the peace talks between the League and the Hsktskt. It may be an attempt to defame your kin, through use of some being alterformed to appear Jorenian."

That theory made the men begin muttering among themselves. Reever had already spoken to me of the new alterform technology, which manipulated DNA to transform beings of one species into another. The bioengineered beings had usually been utilized by the League for intelligence gathering or infiltration during the war, and there had been rumors that the Hsktskt now possessed the technology.

"I am more likely to believe this outlaw an alterform than an escaped Jorenian slave," Xonea said.

This also puzzled me. "Why?"

"No Jorenian would voluntarily live among the Hsktskt," the captain informed me in a peculiar tone, "and none who have been made slaves in the past survived long in captivity."

I folded my arms. "Teulon Jado survived more than two years after being made a slave."

"He took back his freedom, such as it was." His gaze turned as cold as a dark-season ice storm. "Are you certain it was not another humanoid species? One that is dark-skinned and light-eyed, like us?"

I wanted to agree with Xonea simply to be done with the matter, and to remove that coldness from his eyes, but I could not. "He looked like a Jorenian. He had the skin mark of a Torin."

"There is one manner in which we can verify the healer's claim," Qonja said. "With the permission of the Hsktskt, I will scan the surface of the planet for Jorenian life signs. Among this population, they will be simple to locate."

It was an excellent idea. The Hsktskt were cold-blooded reptilians, while the Jorenians were warm-blooded humanoids. The outlaw would show up very differently on long-range bioscans.

"Telling the Hsktskt that a rogue Jorenian may have led the attack on their medical facility would not be wise," the captain said. "They may decide that we are responsible, and attack the *Sunlace*."

"You need not tell them you are scanning for a Jorenian," I said, feeling slightly exasperated. "You need not lie, either. Merely say Qonja is scanning for beings that may be carrying exotic pathogens."

"That is not true."

"It is partial truth," I countered. "Jorenians carry many types of natural bacteria in their bodies that can be considered exotic."

Xonea scowled as if my suggestion offended him. "Deception will not endear us to the Hsktskt."

"Neither will discovering that they have a rogue Jorenian among these outlaws," my husband pointed out, "or that we kept our knowledge of it from them."

"Very well." A light flickered on Xonea's console, and he glanced at the screen. "The Senior Healer summons you to Medical, Cherijo. That is where you directed the female Hsktskt to report?"

The attack on the medical facility had severely damaged the forensics section, so ChoVa had agreed to bring to the ship the body of one patient who had died while in cryopreservation. It was the only way I could convince her to agree to allow me to perform an autopsy.

"Yes, she is waiting for me." I rose and looked around the room. "I may return to Vtaga with Healer ChoVa after we have examined the body?"

Reever and Xonea both started to speak at once.

"I can only do one thing," I reminded them. "Not two. Agree first before you issue orders."

"As long as security is reestablished, and your escort is increased and better armed, I will permit it," Xonea said.

My husband remained silent, but the stillness of his features made me think that he was again displeased with me. I thanked the captain and left the conference room, wondering as I went to the lift if my marriage was going to survive this plague any better than the Hsktskt.

When I arrived in Medical, the Omorr was waiting for me, and bounced across the deck toward me with visible agitation.

"Where have you been?"

"Telling men things they did not wish to hear. Was I needed here?" I turned to view the ward, but several patients had been discharged, and those who remained were quiet and appeared in stabilized condition.

"Your Hsktskt is waiting for you to attend this autopsy." He indicated an examination room on the far side of the bay that was commonly used for laboratory cultures and specimen analyses. "I thawed the remains for her."

"I thank you." His stare made me glance down at my garments, which were soiled with smoke, dust, and suspension fluid. "I did not have time to change."

"The state of your clothing is irrelevant. Are you hurt?" I shook my head, but he removed the headband device I wore, checked it, and inspected me as if I were bleeding from every opening. "You should have come here first. I told Reever that I would have to examine you. What was he thinking?"

"We were escorted from the launch bay to the briefing room on the captain's orders. You should complain to him." I went to a garment-storage unit to remove a scrub gown, mask, and gloves, and then stepped behind a screen to strip. "I see you have released Knofki." I was glad the boy no longer had to be confined to a berth. "Did you decide when we can start the fittings for Dapvea's prostheses?"

He made no reply, and when I looked around the edge of the screen I saw that his gildrells were so stiff they hardly moved. He was angry with me again.

"We will talk about the patients later," I said as I finished dressing. "Why were you not at this briefing? I had expected to see you there."

"You expect me to leave a female Hsktskt here, in my Medical Bay, to do as she pleases?" He sniffed. "I think not."

"ChoVa will not harm anyone. She may be reptilian, but she is no different than us." I came out from behind the screen and pulled on the gloves. "We cannot help her people if we treat them as if they all suffer from filth-born fleshrot."

"Leprosy," Squilyp snapped.

"As you say." Perhaps I had offended him by not asking his permission to bring the female Hsktskt on board. "Senior Healer, I would have performed this procedure on the planet, but the forensic lab at their facility was all but destroyed, and it was not safe to travel to another." I looked at the lower deck. "Next time I promise that I will signal first."

"Stop doing that!" the Omorr shouted, making me jump. When two nurses stared at us, he brought his temper back under control and added in an almost-level tone, "The Adan signaled the ship the moment the facility was attacked. Then, when I saw the Hsktskt walk in here as if she were in charge . . ." He made a swift, frustrated gesture.

"I am well," I assured him. "The Hsktskt will not take over the ship. ChoVa is only here to help me with the autopsy. I regret that our actions caused you worry and concern. Please forgive me."

His facial skin darkened. "If you cringe in front of me one more time, I vow I will give you a real reason to do so." He hopped away into his office.

I frowned as I pulled a scrub mask over my head and tucked it under my chin. I did not fear the Omorr, exactly. The Senior Healer might have a terse and unfriendly demeanor—rather like Hasal, Teulon's second on Akkabarr—but most ensleg males who were not Jorenian seemed to be the same. Still, my attempts to placate his surly moods were not proving to be very effective. Perhaps I would ask his mate if there were some ensleg behavior of which I was ignorant.

ChoVa had already prepared the body for autopsy, I saw as I walked into the isolation room. The Hsktskt healer looked bigger and more alien here, where I was accustomed to only Jorenians, but I felt closer to her than I had on the planet. Perhaps our brush with death at the facility had created an unspoken bond between us, or I simply trusted her more because of it.

"Do you wish to dissect or examine?" I asked her.

"I wish to be a hundred light-years from this place," she said, pulling down the large mask covering her lower jaw. "Naked and basking in the warmth of an alien star."

"I do not think I can arrange that," I admitted. "They have round rooms with machines that simulate such places here on the ship that you may use. After the autopsy, perhaps."

"Yes, the autopsy." She made a soft hiss that was almost a sigh. "You are the surgical expert; I know my species. You dissect, I will examine."

I had not performed many autopsies on Akkabarr—there had rarely been time to worry about how our men died—but the procedure was a simple one and, as before, my hands remembered what my mind did not.

ChoVa switched on the console audio data recorder. "Autopsy on adult male Hsktskt, rank centuron, age forty-four rev," she said as I made a long, three-sided center incision down the middle of the corpse. "Preliminary cause of death thought to be cellular breakdown as a result of infectious unidentified pathogen and extended cryopreservation."

The reptilian's body cavity contained many organs I had never before seen. The same odd familiarity, however, again flooded my thoughts as I studied how the organs were arranged. Some part of me knew what the organ systems were and how they functioned. Following standard procedure, I examined the area surrounding the large cardiac organ before excising it and placing it in a specimen tray.

ChoVa retrieved the tray and took it to the medical scanner console. "Outer cardiac layer displays tissue necrosis consistent with cryo-crystallization," she said as she placed it in the organ processor's recess, which scanned it for other imperfections. "No enlargement, unrelated damage, or other defects. Harvesting specimens for further analysis."

As I continued dissecting, ChoVa examined and removed tissue specimens from several areas of each organ I handed to her. She helped me turn the body to take a sample of spinal tissue and fluid, and then stepped back as I used a lascalpel to cut open the cranial case and remove the yellow-pink cerebral organ.

The Hsktskt brain was much larger than those of most humanoid species, and possessed three distinct hemispheres and a dozen gland clusters that needed separate examination. Once the whole brain had been scanned, I dissected it on a smaller adjoining table and harvested the clusters one by one.

Only one set of glands did not appear normal, and I called ChoVa over to confirm this. "Is this more damage from the cryo?"

She studied the inflamed specimen. "No. From where did you remove these?" When I pointed to the corresponding section, she shook her head and retrieved the cluster with a pair of forceps. "They must be diseased."

As I was finished with the brain, I joined her at the scanner console. The display showed no trace of disease, but it did flag an unusually high concentration of an enzyme not normally present in the cluster.

"Tohykul," she said.

I did not know the word. "What is that?"

"A mistake." After she repeated the cluster scan a second and third time with the same results, she grew impatient. "Do you have another unit? This one is obviously malfunctioning."

I went out and retrieved a portable scanner unit we used on the ward, wheeled it in, and waited as she conducted a fourth scan. The same elevated enzyme level appeared on the portable's display.

"What is it?" I had no knowledge of the enzyme, odd or otherwise.

"These results are not viable," she said as she removed the specimen and stared at it. "Tohykul is present in the Hsktskt brain, but only in trace amounts during gestation and immediately after birth, and never in this quantity."

"Perhaps it is a synthetic form, administered before death?" I guessed.

"No. It cannot be synthesized. We would never . . ." She set aside the specimen and regarded me with wide eyes. "Tohykul was once produced in the brains of our ancestors. We believe it was the result of them being overcome by an abnormal state brought on by loss of emotional control, something we only experience now in utero."

I glanced back at the body. "Does this enzyme cause the same behavioral symptoms as the infected patients have been displaying?"

"No. Tohykul was a survival response and produced the exact opposite. It flooded the body with ten times the average level of blood sugar and increased nerve sensitivity. The result was elevated strength and extreme aggression." She stepped back to the dissection table and looked inside the open cranial case. "The glands of Hsktskt infants produce a tiny trace amount of tohykul after they are born. It is what makes them so dangerous."

The dividing line between fear and aggression was not so wide. "This male is not a newborn."

"Listen to what I say," ChoVa said, very agitated now. "The gland cluster that produces tohykul cannot do so without the specific trauma of birth. The enzyme no longer exists in the infant's body after several days. There is no more reason for adult Hsktskt to produce the enzyme."

"Something caused this male's mind to manufacture it in great quantity," I pointed out. "What could be the reason for it?"

"None." She turned as if to leave, and then faced me. "You do not understand. This only happened to adult Hsktskt in our prehistory, when my people were confronted by threats that no longer exist."

It seemed I would have to pry this information out of her a word at a time. "You surely face threats now. This plague is a very large and frightening one."

"Modern Hsktskt do not feel fear of such things. In ancient times, our ancestors did, but those emotions were necessary to help them survive and fight for control of our world. Larger, more primitive lifeforms like us populated Vtaga in that era. They caused those reactions in our species as a part of the evolutionary process, especially . . ." She paused and her throat worked. "The rogur."

I felt a surge of impatience. "Then this rogur or something like it is the cause of it."

"Not unless this centuron first traveled back in

time," she told me. "The rogur as well as our other ancient enemies are extinct. Our ancestors killed off all of them ten thousand years ago."

ChoVa walked out of the examination room. I covered the body and followed her, only to find her gone and Squilyp in my path.

"What happened?" he demanded. "Why does that Hsktskt look as if she wants to use her talons on someone?"

"I am not sure. She is . . . upset." I was not certain that ChoVa would wish me to repeat what she had said or pursue her further. "She needs time to be alone now. Is there a nurse available to assist me with finishing this autopsy?"

"I will do it." The Omorr hopped across the deck and into the examination room.

The Senior Healer proved to be an efficient forensic assistant, but like the ship's database, could not provide me with information on the rogur or any other ancient, extinct Vtagan life-form.

"The Hsktskt do not share data about their species, history, or planet," Squilyp told me after I finished a series of unsuccessful inquiries. "Even their language has rarely been recorded. We know nothing about their past except that it is lengthy, violent, and ugly."

"The evolution of any intelligent species is rarely a short, peaceful, pleasant business." The clatter of an instrument against a tray drew my attention, and I watched as he tossed another clamp across the table with more force than was necessary. "There may be a connection between these ancient creatures, the abnormal enzyme level, and the contagion infecting the Hsktskt. Perhaps this rogur ChoVa mentioned, or another creature like it, was not rendered extinct, and has somehow infected her people."

"People?" Squilyp rolled the Hsktskt male's remains to one side to lay out an open body bag beneath it. "They are not people."

"Of course they are." I tugged the other edge of the bag to my side of the table. "I think they are more like you ensleg than you know."

"You are wrong." He shoved one of the corpse's limbs into the bag's recess. "Hsktskt are not people. They have little intelligence and no emotion. They enslave other species and treat them like cargo. They are brutes. Unfeeling *monsters*."

I knew most humanoids felt distaste toward slaver species like the Hsktskt, but Squilyp's anger seemed excessive. "Nevertheless, they are my patients. If I am to help them, I must know more about this enzyme and its effect on them." I watched as he finished prepping the corpse for transport back to Vtaga. "What is your opinion as to the cause of death?"

The Omorr looked up, surprised. "Clearly systemic damage from the cryopreservative fluid and being frozen too long killed him. Cellular frost-necrosis was evident in all the tissue samples." His facial skin darkened. "That beast doctor knows this, and yet she continues to freeze her own kind. Is that the sort of behavior an intelligent, compassionate species demonstrates?"

"They are desperate." I shook my head. "Damage

from the cryo is the mechanism, but not the cause. He would not have been subjected to extreme temperature if he had not been infected with this pathogen—"

"No traces of a hostile organism, pathogenic or otherwise, were present in his blood, tissue, or bones," the Omorr said, sounding testy now.

"None that we could *identify*," I corrected. "Cherijo wrote in her journals of a contagion on K-2 that concealed itself by mimicking the cells it infected. Something similar could be happening here."

"This is completely different." Squilyp sealed the body bag and went to the nearest cleansing unit, where he scrubbed his membranes with marked ferocity.

I picked up the chart and finished entering the last of the autopsy data, and still he was scrubbing. I went to stand beside him. "Is this need for cleanliness because you are angry with me, or feel renewed contempt for my patients?"

"Both." He lifted the edge of his single foot from the foot pedal to deactivate the cleanser, but remained staring down at his membranes, which were raw, bright pink. "You do not remember Catopsa, or what these beasts did to you while you were a slave."

"You speak of Cherijo. I was never on Catopsa, or a slave." I folded my arms. "They did nothing to me."

"I weary of thinking of you as two people." His eyes shifted sideways, and they were narrow and very dark now. "The Hsktskt took you from us. They stranded you on Catopsa and forced you to treat the other slaves, most of whom blamed you for their enslavement. The Hsktskt guards were monsters. One of them beat you, starved you, and branded you over and over when your slave marks healed over."

"Those things were not done to me." I thought of my life on Akkabarr, and how terrible things had been for us before and during the rebellion. "I have known my share of pain and deprivation, but the Hsktskt were not responsible for it." I felt chilled and wrapped my arms around my middle. "I am sorry they hurt Cherijo. It must have caused you pain to know your friend had suffered such things."

"You don't *want* her memories." His gaze shifted, going to the body bag and then back to my face. "Is that it? Is that what you're doing? Deliberately suppressing them?" He whipped out a scanner and held it under my nose. "Think about the Hsktskt."

"That is all I do." I pushed the scanner aside. "And I have had enough of this."

"Cherijo's memories may be stored in another region of the brain. She was engineered with enhanced capacity. I never thought to . . ." He glanced at the neuro treatment room. "I must apply stimulation to different areas of your brain."

"No, you will not." I reached for the last of my patience. "Senior Healer, you cannot find memories that do not exist. All I have are of Akkabarr and my life there."

"If that were true, then how were you able to perform that autopsy?" He gestured toward the remains, which two nurses were moving on a gurney. "There were no Hsktskt involved in your rebellion."

I rubbed my aching temple. "As I have told you before, in the past I have performed many such procedures—"

"But not on the Hsktskt, or any other reptilian life-form. They aren't like humanoids. Aside from considerable physical differences, they can't function on ice worlds. The cold kills them. Only Cherijo had the experience to perform this procedure, and that came from her time as a slave on Catopsa. To use her skills, you would have to directly access her memories." He adjusted his scanner and placed it under my nose again. "Now, try to remember the last operation you performed on the Hsktskt."

He sounded as agitated as Reever, and yet curiously excited. It made me feel sick.

"This serves no purpose." I pushed past him. "I must check on ChoVa, and then go to my quarters. Reever will be worried. We will speak of this another time." I moved toward the door panel.

Squilyp seized my shoulder and turned me around. "You can't forget her forever."

"I don't remember her." I was shouting, but then, so was he.

ChoVa abruptly entered the room. "My sire wishes to come to this vessel tomorrow and deliver the official apology for involving you and your team in our domestic problems with the outlaws." She looked from me to Squilyp. "Cease your altercation and advise me as to who arranges such visits."

I felt a quick wave of relief and stepped away from the Omorr. "We should speak to the captain about it. I will take you to see him."

"This is not over," the Omorr called after me.

Once we were outside Medical, ChoVa said, "I regret my earlier, hasty departure. It was wrong to leave you without warning in the middle of the procedure. What did that single-legged one mean by 'this is not over'?"

"The Senior Healer has been attempting to recover my former self's memories." I sighed. "Now he believes I am hiding them, or suppressing them."

"His assumption is understandable," she said. "Irrational and unproductive emotions often compel you warm-bloods into paranoia."

"Indeed." I glanced at her. "You have cold blood. What is your excuse?"

She tasted my air, and then exhaled heavily. "Perhaps I suffer from close proximity to your kind."

My mouth curled. "We are a terrible influence, I am told."

As we walked I told her about what little Squilyp and I had discovered from the autopsy, and then paused outside the lift entry.

"ChoVa, if I am to find a treatment for this contagion, I need a great deal more information about your people, their prehistory, and especially this rogur and the other extinct creatures you mentioned." Even my uttering the word provoked an instant physical response from the Hsktskt female. She tensed, her eyelids flared wide, and the muscles around her jaw twitched. "I know I am offending you. I understand that certain taboos are considered necessary to reinforce the framework of a society. But I ask that you set these things aside and help me, before there is no society left."

"If I can, I will," she said slowly. "It will be difficult. There is nothing I know about the creatures of the past, not even what they were known as. Only the rogur is mentioned by name in some old stories; legends told by the eldest to frighten the youngest among us. I cannot even guarantee they are based on the truth."

"Surely you have some history preserved of these creatures? Data, written records?" She shook her head. "Specimens? Fossils? *Anything?*"

"Nothing," ChoVa stated flatly. "Hatred for these creatures was so complete that when my ancestors exterminated them, they removed every trace of them from our world. No one was permitted to speak of the old ones or what they did. Documents that contained drawings and writings about them were burned. Eventually all the people who had actually seen the creatures died, and their children were left with only a few stories. This is how it has been passed down through the bloodlines for many generations. A collection of myths that make no sense."

"Then that is where we must begin." I felt uneasy, for I knew how powerful legends could be. I had used the legend of the vral to violate the taboo against women healing men—and that had fooled whole armies. "Tell me about the rogur."

TEN

"It is possible that these prehistoric creatures preyed on the ancient Hsktskt in such a way as to inspire ChoVa's legends," I said to Reever the next day as we prepared for TssVar's visit to the *Sunlace*, "but nothing like this rogur she described could have existed."

"Why not?" my husband asked. "The universe is large, and its inhabitants diverse."

"No living thing could grow large enough to swallow a continent, or assume the form of all other living things at will, or take years to digest its victims while keeping them alive by feeding them bits of each other."

"There is one, very ancient, amoebic life-form on a free-trader world in the N-jui system that was reported to have destroyed a large space vessel by enveloping and absorbing it," my husband said as he helped me into the formal uniform jacket I was to wear at the reception in launch bay. "Stories of another shape-shifting species have circulated among the mercenaries for many decades. I know of three intelligent species who often swallow their prey whole. One of them can—"

I grimaced and stopped fastening my jacket. "I

do not want to know those details, I thank you." I noticed he was not wearing his usual black garments, but had put on a modified version of a crew member's blue-and-silver uniform. "Do you wear the Torin's colors now?"

He gave his tunic a look of mild distaste. "Only for this visit."

Marel had gone to play with Fasala, so I had nothing more to do until it was time to greet TssVar. I went to the database console and checked the different inquiries I had made based on the description of the rogur from ChoVa's stories. "All the ship's machines can tell me is that the creature is likely mythic. I already know that."

"Myths are usually grounded in some fact," my husband said as he came and switched off the console. "I never heard TssVar or any Hsktskt speak of this creature, but what ChoVa told you sounds like something her kind would go to great pains to conceal."

"Why?"

"The Hsktskt have no natural enemy on Vtaga or anywhere else." He straightened the front of my jacket as if I were Marel. "They fear nothing. Offworld, they conduct themselves as if the galaxy and all its worlds and beings belonged to them by right of evolutionary superiority."

"So if the rogur did exist, and did do some of these terrible things mentioned in these stories . . ." I tried to follow his logic, but all I knew were the ways of the Iisleg. "The Hsktskt would lose face?"

"It would reduce them to an equal standing with us." Reever ran his hand over my hair and down the length of it. "The Hsktskt see humanoids as irrational, fearful beings, unable to properly defend themselves or their territory. Raiding humanoid colonies, and capturing and selling our kind as slaves for centuries, have not improved their opinion. You look beautiful today, Jarn."

I smiled. I had put some effort into making myself presentable in the ensleg fashion. "I had hoped my appearance would please you."

"Did you please him as well?" he asked, winding my hair around his hand in an idle fashion.

"Him?"

He bent his head and brushed his mouth next to but not over mine. "Teulon."

I frowned. "The Raktar did not care about my appearance, as long as I wore the vral mask around the rebel men. Why?"

"I was only curious." Reever straightened and made a show of checking the time display on the console. "We should go."

We walked into the launch bay, where Xonea and other important men from around the ship had assembled to receive TssVar. None of them looked particularly pleased, but I saw no show of anger or hostility, and no one's claws had emerged. The Senior Healer was present, but I did not see ChoVa.

Reever gestured for me to go stand with Squilyp and the assembled medical staff, and then went to speak to Xonea. Feeling troubled again, I took my place at Squilyp's right side. Across from us I saw the giant walking-and-talking feline called Alunthri. Its ears flicked as it noticed my gaze, but it turned almost immediately to look out at the stars.

The jlorra on Akkabarr had tolerated me, and a few times had shown me affection. I had grown accustomed to sharing our quarters with the small beasts, although I felt sure I would never completely trust them. What was I to do about this creature, who claimed Cherijo as a friend?

"I should be in Medical," the Senior Healer said, distracting my thoughts. A Hsktskt scout ship passed through the buffer barrier and landed on the transport pad. He looked uncomfortable in his formal tunic, and the faint bruise of sleeplessness darkened the flesh around his eyes. "This is nothing but a farce."

"Showing proper respect invites the same," I murmured as I watched Reever and the captain move to greet SubAkade TssVar as he walked down the scout's ramp. "Where is ChoVa?"

"She was showing respect for our efforts to preserve the peace and save her species by rescanning the body we autopsied." Squilyp's gildrells curled and uncurled in an agitated fashion. "Does she really think we would botch the procedure?"

"I cannot say what she thinks. I am not Reever." I noted the number of guards TssVar had brought with him, and how careful Xonea and Reever were to inspect the weapons they carried. I also saw a Hsktskt male beside TssVar who seemed quite small—only a few inches taller than me—and stood looking around with wide eyes. I heard the Omorr release an impatient sound, and turned to him. "Aside from ChoVa's general lack of respect, what else has become lodged in your throat?"

It took a moment for him to comprehend the Iisleg phrase. "My mate had a restless night," he said, his voice lower and tighter now. "Her delivery time draws near."

His confession astonished me. "Why would that bother you?" The Iisleg valued sons who could hunt, protect the tribe, and carry their name and blood, so our males always looked forward to birthing times to finally know the sex of the child.

"Garphawayn has never before delivered a child," he snapped. "Something could go wrong." He shifted restlessly, rocking back and forth on the edges of his broad foot. "I suppose those barbarians on that ice world made their women drop their newborn out on the ice."

"Only if the mother were cast out to die while she was in labor," I said blandly. His visible outrage made me add, "It is a pity you are not Iisleg. Our males do not attend birthings, and they only acknowledge male children they know they have sired. New mothers and female children are always ignored."

Squilyp snorted. "Those males should be whipped, preferably by their own women." At a discreet signal from Xonea, he stopped rocking. "The captain wishes us to greet the beast."

I wondered what he would do if I used my elbow on his rib cage. "Stop calling them beasts."

TssVar did not wait for Squilyp to finish his formal greeting, but stepped forward and held his clawed hands out in a palm-up, humanoid gesture. "The Hanar sends his regrets that your life was endangered, and asks that you return to Vtaga to continue your efforts to cure the plague. I am to make whatever restitution you require in order to facilitate this."

"I require nothing, as no harm was done," I said, glancing at the young male Hsktskt. "My husband and the captain will wish to decide if and when I return. You should make your negotiations with them."

"We will need more security for Cherijo, Sub-Akade," Xonea stated.

Reever took a more direct approach. "What have you done about preventing another attack by these outlaws?"

"We have moved a battalion to occupy the capital. The renegades will not breach our defenses again so easily," TssVar said. "As for security, the Hanar is sending a detachment of Palace Guards to escort the healer upon her return. They have sworn to sacrifice themselves before they allow her to be harmed or killed."

Xonea looked at Reever, who appeared to be in deep thought.

"I want five arena guards added to the detachment," my husband said at last. "They are faster than the Hanar's men."

"Done." TssVar turned to me. "The Hanar would know if you have made any progress in determining the cause of and a cure for the plague."

"We should discuss the results of the autopsy ChoVa and I performed." I smiled at the curious expression on the young male's face. "Would you tell me the name of this one, please?"

TssVar's primary eyelids lowered, and his tongue flickered for a moment before he answered me. "This is the youngest of my line, CaurVar." He hissed something wordless at his son, who stepped forward and dropped his head back for a moment to reveal the pale green-and-white scales covering the front of his throat.

Reever had told me throat-baring was an acknowledgment of respect as well as a gesture of submission among the Hsktskt. As the warm-blooded were considered inferior species, to be shown such was a great compliment.

"You are welcome here, CaurVar," I said.

"You are my sister's namesake," the young male said. "My mother often claims that ChoVa might have become a great military commander, like my sire, if not for your designation over her life."

I raised my eyebrows. "Is this an undesirable thing?"

He gave his sire a sly look and flashed some very adult-looking rows of jagged teeth. "If you dislike the military as much as my mother does, no."

His voice had not yet thickened and deepened like that of an adult male, but had a far more pleasant tone, mellow like the sound of an Iisleg child's wind trumpet. His scales appeared thinner and smaller than TssVar's, and the color pattern was much more spotted with white and yellow. Most surprising was the fact that his claws had been cut back and were blunted.

TssVar noticed my interest. "It is common practice now among our females to cull the young ones of their claws. They believe it somehow prevents them from contracting the plague."

It would also prevent them from harming themselves, I thought, for I had seen several young

Hsktskt at the medical facility. "CaurVar, have you ever seen the inside of a ship like this one?"

He shook his head and turned at once to speak to his sire. "Do we own this vessel, Father?"

TssVar uttered a sharp sound. "No, *kasso*, these people are here as our . . . allies."

"Warm-blooded allies?" CaurVar's brow furrowed. "Does mother know about this?"

Xonea kept his expression neutral, but I saw a glimmer of appreciation in his eyes. "I would be pleased to show your son around the ship while you meet with the medical staff," he said to TssVar.

One of the guards stepped forward and hissed something too low for our wristcoms to translate, but TssVar only made a terse gesture, and the male returned to his place.

"I will permit this." Now the giant Hsktskt looked almost uncomfortable. "My youngest is very curious. He will ask a great many questions."

"Then it is well that I possess many answers." The captain gestured toward the corridor, and in his eagerness CaurVar almost ran to the door panel.

Squilyp cleared his throat. "We may make use of the launch bay scheduling room for the medical briefing," he suggested. "I can access the forensic database from the console there."

"You are the Senior Healer of this ship, are you not?" TssVar asked the Omorr. When he nodded, the Hsktskt's eyes shifted to me. "An interesting choice."

We adjourned to a large area connected to the launch bay, where Squilyp reviewed the results of the autopsy we had performed on the plague victim, blaming cryopreservation efforts as the cause of death and making a formal recommendation that the Hsktskt find alternative means with which to control the infected patients' symptoms.

"You cannot continue to freeze them," Squilyp said as he showed TssVar and his entourage the cellular-level damage inflicted by the cold. "Your daughter tells us that treatment with synthesized neuroparalyzer proves to be equally toxic to your species. I suggest you explore new methods of physical restraint until treatment for symptoms or a cure can be discovered."

TssVar turned to me. "What of a cure? Have you made any progress, Healer Torin?"

"We learned from the autopsy that one of the gland clusters from the victim's brain was saturated with tohykul," I told him. "ChoVa indicated that this enzyme is only present in any significant quantity in newborn Hsktskt, but the victim was a mature male. This is the first physical anomaly we have found among the infected."

"One infected male," TssVar corrected.

I nodded. "That is why we must return to the surface and conduct tests on the other quarantined Hsktskt to learn if they, too, have the same quantity of tohykul in their gland clusters, as—"

A nurse walked abruptly into the room. "Your pardon, Senior Healer, but you are needed in Medical Bay."

Squilyp frowned. "I will report as soon as we are finished here."

"It is your mate, Senior Healer," the nurse said,

making an expressive gesture. "She has gone into labor and is calling for you."

As soon as he heard "labor" the Omorr jumped up and hopped across the room. "Cherijo."

"Excuse me, SubAkade," I said to TssVar, "it is his first child." I didn't wait for a response but hurried out after Squilyp.

I had never seen the Omorr move as quickly as he did through the corridors. I barely had time to catch up and leap into the lift with him before he took it to Medical Bay's level.

"She delivers too early," Squilyp muttered as he bounced around the lift compartment. "There will be complications. Why did I not send her back to Omorr? Perhaps we can stop the contractions. It is too early. I have killed her."

I kept myself flattened against the back of the compartment to avoid his big foot and his gildrells, which snapped and snarled around his face like short whips. "You said females of your species deliver each in their own time. The nurse said nothing about complications, or if she were dead."

He stopped and glared at me. "You are not helping."

"Think of how you would feel if you received this message here and she were on Omorr," I pointed out.

"I cannot think." The lift stopped, and he hovered impatiently until it opened. "Hurry."

We hurried. So much so that the Omorr nearly ran over two nurses and a supply cart on his way into Medical, which appeared as if someone had raided it and strewn the contents of every cabinet on the deck. There Donarea, the chief obstetrics resident, was waiting outside a treatment room and peering anxiously through an observation panel.

"Why are you not in there with her?" Squilyp shouted as soon as he saw her.

"Your pardon, Senior Healer, but the healer said I should wait outside until she summoned me." Donarea had several fresh, thin lacerations on her face.

"The healer? What healer? There are only Cherijo and I and—" He choked on his words. "Not the Hsktskt. You did not give my mate to the Hsktskt. Tell me you did not."

Donarea turned to me. "The Lady Maftuda presented active labor and extreme distress when she arrived. She became violent when told her mate was not here and that I have never delivered an Omorr—"

The Omorr pushed the resident out of his way and burst into the treatment room. I ran inside behind him.

The delivery table was empty and pushed to one side of the room. ChoVa stood in the center, holding a writhing, struggling Garphawayn from behind, and appeared to be pushing her onto the deck. The female Omorr was naked and shrieking out many words, none of which my wristcom would translate.

"Release my mate," Squilyp bellowed.

Garphawayn looked up, her wet face a dark pink color, her eyes bright with emotion. "You did this to me. Pray I do not find a blade before I am ripped apart." She threw back her head and screamed as her upper sternum flexed and one narrow aperture appeared, opened, and immediately closed again.

Squilyp staggered backward. "The child comes." He reached out to steady himself and nearly fell over.

"Stay out of the way, Omorr." ChoVa reached around and tested the opening. "She is ready. Jarn, aid me. I will hold her arms."

I went to crouch before Garphawayn, who hurled more of her incomprehensible words at me. The birthing aperture appeared again, wider this time, but closed before I could see any sign of the newborn.

ChoVa kept the female Omorr's three strong arms pinned from behind. "When it opens again, the infant will present its head. Ease it out to the gildrells and allow the child to do the rest. Do not put your fingers or hand in the birth canal; the contractions will break your bones."

I followed her instructions. The tiny head of the Omorr crowned, and I slipped a hand beneath it and guided it out of its mother's body. Its gildrells were half the size of an adult Omorr's, but they latched immediately onto the sides of the canal and pushed or pulled it open wider. The remainder of the child's body popped out into my waiting hands, and the next contraction was so strong that it severed the umbilical cord. The infant hissed rather than squalling, as Terran children did, but otherwise it was like any newborn: wrinkled, dripping wet, and very unhappy to have left the comfort of its mother's body.

"It is a male," I said as I saw its small, sheathed penis extrude for a few seconds. I wrapped him in a linen blanket and moved to hand him to his mother.

ChoVa did not release Garphawayn's arms to allow her to hold her newborn. "Give it to the sire," she said. "She delivers another."

A second infant? I went to Squilyp and placed his squirming, hissing son into his unresisting arms before hurrying back. The head of the secondborn had already crowned, and the infant wrenched itself from its mother's body without any help from me. It, too, was a male, and identical to the first.

"There." ChoVa released Garphawayn, who leaned back against her with an exhausted sigh. "Give her that child. Omorr, bring the other here so that his mother may look upon him."

Squilyp hopped over and crouched beside his mate, depositing the other twin male in her arms. The two small Omorr males were perfect miniatures of their father.

I smiled at ChoVa. "You are an excellent midwife."

"It was my specialty before I went to serve the Hanar," the Hsktskt said. "I have delivered Omorr slaves in the past, and I know how difficult and violent their labor can be."

Squilyp looked up, his gildrells stiff and straight. "Yes, I expect you would. What did you do with their offspring? Eat them, or sell them?"

"Neither." ChoVa straightened. "I am a physician, not a slaver. Hsktskt do not devour live fodder."

"Your guards did on Catopsa," the Omorr snarled back.

"Senior Healer," I said, feeling the immediate need to intervene, "this is not the time for such a discussion."

"Isn't it?" He didn't move his gaze from ChoVa. "Your young brother is on the ship. How would you feel if I kidnapped him and sold him to slavers? Or cooked him for my next meal interval?"

Rows of jagged, efficient teeth appeared. "I would not suggest you try either, Omorr."

"Fortunately I have no desire to. Your services are not needed or wanted, Hsktskt." Squilyp made a fierce gesture toward the exit. "Take your claws off my mate and leave here at once."

ChoVa blinked, and then eased Garphawayn over to me before she trudged out of the treatment room.

Donarea joined us to help with cleaning up Garphawayn and her sons. I remained silent as I used a scanner to check the female Omorr. "Her uterine cavity is clear, no signs of hemorrhaging. The afterbirth remains in one piece."

"She will eject it in an hour, after her body absorbs the nutrients and compacts it," Donarea explained.

The Senior Healer lifted his wife and his sons into his powerful arms. "Resident, push the table back over here. Cherijo, linens." His gildrells were entwining with Garphawayn's, but his dark eyes were still filled with inexplicable fury.

I helped the resident move the table back into its position, and retrieved linens to cover the female

Omorr while the senior healer scanned both of his sons. "They appear to be perfectly healthy."

"Twin males." Garphawayn looked down at her sons. "My family will be pleased." She seemed less dazed now, and looked around her. "Where is Dr. ChoVa?"

"I sent the Hsktskt away," Squilyp said in a soothing tone. "Did she harm you?"

"She prevented me from harming everyone in here." The female Omorr sighed. "Forgive me, but the pain was more than I could bear. When I could not find you, my distress made me take leave of my senses. All I could think was how much I wished to make everyone I saw suffer what I was feeling. I think I might have injured the staff and myself and the children, if not for that Hsktskt."

I looked across the table at Squilyp. "I will go and find her."

"If you mean to have me thank that beast, or apologize to her, do not bother. You heard what she said—the only reason she knew how to cope with this was because she has delivered Omorr slaves." He sniffed. "Better you have the captain make her leave the ship before she decides to take my wife and children and sell them to the highest bidder."

"That will not be necessary, Omorr," ChoVa's voice said. I looked up and saw her at the observation panel looking in. "We may be, as you say, beasts, but we are civilized ones. We will leave voluntarily."

ChoVa walked away, and SubAkade TssVar looked in for a moment before doing the same. Reever stood at the panel long enough to meet my gaze and shake his head before following the Hskt-skt out of Medical.

I left Squilyp with his mate and their sons, but by the time I reached the launch bay the Hsktskt had already departed the ship.

"They said nothing about returning," the launch supervisor told me. "Shall I contact the surface and inquire?"

I had no idea how serious this breach of protocol was, but ChoVa and her sire had every reason to feel offended. "It is best to ask the captain."

I did not want to return to Medical and listen to Squilyp again disparage the Hsktskt, or go back to our quarters and face Reever's unhappiness over the matter, so I decided to visit one of the simulator rooms. It would be good, as Darea had suggested, to work off some of this strange frustration I had been feeling.

I went to the closest unit and checked the panel. The simulator was not in use, but the program that had just been terminated was listed on the panel display as a sparring exercise. Perhaps the crew members using it would tell me how to initiate one suited to Terrans.

I entered through the door panel and saw Qonja and Hawk standing in the center of the yellow power grid. Both were stripped to the waist and covered with sweat. Two swords and several pieces of protective armor lay discarded to one side of the room.

"You are improving, but you must drop your guard to attack," Qonja was saying to Hawk. He put his hand on the winged man's shoulder. "Do not hesitate. I will counter the move, but I will take care not to injure you."

"I don't care about myself." Hawk covered Qonja's hand with his. "I'm afraid I'll hurt you."

Qonja's expression softened. "I am stronger than you think, *evlanar*." He bent down and for a moment I thought he meant to put his mouth to Hawk's.

"No." Hawk turned his head. "We cannot, not here. It is not worth it."

"You are worth much." Qonja rested his hand against Hawk's neck. "What we cannot do is go on like this, never touching outside our quarters, always fearing someone will see. I honor you, you honor me."

Hawk's wings flared briefly before he stepped away and picked up a cloth to dry his chest. "Someone *will* see us, and report the matter to your ClanLeader, and then Tlore will force you to leave me." He drew in a sharp breath. "Secrecy is more important than displaying our honor."

"Secrecy imprisons us. It makes a mockery of what we feel." Qonja came up behind Hawk and stroked his hands over the other man's wings. "No one could make me leave you now, *evlanar*."

As Hawk turned around into Qonja's embrace, I opened the door panel and slipped out into the corridor. I was confused, not by seeing the two men together, but by what they had said.

"No one knows that they are lovers."

I turned to see the large, talking feline standing

just behind me. "Alunthri." I suppressed a desire to step back. "I did not mean to intrude on them."

"You took pains not to do so." Its whiskers twitched. "I will not harm you. I cannot harm another being."

"Apart from Iisleg hunters, felines are the deadliest thing on my world." I glanced at the entry to the simulator. "Why does no one know about them?"

"Jorenians do not permit same-gender mates."

I had noticed that there were no men together on the ship, but I had thought that a matter of a modesty. Iisleg men who coupled with men were not treated any differently than those who coupled with women. Indeed, males from some of the more primitive iiskars believed that a man could only truly love another man, as women of the Iisleg were considered creatures without real souls and therefore unworthy of such affection. However, Reever had told me every species was different.

The feline's eyes narrowed. "Will you tell anyone about them?"

Qonja and Hawk's relationship violated some Jorenian custom, so they had chosen to conceal it from the rest of the crew. I would have to somehow ask my husband to explain it to me without exposing what I now knew of Qonja and Hawk's relationship. "No."

Alunthri bared its teeth. "You are as kind as she was." Before I could reply, it passed me and disappeared down the corridor.

I went to our quarters, where I found my husband sitting and reviewing data on the console. A server of tea sat ignored beside him, and I went to retrieve it.

"You do not have to wait on me," he said without looking at me as I reached for it.

"I am not waiting on you. I am keeping you from spilling this on the console." I took it to the cleansing unit. "The launch bay supervisor told me that the Hsktskt departed for the surface. Will they return?"

"Probably not."

So they *had* been offended by Squilyp's careless, angry remarks. "I must ask you something else."

"Ask me anything."

I thought about how to say it. "Why are there no men with men on this ship?"

"There are men working with men all over this ship." He finally looked at me. "You mean as couples, as we are?" I nodded. "Most of the crew is Jorenian. They do not practice homosexuality."

I frowned. So what the talking feline had said was truth. "They do not? At all?"

"Their species mates for reproductive purposes, and for life." He switched off the console. "Their males cannot fertilize other males."

"I know that," I said, feeling the odd anger building inside me. "But surely they do not all have to produce children?"

"From what I have been told, breeding is a strong biological imperative with the Jorenians." He removed his tunic and tossed it over the back of his seat. "At some point during their maturity, their bodies make it so that they have no alternative but to Choose a partner and mate."

"They might decide to mate with someone physically incapable of bearing children," I pointed out. "How is that different than mating with one of the same gender?"

"Why are you asking me this?" He eyed me. "Have you involved yourself with another female?"

"Involved?" I was involved with everyone on the ship. "How do you mean 'involved'?"

"While you were on Akkabarr, you were involved with Resa," he said. "And with Teulon as well."

Why was he looking at me like that? "Teulon was my general, and Resa was like my sister. I was deeply *involved* with them both. If not for Marel, I would still be *involved* with them."

"That I know." He gave me a small, cold smile. "Luckily we had a child I could use to blackmail you into becoming *involved* with me."

Ah, so he meant it as coupling. Now I understood why he was always making those strange, pointed remarks about Teulon. And now Resa. He was very possessive of my former self, and doubtless regarded my relationships outside our own as a threat. On Akkabarr the men would have found this very amusing, but they routinely shared their women with other men. To do otherwise was to be considered a poor friend or an impolite host.

"If you wish to know how I was with Teulon and Resa," I said, "all you need do is ask me. I hide nothing from you."

"Such as what you now know about Qonja and Hawk?" He walked past me.

My husband could read my thoughts, it seemed,

any time he wished. "I was not hiding this from you. I was not volunteering my knowledge of it. That talking feline, Alunthri, warned me of the Jorenian taboo. I was attempting to practice what the protocol officer called discretion." I followed him into our sleeping chamber. "There is a difference."

He turned and seized my wrists in his, and continued the conversation inside my head. *There is no difference. You conceal things from me. You hold yourself apart from me. You treat Alunthri, the gentlest creature on the ship, as if it were a killer. Nothing is as it was. You cannot give me what I need.*

Both of us were feeling far too much anger and frustration, and there was only one practical outlet for that.

I cannot? Rather than struggle, I pressed myself against him. *This body that you love so much, it has not changed. What I can make you feel when I touch you is no different.* I felt him stiffen and withdraw from the mind-bond between us, but I reached out through my thoughts to him. *I do not hold myself apart. I am yours, Husband. Your woman, your mate, your companion. Your pleasure. Enjoy me. I will enjoy you. I want that above all other things.*

His hand spanned my jaw and tilted my face back so that he looked into my eyes. *She would never have offered herself like this to me. She reserved her passion for her work and her patients.*

Suddenly I understood. *But you wished her to. You wanted her to need you as much as you needed her.*

Yes, I did. So you see, you have given me what she never could. He bent his head down and kissed me.

As I felt the mind-bond melt away, I wondered if this passion between us would be enough.

"Mama?"

I looked over to see Marel looking in on us. Beside her was CaurVar, TssVar's youngest child. "Marel, where did you find this male?"

"Hiding," my daughter said. "CaurVar didn't want to get sick so he got off his daddy's launch when no one was looking in the launch bay." She placed her small hand in the Hsktskt boy's claws. "I found him and hid with him for a while but now we're hungry and tired. Can he stay in my room, Mama?"

ELEVEN

Explaining to Marel that the Hsktskt chief peace negotiator's son could not share her sleeping chamber was a simple matter. I said "No" and that was the end of it. I then busied myself making a meal for the children, which in CaurVar's case required cross-referencing the menu database for reptilian fare.

Returning the young Hsktskt to his family on Vtaga proved to be much more difficult.

"There may be accusations of abduction made," Xonea said as he came to our quarters to discuss the situation. "The Hsktskt have a large planetary defense fleet in readiness in orbit, and their flight patterns are altering as I speak. We have attempted to signal the surface, but our relays are being jammed."

"SubAkade TssVar was already offended by the Senior Healer's remarks to his daughter," my husband said. "When he discovered his son missing, he made an inevitable if erroneous conclusion."

Xonea frowned. "What sort of remarks did Squilyp make?"

"He threatened to sell the boy into slavery," I said, "or to cook and devour him as his next meal."

The captain muttered something under his

breath and went to look out our hull viewer at the planet.

I went to check on CaurVar and Marel, who had finished their meal and were playing with the small beasts in her chamber. CaurVar seemed fascinated by the way the gray feline and his black mate stalked a ball of twine that my daughter drew slowly across the floor.

"Healer, are they good hunters?" he asked me eagerly.

I gave the beasts a wry look. "Not as long as I dwell here." I heard Reever and Xonea arguing out in the other room and eyed Marel's console. Every moment our men debated how to respond to this crisis, and TssVar refused to communicate with the ship, the boy's mother would be in an agony of not knowing what had become of her son. "CaurVar, do you know the personal relay code for your mother's console?"

"Yes, Healer."

I was betting TssVar had not jammed any family channels. "Would you like to send a signal to her to let her know you are well and not in distress?"

"She will be very displeased with me." He eyed the console with as much reluctance as Marel displayed when she was required to tidy her chamber. "Do I have to?"

"Females of any species can become agitated when unexpectedly separated from their offspring," I explained. "Beneath her anger will be much gratitude and relief."

The young male thought about it, and then nodded and came over to the console. I watched as he input the signal code and enabled the relay.

The viddisplay coalesced into the fury-filled visage of a female Hsktskt. "You dare use this . . . CaurVar. Where are you? What has happened? Why did you not return with your father and the others? Are you being imprisoned?"

This was the female of whom Cherijo had delivered five Hsktskt infants. Faced with the same choice, I suspected that I would not have done the same. I would have treated her like any other threat. My gaze moved from her ferocious countenance to that of her son. As much as I liked children, I probably would have done the same to her offspring. *Which once again makes my former self better than me.*

"I am well, Mother. I am on the warm-blood's ship with my new friend, Marel. She is Terran. No one has imprisoned me. I had Tingalean food for my evening meal." He turned and beckoned to my daughter, who joined him at the console. "I do not want to come home and get sick like fourth cousin GurunVa and have to go to hospital. May I stay with the warm-bloods?"

"My mama says CaurVar cannot stay in my chamber," my daughter chimed in, "but we have many other places on the ship. The captain is my ClanUncle. I will ask him to give CaurVar a nice room like mine."

UgessVa stared at both children before making a visible effort to compose herself. "Is your mother there, child?"

"I am." I stepped in front of the vid lens so she could see me. "Forgive the abruptness of this relay.

Your mate is blocking all signals from our ship, and I knew you would be worried about your son."

"I have been . . . anxious . . . that my son not become caught in the middle of something unpleasant." She turned her head to speak quickly to someone out of visual range before she added, "Tension is escalating, Healer. We must repair the damage that has been done before more occurs."

The Hsktskt, it seemed, were as proud as the Jorenians—and equally protective of their kin. "In this, I must rely on your advice, Khedera."

She nodded and thought for a moment. "In addition to the present difficulties, my mate's superior has just died of plague. If you were to agree to provide a small group as ceremonial escort for CaurVar to his sire's rite of elevation, I believe I could arrange safe passage."

"Who would need to be included in this group?"

"You, your mate, and your offspring. The commander of your vessel." Her inner eyelids drooped. "If you could bring the one who made the unpleasant remarks about CaurVar as well, and have him make formal apology for them, it would alleviate much of my mate's ire, and put an end to this situation. I will give you my promise that no one will try to kill him."

"Reever and I will attend the boy. I may be able to convince the captain and the Senior Healer to accompany us as well. Marel . . . " I had been doing everything I could to keep her away from the Hsktskt and the planet, and I certainly didn't want her near this powerful-looking female while she still might be feeling vengeful. It was not safe, and Reever would never agree to such a thing.

"You now know how *I* felt when TssVar told me he was taking our youngest to your ship," UgessVa said, reading my silence with lethal accuracy.

That decided me. "I can do no less, then." I gave her a hard look. "Perhaps, next time, you will keep your son home."

UgessVa inclined her head, and then her voice went low and soft. "I am grateful you found this way to contact me. CaurVar is the last of my brood, and very special to me. Whatever happens, I was right to choose you to be my daughter's Designate."

I did not tell her that if she had chosen me, her daughter and the rest of her offspring might never have drawn their first breaths.

A formal escort flew to the ship and took position, waiting for the launch that would carry us to Vtaga to attend TssVar's elevation rite, and permit us to formally return his son and apologize for the offense caused to his bloodline. The presence of the waiting scout ships eliminated much of the usual objections and debate over the situation, and the captain reluctantly agreed to fulfill UgessVa's terms.

Squilyp might not have done the same, if his mate had not overheard me requesting he make the jaunt to the planet and offer an apology for his insensitive words. Garphawayn was already up and hopping around the Medical Bay, however, and she insisted he accompany us to, in her words, "prove to the Hsktskt that Omorr are honorable and ethical, and only behave as utter barbarians under extreme duress."

Marel was excited about making the journey, and infected CaurVar with her enthusiasm. The two never stopped chattering away about CaurVar's home and Vtaga and the many wonders he could show her.

Reever said little beyond his terse agreement to bring our daughter along, and his inquiry as to which weapons I would be carrying. He armed himself as though preparing to enter a battle zone.

When I reported to the launch with Reever and the children, I wanted nothing more than to slip away as CaurVar had when no one was watching, and hide until they were gone. So much rested on what happened over the next few hours; perhaps even a renewal of war. I was a healer and a mother; I had already fought one war. When would come my time of peace?

The Adan sent every warrior they could fit on the launch with us, and no one protested their presence. If I could have squeezed every warrior on the crew into the passenger compartment, I would have. Like Xonea, they wore the Jorenian silver-blue formal uniforms that were reserved for important ceremonies, although the dignified garb only partially concealed the number of powerful weapons they carried.

The children seemed oblivious to the tension, or so I thought until we had left the ship and were en route to Vtaga. My daughter released her harness and unexpectedly climbed onto my lap.

"Mama," she whispered, "why is everyone upset? Is CaurVar in trouble?"

I glanced over at TssVar's son, who had been seated across from us and appeared to be engrossed in a discussion with Xonea. "No, Marel. It is just that tempers are strained, and everyone wishes to ensure that nothing bad happens to us while we are visiting the surface."

"Nothing bad will happen if we do nothing bad," my daughter said with the absolute assurance of a child. "Only sickness does bad things."

"Sickness?"

Marel wrinkled her nose. "The one on the planet. CaurVar told me about it. He said it scares him to see grown-ups hurting themselves. He hid on our ship because he doesn't want to catch it." She rested her head against my heart. "You should mix up a medicine to make the sickness go away, Mama. I don't want CaurVar to get sick."

"None of us do, daughter." I held her against me, and the precious weight of her made me feel exhilarated and exhausted. How much I wanted to protect her, and how inadequate I felt to the task. "I will find a medicine that will help them if I can."

She gave me one of her brilliant smiles. "I know you will, Mama. ClanUncle Squilyp said that you are the best healer in the universe, even if you can't remember that you are."

I turned to look at Squilyp, who had been sitting in a frosty silence ever since we left the ship, and was now staring at it through the back view panel. "Did he."

Reever was watching us, and some of the coldness left his eyes as Marel climbed down and wandered over to talk to one of the tall, fierce Adan guards. "How simple things would be if we were to put the children in charge of these matters," he murmured, bemused.

"I will suggest it to the council when next I contact them." I sighed and rested my head against the hull wall. "It is good that Marel has this friendship with CaurVar." Something occurred to me. "Can Terrans and Hsktskt become mates?"

"It has never been attempted," my husband said. "Nor will it, if you are thinking of someday pairing our daughter with TssVar's son."

"If Terran females can mate with Hsktskt males, it would be a good match." I studied the young male. "His sire has great status on this world. She might never find another male with as much promise."

"Jarn."

I glanced at him. "Yes?"

"You will arrange an Iisleg-style marriage for Marel only over my dead body," he said flatly.

I shrugged. "It was only a thought."

The elevation rite was to be held on TssVar's family estate, which was located on the outskirts of the city. Reever had told me that the Hsktskt lord's estate was one of the largest in the vicinity, but what came into view as we flew through the lower atmosphere appeared to be more like a small city, with an enormous cluster of towering structures in the very center. The heart of the estate was surrounded by all manner of walls and heat-collection domes and watchtowers, as well as long tracts of cultivated land. So many satellite dwellings lay beyond these that I wondered just how large a family TssVar had.

Compared to the Hanar's Palace, the design of TssVar's main compound dwelling was more formal and stark, all smooth brown and white stone following simple, rounded lines. It seemed much older than the Hanar's Palace as well, but its simplicity made it all the more impressive. Perhaps his many kin had occupied this estate for generations, as the Kangal had in the skim-cities of my homeworld, with each new generation building outward to accommodate their growing numbers.

"This is nothing," a female voice said suddenly. *"You should see what's buried out in the desert."*

I tensed as I looked around. Aside from Marel, I was the only woman on the launch.

I had heard that voice before, and it only took a moment to remember when. The same voice had called to me just before the *Sunlace* transitioned.

Just before I had fallen into a coma.

Was this the Maggie Reever had spoken of when I regained consciousness? Why was she speaking to me now? Would this have the same effect as the last time? If I told the others, they might turn the launch around and return to the ship. Such a thing might make the Hsktskt believe we had decided against bringing the SubAkade's son back to the planet. Given the tension on both sides, this dangerous situation then might very well turn lethal.

I did not know what to do, so I sat quietly, listening for the voice, but it did not speak again.

Once we landed, we were thoroughly scanned and submitted to another extended biodecon before we were permitted to disembark. I made a point to keep both Marel and CaurVar close to me and Reever. If there were to be any violence, I intended to pick them up and carry them back onto the launch. Whatever the tensions were between our peoples, the children did not deserve to be caught in the middle of them.

A large and nervous-looking female stood waiting with SubAkade TssVar at the base of the docking ramp, and relaxed only when she saw CaurVar.

"That is my mother," the young Hsktskt male said, sounding more subdued now. "She does not seem pleased to see me."

"Make no mistake, child," I said, holding Marel's hand a little tighter. "She is."

I walked up to UgessVa and made a cautious gesture of greeting. What would a mother say to another mother? "Your son's behavior while he was with us on our ship does you credit," I said. "I regret the mistake that kept him parted from you."

"You cared for him as I would, which is all I could ask," she replied, turning her head to glare briefly at her mate. "You have our gratitude, Healer."

I did not see ChoVa present, but thought perhaps she might have been summoned back to attend the Hanar. I rested my hand on Marel's curly blond head. "This is Marel, the daughter of my body. She played a small part in concealing CaurVar until your men had left the ship. Marel wishes to express her regret for that."

"We didn't want to make you sad, Lady TssVar," my daughter said, her big eyes wide as she looked up at the relieved mother. "Please don't be angry at CaurVar. I helped him hide from the crew until we got hungry." Her bottom lip wobbled. "It's my fault he's in trouble."

CaurVar shuffled and looked slightly embarrassed. "No, the fault was mine. I did not wish to come home. I am afraid of the plague, Mother. I thought I would not become infected if I stayed with the warm-blooded—with Marel and her people."

"Is there to be no blame assigned to me?" TssVar asked quietly. "I did not attend to CaurVar when we departed the ship. He should not have been able to escape my notice to remain behind." He seemed almost proud that the young male had.

"My careless remarks drove you and your people from the *Sunlace*," Squilyp put in. His face turned dark pink as everyone looked at him. "The blame lies with me. I should have given my gratitude to your daughter for providing assistance to my mate while she was in labor. What I said instead was selfish and ungracious. I beg your pardon, SubAkade TssVar."

Marel smiled up at the huge Hsktskt. "Can we all say we're sorry and no one will be upset anymore?"

"Sometimes it is not so simple, child," he said, squatting down so that they were almost on eye level. "Words and actions can be used to make peace, but they can also be wielded as weapons to start a war."

"Do we have to have war again?" my daughter complained. "It hurts people and makes my mama go away for a long time. She doesn't remember who she was before the last war yet."

"I will work on that with your people." TssVar stood. "My superior, Akade OtokVar, died while in cryopreservation at his family's private medical facility. My daughter has returned to the palace to ensure that our ruler has not yet contracted the pathogen." He looked across the compound at a large group of guards and other Hsktskt. "After the rite of elevation, I will be relocating to the palace to assume the Akade's offices. It will likely be some time before I am able to become personally involved in your efforts to cure this plague."

He was worried that we would not, that much was obvious. I sensed something more to what he was saying, as if he were trying to deliver a warning. Was the Hanar prepared to use our lack of progress as an excuse to attack us, or the League?

"If I may work with ChoVa," I said, "I will do whatever I can to find treatment and, if possible, develop a vaccine to protect those who have not been infected."

"That is all I can ask of you," he said, mocking his mate's earlier words to me. He moved two limbs to indicate those waiting on the steps of the main dwelling. "I consider this matter settled between us. We must begin the rite now, before the sun reaches its zenith."

"I will take the children to the recreation area," UgessVa said, gesturing to a little garden a short distance away. She exchanged a look with me that promised they would be safe there, and I nodded.

I knew nothing of Hsktskt ceremony, and found

the solemnity of TssVar's rite touching. With his family gathered around him, he and several older males recited the names of all those who had shared their blood back some thirty generations. This was done rapidly and in hissing monotones, but the blending of the differently pitched male voices almost made it sound lyrical.

One of the older females brought forth a large silver alloy ring set with a strange multicolored stone, and knelt before TssVar with her head angled back in the submissive position. A second female took the ring and, after producing a sharp, thin-bladed dagger, stabbed TssVar in the throat.

The sight of blood made me tense, but Reever put a hand on my arm.

"She pierces his hide to accommodate the Akade ring of office," he murmured to me. "It acts as one of our location and monitoring implants as well as a visible reminder for other citizens of his status."

"Why must it be implanted?"

"As proof of identity and successive right," my husband said. "Once inserted, the ring cannot be removed until the wearer is dead."

I would have questioned why TssVar would need such a thing, but an odd sense of being watched came over me, and I scanned the area. Other than our landing party and the assembled members of TssVar's line, there was no one else present. Something seemed to brush past me, though, and I heard a series of cracking sounds.

Reever must have heard it as well, for he turned completely around, looking as I did.

UgessVa came to join us, holding CaurVar and Marel by the hands. "It may be a ground tremor."

The wall nearest to us began to shake, the stone creating more of the noises as it cracked. Bits of mortar popped from the closely fitted seams as if the wall were spitting them at us.

"That," I said, pointing to it, "is going to collapse."

Reever followed my gaze and snatched Marel up, pushing her into my arms. "To the launch. Now. Run."

A rumble roared from behind the wall, which did not collapse but instead exploded. Hissed orders and stone falling blended with the whine of weapons being enabled. Oddly shaped shadows chased each other on the ground, and as I ran with Marel for the docking area I tilted my head back to see what was making them.

The sky above us filled with strange, dusty-colored vehicles with wide half domes on the bottom that absorbed the displacer bursts that TssVar's guards fired at them. Two more blasts hit the walls on either side of us, destroying them. I held my daughter close and stopped, peering through the dust and falling debris to find the clearest path back to the launch.

Something swooped down in the madness and, like the claws of a ptar, seized my shoulders. One of the Adan wrapped his arms around us, trying to pull us back, but only managed to pull Marel from my arms. He fell as whatever had me fired at him, rolling over to shield my daughter with his body while I was jerked into the air.

I fought wildly and screamed for my husband until something struck the back of my head and I fell against my captor. I felt my consciousness slipping away even as powerful hands dragged me to my feet.

"*Etavasss,*" a Jorenian voice said.

"No," I muttered, and fell into the black.

TWELVE

I woke to bright light, silence, sand, and chains.

The landscape around me rolled out, a flat and lifeless ocean of dark sand forming motionless waves that curled and stretched unto the horizon. Four poles had been sunk into the sand and a rough, thick cloth stretched between them to form a canopy over my head. My wrists, knees, and ankles had been bound together with lengths of alloy links. I tested them, and found them to be lightweight but impossible to break. All around the canopy were other temporary shelters and structures, although they appeared much more hastily erected than those the men of the iiskars regularly erected for their tribes.

I tucked in my chin. Beneath me, more of the crudely woven material made a rug to cushion me, and through it I felt the heat of the sand. I smelled the sharp odor of a Hsktskt and rolled, almost bouncing into two brown, scuffed boots and two blue, six-fingered hands.

I looked up into white-within-white eyes, and the scarred face of the outlaw I had seen at the medical facility. He crouched by the edge of the rug and watched me with visible interest. He smelled and dressed like a Hsktskt, but he had the body hair and skin of a Jorenian.

To know I had not imagined him was a small relief; one I discarded as soon as I remembered the attack on TssVar's estate and the Adan rolling to the ground with Marel.

"Reever." I jerked my head up and tried to see around me. "My daughter. What have you done with them?"

The sound of my voice made him nod. He reached to one side to retrieve a round, manacle-like device that he clipped around my neck. The rounded, heavy alloy pressed odd bumps lining the inside of it against my skin.

"You must wear this," he said, his lips moving differently than the sounds I was hearing in my ears. "It will translate our words so we may understand each other."

He was speaking the soft, hissing language of the Hsktskt, not Jorenian. I felt too startled by this to do more than nod.

"You are a healer, yes? And flesh, not scaled, like me. I have never seen one of my kind up close." He shifted around me, studying me as he might a carcass he wished to butcher. One of his hands briefly covered my left breast. "You are female, yes?"

I wanted to scream at him to stop, and barely restrained myself in time. "Yes. I am Iis—Terran. I am female. I will answer any questions you have, Kheder, if you remove my chains."

He cocked his head. "What is a kheder?"

"A leader. A male who is shown respect."

"I am the seduhanar here. You will show me

respect." He reached over to brush some of the sand from my face.

"What does that mean?" I asked, not understanding his title. "Seduhanar?"

"Master of war." He inspected me from head to toe. "You are young and very small. When I saw you at the killing place, I thought you a child. Then I saw you with the smaller female at the Akade's estate, and thought differently. You are full grown, are you not?"

I nodded. I had to bite my lip to keep from asking about Marel, and if she had been harmed during the attack.

"What are you called?"

"Jarn." The chains around my wrists shifted as I did, and I grimaced. "Why did you abduct me?"

"I ask. You answer." He reached out and fingered a strand of my hair. "You have this, like me. Why?"

"Hair? Why do I have hair?" I felt bewildered. "It grows from my scalp. It covers it and helps me retain my body heat."

"The people do not have hair. They have scales. They use thermals to maintain body temperature." He looked down at himself. "I am flesh. I do not have to do that." He didn't seem happy about the differences.

By "people" I assumed he was referring to the Hsktskt. "They are reptilian. We are humanoid."

"I had scales, once," he told me. "When I was younger. They fell off before I was grown to this size. Did you have scales when you were smaller?"

"No." Why would a Jorenian male believe that he had once been covered in scales? Either the translator device was malfunctioning, or he was mentally defective. "May I ask one question?"

He considered that for a long moment. "One."

"May I speak to your leader, Seduhanar?"

He sat back on his haunches. "I am PyrsVar, the leader in this place." He smiled, and white Jorenian teeth filed to sharp points flashed. "I am a good war master, am I not? We evaded the new Akade's guards with little trouble. This was because I scouted the Akade's defenses. He let many attend the rite, so there were gaps in his grid. They were simple to exploit."

I did not care how easy the raid had been for him and his men, or how foolish TssVar had been about security. I needed to know his status in this group, and how I could use that to free us.

He unnerved me, particularly with how still he was when he spoke. I had never seen a Jorenian talk so much without once using his hands to make the accompanying gestures. He also seemed to enjoy boasting of his status and accomplishments, something I had never known the Jorenians on the ship to do.

I would appeal to his vanity first. "You are the leader of the group of outlaws that attacked Akade TssVar," I said, as if unsure.

He sighed. "Yes, outlaws, that is what the people call us. All of us, we are without line. I lead. You are my captive, and you will answer me. Why do you come here to Vtaga? Why were you at the killing place?"

"I was brought here to help the people. Some of them are very sick. The killing place is a hospital where those who are ill stay and are cared for until they are better." There was no surprise on his face as I said this, and I wondered if he even believed me. "In any case, I am a healer, not a soldier. It is not necessary to chain me."

"You might try to run away. The desert will eat you if you do." He stroked my hair as if I were a pet. "You are small and thin, and your skin is a strange color, but you please me."

"I am happy that I do." No, I wasn't. "If you remove my chains, I promise I will not run away from you. I do not want the desert to eat me." I had the feeling all of my blades had been taken from me, but they might have missed one or two.

PyrsVar thought about it as he toyed with my hair. "My men will shoot you if you try to run."

"I have told you that I will not." Running would be useless. I was going to have to steal one of their skimmer vehicles. "I am only a female, and a healer. What harm can I do to one such as you? You are a seduhanar, a master of war. You are more clever than the new Akade."

My flattery seemed to work, for he nodded and began removing my chains. This made him draw close enough for me to see all the details of the terrible scars on his face. From the size and shape of the old wounds, they might have been made by Hsktskt claws.

Despite my fear, I felt a pang of pity for him. "How did you receive the scars on your face?"

He didn't answer.

"Were you a slave of the people?" I asked him. Perhaps he had been taken from his Jorenian family as a child and was thought dead by now. "Were you abused?"

"Most of the people do not know me. Slaves are flesh; I have flesh." He tossed aside the chains that had bound my ankles and knees, and then removed my footgear to examine my feet. "You have five of these." He touched my toes. "But I have six. Like these." He showed me the fingers on his hands by wiggling them. "Why is that?"

"We are humanoid, but we come from different species." Did he know nothing of Jorenians and Terrans? Perhaps if he had been slave-born, and had never left Vtaga, he would not. If that was the case, the Torins were in for a rude surprise. "I am Iis—Terran. You are Jorenian. That is why your skin is blue and mine is not."

He grunted and went to work on the chains around my wrists. One of the outlaws approached us, but he did not look up.

"We should have done as the leader said," the outlaw told PyrsVar. "You should not unbind her. Frightened warm-bloods are foolish with their fear. She will attempt an escape."

"I will catch her and beat her if she does." He gave me a hard look before he dropped the chain that had bound my wrists and pulled back the sleeves of my tunic. "You bear no slave brand."

"I am not a slave. I came to Vtaga by my own choice." I rubbed my wrists with my hands.

"The other one awakes," the waiting outlaw told PyrsVar. "What should we do with him?"

"Bring him to me." PyrsVar helped me up, and walked in a circle inspecting my form. He stood almost three feet taller than me. "There is not much to you. Are you certain that you have finished growing?"

"Yes." I watched as the outlaw went into a tent and emerged with another Hsktskt. Between them they held my husband. I crossed my arms and surreptitiously checked my tunic sheaths, but all the blades had been removed. "War Master, may I ask another question?"

"Later." PyrsVar lifted my arm and bent over to study the side fastenings of my tunic. "How do I take you out of this garment to see how the rest of you is made?"

Bruises marred Reever's face, and blood still oozed from a deep gash on his brow. He did not struggle with the Hsktskt marching him to us, but locked his gaze with mine. *Are you injured?*

I was jolted by the impact of his thought, as fast and hard as a physical blow. *No, I am well.*

Stay out of my way. He turned his attention to PyrsVar, and nearly stumbled as the outlaw war master turned and Reever saw his face for the first time. In my thoughts appeared the image of another face, identical to PyrsVar's except for the scars. *It cannot be.*

"That one is a male of your kind," PyrsVar was asking me. "Is he not? He is the same color."

The mental link between Reever and me ended, so I didn't understand my husband's reaction. It was almost as if he recognized the Jorenian outlaw.

When PyrsVar didn't receive an answer from me, he lost interest in Reever and began prodding the hidden fasteners of my tunic, as if trying to determine how to release them. Finally he straightened and looked down at me, his expression mildly exasperated. "Take off your garments."

Reever broke free of the guards holding him and lunged silently at the Jorenian outlaw, who pivoted and countered his kick with a sweep of one arm. I moved forward, trying to distract PyrsVar from the other direction, but I caught my heel on the edge of the rug and fell. One of Reever's guards used my hair to drag me to my feet, and put one of his limbs across my neck, pinning me against him.

My husband and PyrsVar fought in total silence, only the sound of their fists and feet connecting with each other's flesh making muffled thuds. They moved faster than I could follow, each whirling around the other in tight circles and half circles, as if they were performing some savage, violent dance.

A dance that came to an abrupt end, as it happened. PyrsVar produced a short whip that he wrapped around my husband's knee and jerked to send him off balance. As Reever went down, the Jorenian used his fist to hit him at the base of his skull, which knocked him unconscious.

"Tie him up," PyrsVar said to the other guard. "See what he knows about the Akade, and then kill him."

"Wait." I fought against the outlaw holding me. "War Master, please. Two captives will be more valuable to you than only one."

His all-white eyes met mine. "He is a good fighter. With a blade, he might have bested me. That means he will be troublesome. It is better this way."

"It is only that I belong to him, and he fought to

defend his claim on me," I said. "Spare him, and I will do anything that you wish."

"Anything." PyrsVar flashed his pointed teeth. "Whatever I ask of you."

"Yes."

"Very well, Terran. He may live a little longer." He looked at the guard holding me and gestured toward the largest tent. "Take her."

The guard hauled me to the large tent, pulled back the flap that formed the entry, and shoved me inside.

I waited to see if he would follow, but the flap slapped shut and through the thin stuff of the wall I could see his shadow as he took up a guard position. I then looked all around me to see if there was another avenue of escape.

The outlaw's shelter shared many similarities to those of the Iisleg, and despite my anxiety part of me relaxed. All these weeks on the ship and in the Hsktskt city I had been surrounded by the unfamiliar; here was a place that made sense, at least to my eyes.

Now if only I could understand this Jorenian living among and leading the Hsktskt. A slave might lead a revolt of other slaves, but a band of renegade slavers? Why would they make him their war master, much less follow him into combat? As a warm-blooded being, he was their natural enemy.

Jarn.

I felt the whispering brush of my husband's thoughts, and closed my eyes to focus on them. *I am here.*

I am in restraints and alone in a tent. Can you come and release me?

Not yet. I looked up as I heard footsteps. *Someone is coming.*

PyrsVar ducked into the shelter without warning or ceremony and proceeded to ignore me. It was the exact sort of thing a male of the iiskar might do, so I decided to respond as an Iisleg woman: I found a space against one wall flap and crouched there to wait and see what he would demand of me.

The outlaws had few comforts, and like the Iisleg, they were economical about their use of them. PyrsVar stripped off his outer robe, revealing a form-fitted sleeveless garment underneath that was made out of plain material and cut to resemble the thermal garb Hsktskt wore under their outer clothing.

Do you recognize him? my husband asked me through our tenuous link.

He was the one at the hospital, the one no one believed I saw, I thought.

Look at him. Let me see him through your eyes.

I looked. PyrsVar had been a warrior for a long time. Ladders of blade and weapons-fire scars ran the length of both of his arms, and I saw pits in his muscles here and there, left by deeper, gouging wounds. His hair hung longer than any Jorenian's I had seen, and appeared coarser, but it was a solid black in color with no purple streaks indicating any significant age. His features were weathered, doubtless from the heat, but the skin of his throat was as young and tight as a boy's.

The more I looked at him, the more I wanted to

ask him questions. *Reever, he is not like the other Jorenians except in form and coloring. He moves as the Hsktskt do. He smells like them.*

Crossbreed, Reever thought. *He must be. There is no other possible explanation for the resemblance.*

I had been right; Reever had recognized him before he started the fight. *Who does he resemble?*

PyrsVar caught me watching him. "That male with flesh like yours, he is your mate?"

Reever answered inside my mind. *Hsktskt will kill to take a mate from another male. Tell him no. Tell him you are my servant.*

I shook my head. "I serve him. I take care of him and his child."

"You said you were not a slave," he pointed out.

"I am not." Reever's thoughts had suddenly faded from mine, and the link dissolved. "Servants are compensated workers, not owned property. I can choose to leave his service anytime I wish."

He dropped down by an elongated container and, after removing the end, drank from it. Slowly he rose and brought it over to drop it in front of me. "Drink."

I took a sniff of the liquid before I obeyed him. It was water mixed with something vaguely salty. I swallowed only a mouthful before I offered it back to him.

"What do you call the male you serve?" he asked as he hunched down in front of me.

He was using the past tense. Was Reever dead? Was that why the link had ended? "Reever. That is his name."

"One of my men recognized this Reever. Long

ago he fought as an arena slave called HalaVar. He prevailed over everyone who faced him on the sands. He left the arena a free being after he saved the life of the new Akade. He then served the Faction for many years as a spy." He put his fingers against my face, tracing over my features. "Your skin is soft. Why is that?"

I held still, trying to process everything he was telling me about Reever while managing my own fear. "Females of my kind are that way. Have you killed Reever?"

"Not yet. You would be easy to injure." He dropped his hand. "Why does a healer serve one like him? He is a killer and a traitor to your kind."

All these questions. Physically he was an adult Jorenian male, and he fought as well as Reever, so why did he have the curiosity level of a child? "It is work." I drew on the last of my patience. "One must have purpose. Mine is to serve others."

He grunted. "You need new purpose."

"Seduhanar."

PyrsVar looked over at the guard who had come through the flap. "What is it?"

"The leader has signaled. You are to bring the captives to the stronghold." His tongue flickered out to taste the air. "At once."

"When I am ready." PyrsVar made a sweeping movement with his arm, a common Hsktskt gesture of dismissal. The guard vanished.

Why did he move like them, and not at all like the Jorenians on board the *Sunlace*? The longer I was around PyrsVar, the more confused I became.

"This is not your permanent base," I said carefully.

"We have many sand warrens like this one in the deep desert." He pushed my chin up and examined my throat. "You are bruised."

I touched the sore spot on the front of my neck. "Your guard is much stronger than I am." I took in a quick breath as I felt Reever once more in my thoughts. *What happened? Are you hurt?*

No. I was distracted by something. Focus on the war master again.

"At the Akade's estate, you were with many men who look like me." PyrsVar sat back on his haunches. "They are my kind, my . . . species, you said, yes?"

Tell him the truth, my husband directed.

"Yes," I said. "They are called Jorenians, from the planet Joren. It is your homeworld."

PyrsVar released some air. "No. I have never been there. The first time I saw you and others like me was during the raid on the killing place."

Reever's thoughts grew dark and angry, but he did not show me why. *We must hurry now, Jarn. Find out how he came to be on Vtaga.*

"How did you come to be here?" I asked. "Was your mother a slave?"

"I do not know. The male who raised me is one of the people. I have never been near anyone but the people, and those without line." PyrsVar rose and walked away from me. "You will tell me about the Jorenians. About their ship and their world, and how they come to be here. Why do they help the people?"

Tell him nothing more than you already have. Reever sounded adamant.

His urgency made my heart pound, and I curled my fingernails into my palms, fighting for calm. "I only came on board the ship a short time ago. I do not know much of the Jorenians, or why they came here, other than to help the people who were sick."

PyrsVar didn't appear convinced, and bent over to put his face very close to mine. "You sweat, little healer. Do you tell me the truth, or do you seek to deceive me?"

"I am hot. I tell you what I know of those I serve."

"This I know." He showed me his pointed teeth. "You serve *me* now."

His interest had grown from casual curiosity to something more menacing. I suspected there were few if any females in the camp, and his curiosity about humanoids appeared endless. Of course I was also at his mercy. It was not hard to imagine what was going to happen.

"If you wish." I felt his hand in my hair and tried to disconnect my thoughts from my husband's. There was no reason he had to witness this part of the ordeal.

It will not happen, Reever assured me.

Something in PyrsVar's eyes changed. "I know your scent." He said this hesitantly, as if he wasn't certain. He took in a deep, slow breath. "I thought I had tasted it before when first I saw you."

Had Cherijo known this male on Catopsa, where the Omorr said she had been a healer among slaves? Had PyrsVar been taken from there and brought to

Vtaga? How could the Hsktskt have trained him to think and move and smell as they did?

"You have felt the same thing, yes?" he was asking me.

"I have never seen you before, but at the hospital, I thought you looked like someone I know." I wanted to know why I felt that sense of familiarity, too, but I would not jeopardize the safety of the captain or any of the Torins by telling him more about them. My eyes went to the clan symbol on his throat. Like all the Torins, it was black and shaped like an upswept wing. It was faintly blurred, though, as if smudged. "Were you brought here from another world? Have you ever left Vtaga?"

"I have always been here, nowhere else. I think that we were meant to meet." He spoke with more assurance now. "You were meant to come to me, and belong to me."

"*He had his chance,*" the female voice that had spoken to me on the launch said from some place behind my eyes. "*He blew it. Don't listen to him, Cherijo. Do you hear me? Don't listen—*"

I pressed my hands against my ears. No one but me and PyrsVar occupied the shelter. Was I going mad, like some skela did after too many years of skinning the faces from the dead?

No, beloved, Reever's thoughts flooded over mine. *You are not mad. It is only something from your life before—Maggie, the woman who raised Cherijo, is trying to come back into your life now. But you are not Cherijo, and I do not think she can take over your mind.*

Duncan. I took in a quick, sharp breath. *I'm afraid of what she will do to me.*

For now, only know that I love you. Whatever happens. Whatever comes between us. Nothing can change what I feel for you, Jarn.

Soothing warmth enveloped me from the inside out as Reever sent a continuous stream of wordless reassurance that flowed from his emotions. He did love me, as he had said, and it was beyond anything I had felt, beyond my love for our child, beyond my love for the work, Teulon, Resa, and the few beauties of living I had known thus far. Reever's love was a universe surrounding me, endless and unfathomable, and it would never end.

He knew I was not Cherijo, and yet he gave this love to me as freely and completely as he had to her.

As this happened, PyrsVar wound my hair around his claws. I did not fight him. Whatever he did to my body didn't matter. Reever was inside me. Reever kept me safe. Reever would be there waiting when this was over, and we would go on together, and I would learn how to be worthy of such a love as he had for me.

"Seduhanar," one of the guards said from the entry.

"Not now," PyrsVar muttered.

"We have discovered two intruders in the warren."

"Kill them," PyrsVar said, and then moved back when I took a sharp breath. He turned to glare at the guard. "Hold. Who are they?"

"Juveniles. One male of the people, and one female"—the guard nodded toward me—"like her."

There was only one other female Terran on the

planet. I scrambled to my feet and would have run out of the tent, but PyrsVar caught me with one arm.

"She is my daughter," I said, struggling to free myself even as I knew it was hopeless. "He is the son of TssVar. They are only children. Please."

"Bring them to me," the war master said. He lifted me off my kicking feet and put me on his eye level. "We do not harm young ones if we can help it."

I stopped fighting his hold. "You won't hurt them?"

He shook his head. "They pose little threat, and I can use them in other ways." He set me down. "Tell me, Healer, will everyone who came with you on the ship end up in my warren?"

I hoped not. "I do not know how they could come here by themselves. Your men must have taken them when you abducted us."

"My men only had orders to take your kind, and when we left the Akade's land we had only you and the male. Or so I thought." PyrsVar turned as Marel and CaurVar were marched into the tent. Both appeared dirty but otherwise unharmed. "Who are you, and what do you want here in my camp?"

"You took my mama and daddy, you bad man," Marel scolded him without the slightest hesitation or show of fear. "I want them back."

CaurVar's gaze caught mine, and he shook his head slightly before he spoke to PyrsVar. "I am the youngest son of Akade TssVar, second to the Hanar," he told the Jorenian outlaw. "I will serve as hostage. Release these warm-bloods, for they are useless to you."

PyrsVar's mouth curled on one side. "I see that you are blood of the Akade. The warm-bloods will remain. You will all be made useful." To the guard, he said, "Take them and put them with the male."

"Wait. May I first check them and see that they are uninjured?" As soon as he inclined his head, I rushed over to my daughter and pulled her into my arms. "How did you get here?" I whispered as I ran my hands over her small form.

Marel glared at our captor before hugging me tightly and murmuring against my ear, "I took CaurVar and moved us to one of their fliers. They have spaces in the back where we could fit without them seeing. We were going to rescue you." She slipped something that felt like a weapon into the waistband of my trousers. "Only I went to sleep after I moved us, and then the bad men found us when CaurVar woke me up."

She had done the same thing during the Jado Massacre, teleporting herself, Reever, and Teulon's son Xan from the Cloud Walk before it had imploded. I kept an arm around her as I quickly checked TssVar's son, who was also unharmed.

"I am sorry, Healer," he said in a low voice. "I do not know how Marel did this thing. One moment I was running toward my father and the next I was in a cargo hold with her and . . ." He shook his head.

"Take them," PyrsVar said to the guard. I quickly kissed my daughter and touched CaurVar's shoulder before the children were led out of the tent.

Reever, I thought, trying to reestablish our link, but he did not respond. *Reever, Marel and CaurVar are*

*here. Try to free yourself and get to them. Take them away
from here.*

"So now I have four captives," PyrsVar said
thoughtfully. "Many more and I will have to send
for more supplies."

I wiped the tears from my face before I turned to
meet his amused gaze. "Release Reever and the children. They are not as valuable as I am. I will stay
with you willingly and not attempt an escape for as
long as you wish. You have my word."

"I do not need your word. I have your child. That
will make you do whatever I say." He went to a
storage container and opened it. From it he drew
out a more casual robe, into which he shrugged.
"Our leader will wish to interrogate all of you, but
that will wait. We will share a meal and rest together, and you will tell me everything you have not
about the people on the ship."

THIRTEEN

I tried to remain calm and clearheaded. If we were to escape the outlaws' encampment, I would need to focus on that and not the fear that this renegade Jorenian would have us all executed.

The meal PyrsVar shared with me consisted not of the vegetarian fare Jorenians preferred, or of the synthetic raw, bloody flesh that was the usual diet of Hsktskt. Instead, he opened a cloth bag and drew out what looked to be Iisleg journey strips, formed from some sort of fruit paste mixed with shreds of meat and grain kernels.

"You eat meat," I murmured, surprised.

"I cannot eat the raw food the people make," he said as he handed me two strips. "Do my kind eat raw food?"

"No, the Jorenians are vegetarians. They grow flowering plants on their homeworld for food, and eat synthetic vegetables when they travel." I took a small bite from the strip and found the leathery substance strange-tasting but not unpleasant. If I had not been so nervous, I might have enjoyed it. "This food must travel well."

"It does. We move camp every third day." He devoured his portion and nodded toward mine. "Eat."

With small bites I managed to force down one of the strips, but handed back the second. "I am not as large as you," I explained. "I do not need as much to eat as a Jorenian."

"My kind are like me in size, yes? What do they look like?"

"Yes." I thought of the captain. "They have blue skin and black hair, and eyes like yours. They move their hands when they speak their language. They are very fond of children."

He looked disgusted. "So fond they bring them on their ships to other worlds? Foolish people. Young ones do not belong in space. They should be protected, as the people here protect theirs."

"Perhaps someone brought you here," I said tentatively.

"No. This is my world." He sat back and peered at me. "You have blunt teeth. Like a grazing animal."

"My people hunt animals for food. We eat some plants when we can find them. That is why four of our teeth are pointed." I felt a little foolish as I displayed my teeth and showed him my incisors, but it might establish some common ground between us. As it was, his only kinship bond was with the Hsktskt. "Your people have the same sort of teeth, so perhaps in ancient times they ate meat as well."

He grunted. "They should not have stopped."

"You should meet your people, War Master. They would be glad to know you." Or they would be after they recovered from the shock of it, I thought. "I could arrange a meeting."

"Why? I only look like them. My men are my

people." He seemed interested, though, as he handed me the container of the salty water I had tasted before. "Tell me about this world of theirs. Joren, you called it, yes? What is it like?"

I did not have Cherijo's memories of visiting the Jorenian's homeworld, but the crew had told me enough stories of the planet that I could give him some details. "The sky is said to be all colors, and the seas are purple. They grow many things, but the land is mostly covered with a silvery grass. There are grazing animals they raise for their milk called *t'lerue*. The Jorenians live together with their family HouseClans, in huge dwellings of white stone quarried from their mountains. There is little crime and no war or strife. Each family shares one name, and will die to defend its kin. They tell me no one is ever lonely because they always stay together."

"There is always loneliness." For a moment he looked wistful. "If there are no wars or strife, it must be crowded on this world. They would not have room for me."

"They would make room. They are very devoted to family." I decided to take a calculated risk and gestured toward his throat. "The mark on your neck is the same symbol I have seen on those who belong to HouseClan Torin. The Torin adopted me, and the ship on which I traveled here belongs to them. They could be your family."

PyrsVar made the odd, choppy sound of Hsktskt amusement. "I do not wish to live among the warm-blooded. They may look like me, but they are weak and foolish. My people are right. You are only fit to be slaves." He gave me a long, intent look. "I have never had a female of my own."

"Is that what I am to be? Your slave?"

He imitated my smile for the first time. "Do not be afraid. You are mostly docile, and you breed small children, but the young one has interesting coloring, and some courage. The leader can have the others, but I think I will keep you for myself." He moved to his feet and walked toward me. "I will not harm you, so long as you please me. Perhaps I will let you be mother to my children."

I did not want to kill him, but to save Marel and CaurVar I would. I turned slightly away to hide the hand I eased under the hem of my tunic. Marel had not passed a weapon to me, I discovered when I touched the object tucked into my waistband, but an infuser like the one ChoVa had given me at the quarantine hospital. How she had obtained the instrument, I could not guess, but it was almost a relief to press the buttons that filled the delivery chamber with neuroparalyzer.

PyrsVar crouched down in front of me. "Why do you cringe?"

"You say I should not be afraid, but you have given me every reason to fear you," I said.

"I have said I will not harm you, and I always keep my vows." He looked down at my body with some interest. "I still have not seen what is under your garments. You will show that to me now."

I placed a hand on his shoulder and leaned close, pressing my cheek against his. "Please do not hurt me," I whispered as I drew out the infuser.

"Do not give me reason to." He wrapped an arm

around me and rubbed his face against mine. "I like your scent. It is like the air in the high places."

I moved my head back to smile up into his face, and quickly jammed the infuser into his neck and released the drug. He threw me away from him with a roar of surprise, then staggered and fell to his knees.

The sand beneath the tent rug had cushioned my fall, so I was back on my feet in a moment. I picked up the whip he had tossed to one side and uncoiled it, holding it ready in the event I would need to defend myself.

"You lied," PyrsVar gasped, pressing a hand to his neck and struggling to stay upright.

"Yes," I said as I watched him topple over. "I did."

I waited a few moments before I went near him, and then checked his pulse. His heart beat faster than a Jorenian's should have, and his body temperature felt lower, but he was in no danger of dying from the dose. I rolled him onto his side so that his airways would remain clear and open, and then went to the flap to open a gap in the seam and look out.

Night had fallen, as had the temperature, and no one was standing guard by PyrsVar's tent. From the lights and shadows inside the other shelters, I assumed the outlaws had retreated inside to protect themselves from the colder night air.

Reever?

Here. Reever sent me a mental image of the tent where he was located. *Cover yourself with something, and bring weapons.*

I picked up PyrsVar's robe and two of his blades before I stepped out of the tent. I waited in the shadows to make sure no one was about before I crossed the sand to the next tent. Inside, two guards were having an argument about where to move the camp. One wanted to go to the mountains in the east, while the other thought they should relocate to an underground network of caves to the south. I committed what they said to memory before moving away.

The tent where Reever and the children were being held was at the very edge of the camp, and no measure of security had been made to keep them inside. I saw why when I released the entry flap and slipped in.

Reever had been chained to the tent's center pole. The children were manacled to his ankles. Reever had also been bound with a wire studded with sharp spikes and thin-edged bits of alloy that had been positioned to cut into his limbs if he moved. From the amount of blood running from both of his arms, he had tried to move more than once.

"Mama," Marel said, her dull eyes lighting up as soon as she saw me.

I lifted a finger to my lips and looked around the tent for something to use on the wire.

"There is an alloy cutter in there." Reever nodded toward a container shoved in one corner.

I used one of the blades to pry off the lock and retrieved the cutting tool. "I used neuroparalyzer on the leader. It will only last a few hours."

"That is enough." Reever made no sound as I cut away the wire binding him, but caught my hands as

I tried to examine his wounds. "Time for that later. The guards come to check on us every hour. We have to go now."

He helped me release the children by cutting through the manacles' locks. I wrapped CaurVar in the cloak I had taken from PyrsVar's tent and checked outside the flap. "We are in the middle of the desert—how will we get back to the city?"

"The same way we got here," my husband said as he picked up Marel. "By air."

The outlaws' sand gliders had been concealed beneath immense cloths dyed to appear like the desert sand. Reever did not remove the cloth from the first we came to, but reached under it and removed something from the glider before moving to the next.

"What are you doing?" I whispered as I led CaurVar and Marel by the hands behind him.

"Slowing them down." He collected a dozen more of the devices before dumping them onto the ground and covering them with a mound of sand. "They will not be able to fly the other gliders without those."

He uncovered the last of the gliders and strapped me and Marel to the back of it. CaurVar took position in front of Reever at the controls.

A shout came from the encampment, and the sand beneath my feet shook as heavy footsteps came toward us.

"Don't look down," my husband said as he engaged the engine, and immediately launched the glider. We soared straight up into the sky, weaving wildly as Reever avoided the displacer rounds being fired at us from below.

I did not look down, or anywhere else. The speed of the glider caused the wind to rip at us, the displacer rounds were exploding all around us, and I thought I might scream if I did. Instead, I closed my eyes and clutched Marel tightly.

"Faster, Daddy," my daughter crowed, evidently delighted. "This is fun."

I promised myself to have a long talk with my child about her concept of entertainment as soon as we were not in imminent danger of being blown up or crashing to the ground. When I gathered the courage to open my eyes, I saw Reever studying a holomap on the glider's control panel.

"How far?" I asked.

"Approximately two hundred kilometers." He turned the glider north and increased our speed.

Even as fast as Reever was flying, it took nearly an hour before I saw the first sign of civilization below; the outlands of one of the large Hsktskt family estates beyond the Hanar's city. The scent of the air changed as we crossed over the city's airspace, and I saw smoke rising from the rooftops of the dwellings beneath us. Many small fires were burning, but they did not appear to be the result of weapons fire or any sort of attack. The flames seemed to be emanating from large black torches placed in the centers of the rooftops.

Marel had fallen asleep in my arms, and I rubbed her back absently. Had PyrsVar and the outlaws had time to make it to the city and do this? It seemed unlikely. I had injected the renegade Jorenian with a massive dose of neuroparalyzer, and I doubted his men would abandon him there to give chase. If the war master were to attack the city, he would do more damage than what would leave a few small fires burning.

Something bothered me more than the smoke and flames below us. Reever had concealed but not destroyed the devices he had taken from the other gliders—something he could have easily done with the displacer weapons he had taken from the camp.

I leaned forward. "Why did you only disable the other gliders? Why not destroy them?"

"If I had, those men would die out there."

I had seen Reever fight PyrsVar. He had been in a killing rage. "Why let them live after what they did to us?"

Reever did not answer me for a long time—so long I was sure he would not. Then he said, "Because the one who leads them is Xonea's Clan-Brother."

TssVar's guards and retainers swarmed around us as soon as Reever landed, and held their weapons trained on us. All of the guards wore garb that reminded me of decontamination suits.

"Stay where you are." One of the guards stepped forward and scanned us quickly. "Do not approach the Akade's compound."

"We were abducted by outlaws," Reever said. "I must speak with the Akade at once."

I saw two forms moving quickly toward us, flanked on either side by the Adan. "I think he comes there."

The pair were TssVar and his mate, although they, too, were wearing full protective suits. The Adan were not. UgessVa went directly to her son to inspect him.

"Mother, why do you wear that?" CaurVar asked, trying to touch the sleeve of her suit.

UgessVa backed away. "No, my son, make no contact with me." She looked at her mate, her gloved claws curled into shaking fists. I realized that it was taking all her self-control not to sweep her child up into her arms.

Qonja came to me. "Are you well?"

"Yes, but why this?" I gestured toward the Hskt-skt's envirosuits.

"They do not want to infect the boy," Qonja said, nodding toward CaurVar.

"It would have been better if you had stayed in the desert," I heard TssVar say to Reever. "After the attack, thirteen members of my household came down with second-stage symptoms of plague. ChoVa is here and has confirmed that we all have some amount of this enzyme, tohykul, in our brain tissue, which would indicate some degree of infection. I have quarantined the estate."

"Can your family not be moved to the hospital in the city?" I asked.

"ChoVa came to tell us that the plague is sweeping through the city as well," UgessVa said to me, her voice low and tight. "There is no more room at the facility. Those who become infected are being quarantined where they fall sick."

"That cannot be done." I thought of the violent symptoms the infected had displayed. "Outside a medical facility, there are few viable means to control them." I drew in a sharp breath as a spike of terror and anger twisted inside me. What I had thought were large torches being burned might not be torches at all. "Are they being killed as soon as they display symptoms? Is that why they are burning the bodies in the city?"

"ChoVa reported that some families are doing so, to protect those who are still well." The Akade looked as exhausted as I felt. "I directed my daughter to bring her equipment from the city and work from here now. She will do what she can for our people." He looked at Reever. "CaurVar has none of the enzyme in his brain tissue, and has shown no sign of symptoms yet. I wish one of my blood to survive this thing, if that can be done. Will you take him back to your ship?"

"Father," CaurVar said, shocked now.

My husband said something under his breath.

The Akade put a gloved hand on the boy's head. "I know what I ask of you, HalaVar, but he is the last of my line. There will be other Hsktskt not on Vtaga whom he can join with when he is older. Until then, I trust you to look after him."

" 'Grieve when the heart is still,' " I said, invoking an old Iisleg proverb, " 'not while it is still thumping.' " I turned to Reever. "Even if you do not care about TssVar's concerns, we will still need some healthy subjects removed and kept segregated from the infected for test purposes. Under the circumstances, it is wisest to take the boy to the ship while I remain here and work with ChoVa toward finding a treatment."

"There is the small matter of the outlaws who abducted us," my husband reminded me. "They will try again."

"The Akade will ensure that they fail this time." I handed Marel to him. "The Adan will be happy to assist him with that."

"As long as you are here, I am staying," Reever said. He turned to Qonja and handed our sleeping daughter to him. "Take the children back to the ship. Have Xonea signal me as soon as possible."

I did not want my husband to have to choose between me and Marel. "You need not remain here. We have little time left. I know I will be spending all my hours working with ChoVa."

"The only thing that will ever separate us again," Reever said flatly, "is death."

Even as the look in his eyes frightened me, I remembered the enveloping warmth of his love flooding through the link we had shared in the desert. That emotion had been for me, not Cherijo. He may have loved her, but now I knew he loved me as much. After losing her during a separation, obviously he did not wish to leave me. It also had something to do with PyrsVar, and Reever saying he was Xonea's ClanBrother.

"Very well." I had to concentrate on what I could understand: creating a vaccine to combat the pathogen. I would be safer with Reever there to personally guard me, too. "Qonja, look after my daughter and the Akade's son. CaurVar, wish your parents farewell."

The young Hsktskt went to his father, his blunted claws curled as tightly as his mother's were. "I thought I wanted to stay on the Jorenian's ship, but now I do not want to leave you." His eyes clouded. "Will you and Mother and our line die?"

"We all die," TssVar said. "But if your sister and Dr. Torin are successful, I hope not for many years." He placed one hand on the boy's head. "The line continues with you."

CaurVar nodded and faced his mother. "I will not disgrace you or our blood."

"I know you will not." UgessVa gave him a direct look. "You are the son of the Akade, second to the Hanar. You will conduct yourself as such, and remember that you are in my thoughts, and will be so until we are together again."

CaurVar bowed his head. "I will remember."

I found it difficult to watch the Adan board the launch with the children and initiate the engines. Each time Marel and I were parted, I felt the wrench more keenly. Perhaps I did understand Reever's strange attachment to me, after all.

"Your people," UgessVa said to me. "They will treat my son with respect?"

I nodded as the launch disappeared into the dark sky. "The Jorenians cherish children of all species."

"A pity we have not followed suit." TssVar's mate didn't wait for me to answer but trudged away toward the main dwelling.

FOURTEEN

There was no time for any of us to stand and mourn being separated from our children and friends, for every minute would count now. I asked TssVar to take me and Reever to ChoVa, whom I learned had commandeered one of the large outbuildings for use as her laboratory.

The Akade was silent as we crossed the compound, but a sharp cry from the inside of his main dwelling made his head turn and his tongue flicker.

"The symptoms can be controlled for a time with neuroparalyzer," I said quietly to him. "At least for the next day or so."

"ChoVa indicated the same." He removed a device to open one of the secured gates in the innermost compound wall. Reever went ahead of us, but TssVar gestured for me to remain there with him. "I have never been defeated by anyone but your mate. But this sickness—I cannot fight it. I cannot even see it. I have never feared anything in my existence as I do this thing."

After what Reever had told me about the Hsktskt attitude toward fear, the admission startled me.

"An epidemic is like standing in the center of an ice field during a thaw and watching the cracks from crevasses forming race toward you from all sides. There is no evading them. They cannot be reasoned with or fought. Ptar wings do not magically spring from your back to permit you to fly away from them. You can only stand still and endure their passage and hope that before it is over the ice does not collapse under you."

TssVar stared down at me. "So what is it that we can do? Walk to the edge of this crevasse?"

"We stand upon it now," I suggested. "Our task is not to look down or dwell on how far we might fall."

We continued on to ChoVa's temporary lab, where TssVar unlocked the outer access door. "My daughter is very angry with me, and with you," he mentioned. "I think what the Omorr said to her when she was on your ship shocked her. She has never confronted the reality of what other species think of us. A painful revelation, but I think . . . a valuable one. ChoVa thinks too much like a warm-blood."

I hid my amusement. "I cannot say that is a bad thing."

ChoVa had hastily rigged her lab equipment into a workable arrangement, in the center of which she now stood measuring what appeared to be doses of some pale green liquid. She glanced up briefly to nod to her father and Reever before she handed a datapad to me.

"That is the data on an enzyme blocker I wish to use on those who have been infected," she told me. There was no friendliness in her voice, and no deference in her manner. "I am combining it with a mild dose of neuroparalyzer. Together they should stabilize the level of tohykul in the brain and keep the infected calm for a short period, perhaps thirty or forty hours."

Her voice sounded strained with more than annoyance. Of course, she served the Hanar. The pressure being put on her to find a solution must be tremendous.

"Are you infected?"

"Not yet, but as I have been exposed to everyone here who is, I think it only a matter of time." ChoVa handed me one of the vials and gestured toward her father. "Would you infuse the Akade while I prepare more doses for the rest of the household?"

I went to TssVar and administered the treatment. There were no signs of relief or any change in his expression, but most of the tension in his muscles relaxed to a small degree, and his breathing slowed and deepened.

"I am going to scout the perimeter of the building," Reever said abruptly. "Signal me if you need me." He walked out into the night.

"I must go and attend to your mother," TssVar said to ChoVa. "If you need anything, you have but to ask."

"I will, Father." ChoVa watched him leave, and then set down the dosage of blocker she was mixing and bowed her head. "Just an hour ago he asked me to give him the means to kill himself. He would rather end his life sane, he said, than die like a raving, wild animal." Her huge yellow eyes met mine. "I am afraid I will fail, Jarn. Just as he is. I do not know how to cope with such fear. It wants to paralyze me."

"There is still time," I promised her. "We know one of the signs of infection now. We will work from there and find a way."

"If I do not go mad first." ChoVa sighed and picked up her dosage beaker. "My father said that you were abducted from his elevation rite by outlaws. Were they the same ones who attacked the hospital?"

I nodded. "They are encamped in the desert—or were—about two hundred kilometers from the city." Telling her that the head of the criminal group was a Jorenian did not seem like a good idea. "They live out there like outcasts. Is that what is done with those who are no longer accepted among your society?"

"Those without line are driven from us. Many go into the desert to live secluded and die alone. I have never heard of them banding together, but perhaps that is what these outlaws have done." ChoVa handed me an infuser and pulled up the sleeve of her jacket, baring yellow- and green-scaled flesh. "You must inject me with the blocker."

"You told me that you were not infected."

"The tests I performed on myself showed no trace of the enzyme, but that may change now that I have been exposed to my father's household." She stretched out her arm. "In any event, it is the closest thing we have to a vaccine. Infuse me."

I watched her as I did so, and her reaction was almost identical to the Akade's. "How long before the amount of neuroparalyzer in your bloodstream reaches toxic level?"

"With regular infusions," she said as she rolled down her sleeve, "three days."

ChoVa and I worked through the night examining and testing the tissue from the patient we had autopsied on the *Sunlace,* as well as blood samples she had collected from TssVar and the other members of his household. No trace of the enzyme showed up in any of the specimens, which indicated several things.

"The enzyme could be an immune response to the pathogen," ChoVa decided. "Very specific, very localized, and the levels increase as the infection worsens."

"We have biopsied that gland cluster seventeen times." I lifted my tired eyes from a scope viewer and switched off the light emitter. "We have found nothing but healthy tissue."

"Cryopreservation is killing the carriers, but it may also be destroying the pathogen in the process." She collected the cellular slides and placed them in a cold case. "Considering how hypersensitive my species is to low temperatures, it also seems logical."

I considered the theory. "The only way to know is to biopsy the gland of a living patient."

"That would prove fatal to the subject." She pulled up a diagram of the Hsktskt brain. "The gland cluster regulates most of the vital involuntary nerve and muscle functions. Respiration, muscle contraction, and conscious thought processing cannot take place without the gland functioning."

"How can the pathogen invade only the brain tissue without spilling into the bloodstream?" I regarded her head and then consulted the diagram. "The back of your sinus cavities is three centimeters from the frontal region of the gland cluster. Could an airborne organism be inhaled and infect the cluster?"

"There is a membrane between the two that prevents any such contamination," ChoVa said, and then she jerked as if she had been punched in the abdomen. "Did you see an intact membrane in the skull of the patient we autopsied? It would look like"—she pulled up another image on the console, this time of thin, pale tissue stretched between two curved bones—"this."

I concentrated and recalled the dissection of the corpse's cranial case. "There was tissue, but it was not that color. It was black."

"It may have been diseased." She went to the case with the autopsy samples and threw it open. "Did you harvest a sample?"

"No, I did not," I said.

ChoVa slammed the case shut. "We must retrieve another corpse and examine the membranes."

"The estate has been quarantined," I reminded her. "We cannot leave."

"We cannot wait until one of my father's household dies," she snarled at me. "Assuming they will. We have no cryolab here. I cannot freeze them to death to suit our purpose."

"Would you rather kill one of the infected, to save

time? Who will you choose? Is there one of your father's retainers you particularly dislike?" I watched the anger fade from her eyes. "There has to be another way. You serve the Hanar, so you must have some influence with him. Ask that one of the victims from the city be brought here for us to autopsy. If they are afraid of contamination it can be delivered by humanoid slaves."

"The Hanar will not do so," she informed me. "I did not tell my father, but the Supreme One issued orders that all of the dead are to be burned."

The Hanar was afraid of being infected himself, that much I could see. "Ask him not to burn one. Only one. It may be what helps us find the cure."

"I would, but he will not listen. He is almost mad with fear—" She closed her eyes and slammed her fists into the nearest flat object, which turned out to be an exam table. Her blows made the surface of the table buckle, and she stepped back, staring at it with bleak astonishment.

"I have always wanted to do that." I admired the depth of the indentations. "I wish I had your strength."

"And I your composure." Her shoulders sagged. "Jarn, I can do nothing right, and I become more frustrated by the hour. Even if I am not infected, soon I will be of no use to you."

"Nonsense." I felt more inclined to agree with her, but that would not provide any motivation. "This is only a small setback. All we need do is remain calm and think clearly."

We were still debating how we might obtain a corpse when the locks on the outer door disengaged and a pair of Palace Guards entered the lab. Both were in envirosuits and carried rifles held at ready.

"What is it?" ChoVa demanded, clearly outraged at the interruption.

"The Hanar has ordered you to return to the Palace," one of the guards said. "Gather what you need. You will not be returning here."

I touched her shoulder. "Go. Explain what we have discovered and what we need to continue."

"No," the guard said before ChoVa could reply. "The Hanar's orders are to bring you to him as well, Warm-Blood."

ChoVa quickly grabbed two medical cases and what light instruments and scanners she could fit in them, and handed one to me. The two guards held their rifles trained on us as we were escorted from the lab.

"Do they think we are dangerous?" I asked ChoVa in a low voice.

She glanced at the weapons. "Evidently the Hanar does."

Outside more guards stood holding rifles on Reever and the Akade. My husband was bleeding from the nose and mouth again, and when he saw me something in his eyes glittered like light on a blade.

I had the feeling that ChoVa and I would not be at the Palace for very long.

The trip from TssVar's estate to the heart of the city took only a few minutes. The Hanar's guards would not speak to ChoVa or answer her questions about why we had been ordered to court. The further into the city we moved, the more fires I saw burning above on the rooftops. The smell of the smoke-filled air came through the transport's vents, and the stench of cooked flesh became so strong I thought I might retch.

"Breathe through your mouth," ChoVa advised me as she studied my face. "Do you know your skin turns the color of bone when you are nauseated?"

I tried her suggestion, and it did help. "At least I am not green all the time."

It was ridiculous to jest when we were possibly facing imprisonment or execution, but I was tired and feeling a little defeated. I had come here to help these people, and I had failed. Worse, I had caused my husband and daughter to be abducted and nearly murdered by outlaws in the process. Doubtless my former self would congratulate me for my dedication to the work; but then I was turning out to be almost as reckless and impulsive as *she* had been.

"You're not half the doctor she was," the disembodied female voice I had heard on the launch and in the outlaw camp told me. *"You're small and scared, and you're always avoiding confrontations. Cherijo never ran from a good fight."*

I was hearing Maggie's voice in my ears, but from the lack of reaction around me, no one else did. I wondered if the entity or whatever she was could read my thoughts.

"Like they were made of plas," she said. *"And I'm Maggie, not an entity. I was the only mother you've ever had."*

I frowned. She sounded resentful, almost sulky,

as a boy child did when he was thwarted. I rather expected more from the being Reever had described. How was she transmitting these messages to my mind? Was there some organic implant in my brain that had never been discovered?

"*It's organic, all right,*" Maggie said. "*You'll never understand it, or the how and from where and why, but that doesn't matter. I'm disappointed in you, Jarn. I expected you to at least try to recover Cherijo's memories while you were screwing her husband and loving up her kid.*"

She wished me to address her. That seemed as crazy as talking to myself, but I decided to try a direct thought. *Why are you contacting me like this?*

"*I have nothing better to do,*" Maggie snapped. "*Sure, I could float here in oblivion and wait for the end of time, but it's going to take a few million more centuries. I need some quality entertainment. Which, by the way, you are piss-poor at providing. Why don't you try to break free of these guards? Why don't you get that big female lizard to help you?*"

Some of the guards were giving me curious looks, and I glanced down to see that my hands were clenched so hard that my short nails had cut small, bloody lacerations into my palms. This was neither the time nor the place to confront Cherijo's ghost-mother. *Why don't you close your mouth?*

"*Okay.*" The voice went silent.

Once we arrived at the Palace, we were moved from the transport onto one of the lift-vessels, and given only a desultory scan before being whisked up to the Hanar's level.

"If the Hanar fears being infected by the

pathogen," I murmured to ChoVa, "why does he not have us decontaminated more thoroughly?"

"I cannot say." She looked around her. "Most of his guards have gone, too. Have you noticed?"

The Palace did seem somewhat deserted. We walked through the corridors to the Hanar's throne room, but the guards remained outside as we passed through the entry doors, and closed and secured them behind us as soon as we had done so.

The smoke from the city's burning dead tinged the pervasive heat of the throne room, but otherwise the chamber appeared empty. Everything had been removed, even the Hanar's dais. I glanced at ChoVa, who shook her head slowly as she scanned the room.

"He must have ordered everything taken to be burned," she murmured. "When last I saw him, he was worried that the infection could be in everything, all around him."

"Perhaps he is already infected," I suggested in a low tone.

She took in a quick breath. "The paranoia, yes, it makes sense now."

"Here now, my personal physician and her pet Terran." The ancient Hsktskt came limping into view, kicking something out of his way. In both hands he held long swords dripping with dark fluid.

"Hanar, what has happened to you?" ChoVa said.

He hissed, baring bloodied teeth. It was only then that I saw what he had been kicking were the remains of a guard, partially covered by the sweeping hem of his robe. The guard's throat had been torn out, and large chunks of his flesh were missing. A bulge in Hanar's throat told me how at least one of the wounds had been inflicted. "ChoVa."

"I know," she said to me.

"This is your doing, Terran," the Hanar said, his voice thick and distorted by the flesh still lodged in his gullet. He swallowed it, and then lifted and pointed one of his swords at me. "I should cut you to pieces and feed you to her."

ChoVa stepped forward with a slow, deliberate movement. "Hanar, you are the light and reason of our people. We are lost without you. Permit me to ease your suffering." She reached into her case and removed an infuser.

"No." Although there were many yards between them, he swiped at her with the other sword as if he thought to strike her. "I know what you do. You mean to end me so that your blood assumes the throne. Your cursed father will never wear the mantle of leader. I will devour him myself before I allow him to kill me."

"That is not the truth. You have known my father since he took his first breath," ChoVa argued. "He lives to serve you, as do I."

"You will die serving me." The Hanar turned and bellowed, a roar so loud I had to clap my hands over my ears. "Come out, you filth. They are here. I have fulfilled my part of our bargain."

ChoVa hissed as a shadow detached itself from the wall and moved into the light. It was PyrsVar, the war master of the outlaws.

"Hanar, this male is the leader of the outlaws

who have attacked your city," I said urgently, ignoring the wild look ChoVa gave me. "He cannot be trusted. Summon your guards at once."

"He knows who I am, Healer," PyrsVar said. "I came here alone and surrendered myself to the Hanar. I have since been granted amnesty for my crimes, have I not, Supreme One?"

"Only for the cure you promised me." The old ruler's arms fell, and his swords slipped from his claws and clattered to the floor. "You have them now, renegade. Give me what you vowed, and then take them and get out."

I turned toward the grinning Jorenian. "*You* have a cure for the pathogen?"

"Indeed. I vowed to use it to put an end to the Hanar's suffering." PyrsVar strode up to the exhausted ruler and placed one of his hands on the old Hsktskt's arm, as if they were old friends. "Did I not?"

"I cannot bear another moment of this madness. Not another moment. Do as you said." The Hanar closed his eyes and would have fallen if not for the war master. "End this before I end myself."

"As the Hanar commands," PyrsVar said softly.

A weapon fired. I watched in horror as the Hanar jerked, and then crumpled in a heap of tangled limbs and robes. ChoVa screamed in fury and rushed at the renegade Jorenian, but was knocked backward by a displacer shot to the side of her head and fell, unconscious and bleeding, to the floor.

I did not think, I ran. A gaping hole in the Hanar's abdomen told me his fate, but I checked for a pulse anyway and found none. I moved over to

ChoVa and tore off my jacket, using it to stanch the flow of blood from the deep gash creasing the side of her head.

"Healer."

I looked up. In my face was the pistol PyrsVar had used to kill the Hanar and shoot ChoVa.

"You see?" he said in a reasonable tone. "He no longer suffers from the plague. I told you, I always keep my vows."

FIFTEEN

PyrsVar left the Hanar where he had fallen, but dragged ChoVa over to a small adjoining room and shut her inside, using the pistol again to fuse the door-locking mechanism.

I used the opportunity to run to the doors and pound on them with my fists. "Help," I screamed, hammering as hard as I could. "Open the doors. The Hanar has been murdered. Open—"

"You are wasting your breath."

I did not look back or stop shouting.

"The throne room is completely soundproof," PyrsVar said as he dragged me back from the door. "You can scream until your throat swells shut, and they will still not hear you." He lifted me under one arm as if I were nothing more than a pack of supplies and strode toward the observation deck. "Now that I finally have you again, we will go."

I tried to look up at him. "You did all this for me?" You shot the Hanar only to get to *me*?"

"I would have shot anyone else who came between us," he assured me as he shot out the protective screen covering the deck viewer and stepped through it. Outside a small scout ship hovered, and then swooped closer to extend a ramp. "You should not have drugged me, or run away from me."

"You abducted me and my family," I said, struggling with him as he put me down on my feet inside the scout's small passenger bay. "What did you expect me to do?"

"Keep your vow to me." His hand clamped around my neck, and when I felt the tips of his claws I went still. He used his other hand to retract the ramp and close the bay door, trapping me inside the scout with him. "You promised me that if I let the male and the young ones live, you would not attempt to escape. You lied to me."

"Yes, I did," I admitted. "But your grievance was with me, not the Hanar. You had no reason for murdering him."

"Perhaps you should not lie to me again." PyrsVar flung me into a small alloy cage made for some sort of animal and locked me inside. "For who knows who or how many I will kill to get to you the next time?"

He went up to the helm and spoke to the pilot, who was presently flying at high speed out of the city. Try as I might, I could not hear what they were saying. Through the viewer civilization rapidly disappeared, replaced by the featureless and endless sands of the desert. Dread settled inside me as I realized there was no one who knew I had been abducted. Back at the Palace, the Hanar was dead, and ChoVa lay unconscious in a locked room. It might be days before she was found. By then everyone might assume I had been killed.

No, Reever will know, my common sense argued.

He knew my body lived the entire time I was on Akkabarr.
But with no witnesses, and no means with which to
track me, how would Reever find me this time?

PyrsVar sat down at the copilot's console and
proceeded to ignore me for the rest of the flight. He
might have meant to unnerve me, but I was glad of
it. I needed time to think, and to plan better. My
daughter would not be here to slip me an infuser,
nor my husband to fly me back to the city. If I was
to escape, I would have to do it on my own.

Hours passed. Once the scout stopped, possibly
to refuel, but it took off before I could see what was
happening outside the ship. I thought I would end
up in yet another outlaw encampment, but we soon
passed over the last of the desert and moved into a
maze of towering mountains and narrow, rocky val-
leys.

This was one of the unsettled regions of Vtaga,
too cold and steep to appeal to the heat-loving Hsktskt. I sat down in the cage, exhausted and defeated,
and watched the snowcapped peaks flash by as the
scout flew between them. Back at the Palace I had
managed to bandage ChoVa's head by tearing off
the sleeve of my jacket, but until she regained consciousness and was subjected to head scans, there
was no way to know if being shot had caused any
more serious damage. Then, too, someone would
have to find her, something I doubted would happen soon. Whoever entered the throne room would
see the Hanar's body first.

What will they do without a ruler? I closed my burning eyes. *Who will succeed him? Will it be TssVar, even
though he is infected?* At least ChoVa had seen

PyrsVar shoot the Hanar. If she had not, they might have blamed it on me, and taken out some sort of retribution on Reever and the Adan. My hand crept up and touched the place on the side of my head where I had been shot twice at point-blank range by Daneeb. *Unless she has no memory of it.*

I must have slept, for the next time I opened my eyes the muscles of my neck were stiff and the launch engines were reversing. We were landing again, somewhere, and from the change of scenery in the viewer it was someplace so high that there were cloud formations floating by and beneath the scout.

Through tired eyes I watched PyrsVar walk back to me. He opened the door of the cage, and then reached in to help me out. His claws had retracted, but his expression was, if anything, more uncompromising than it had been.

"Are you not going to ask me where we are?" he asked as he bound my wrists together in the same type of manacles he had used on the children at his desert camp. "Or are you thinking of how you will plead for my mercy this time?"

"On my homeworld, women are taught to be silent when they are being beaten or punished." I turned my face away from him, bracing myself to endure what would come. "Do as you will, War Master."

He jerked me around to face him. "You would like that? Is this what that Terran male, your master, has done to you?" He looked all over me. "You are not afraid of me or him. Why do you pretend to be so?"

"There are more important things than what happens to me." I nodded toward the pilot. "The people are dying. ChoVa and I were working on a cure for their sickness. Without one, their symptoms will overwhelm them, as they did the Hanar."

"The fear." His eyes narrowed. "I could smell it on him."

"Fear is an emotion that Hsktskt do not experience," I said. "They do not know how to cope with it. They are already burning the dead. Soon the madness will set in and send them into the streets, where they will fight each other like wounded animals."

"The strong will survive," he assured me, taking my arm and making me walk to the hull access panel. "Those who do will be worthy of my rule."

So he wanted to be the ruler. "You will survive, no doubt, because biologically you are not like them. But who will you rule, War Master, when the last of your outlaws has gone insane, and all of the cities on Vtaga are empty or burned to the ground? What will it be like for you, Hanar of a lifeless world?"

PyrsVar hesitated, staring down at me, and then flashed his pointed teeth. "That was better than the begging and pleading. You should have said this in the desert; then I might have let you go." He jerked me out of the scout and into frigid, snowy wind.

We had landed atop a high mountain, on a transport pad so small the scout barely fit on it. Above us, a round structure made of rough-quarried stone had been built into the side of the mountain and camouflaged to appear as nothing more than natural outcroppings. A primitive-looking lift descended, so small as to barely accommodate the two of us, and raised us up to an aperture in the lower stone vault of the structure.

As the lift halted, I saw someone standing just beyond it. A Hsktskt male in his prime, from the shape of his body, but he had draped his head and shoulders with a curious headdress made of dimsilk. I recognized the alien material because Resa and I had made use of it to disguise our own bodies when we had posed as vral on the battlefields of Akkabarr.

PyrsVar hauled me out of the lift and shoved me down on my knees. I did not resist, but I showed no particular deference toward the disguised male.

"How long I have waited for this moment," the Hsktskt waiting for us rasped. "Dr. Cherijo Grey Veil, here on Vtaga, come to save the Hsktskt from themselves."

He called me by the name Cherijo used before she had mated with Reever, but why?

"I remember you being larger and noisier, but perhaps the years have taken their toll on you." Beneath the dimsilk, some sort of mechanism clicked and whirred. "Well, Doctor, have you found a cure for *this* plague?"

"Not yet." I had an eerie sense that I knew this male, but it might have been the voice. He spoke with the synthetic speech sounds of a drone.

"Such optimism, even under the duress of being a captive held at the mercy of a killer. Your bravado is useless here, although I do appreciate the effort." The shifting lines of the dimsilk concealed his head movements, but his body turned slightly toward PyrsVar. "Does the Hanar yet live, or did you manage to neutralize the correct target this time?"

The renegade Jorenian bowed. "The Hanar is dead, as you commanded, sire."

My shock must have shown on my face, for the veiled Hsktskt made a low, chuffing, mechanical sound. "You are not mistaken in what you are thinking, Doctor. PyrsVar is my son."

I did not know what to say. How could this Hsktskt father a Jorenian? Given that one was a reptilian life-form and the other humanoid, crossbreeding seemed unlikely even if he had used a female Jorenian captive.

"Have you not guessed who I am? I am disappointed." To PyrsVar, he said, "Go into the desert and gather up your men. The city will fall into anarchy now that the Hanar is no more. We have only to wait a few more days."

"What of the sickness?" PyrsVar demanded. "What if my men grow sick?"

"I have told you that they will not." He made an abrupt gesture, and the renegade Jorenian slowly turned and went to the lift.

Part of me wanted to jump up and run after him. Of the two males, even as angry as PyrsVar was with me, he was definitely the less menacing.

"Come inside," the veiled Hsktskt said, gesturing as he might to a guest. "The air is warmer, and we have much to discuss."

The interior of the structure held a large, sophisticated laboratory, more massive than any I had yet seen on Vtaga. Twice the size of the scout, the main lab area served as a wide hub, ringed by many door panels and open corridors that twisted out of sight. It did not seem right that it was empty, barren of anyone but me and the disguised Hsktskt. There should have been an army of technicians and workers making use of the place.

That the complex had been built into the mountain rather than on its surface also troubled me. On Akkabarr, the Toskald had made my people dig trenches deep in the ice to conceal and store massive armories of weapons, as well as the control crystals to command a thousand different armies.

What was this Hsktskt trying to hide?

"I see you are admiring my stronghold," my captor said as he led me toward a comfortable-looking area set with chairs and other furnishings. "It took some years for me to gather the funds and means to return to Vtaga and build it."

"What purpose does it serve?" I asked. "Do you provide sanctuary for the outlaws?" That might explain the absence of others.

"Please, sit down." He gestured toward the furnishings. "I hardly ever entertain, but I have both Terran and Jorenian teas. My son is naturally fond of the latter."

He had PyrsVar abduct me, and yet he treated me as an honored guest—and competently ignored my questions. The latter frightened me more than if he had tossed me into a detainment cell or had me seized by interrogation drones and tortured.

"I thank you." Cautiously I sat down in one of the chairs closest to a door panel and looked about for something I could use as a weapon to defend myself. I saw nothing. "Why have you brought me here? Am I your hostage?"

"I have no need of a hostage, Doctor." He moved to a food unit and prepared a server. "But if it pleases you to think of yourself as such, you may do so. I doubt anyone will be coming to save you. This region is too cold for my kind to attempt it, and your kind has no idea where you are, do they?"

"No." I might have lied, but he had to know how effective PyrsVar had been in abducting me. "No one does." I paused. "Yet."

He brought the server of steaming liquid to me, but I only warmed my hands with it. I was not ingesting anything until I knew why this male had gone to such lengths to bring me here.

"I admit I am surprised that you have not guessed who I am." The Hsktskt began slowly removing the dimsilk covering his head. "We spent so much quality time together on Catopsa. I think of all the slaves there, you proved to be my finest test subject. We might have discovered great things together, you and I."

I suddenly knew who he was, for I had read about him in Cherijo's journals. "You are SrrokVar, the Hsktskt scientist who tortured Ch—me?"

"I was." He pulled back the last layer of dimsilk and revealed what sat on his shoulders in place of his head. "Now I am something quite a bit different."

The journal descriptions of the Hsktskt scientist and physician who had tortured Cherijo on Catopsa did not match the appearance of the creature before me. What had once been a Hsktskt male was no longer completely organic in form. The Hsktskt's neck ended just above his shoulder line, disappearing under a wide alloy gasket affixed to what must have been an artificial skull made of transparent plas.

The server of hot tea fell out of my hand onto the floor, splashing my right leg. I barely felt the scald, so horrified was I. "What happened to you?"

"*You* happened to me, my dear doctor," SrrokVar said through the bubble's com unit, shaped and moving like a mouth to imitate speech. "You remember how cleverly you manipulated the safety controls on the bonesetters that you clamped to my head. I could not remove them before they crushed my skull."

I wanted to deny that I had done such a thing, for Cherijo had not written of inflicting mutilation so severe as to make it necessary for this male's brain to be transferred to a plas bubble. But here was the proof in front of me: a drone's head atop of a living body.

"I could not immediately remove the bonesetters, and by the time I did the damage was done." His artificial mouth stretched wide. "I barely escaped Catopsa alive. I put myself into cryostasis and set the escape ship on course for a colony of mercenaries who would give me sanctuary. By the time they recovered and revived me, necrosis had taken hold and the tissue damage had become irreversible. Happily, these mercenaries also specialized in creating new identities for fugitives through reconstruct technology."

The thing atop his shoulders was not quite a drone's head. The artificial skull appeared to work just as a drone's did, with audiovisual sensors that fed data to its contents. Yet instead of a central processor and data-storage banks, SrrokVar's control center was his intact, living brain, floating in cloudy green fluid and connected to a web of input leads.

I had to say something. To apologize seemed obscene. I could not believe Cherijo had done this deliberately to another living being, if she were indeed responsible. Desperately I searched for some neutral response.

"How is it that you are PyrsVar's sire?" I asked quickly. "Whatever was done to your head, you are still biologically Hsktskt. He is Jorenian."

"As unlikely as it seems, PyrsVar is my son, as much as you were Joseph Grey Veil's daughter." He sat down across from me and laced his clawed hands together. "The reconstruction I underwent originally gave me the idea, and then alterform technology became available. What reconstruct surgeons did for me by grafting drone components onto my body could suddenly be done with living cells."

Now I understood. "You made him in a machine, as I was made."

"How charming your speech is. I remember it being primitive, but not quite to this degree. Yes, PyrsVar is a bioengineered construct, cloned from my cells and others. In fact, your father's research proved as valuable to me when I was creating my son as the alterforming data my people stole from the League." He waited, as if he expected me to say something.

I spotted a piece of broken plas near my ankle, and bent over as if to check my scalded leg. "Why use Jorenian cells if you meant to re-create yourself? Where did you get them?"

"You mistake my purpose. My son's genetic frame had to be a biomatch to that of the Hsktskt, but humanoid in appearance. The Jorenians are one of the few species comparable in size to us. Your adopted people are so admired that they are welcomed on virtually every world; thus, appearing Jorenian gives my son an instant passport to the rest of the galaxy." He leaned back as if enjoying himself. "As for the cells, harvesting the DNA was simple, once I had obtained the cadaver that I wanted."

"Jorenians do not preserve the bodies of their dead," I said, pulling down the leg of my trousers and palming the jagged bit of plas in the process.

"This is the amusing part of my tale." He made one of the Hsktskt's sweeping gestures. "Shortly before you and I met, I had purchased a number of Jorenian cadavers from a solar salvage operation. The Jorenians hurtle the bodies of their dead through space toward stars as a form of celestial cremation, but do you know, sometimes the dead do not arrive. Often they are whisked away by magnetic fields and solar winds, and end up orbiting a nearby planet."

As he spoke, SrrokVar kept pausing now and then, watching me intently as if expecting a reaction. Clearly he had no idea that Cherijo's memories were lost to me, or of the scant amount of actual information I had about him. I saw no merit in revealing this.

"I harvested DNA from a Jorenian cadaver that had died of blood poisoning, and used it to alterform a young adult Hsktskt outlaw," SrrokVar continued. "It required me to perform a complete cerebral memory wipe, of course, so that the unwelcome memories of the Hsktskt's former life would not interfere. The result is PyrsVar."

If he had had a mouth, and had been humanoid, he would have been smiling. I could tell this from the smugness of his tone, even filtered by the drone tech delivering it.

"That is why he seems so young sometimes," I murmured, fascinated and appalled. "How old is he?"

"In Terran terms? A child yet. Much younger than Kao Torin, the donor of the Jorenian cells."

So PyrsVar was a Torin, in a roundabout sense. "The Torins have no idea you took cells from their dead kin."

"Neither did you." SrrokVar rose to his feet. "I expected more of an emotional reaction from you, my dear doctor. I chose Kao Torin with such care, not only for the Jorenian DNA that would allow my alterformed progeny to travel throughout the galaxy unhindered, but in hopes that he would find you someday. I imagined how you would squirm every time you looked at him, the living ghost of the lover you killed."

"I have no memory of Kao Torin, or of any feelings we shared between us," I took pleasure in telling him. Perhaps it was unwise, but the outrage I felt on Cherijo's behalf would allow me to remain silent no longer. "Two years ago I was shot twice in the head. I healed, but in the process I lost all of Cherijo's persona."

He went still and some of the things on his head whirred faster. "Are you saying that you suffered brain damage? That your memory center was compromised?"

"I have no memory center. All of Cherijo's memories were destroyed. I do not remember you, or Catopsa." I gripped the broken piece of plas tightly. "I do not remember this Kao Torin, or that he was my lover, or that I killed him. I cannot feel the pain you wished to inflict upon her."

"You will. You will remember everything, and feel it down to your bones." SrrokVar seized me and dragged me out of the chair. "Let us see to that now."

I used the broken piece of plas like a dagger and drove it into the side of SrrokVar's neck, hoping to sever one of the power cables enabling his visual emitters. It would have been the same as blinding him.

It did not work. I misjudged the shielding of the cable, and only cut it partway before he snatched the plas from my hand and threw it across the lab.

"Reviving the past is my specialty now, Doctor," he told me as he pinned my arms to my sides and carried me effortlessly toward a small chamber with a large view panel. He did not seem in the least upset that I had attempted to kill him. "I have devoted all of my intellect to bringing what was back to life. Very soon this plague you came here to cure will return my people to the glory of what we were before we allowed civilization to tame us, and clever humanoids to pollute our thinking."

"You are responsible for the plague?" I writhed, trying to free myself. "How can this help the Hsktskt? You're killing your own people."

"What I do will free them." He shoved me into the chamber and sealed me inside. I rushed at the door panel, but the seam was too tight for me to force open. I whirled around, looking for the means with which he meant to hurt me. There were only a few round nozzles set into the smooth walls.

"This is meaningless," I called out. "Whatever you do to me will not bring back my former self, or yours. Others will find a cure to the plague."

"Nothing can stop it now." SrrokVar tapped his claws against the front of the plas bubble. "I will never be what I was—Dr. Grey Veil—but the damage done to you can be repaired." He disappeared from view, but his voice kept speaking. "It must be, if you are to witness the restoration of my people and give me the secrets to immortality."

SrrokVar appeared at the console on the other side of the viewer panel. He input some command, and a white powder as fine as dust began pouring from all of the nozzles into the chamber.

"What you are about to breathe in is the pulverized bone dust of a shape-shifting species called the Odnallak," he said over the audio panel. "Their primary survival mechanism is to acquire an image of their enemy's deepest fear and assume that form, both made possible by a unique chromatophoric organism in their bloodstream. That organism remains dormant in their skeletal structure even after the host body dies. Inhalation by a sentient being activates its ability to attack, only without a host it does it through brain chemistry."

As it must have for all the people of this planet. "When Hsktskt breathe it in, they remember the old ones like the rogur. Ancient terrors so horrifying that they would rather kill everyone around them than think."

SrrokVar inclined his drone head. "The perfect soldiers, wouldn't you say?"

"They will be driven to suicide before you can use them in battle. As will I, if you use this dust on me." I moved to the center of the chamber to avoid the growing piles of dusty powder on the floor.

"My people are suicidal only when not provided with an outlet for their fear. You saw that yourself at the medical facility in the city. As for you, I have been told you are almost impossible to kill, and I am more than willing to risk your death to revive your memories." He pressed more keys, and a vid unit appeared in the viewer. "You shouldn't have forgotten what you most feared, Doctor. You should never have forgotten me."

The ceiling opened, and large fans began blasting air into the chamber, stirring up the Odnallak dust to swirl around me. I held my breath as I tore a strip from my tunic and covered my mouth and nose with it, but my efforts proved useless. The fine particles in the air went straight through the cloth and into my chest and head.

I coughed and choked as a deep burning sensation spread through me. Then the chamber and SrrokVar and the floor vanished, leaving me alone in the dark and unable to breathe.

SIXTEEN

"You can breathe all right, Joey. Just suck it in and blow it out."

A fist struck the center of my chest, and I breathed in reflexively. I was not choking, the air was clear again, and the unbearable burning sensation inflicted by the dust had disappeared.

I am dead, I thought. *He smothered me with that filth and this is death.*

"You're not dead," the female voice said.

I opened my eyes and discovered the voice was correct. I was not smothered or dead or in the dark anymore. I lay in a narrow place enclosed in clear, jagged airstone shot through with thin veins of darker stuff. An older, red-haired Terran female sat cross-legged beside me. She was dressed in an Iisleg woman's robes, but had removed the proper head covering. In her hands was the head wrap, which she was slowly ripping into smaller pieces.

I recognized the voice if not the face. This was the one who had been speaking to me when no one else could hear. I did not know how I knew that; only that I did.

Green eyes flashed as she looked up at me briefly.

"You know because I've given you back that memory."

I sat up and looked up and down. There was no beginning or end to the crystal prison, no ceiling or floor. We were floating on a column of air.

"This is what I fear?" I asked no one in particular. "Being stuck in a plas tube with a Terran who dislikes covering her face and meddles with my brain?"

"I'm not Terran. I only look like one for context purposes," she said. "This is a mental construct, which is a fancy way of saying you're just imagining things. Well, except me. I'm Maggie. Chief brain meddler."

"Maggie." The name was painfully familiar on my tongue. Was it as she said? Had she given me my memory of her? I did not want it.

"Your mother. Sort of. Yes, I gave you the memory. It took damn near forever, too. You'll take whatever I give you, Joey."

I curled my hand into a fist. "You will stay out of my head, alien."

She laughed. "I'm not an alien."

I studied her. She did look Terran, but Reever had told me she was not. "You are a machine?" Had Cherijo's father constructed her as some sort of bizarre incubator device, to simulate Terran gestation?

"No." She tossed aside the shreds of her head covering and sighed. "I was, am, and will be Jxin, and no, I'm not going to explain all that over again. You didn't believe me the last time I did anyway."

She spoke to me as if I were still Cherijo. Perhaps

she meant to somehow erase me and bring back my former self. I could not let that happen, so I stood and looked up, reaching to touch the crystalline surface of the wall. It felt as smooth and slippery as ice after a windless freeze.

"You can't get out of here unless I change the construct, and we don't have time for that," Maggie told me.

I turned to stare down at her. Bits of weave from the head wrap made her hands appear furry. She had an unpleasant amount of amusement in her green eyes. "Release me from this."

"I didn't bring you here. Domehead did." She threw a wad of fabric over her shoulder. "I did try to reach you several times while you were on Akkabarr, but when that skela bitch on the iceball tried to kill you, she damaged the implants and ruined the connections. I never planned for you to get shot in the head, which, I might add, was stupid of you to let happen."

"What implants?" I demanded. "What connections?"

"They're what I placed inside your thick skull so that I could continue to guide you after I transitioned from physical form to something a little like controlled energy." She sighed heavily. "I shed my body too soon, or I could have gone there and rewired you before the old pathways degraded. Not possible anymore; I can't cross distance except as light and thought."

I had no time for mysterious conversations with alien women who didn't exist, and who might or might not be my machine-mother. I needed to return to Vtaga, and find a way out of the stronghold and back to the city. "How do I leave this place?"

"When I'm done talking to you, you'll regain consciousness, spit up the dust you've inhaled—that's going to be nasty, by the way—show the mad scientist that you're not suicidal, and convince him to let you go." She rolled her eyes. "Which is pretty much your job description whatever mess you're in, honey."

"He tortured Cherijo, and claims she destroyed his head," I informed her. "I do not think he is going to release me. Not when he could harm me again. Help me to escape him."

"Jesus, you've completely lost your backbone, too." She seemed disgusted. "Is that what that iceball was? The Planet of Spineless People?"

"Akkabarr was a slaver world." Her irreverence became more annoying by the moment. "As we speak, people are dying. I am needed elsewhere. *Help me.*"

"People are always dying. Actually, it's one of the few things they do very well. Right up there with breeding and killing." She yawned and stretched out her arms before rising to stand, and then tilted her head and looked past me at nothing. "Wait, something interesting is developing out there. We might have a backup plan. Those big blueberry people certainly do get attached to you."

"The Jorenians?"

"Never mind; we have more important things to discuss. I haven't exactly explained myself and your mind is accepting the physical memory of me but nothing else. So, here's the deal." She squared her shoulders. "We'll call me an alien life-form, never mind which kind. I'm dead and I will not be coming back in an altered or more evolved form."

"How terrible for you." I had to force the words out, but I needed her.

"Don't pretend you're sorry for me. You don't even know me." She placed her hands on her hips. "Your dad could not have engineered you without my assistance. I meddled; you were born. You were created by him to be the perfect physician, and although you're a lot more I still don't have a problem with that."

"I am so glad." No, I wasn't. "Can we leave here now?"

"Pay attention." She tapped the side of my scalp where the old wound had been. "There is one very tenuous connection left, and that's what is letting me speak to you and pass some memories to you now. That and a little of the really ugly guy's freaky dust, which is acting like a booster."

"He said it was powdered bone." If SrrokVar was correct about the properties of the powder, then my former self had been afraid of Maggie. More afraid of her than anything else. But why?

"This is the genuine, scary, fucked-up part of the whole situation," she was saying. "Somehow, someway, that tin-headed psychopath managed to get his claws on some Odnallak bones. That's the reason you've got to shut him down. They can't leave this world. They have to be destroyed here and now."

"I am locked up and evidently unconscious," I reminded her. My head hurt, and I could feel a stream of images and sounds pouring into it. "I have no weapons, and no help. I rather doubt I am going to be doing anything." I stared into her face. "Unless you do something."

"I told you, I can't," she snapped. "The Odnallak were very nasty people who lived a long time ago. They were the last of the ancient shape-shifter crowd. We didn't like them. We really, really didn't like them."

"We . . . ?"

"Me and the Jxin, mysterious alien beings that also no longer exist in your reality." She produced a slim tube of white, lit one end with a flame from one of her lengthy crimson nails, placed the unlit end between lips, and drew in. "It's the Odnallak's fault; they wanted to improve their shifting ability." She blew out a small stream of smoke. "They manipulated DNA the same way my people did, but, I'll admit, they were a little better at it. And they weren't exactly interested in doing nice things like me and my people. That's when it happened."

I waved a hand in front of my face to disperse the smoke, and in that moment remembered everything about Cherijo's life on Kevarzangia Two. "It?"

"The disaster. The infection. Whatever you want to call it. The Odnallak pushed things too far, and created the black crystal." Maggie turned and gestured to the series of cracks running through the clear plas tube. "That stuff."

She was talking about the rock cracks while I was reliving the memories of a plague on K-2. Perhaps SrrokVar's dust had driven me insane already. I caught my breath as I discovered through the flood of memories that Cherijo had been in love with a Jorenian who looked exactly like PyrsVar.

"It looks harmless, but it's not. It's malignant. It's aggressive. And over the seemingly endless stretch of linear time in which it must exist, it's gotten hungry." She gestured with the thing in her hand. "It now wants to eat up everything living in your universe."

The smoke made my eyes sting, as did the memories of what the plague had done to the colonists of K-2. "You speak of this mineral as if it were sentient."

"It's not a mineral. It's not a vegetable, or an animal. We don't know what the hell it is. It just shows up and starts causing problems, generally for our little soldiers like you."

"I am a soldier? I thought I was the perfect physician." I remembered Reever linking with me the first time, kissing me the first time . . . and having sex with me the first time. "Which is it, and will you put out that thing? It's making me sick."

"Stop taking me literally, and complaining about my cigarette. It's annoying." Maggie pushed some of her curly red hair back from her face. "There is some justice in the fact that the first species the black crystal ate was the Odnallak, because they were trying to use it as a weapon."

"A wise crystal."

"Yeah, it's a smart little bugger. It turned on them at a crucial moment during a very large war and gobbled up most of them. Then it came after me and my people, and we tried fighting it. Big mistake, and PS, it ate most of us, too." She regarded her cigarette. "Those who survived—that would be me and a couple of others—scattered and began to prepare the countermeasure."

I watched Kao Torin's death through Cherijo's eyes, and wiped tears from my face. "What has this to do with me?"

"The few Odnallak who survived the crystal invasion were changed by it. They lost all the knowledge they had gathered to create the damn thing. They don't know how to control it or kill it, the way their ancestors did." She rested her hands on my shoulders. "They're no longer a threat to anyone but themselves. It's the black crystal that is becoming a very big problem for your reality. It's traveling now, and it's infiltrating planet after planet. It's indestructible, and it will only remain dormant for a few thousand more years at the most. Once it has spread through the universe, and contaminated every inhabited world, it will wake up and it'll be dinnertime."

"If there are thousands of years before this happens, why tell me?" I demanded. "I need to know how to get out of here, now, and help the Hsktskt."

"Screw the Hsktskt. We made you and the others to take up the fight where we left off." Maggie smiled. "That's why you were made immortal, Joey. We need you to stay alive for a long, long time."

Her logic made my head ache—or perhaps it was the smoke wafting into my face. "I could be killed any number of ways. Why didn't you wait?"

"Christ, you're as oblivious as the Hsktskt." She made the cigarette vanish, and with it the smoke she had exhaled. "I didn't want to have to do this. We wanted you to have a certain amount of free will—it motivates you better than we could—but there's no other way now. You're not going to develop a spine until you have Cherijo back in your head." Her long, crimson fingernails began lengthening and forming sharp points.

"How do you intend to put her there?"

"I can imprint my memories of her on you." Maggie flicked a hand at one wall, which moved away, creating a larger space. "Lie down. This is going to take awhile, but as long as you cooperate I can give you back yourself, and you can—"

I resisted the memories of my former self, shoving them away from me. The flood of that life stopped. "No."

"—get the hell out of . . ." She stopped and squinted at me. "What did you say?"

"I do not want her memories, or yours. I do not need them." When Maggie lifted her hand, flashing her daggerlike nails in my face, I ducked and lunged, driving my shoulder into her abdomen and pinning her against the rough plas wall.

"Joey!"

I caught her neck with one hand and grabbed her hair with the other, and put my face close to hers. "You release me from this place now, or I will choke the life out of you."

She didn't breathe, and didn't seem to need air to talk. "I guess it wasn't the Planet of Spineless People. It was the Planet of Psychopaths." The corners of her mouth curled. "I told you, little girl, I'm already dead. You can't hurt me."

"I will find a way," I assured her.

Maggie stared into my eyes. "Yes, I believe you would. Two personalities, completely opposed. The things you discover in your experiments when you don't have a body or a lab anymore."

"You need me," I said, "and I wish to live. There is still a great deal of time before the black crystal becomes active. The Hsktskt do not have such time. I will do as you wish, but you must help me now." When she said nothing, I added, "Will Cherijo be as cooperative as I have offered to be?"

"Probably not." She thought about it for a long moment. "All right . . . Jarn, isn't it? Let me go now, and I'll kick you out of here, and you can go and save your Hsktskt pals. But you will keep your promise to me."

"The word of an Iisleg cannot be broken." I didn't move my hands. "You're coming with me."

"I'm energy—"

"Shut up." I gave her a shake. "This is a mental construction, you said. So you will move it into my head and stay in my mind. Guide me. That is what you're supposed to do, isn't it?"

She nodded. "It's going to hurt."

I released her. "Everything hurts."

"Not like this." Maggie smiled a little. "Take a deep breath."

I inhaled.

The daggers of her fingernails stabbed into my temples and began slowly pushing in toward my brain.

The pain became everything for a time, and I endured it as I had everything else in this bizarre place. After a time, how long I did not know, I moved through the pain and fell into a strange dream.

Maggie was there, standing and watching me from a distance. So, too, was Reever, on the other side of my consciousness, but he was running toward me instead of standing. The distance between us never changed.

Was this my choice? Had I somehow betrayed Reever by agreeing to Maggie's demands?

"Healer."

The vision faded from my eyes, and I became aware of my surroundings. I stood in the chamber where SrrokVar had left me. I turned toward the viewer and saw PyrsVar standing beyond the clear barrier. Snow—no, Odnallak bone dust—whirled around me as I watched him lift a pistol. He meant to shoot me, and part of me felt an inexplicable flood of relief. I opened my arms wide, ready, almost eager, to accept my end.

The clear barrier shattered, and the dust rushed out of the room.

SrrokVar appeared then, and tried to wrestle the pistol from PyrsVar, who was covered with dust. He struck the renegade Jorenian in the face, but PyrsVar returned the blow. The monstrous Hsktskt fell away out of sight.

I will have to wait my turn, I thought, and lowered my arms. As I did, darkness closed around me, jerking me away from PyrsVar and into the blessed blackness of oblivion.

My skull felt as if it were still splitting in half when I next opened my eyes. I was being carried in strong, blue arms. I could smell blood, but not my own. I focused on the face above me, and went stiff as I recognized PyrsVar as the one carrying me.

He was muttering under his breath. "Not one. Not the other. Not one. Not the other."

"War Master?" I said, my voice strained. Icy wind slapped my face as he walked from the stronghold to the small transport pad. "What happened? Where are you taking me?" My wrists and ankles were bound again, but I couldn't see SrrokVar.

"He deceived me, just as you did." PyrsVar's white eyes shifted down. There was green and purple blood on his face. "My chest hurts. Burns."

I saw traces of the Odnallak dust on his nostrils and in the corners of his mouth. "You took me from the chamber." I could remember it clearly now.

"He was going to suffocate you in that dirt." He carried me onto the scout and snarled something at the pilot before dropping into a seat with me. The scout's engines engaged. "I should have known. He has suffered much, and cannot . . ." He looked down at me, and his expression changed as he pushed me off his lap. "Warm-blooded. He should have killed you."

I remained where I had fallen on the deck. "He meant to, I think. When he was finished tormenting me."

The renegade Jorenian pressed his hands to the sides of his head, and then pulled them away and stared at them with visible horror. "What has he done to me? He has made me like one of you. How can this be?" Now he was speaking in the hissing tone of the Hsktskt.

"You were like the people once. He said you were an outlaw and that he changed you. Alterformed you to look like a Jorenian."

"ToruVar." He stared past me. "That was my name. ToruVar."

"He made you with Jorenian DNA, so that you would be able to travel to other worlds." I felt a terrible pity for him. "The Jorenian he used for this was someone I once knew."

Too much information, Maggie's voice said from inside my mind. *He's going to lose it if he doesn't reconcile the two sides of his persona. Which makes him a far better match for you than Reever is, now that I think about it. Pity I didn't know about him when I designed your comeback.*

"Whatever SrrokVar did to you," I said to PyrsVar through gritted teeth, "cannot be changed. I know. I was another woman before I, too, was harmed and changed. I have to live with what she was, and the things that she did, but I do not have to be her. I am myself."

PyrsVar's rapid breathing slowed. "I was a thief. I remember it now. I stole because we had nothing. My siblings were starving. The war . . . the dishonor my father brought upon our line when he deserted . . ." He shook his head and met my gaze. "We are going back to the desert. You will stay there with me until I can think of what I must do."

"What happened to SrrokVar?"

PyrsVar did not answer me, and sat for the remainder of the flight in silence, staring at the mountains we passed.

The outlaws had moved their encampment to a

bleak region of stone cliffs, enormous boulders, and lifeless sand. The scout landed on a flat-topped outcropping and remained there only long enough for PyrsVar and me to disembark before flying away.

After the frigid climate of the mountain stronghold, the heat and humidity-heavy air seemed particularly thick and unpleasant. I saw the outlaws had tucked their camp below, in the maze of rocks and passages at the base of the hill.

"Come." PyrsVar took hold of my arm and led me to a winding passageway that had been cut into the rock, and gradually descended into the dark interior.

SEVENTEEN

I thought he might tie me up or lock me in another cage, but once we had entered the rough, cavelike enclave he was using as a shelter, he removed my bonds and gestured for me to sit.

"Be very careful, Jarn," Maggie said. *"The self-controlled bastard may not look like it, but he's just about to go over the edge."*

I knew what she meant, for I could see it in his eyes. Tension and fear, and a curious confusion that muddled the mind reeling beneath them. I had been to that same place too many times since waking up in Cherijo Torin's body.

"You should tell your men to stay away from us," I said cautiously. "They will become infected by the dust."

"They are raiding one of the outer settlements," he told me. "They will not return for several hours."

"All right, he's calmer, but you have to talk fast now," Maggie said. *"He needs help with accepting the truth of what he just learned about himself."*

Which is? I thought back.

"The fact that he was created by Dr. Tinhead solely to torment you," Maggie said. *"SrrokVar told him that*

just before he shot out the viewer and dragged you out of there. What he needs is a friend now, Jarn. Someone who will tell him the truth."

If I could befriend the renegade Jorenian, and somehow convince him to take me back to the Hsktskt city, then I might still have a chance to stop the plague.

"I can see your thoughts on your face now," he said, crouching down by the fire and warming his hands. They had patches of dark skin on them, as if he had snowbite. "I could not do that before I breathed in the dust. It is changing me."

"SrrokVar said that it invokes our deepest fears." I sat down on the rug nearest to him. "I think it brings some alteration of awareness as well."

"Oh, thank you so much," Maggie said sourly. *"I've always wanted to be a phobia crossed with a drug-induced hallucination."*

"My sire is not a simple man," PyrsVar said slowly. "I knew this as he brought me into being. I admired him for it. I believed the things that he told me. But the hatred he has for what the people have become . . ." He shook his head. "It is like his hatred of you. They became entwined. Whatever happened between you altered him inside. It drove him insane."

I couldn't disagree with that. When he said nothing more, I went to his stores and busied myself preparing a pot of the dark beverage the outlaws brewed.

"You aren't afraid of me anymore," he murmured.

"If you intended to harm me, you would have

left me with your sire. He is an expert in torturing slaves. That is what he did to me, before I hurt him." I brought him the tea and the meat strips I found in one of his supply bags, and presented them as an Iisleg woman would. "I am in your debt."

"I saw so many strange things in my head when I released you from that chamber," he admitted. "A world of flowers, and people with my skin and features. That was Joren?" I nodded. "It is as you said. And you. I look at you and I want to embrace you." He looked down into the server I had handed him. "I was right about you. This is not the first time we have met."

No, it was not. Thanks to the stream of memories Maggie had put into my head, I could now remember the first time I had kissed Kao, and made love with him. How hard I fought to keep him from dying of the Core plague, and how my extreme measures had eventually been the thing that had killed him.

It upset me for a moment, thinking of those memories as my own when they were Cherijo's alone. But Maggie and the effect of the bone dust had done this, and I could not reject experiences that now felt as much a part of me as if I had lived them on Akkabarr.

"We knew each other once," I said, banishing the memory of Kao dying in my arms. "You were someone for whom I had great affection. I was a different person. SrrokVar did not know I had forgotten you. He deliberately used my dead lover to create you in hopes that someday he could use you to harm me."

"I do not understand. Why go to all this trouble

for a Terran? We were to conquer Vtaga, and destroy the lines. We were to make everyone the same, so there would be no more outcasts, or hunger, or shame. A great equalizing revolution, he called it." He sounded like a lost child now. "I believed him, and it was all a lie. He did this so that he could make the people into animals, and have me spread this plague to other worlds. He wanted nothing but power and revenge."

"The woman I was hurt SrrokVar," I said. "He told me that he performed experiments on her when she was a slave. When she was finally freed by her people, she caused the injuries that made him as he is now. So I am partly responsible for his madness." I saw the medical case that I had brought to the Hanar's Palace sitting to one side. "The dust you breathed in at the stronghold is what causes the plague symptoms. You may still be Hsktskt enough for it to affect you as it does the people."

He followed the direction of my gaze. "What do you wish to do? Freeze me? Kill me before I go completely insane?"

I told him about the enzyme blocker ChoVa had created. "I think it will help until I can return to the lab with a sample of this dust."

PyrsVar nodded, and I removed an infuser and a specimen container. I set aside the instrument and opened the container, over which I shook my hair. Odnallak bone dust lodged in it drifted into the container. He came over and did the same, also brushing the dust from his tunic and face. Once I sealed the container, I prepared an infusion and rolled up his sleeve to administer it.

He watched as the green fluid slowly emptied from the chamber into his blood vessel. "You do not blame me for what my sire did."

"Cherijo, the woman I was, accidentally poisoned the Jorenian whose DNA was used to create you," I pointed out. "Should I be blamed for that?"

"No. It is only . . . " The tension left his shoulders. "SrrokVar created me as a weapon. I understood this—the Hsktskt I was volunteered to do this—but now I have no purpose. I cannot continue attacking the people as he slowly kills them. I do not belong on this world or any other."

"There is a place for you," I assured him. "You have only to find it."

"Jarn," a cold voice said from the opening to the cave shelter. "Move away from the outlaw."

I looked up and saw Reever standing only a few feet away, the rifle in his hands pointed at PyrsVar's head. "My husband," I murmured, unable to quite believe my eyes. "How did you find me?"

"I planted a locator in one of the outlaws' supply packs," Reever said. "I thought it might be useful to know where they were hiding." He enabled the rifle's power supply. "It is good to be correct."

"You know, the guy may be as passionate as a geranium," Maggie said from inside me, *"but occasionally he does have his moments."*

PyrsVar did not move. "So this is the day I die." His eyes moved to the Hsktskt who came up behind Reever. "The Akade himself. You must be an important female, Healer."

"TssVar." I rose to my feet, but I kept my body between Reever and PyrsVar. "Did they find ChoVa at the Palace?"

He nodded. "She is recovering at my estate."

"This is PyrsVar, war master of the outlaws," I told the men. "He saved my life."

"He abducted you twice," Reever said. "He shot ChoVa and killed the Hanar."

"If you don't want little bits of Hsktskt-Jorenian alter-formed crossbreed all over you, Jarn, you'd better start talking," Maggie advised me. *"Fast."*

"The Hanar intended to give me to him, and kill ChoVa for what he imagined was a coup attempt," I said, and saw a flicker of confusion pass over TssVar's features. "The Hanar was infected with the plague. He was almost insane by the time we were taken to the Palace." When Reever did not lower his rifle, I added, "Who did you think was eating his guards?"

"It makes no difference," my husband said. "Step aside, Cherijo."

"I am not Cherijo," I said for what I hoped was the last time, "and PyrsVar is not Kao Torin." I nodded as Reever's gaze finally tangled with mine. "I know about their relationship when she worked as a doctor on K-2, and how she chose Kao over you. Maggie is with me now."

"Maggie." He said the name like a death curse. "Maggie was a disease you were well rid of."

"I love you, too, you unfeeling, obsessive jerk," Maggie said from behind my eyes.

"Husband," I said softly. "Kao Torin died on the *Sunlace* in my arms. He could not be brought back. That PyrsVar was created with some of his cells is meaningless. He began life as a Hsktskt. He was only made to resemble Kao. This has nothing to do with us."

"It has everything to do with us," Reever said, enabling the rifle. "I will not let him come between us again. Not after all we have shared together."

"I can't believe he's still this jealous of Kao." Maggie made a clucking sound. *"Honey, you better work with him on this."*

Shut up, Maggie. "I was made from Joseph Grey Veil's cells," I reminded him. "Does this make me my father?"

TssVar put his hand on the barrel of the rifle. "She is right, HalaVar."

PyrsVar's expression did not change even as my husband lowered his weapon. To TssVar, he said, "I was deceived by my sire, but it matters not. My men are raiding a settlement. When they return, I would ask a measure of mercy for them. They are all without line. It was to become what we are, or die alone on the sands."

"We have greater concerns at the moment than your criminal activities," the Akade said. "The entire city is infected with this plague. When word of the Hanar's death spread, many went mad with fear. There is rioting in the streets, and the citizens have taken to the street. They are burning buildings, and killing each other indiscriminately."

"I know why." I gave TssVar a short explanation of the bone dust, and how it had been used to induce the fear. "I still do not know how it is being distributed, but I imagine it is by air. The dust must be breathed in to affect the victim."

Reever rubbed his temple. "Like the plague of K-2."

"So many happy memories of that place," Maggie chimed in.

"This is not a sentient colonial microorganism," I said. "We do not have to kill it. We only have to find a way to neutralize its effects on the brain." I gestured toward PyrsVar. "The war master has been exposed to a large amount of the dust, as have I. It can affect humanoids as well as Hsktskt. We need to find ChoVa and begin testing countermeasures immediately, before SrrokVar releases more dust into the atmosphere, or tries to smuggle it off planet."

"SrrokVar?" TssVar hissed the name with disgust. "That coward should have died after the fall of Catopsa. As it was, he nearly did, but then it was said that he elected to have reconstruction. His line was terminated and his name stricken from the official records. He was exiled from Vtaga for life."

"He has been here for years, building his secret stronghold and preparing his revenge," I said, and nodded toward PyrsVar. "The war master and the plague were merely components of his plan to take control of Vtaga and revive the war."

Now TssVar looked furious. "All of this was SrrokVar's doing? Tell me where this stronghold is."

"We'd better get moving on the plague and leave the big shoot-out revenge scene for later," Maggie reminded me. *"Unless you want all the lizards dead."*

"First take me to ChoVa," I said.

Some of the small army with which Reever and TssVar had invaded the desert warren remained behind to capture the band of outlaws, but the bulk of the men escorted us back to the Akade's estate. I saw ChoVa waiting at the landing pad, her head bound with a thick bandage.

PyrsVar walked between me and Reever, and scowled when he saw the Hsktskt physician. "She does not look pleased."

"You shot her in the head and killed her ruler," I reminded him. "She is entitled to be displeased."

Reever and TssVar went to speak with the Akade's personal guard. ChoVa ignored the renegade Jorenian as she greeted us.

"I was able to obtain several partial cadavers from the Hanar's Palace," she told me, glaring briefly at PyrsVar. "We must begin the autopsies immediately."

"I have a sample of what is causing the plague." I took the container of bone dust from my case and passed it to her. "It is a form of natural hallucinogen that stirs primal memory in your species. The plague is not viral or bacterial. It is drug-induced."

"If this is so, why did this substance not show up on our scans?" she demanded.

"That we will determine once we test PyrsVar," I said, gesturing to the war master. "He was exposed to a large amount of dust only a few hours ago."

"Excellent." ChoVa bared her teeth. "Will you kill him before I begin dissecting him, or will you allow me that small pleasure?"

Maggie whistled. *"Oooh, she's still a little pissed off."*

PyrsVar's dark brows elevated. "I only shot you in the head. I could have killed you easily. You should be grateful to me."

ChoVa made an ugly sound.

"PyrsVar? Shut up." I turned to the Hsktskt female. "We need him alive and responsive so that we can test neutralizing agents."

"I will not mutilate him," ChoVa said. "Badly."

"You can try." He showed her his own pointed teeth.

"Stop it, both of you," I shouted. "We have no time for this. People are killing each other. Now, are you going to assist me in finding the means to stop them, or must I shoot both of you and do it myself?"

ChoVa and PyrsVar stared at me, and then at each other.

"I can tolerate your presence," the Hsktskt physician muttered. "For a few more hours."

"And I you." PyrsVar turned to me. "As long as she does not attempt to dissect me."

"I do not have the means to determine the level of infection on a live specimen," ChoVa said to me. "Can you have your ship shuttle down what we will need?"

"Better yet," I said, looking at my husband and thinking of SrrokVar, "I think we should take PyrsVar to the *Sunlace*."

TssVar did not refuse my request to return to the ship, but he would not leave Vtaga to accompany us. "With the Hanar dead, and two of the other Akade missing, we need a semblance of leadership. I am going to the Palace to see what troops have not abandoned their posts."

"Eventually they all will," Reever said. "You

need non-Hsktskt troops to provide riot control and restore order."

"The only species I would trust to do so without massacring our citizens would be the Tingalean, and in situations of war they are neutral," the Akade told him.

"This is not a war," my husband said. "When we arrive on the ship, I will ask the captain to signal Tingal and request peacekeeping troops be sent to provide assistance."

TssVar nodded, and clasped Reever's forearm. "Tell my son his mother and I think of him with much affection and longing."

We gathered what we needed from ChoVa's lab and took the launch from the estate up to the ship. Maggie's voice inside my head finally quieted and gave me a chance to think about SrrokVar and the bone-dust hallucinogen. Reever stayed by me and held my hand, unwilling to let go of me.

I saw PyrsVar staring at both of us, but for Reever's sake I ignored him. When we reached the ship and flew into the launch bay, I realized what a shock PyrsVar's presence was going to be to the Torins.

"PyrsVar."

He stopped unfastening his harness and looked at me.

"You resemble someone who was held in high esteem by these people," I reminded him. "For them it will be as if the dead have come back to life. Remember that when they see you, and in how they react to you."

He nodded and finished releasing the harness.

ChoVa passed between us and gave him a hard look. "And try not to kill anyone."

"Refrain from tempting me," he muttered back.

I walked out between Reever and PyrsVar. The captain stood waiting on the deck below, and was in such an agitated state that at first he didn't seem to notice the renegade Jorenian.

"Cherijo, we were ready to begin sending warrior squads down to search for you. Reever." He turned and went very still at the sight of PyrsVar's face. His features turned a chalky pale blue, and his lips shaped the word "ClanBrother."

"Captain Xonea Torin, ClanLeader of HouseClan Torin, this is PyrsVar, war master of the Hsktskt outlaws." I awkwardly made the Jorenian gesture of introduction and decided to quickly relay the most important details of the situation. "PyrsVar is a bioengineered construct, as I am. He was alterformed with DNA taken from Kao Torin, your Clan-Brother."

"How can this be?" Xonea took a step backward. "Kao embraced the stars. He no longer travels this path."

"His body was stolen before it reached the twin stars of K-2," I said. When the captain's eyes filled with outrage, I added, "This was not PyrsVar's doing. He was created by SrrokVar, the scientist who tortured Cherijo when she was a slave of the Hsktskt. SrrokVar survived the fall of Catopsa."

Before Xonea could reply my daughter and Caur-Var rushed across the deck to meet us. Marel cried out her delight as she went first to hug her father's legs, then launched herself at me. As I picked her up and hugged her, I saw CaurVar exchanging words with his sister.

"Mama," Marel whispered when she had bestowed a damp kiss on my cheek, "why did you bring that bad man here?"

I glanced at PyrsVar, who was looking all around with keen interest.

"He is not a bad man," I promised her, and hoped that was the truth. "In a way, he is like your Clan-Uncle Squilyp. Only larger and . . . bluer."

Salo and Darea came forward, but both also stopped cold at the sight of the outlaw. Darea's eyes filled with tears. Salo curled his hand around the hilt of a dagger he wore at his waist.

"How can this be?" Darea whispered.

"I will explain," I told her. "But PyrsVar is not Kao. He was alterformed to appear like him."

"He smells like Hsktskt," Salo said, sounding cold and not at all inclined to weep.

"That is because he is part Hsktskt as well," I told him, shocking everyone anew.

Evidently unaware of the disturbance he was creating, PyrsVar turned to me and smiled at Marel. Even with the pointed teeth, this time the expression seemed more natural for him.

"She is fierce for one so small," he murmured, reaching out to touch her curly blond hair. "She would make a fine addition to my band."

Before he could, Reever seized his wrist. "Marel is my daughter," he told PyrsVar in a flat voice. "You will not touch her. Ever."

"As you wish." The renegade Jorenian dropped his arm. "I do not harm children."

"You will not be given the chance to start," Reever promised, his gaze lethal.

Xonea stepped forward, still pale but apparently recovered from the shock of seeing his Clan-Brother's physical twin. "We will have a briefing now, I think."

EIGHTEEN

ChoVa and I excused ourselves from the briefing, and accompanied PyrsVar to Medical, where we isolated him from the other patients and prepared what we would need for testing. We monitored the briefing from Medical while Squilyp scanned the three of us and treated the injuries PyrsVar had received while struggling with SrrokVar.

I felt glad when I heard Xonea agree to contact the Tingaleans and request their help in bringing the citizens of Vtaga under control until a treatment for the bone-dust epidemic could be formulated.

"A good choice," the captain said. "Tingalean venom is so lethal that they have learned to exercise great restraint during any manner of confrontation. As a reptilian species, they will also have some sympathy for the Hsktskt, and concern for finding and destroying this dust before it is taken and used on other species like theirs."

"One Hsktskt on the ship was stressful enough," Squilyp complained as he hopped into the forensics lab after me. "Now I have a Hsktskt, her brother, and a Hsktskt-Jorenian crossbreed who looks like a barbarian and behaves little better."

"He has been living in the desert for some time,

so he will seem a little primitive," I told him as I stored away the specimens ChoVa and I had brought back from the surface. "We need to run extensive analysis on the bone dust, and begin applying potential neutralizers as countermeasures. We can only do this with a living test subject, and PyrsVar has agreed to serve as one. I cannot send him back."

"PyrsVar." The Senior Healer shook his head as he followed me back out onto the ward. "What a name. Does having Kao Torin's DNA make him a ClanSon of the Torin?"

"I cannot say. You must ask the Jorenians. How are Garphawayn and your sons?" I asked, trying to distract him from the subject, which had drawn the attention of several of the nurses.

"My mate is fully recovered. The boys are thriving but need constant care. We enjoy little sleep." He sighed. "Fasala volunteered to help during the day to give Garphawayn an additional rest interval. I had no idea that two infants would require so much attention."

"Two are twice the work and joy of one." I retrieved a biopsy kit and checked it. "We are going to take samples of his nasal membranes. Do you wish to participate?"

"No, I will leave that to you and the Hsktskt. ChoVa," he corrected himself at my look. "Reever has been here three times since you returned from the surface. What is wrong with him?"

Reever felt as nervous as everyone else was, but for different reasons. "Kao Torin and my former self were lovers," I said. "Evidently Cherijo chose Kao over Reever. PyrsVar's presence brings back unhappy memories."

"Ah." Squilyp grimaced. "That all happened before I joined the crew."

"Imagine how I feel." I went into the isolation room, where ChoVa was arguing with PyrsVar over removing a talisman he wore around his neck. I had to clear my throat twice before they fell silent. "I would like to take this biopsy before there is no reason to find a cure for this epidemic," I said. "Can we proceed?"

"I want you to do it," PyrsVar said to me. "I do not want her to part me from any of my flesh."

ChoVa chuffed her amusement. "So speaks the fearless outlaw." Her eyelids drooped. "Perhaps not the best choice of words. Of course Dr. Torin will take the biopsy. I might mistake that tiny brain of yours for the needed tissue and extract it instead." She stalked out of the room.

PyrsVar settled back on the berth. "She does not despise me as much as she thinks she does," he said with a certain amount of satisfaction.

"Don't push it," I said, and frowned. Some of the words and phrases coming from my mouth since being exposed to the dust were beyond odd. "What I mean is, do not provoke her. She may be slow to lose her temper, but I have seen what she can do when she does."

"Indeed, and what can a female healer do?"

"She can perform this biopsy," I told him, showing him the tissue probe. "Without giving you anesthetic. And with the application of a little pressure, can drive this instrument up into your brain."

The sight of the thin, sharp-ended, hollow biopsy tube made PyrsVar swallow. "So I will not provoke her or you."

I smiled. "That is best."

Complete scans of PyrsVar's body had to be performed before the biopsy could begin, and when they were finished I transferred the results onto a data-and-image projector so ChoVa and I could analyze his unique physiology.

"I have never seen the like," ChoVa said with a certain amount of awe as she inspected the data. "Outwardly he is little different from these Jorenians, but inside, he is a warm-blooded version of a Hsktskt."

"The organ arrangement is not Jorenian," I agreed, "but it is not altogether Hsktskt, either."

"You are correct." She peered at the circulatory scans. "He has humanoid vessels and several organs we do not possess. But look, his bone structure and muscle mass match that of my kind. How did this SrrokVar achieve such a sophisticated integration?"

"He had much practice experimenting on humanoid slaves on Catopsa," I told her. "Then there is this new alterforming technology. Genetically PyrsVar is exactly between Jorenian and Hsktskt. I wonder if SrrokVar purposely left enough of him unchanged to someday return him to his original form."

ChoVa shook her head. "Alterforming is irreversible; it would kill him. Then, too, there is this peculiar crossing of the two species' physiologies. Look at the heart and lungs. They are fully integrated with these other Jorenian organs. To alter them back to those of the Hsktskt would cause immediate renal failure. His liver would enlarge and likely hemorrhage. We could not transplant replacement organs in time to prevent it."

"He will always have to be like this," I murmured. "A true crossbreed."

"His children would not," ChoVa said as she pulled up the reproduction system analysis. "He is fertile. His children would inherit some of his Jorenian characteristics, but if he mated with a female Hsktskt, three-quarters of their DNA would match my species."

I chuckled. "There is only one way to know."

"What do you mean? It does not bear thinking about." ChoVa's expression indicated the exact opposite, and several other times during the course of the procedure I caught her eyeing our patient with a less than professional scrutiny.

The biopsy of the nasal membrane produced small samples of tissue that had darkened but were not yet black. All were liberally impregnated with the bone dust, and the levels of tohykul in his gland cluster were rising. I administered another dose of blocker before ChoVa and I went to consult with the Senior Healer. Given our experience with the progression of the disease, we could make only one diagnosis.

"He will succumb to this, more slowly than a pureblood Hsktskt, but in time as fully," I reported to the Omorr. "Given the rate of escalation in his enzyme levels, I would say we have four, perhaps five days at the most, before the final-stage symptoms are presented."

"As we speak on symptoms, I have a request." ChoVa handed a datapad I had not seen to Squilyp. "These are my readings, taken just before we left the surface. "If they elevate to the saturation level, you are to sedate me and put me into cryopreservation."

The Omorr shook his head. "That will kill you."

"There is nothing else you can do, except let me run rampant on this vessel. No one would be safe from me," the Hsktskt female said in a practical tone. "Whatever you may think of my kind, I did not deliver your brood to see them die under my claws."

Squilyp looked uncomfortable. "I spoke in anger. I have apologized for it."

"But you still think the same way," ChoVa said. "I saw how you looked at my brother and PyrsVar. You see us and you only see slavers beneath the scales. I suggest that for once you heed your own prejudice." She rose from her chair. "Excuse me. I will check on the patient." She left.

"Nice going, Squid Lips." I took in a quick breath and touched my fingers to my mouth. "Why do I say these things? I am sorry, I never meant—"

He smiled at me as if he were pleased. "Your memories are speaking for you. Cherijo used to call me that when she was annoyed with me."

"*You see?*" Maggie, silent for so many hours, suddenly laughed inside me. "*You may think you can kill her by ignoring what few memories I passed to you, but you can't. She's still in here somewhere. She's still part of you.*"

"She should let me run my own mouth," I muttered. I saw the Omorr frown and got up quickly. "I'll go and report our status to the captain."

I spent the next two days in Medical, working around the clock in the lab with ChoVa and testing various compounds on the bone dust and PyrsVar. When I tired, I went to rest in one of the patient berths, but rarely slept for more than an hour. I was too conscious of the time slipping away, and we knew from sporadic reports from the surface that the situation on Vtaga was growing worse by the hour.

Reever stopped in frequently, sometimes bringing Marel for a quick visit, and other times to stand outside the lab and watch ChoVa and me as we performed tests. Often I would look up and prepare to set something aside so I could go and speak to him, but he would only shake his head and retreat.

"Your mate watches you a great deal," ChoVa mentioned after the fourth or fifth time she saw Reever outside the observation viewer. "Does it not irritate you?"

"Not especially," I said. "He is worried about me. He does not like it when I work extended shifts." I rubbed the side of my head. "It is a show of affection."

"Ah." She nodded. "He wishes more attention. My mother can behave that way when my father becomes consumed with his work."

I didn't tell her that Reever spent as much time, if not more, watching PyrsVar. When he did, his expression was far from pleasant. He had a deep and abiding dislike, if not hatred, for the renegade Jorenian, and I knew it was because of my past relationship with Kao Torin. Had he hated Cherijo's first love just as fiercely?

I could not bring myself to ask.

The equipment speeded up the process somewhat, but after ChoVa and I had tested two hundred unique chemical compounds, we still have no viable treatment for the bone-dust infection.

"Nothing neutralizes the effects or flushes it from the body," ChoVa complained as we left Medical to have a meal in the galley. "It will dissolve in nothing but the most corrosive acids which, as much as I would like to apply them to the patient, is not a treatment option."

"It is bone. Bone is usually the hardest and most resilient tissue in any organism's body." I nodded to two passing crew members as we entered a lift they had just occupied. "I think we are taking the wrong approach. We are treating this dust like a viral infection when we know it is not."

"What else would you have us treat it as?" she inquired as she walked up to the food machine and examined the menu. "Dirt?"

"That is all it is, when you stop to think about it," I said, leaning in front of her and pulling up the specialty menu for reptilian visitors. "Inert dust, impregnated with an organism that provokes a specialized autoimmune response. Like an allergen in humanoids. When certain Terrans aspirate plant pollen, for example, they sneeze violently and become congested. It is a defense mechanism on the part of the body, to eject the invader and protect the membranes from being further exposed. Were it viral or bacterial in nature, it would multiply. It does not reproduce."

"But if you are right," ChoVa said, taking the bowl of synthetic, shredded, raw flesh she had selected from the unit, "why would our symptoms manifest as extreme fear, suicide, and general insanity?"

I dialed up a traditional Iisleg stew and followed her to an empty table. "What if these ancient terrors your people feared, like the rogur, shed chemicals, or cells, or some other sensory evidence of themselves? The Hsktskt of that time would have inhaled them. We know that the body's response was to induce panic so that the victim would run away, or fight to get away."

"That does not explain the feelings of suicide."

"What awaited the victim who did not get away from the rogur? A lingering and horrible death. Perhaps it was a last-resort defense mechanism, to spare the victim and spite the monster."

"Spite the monster?"

"You told me that the rogur was said to have digested live prey slowly," I reminded her. "Perhaps it would not eat the dead."

ChoVa looked down at her meal. "Suddenly I am not very hungry."

I pushed my bowl toward her. "It's cooked, and it's synthetic for humanoids, but it was never anything but anonymous organic matter."

"I cannot digest any manner of cooked food." She poked at the raw flesh in her bowl. "It makes me regurgitate."

I gave her a sympathetic look. "I feel the same way about vegetables."

Her head snapped up. "That is it. Regurgitation."

"Not here," I said, alarmed, and pointed past her. "There is a lavatory unit just around the corner."

"No, I mean the process. What my body will not accept it rejects, as you said, like an allergen." She tapped the side of her head. "Only the process in Hsktskt is not the same as it is for humanoids."

"You vomit differently?"

"No, we vomit the same. It is just that a pair of enzymes is released in our brains before we vomit," she explained. "One triggers the sensation of nausea, warning us that we are about to purge. The other causes the physical act of regurgitation."

"In humanoids, stomach fluids do both."

"I know. In my kind, however, we cannot vomit unless both enzymes are present. All such reactions in my people are created by enzyme pairs." She took out her scanner and showed me the latest of PyrsVar's brain scan results. "Inhaling the bone dust released the tohykul enzyme. That we know. But the enzyme it was paired with in ancient Hsktskt, barolyt, has not manifested. The result is the brain disorder. Our minds are being told to do one thing, but our bodies are not coping with the mechanism delivering it."

I understood her point. "If you have one enzyme for regurgitation, you feel sick, but you can't vomit without the other, so the sickness never goes away."

She nodded. "Here is what I think. The enzyme being produced is only present in our bodies when we are infants, and then it disappears. A tiny amount of barolyt, the other half of the pair, is what makes it vanish. Like tohykul, it is only produced in healthy Hsktskt immediately after birth."

I felt skeptical. "Why have you never detected it?"

"We have had no reason to go looking for it," she said. "I believe it is produced, but in such small amounts and for such a short period of time that it is almost undetectable."

"The only way to know would be to test the brain of a healthy, living Hsktskt infant," I pointed out, "which we do not have and I would not let you do if we did."

"The number of enzymes the Hsktskt brain is capable of producing is finite," ChoVa assured me. "And even better, the ones we know of have the same basic chemical structure. All we need do is recombine enzymes until we find the one that neutralizes the tohykul, and that should cause the body to eject the bone dust from the respiratory tract."

My wristcom light came on, distracting me. I switched on my personal com. "Yes?"

"Jarn, I need you and ChoVa back in Medical," the Omorr said. He sounded breathless, and someone was shouting in the background. Someone using the Hsktskt version of profanity. "At once."

We abandoned our unwanted meals and hurried back. I heard the banging of alloy and shattering of plas from outside in the corridor, and had to duck as we entered to avoiding a patient's chart flying through the air.

In the center of Medical stood the Omorr and PyrsVar. PyrsVar was bleeding from his neck, arms, and chest, where he had wrenched out the intra-venous tubes we were using to administer test compounds.

"The enzyme-suppression therapy isn't working as well as we hoped," Squilyp said as he hopped to avoid one of PyrsVar's fists. "Our patient seems to have developed a tolerance for it, and has indicated that he would like to leave ship at once."

ChoVa stepped forward. "Outlaw, control your-self."

"Hold your tongue, female," PyrsVar shouted. "I am not staying here another moment. Get out of my way, Warm-Blood, or I will dine on your flesh."

I picked up an infuser and dialed up a powerful sedative used primarily on Jorenians, and tossed it to ChoVa before I approached the pair.

"PyrsVar, I will escort you to the surface." I held out my hands so that he could see I held nothing.

"You." He pointed an enabled lascalpel at my head. "You stay away from me."

He did not understand the power of the surgical instrument he held. I did. "If you trigger the cutting beam and sweep it across my throat, you will sever my head from my shoulders. Hold it steady, and it will bore through my skull and brain." I lifted a hand to my hair, touching the spot where Daneeb had used her pulse weapon on me. "Use it here, and my body will live, but I will die. As you died, Clan-Son Torin."

"I am not one of them," he shouted.

A curious tenderness for him came over me, what a scarred adult would feel for a bleeding child. "I know, PyrsVar. I know, better than anyone."

ChoVa came up behind PyrsVar, pinned him back against her with two limbs, and infused him with the drug. He roared, groaned, and then slid down to the deck. She picked him up with some difficulty, hoisted his body over her shoulder, and carried him back into the isolation room.

"He has been displaying signs of aggressiveness since yesterday," she said as we strapped him down in restraints. "But I had thought he would last longer than I."

"He received a much higher dose of the bone dust than you or the other Hsktskt. He was covered in it." I looked down at his closed eyes, and brushed a tangle of black hair away from his brow. "He has some humanoid characteristics. As a warm-blooded being, he may fare better in cryostasis."

"No." The ferocity of her reply seemed to surprise her as much as it did me. "No," she said, more gently. "We will find the right combination for the neutralizer. We will keep him sedated until we do."

I nodded and saw Squilyp in the doorway. "Did he hurt anyone?"

"Not this time." The Omorr looked grim. "Jarn, TssVar signaled. The rioters have surrounded the Palace. He is barricaded inside, but it is only a matter of hours before the fires they are setting overwhelm the Palace defense system."

Time, our most precious commodity, had just run out.

NINETEEN

Skipping the meal interval had no effect on me for several hours, but the close proximity to ChoVa did. She had begun muttering to herself under her breath, and cursing softly when the bone dust and PyrsVar's biopsies showed no reaction to the synthetic enzymes we were testing.

"I think I will go and visit my daughter for a short time," I finally said after she called the fourteenth enzyme the sort of names I would not have used to describe a Kangal prince, the lowest order of life-form that I knew. "I miss my kid. When I get back, you should also take a rest interval."

She glared at me. "I am not insane yet, you know."

"I know. You're worried about your dad." The fact that Cherijo's speech patterns were taking over my own didn't bother me anymore. They felt right, mixed in as they were with my own manner of speaking. "He's an experienced warrior. He'll be smart, and he'll fight to the end."

ChoVa straightened and pressed her hands against the back of her neck. "You are correct, of course. I apologize. This thing . . . consumes my self-control."

I left her and disdained the lift to make the short walk to my quarters. It felt good to stretch my legs after so many hours of sitting at the scope and studying specimen slides. I yawned as I turned a corner and nearly ran into Xonea, who was striding quickly down the corridor.

"Cherijo." He caught me and steadied me. "I had thought you would be in Medical."

"I needed a little exercise, and some time away from the equipment." I saw him looking past me. "What is wrong?"

"Nothing too dire. Your ClanDaughter and that Hsktskt child have been getting into mischief," Xonea said. "Fasala told me that she believes they have been slipping away to use one of the envirodomes without adult supervision." He continued down the corridor.

Guilt swamped me, and I hurried after him. "Captain, I am sorry. I should have made arrangements for someone to care for them."

He smiled. "Have you not enough to do in Medical?"

"Marel is my child, and Reever and I agreed to be responsible for CaurVar while he was on the ship," I reminded him.

"Children belong to the House. We all of us are responsible for them." He nodded toward a secured envirodome. "There, that one was not scheduled for use this day." He went to the panel and punched in an override code. "We will catch them at their mischief this time."

The entry panel slid open, and I followed Xonea inside. The simulator was running a program of a shoreline by an alien ocean. The pair lying together on the purple sands, however, was not Marel and CaurVar.

"Qonja." Xonea's gaze shifted and his smile flattened. "Hawk."

As soon as I saw that the two men were almost naked and in an intimate embrace, I turned around. "Captain, we should try the one on the next level," I said quickly. "I have seen Marel near there in the past. Come, I will show you."

"I cannot leave, Cherijo." Xonea's voice lost all warmth as he spoke to Qonja. "Your pardon, I did not intend to intrude upon your privacy."

I looked over my shoulder. Qonja was helping Hawk to his feet, and although the winged Terran looked pale, the Jorenian did not seem upset.

"No matter." Qonja put his arm around his companion. "We no longer wish to hide our affection for each other."

The captain made a quick gesture. "Warriors often form close bonds with one another in times of duress, when they are far from their Chosen. There is no shame in it."

"No, Xonea, this is not what you wish it to be." Qonja took Hawk's hand in his. "We are not on the field of battle, and there are no women waiting for us on Joren."

"Terran," Xonea said to Hawk, ignoring Qonja now. "Our ways are not the same. You have no obligation to the future, but Qonja does. He cannot indulge in this . . . pleasure with you. He must bond. He must produce children for his House. That is his path."

"I understand," Hawk said quietly. "I know the Jorenian customs. I have tried to respect them."

"I have not shown the proper respect," Qonja said, looking angry now. "Perhaps it is time that I do." He turned to Hawk. "You know how I feel for you. There is no other I honor more. You honor me as well. We walk the path together."

"Qonja," Xonea said, stepping forward and reaching out as if he meant to grab him. "Do not say more. You have already violated HouseClan law."

"I must show respect for the one who holds my heart," the Jorenian said simply. "That is why I Choose you, Hawk." He kissed the Terran's forehead, and then his cheek, and then his mouth. "There are no ritual words for what we are, and what we feel. I offer you my honor and my kinship for as long as we walk the path together."

Xonea closed his eyes for a moment. "I must summon your ClanLeader and inform him of this. It is my obligation to the Adan."

"Please don't." Hawk suddenly panicked. "Qonja spoke in haste. He is not thinking of the consequences."

"Too late," Qonja said softly as Xonea nodded and left the envirodome.

Hawk looked at me. "What will we do now?"

I did not know how to answer.

Even isolated as we were in Medical, the scandal of Qonja Choosing Hawk swept through the ship and served as the source of a hundred whispered conversations an hour. The nurses spoke of it only when they thought we could not hear, but the consensus was obvious and smothering—what the two men had done was wrong, and had to be met with dire consequences.

"I do not understand Jorenians," I said as I passed a slide with a negative reaction to the latest test enzyme to ChoVa. "What does it matter if two men care for each other so much? Can they not spare one breeder to live life as he wishes, with the one he loves?"

"I do not know. There are some like them among us, but it is not a condoned practice among Hsktskt, and so they keep to themselves. Mating for us, like the Jorenians, is to proliferate and strengthen the bloodline." She shrugged. "Some are said to form mating bonds simply to conceal the other relationship."

The amount of gossip was what most disgusted Squilyp, whose people were extremely circumspect about their personal relationships. He did admit that there were same-gender couples on Omorr, but they were treated the same as mixed-gender couples.

"One cares for whom one cares for," he muttered to me after reprimanding two nurses for passing gossip on to one of the patients. "Whether they can reproduce or not. In every society there are always orphans in need of good homes, are there not? It is no one's business what genders are listed on the mating contract."

It seemed faintly ridiculous to me for the Jorenians to be so obsessed about Qonja's Choice when we were fighting a losing battle against the genocide of the Hsktskt species, but a meeting of the department heads was called to bear witness as Clan-Leader Adan levied punishment on Qonja for making his forbidden Choice.

Squilyp refused to attend and sent me in his place. "If I go, I will say something thoughtless, and possibly start a war between Joren and Omorr. You know how to be silent." He glanced at me. "You do still know how, do you not?"

"Even when I do not wish to," I agreed.

I went, and sat beside Alunthri. The talking feline nodded to me, but only watched in silence as Qonja and Hawk were brought before the Adan.

Xonea was called upon to recount what had happened. He did so, leaving out all but the most relevant details, and then ClanLeader Tlore asked Qonja and Hawk to verify the captain's version of the incident.

He was giving them one last chance, I realized, to back out of their relationship.

Qonja never hesitated a moment. "It is as the captain has said. I was with Hawk, as I have been for some time now. We honor each other deeply. I Chose him before Xonea and Healer Torin. He will be mine by bond."

Tlore Adan turned to me as if seeking one hint of denial. "Healer, it is good that you are here. Is that which the captain and Qonja Adan have said the same as what you saw and heard?"

I thought of all the things I could say. I was, after all, one of the rulers of these people. Perhaps I could change the law to make things equal for Qonja and Hawk. But I recalled what the Omorr had said, and how little I still knew of Joren and its people.

"Tell them the truth," Alunthri said softly. "It is all that ever matters."

I met its clear gaze before I turned to the Clan-Leader and nodded.

The Adan sat back and covered his face with his hands for a moment. It was an awful gesture, like that of an Iisleg male shamed into weeping. The other members of his HouseClan looked just as miserable. At last the ClanLeader stood and addressed the two men.

"Few Jorenian customs cannot be circumvented by some means, but our survival as a species depends on the matter of Choice and Bond. You are much beloved by us, Qonja, but I cannot make an exception for you. In our society, men Choose women, and that is the law. Anyone who violates the law cannot go unpunished."

"I understand, ClanLeader," Qonja said, and bowed. "I am willing to face the consequences."

"Very well." He stood very straight and looked directly at Qonja. "ClanSon of HouseClan Adan, you are repudiated. No more are you a member of our House. No more do you enjoy a place among us. No more will you be counted as kin. All Adan shall be made aware of this."

I could not stand to watch another moment of the ritual, so I slipped out of the briefing room and walked for a time. The sadness I felt for the two men outweighed my anger at the Adan. Custom or law, people had their ways, and one could not defy them without knowing the price of punishment. Still, it seemed a terrible thing, as if the Adan had killed Qonja rather than simply disowning him.

I ended up standing outside our quarters, staring at the door but unwilling to go inside. Qonja had sacrificed everything for Hawk. I knew how that felt, for I had done the same for Marel.

What had I done for Reever?

"You witnessed the repudiation," my husband said from behind me.

I turned and pressed a hand over my pounding heart. "Yes. The Senior Healer felt the process was too embarrassing, and so he sent me in his place. I sat with Alunthri. You scared the living hell out of me. Cough or something . . . next . . . time . . ." I swayed on my feet and then clenched my fists. "I am sorry. Sometimes . . . sometimes the memories make her words come out of my mouth."

Reever came and put his arms around me, and gently led me inside. "You are trembling."

"I'm so afraid. Every other time I go to speak now, it is as if she chooses my words for me." I buried my face against his chest. "I know you wish her back with you more than anything, but I don't want to die, Husband. I am greedy. Greedy for my life, and this body, and you and Marel."

He picked me up and carried me to the big chair where he often sat and read to Marel.

"Where is the little one?" I asked wearily.

"She is staying the night with Garphawayn and the twins." He stroked a hand over my hair. "There is no reason to be frightened. The speech patterns are likely due to the transfer of memories. Nothing will take you away from us."

I covered my eyes with one hand. "But you want

me to be her. It is all you have ever wanted from me."

"In the beginning, when I didn't understand, perhaps I did. But now . . . " He tugged my hand down so that I could see his eyes. "You do not have to be Cherijo. You have only to be yourself, Jarn. Marel and I have come to love you for who you are."

"*Ask him about Kao,*" Maggie said sweetly. "*Ask him about the oath he took for him.*"

I pulled back. "You took an oath for Kao?"

He blinked, and then nodded. "Maggie is still with you, I gather."

"I hardly understood anything she said until she gave me back some of Cherijo's memories," I admitted. "If it is painful to you, you need not tell me."

"I never told you," he murmured. "Cherijo never knew how . . . damaged . . . I was when we met. In spite of that, she healed me. Almost exactly as you did when you found me on Akkabarr."

Disbelief made me shake my head. "I have read Cherijo's journals. She never saw anything wrong with you other than your lack of emotion and the ways in which you were not very human." I remembered how I had first met him, battle-blind and wounded on a rebel battlefield. "I had thought you only a very fortunate soldier."

Reever looked into my eyes. "I will link with you, and I will show you what you don't know, but you must be sure that this is what you want. They are not happy memories, Jarn."

"I was damaged, and I did not have a happy life," I told him. "Until I found you and our child."

He nodded and joined his hands to mine. *Relax,*

he thought as the link seized me. *See through my eyes.*

One moment I was Jarn, in a female body, filled with knowledge and skills of my own, and the next I was tall and lean and dangerous, an alert male, seeing everyone and everything as threats or tools.

I had not achieved the balance I had sought, but I could not go on pretending that I would. I would never save as many lives as I had taken in the arena. What I had done would have to be enough.

It was time.

Obtaining what I needed presented a minor problem. I owned several pulse weapons, but using them would trigger the colony surface-security grid. Subsequent medical attention might foil my attempt, so it would not be advisable to use any weapon that might summon assistance. I disliked the thought of using a blade—I had seen many do the same in the slave cages before arena games, and it took too long. I preferred something more efficient. The most logical solution was chemical, but as I had no knowledge of drugs or access to medical stores, it would be difficult to obtain them. The Bartermen might possess what I needed to accomplish the task, but I was not inclined to trade with them for what I could steal myself. What I needed to know was the precise compound and amount that would bring a swift resolution. I would have to access the medical database and make a discreet inquiry, then visit the FreeClinic to retrieve the drugs.

I jerked back, breaking free of the link to stare at my husband. "Suicide. You were planning to kill yourself while you were on K-2?"

"Yes. I was very tired, and I felt defeated. I had no place, and no one with whom I could share it. I feared what I might become if I continued on as I had been, betraying the only people who had valued me to save humanoids who would never understand me." He took my hand and held it over his heart. "And then you came and ruined everything."

Satisfied that I had found the proper solution to my problem, I finished my coffee, and was preparing to leave when I became aware of something strange.

Someone was near. Someone like me.

My years in the arena had helped me develop a kind of proximity sense, a defense against unexpected assaults or attacks while I was asleep. This was like that sensation . . . but at the same time, it was not. I concentrated, opening my mind in order to locate the source.

"Here we are," a familiar female voice said. "Lisette Dubois's foster family owned a restaurant in Paris."

I saw Administrator Ana Hansen escorting an unfamiliar Terran female through the café. The strange woman was quite short, barely five feet in height, and very thin. She wore her dark hair in a woven cable, clipped against the back of her head. Her hair appeared clean, if somewhat in need of better grooming, and there was an overcast to it—a faint, silver sheen I had only seen among elderly Terrans. Yet, from the texture of her skin, I assumed she was quite young. Her features betrayed some elusive ethnic ancestry I could not identify.

The little Terran female noticed a group near my table, and as she watched them the corners of her mouth went up—she smiled, I corrected myself—before she encountered my own gaze.

I did not find her particularly attractive in any physical sense—she had as much allure as a malnourished child—and Administrator Hansen's presence indicated she was a new transfer to the colony. I always avoided humans like her, but I felt a compulsion to continue watching her. I wanted to speak to her and learn her name. Yet I had no justification for the interest.

Her expression changed as she returned the visual assessment. Of all her physical characteristics, her dark blue eyes were the most remarkable. Her gaze was direct and intent, almost fearless. She appeared perfectly at ease, in command of the situation. However, she did not feel as confident behind that carefully schooled countenance.

She is afraid.

She may have been unconsciously projecting her emotions. The only way I could be sure would be to go to her and place my hands on her. I only touched another being to establish a telepathic link to that individual's speech center, and I already thoroughly comprehended all Terran native languages. I doubted I could actively probe her mind. I had not been successful with the Hsktskt, but I had never had much opportunity—or desire—to link in such an intimate manner with other humanoids. Perhaps if I could strengthen the involuntary connection between us, it would help me understand what she was, and why she was afraid.

My own thoughts bewildered me. There is no reason for this. I didn't care how she felt. Our present situation did not justify even the most limited physical contact. She could give me nothing of use. Even as I acknowledged that, I still wondered—Why is she afraid? Am I frightening her?

That was when a strange vision came to me.

I saw the small Terran, dressed differently, standing before me. We were alone in an agricultural area where I had often worked. All of my attention was focused on her.

A violent determination filled me, and I took her wrists in my hands. I could feel the thin, delicate bones shift as I lifted her hands up to my face. I was focusing on her, reaching in to gather—

The link faded, and I found myself standing in front of Reever, staring down at him. "That happened. I remember. And you saw it before it did."

"I had never had such a vision," he said. "It intrigued me. It kept me alive until I could know better. I kept my distance, however." His mouth twisted as he stood and took my hands in his. "And I paid for it."

The Jorenian pilot stood waiting by my door panel. "You are Duncan Reever?"

"Yes." I studied him. He had the physical advantage of height and weight, but I was probably faster. "What do you want?"

He wore his black hair in a warrior's knot at the base of his skull, and it gleamed as he made a formal gesture. "I would speak with you."

I knew his kind declared their intention to kill before fighting, and he had no reason to be polite to an enemy. Based on that assumption, I invited him in, and offered him the tea his people preferred. He refused. We moved into my living area. There we faced each other like opponents, neither of us making any unnecessary movements. I concentrated on remaining calm and nonconfrontational. If he attacked me and I killed him—even in self-defense—she would never forgive me.

"I am told you traveled with Cherijo Grey Veil, to Caszaria's Moon." His blank, white eyes met mine. Jorenians had no pupils or irises, which was somewhat disconcerting. "Cherijo is my Chosen."

"Yes. Her friend, the Oenrallian Dhreen, also accompanied us." I knew Jorenians were notoriously possessive about their lifemates, and chose my next words carefully. "I was not aware that she had Chosen you until after we arrived. I accept her Choice." No, I didn't, but I could make a show of it. "I would not have accompanied her, had I known."

"A Jorenian female would never have accompanied you alone, but Cherijo is still . . . unused to the ways of my kind." He made a fluid gesture with his hands. "That is not why I am here."

I tensed as he drew an ornate dagger, but he only offered it to me. "Why do you give me this?"

"The Oenrallian told me how you protected her at the resort. I wish to express gratitude for that." He placed the hilt in my hand. "My thanks for your care of my Chosen, warrior."

I studied the blade. It was beautifully worked, honed to a razor's edge. I could bury it in his chest with a simple sweep of my arm. I also knew many ways to dispose of a body. "I do not require thanks."

"It is difficult for rivals to exchange gifts, is it not?" He smiled a little. "Perhaps you will wish to keep it after you hear what I ask of you in return."

Only a Jorenian would have the spine to do that. "What?"

"You know that war is coming."

Suddenly I felt very tired. I went to my console, and saw the reflection of the blade in my hand. "Yes. Very soon."

"It will not be a simple act of aggression. It will be the League against the Hsktskt. Their battles will consume whole systems, quadrants. The conflict will divert many *paths—particularly among those of us who serve in space."* His voice took on a strange note. *"It is not my war, but I suspect I will fight it—and I may perish in it."*

I spun the dagger like a top. "Death comes to us all."

"I do not fear it. That is not the way of my people." He went on to describe the traditional Jorenian preparations for a death ritual, and finally asked, "Duncan Reever, when I embrace the stars, will you serve as my Speaker?"

His request made me catch the dagger in midspin. From what he had told me, a Jorenian's Speaker brought the deceased's last wishes to his kin. It was a task given only to a trusted family member or close friend. "Why ask me?"

"You honor her as much as I."

I flipped the blade into my palm, made it dance over my fingers. "I could kill you."

He nodded. "And I you."

Yet we would not, for her sake. It seemed we understood each other perfectly.

"Yes. I will Speak for you."

"When the time comes, I will send for you." He bowed and departed.

I did not want to admit it, but I liked Kao Torin. He was not Cherijo's balance, but I suspected he would give her a great deal of happiness. Since I could not do that, and I could not kill him, I would have to be content with that.

Slowly I emerged from the link. I was in my husband's arms, and he was carrying me into our sleeping chamber. I felt exhausted.

"That is enough for now," he told me.

Now that I knew why he had been so jealous of

Kao, I had to make him understand what had happened on Akkabarr.

"I never coupled with Teulon or Resa," I told him. "Our involvement was of mutual affection. There was a night when I might have, when Resa and I went to him, but after Teulon woke I chose to leave them. Teulon had no desire for two women, as Iisleg men do. I knew if he and Resa could be alone together, they might heal each other."

Reever sighed. "You did not have to tell me this."

"We must be open to each other." I had sensed something more waiting beyond the memory of Duncan's first meeting with Kao Torin. "I can feel you. You are still holding back something from me. Show me the rest."

Reever placed me on our sleeping platform and stretched out beside me. For the first time he looked hesitant. "It may make you angry."

"I think I have to know."

He nodded, and bent his head to mine, and kissed me.

As I was bandaging my self-inflicted wound, I received a summons to the FreeClinic. It was not from Cherijo, but from her Jorenian pilot. Kao Torin wished to see his Speaker.

I encountered Cherijo on my way to see him. She strode out of the back entrance of the facility and hurried past me. I went after her.

"Get away from me, Reever."

I couldn't, not without speaking to her. "Cherijo, stop."

She walked blindly on. We entered a dead-end alley,

but she kept going until she reached the back wall. Then she shouted, "No!"

I caught up to her, and reached for her.

She turned and nearly went to her knees, her hands curled and pressed against either side of her brow. "I can't stop it! I can't!"

"No, you can't." *I didn't know what else to say. I was going to see her dying lover, to receive his last wishes. I should have felt it like a victory, but all I felt was her pain.*

He was dying because she had injected him with her own blood, and it was poisoning him.

She lunged at me and knocked me to the ground, screaming in my face. I did not defend myself as she struck me, over and over. She was wild, sobbing, completely out of control.

I linked with her. Cherijo, stop.

No! I will not! Let me go!

It felt as if my chest was torn in two. Cherijo. Stop fighting me. Let me help you.

Pure hatred poured into my mind from hers. I never wanted you. Never wanted this. Get out, just get out of me!

Let me help you. *I showed her everything she denied—her own memories. The epidemic. Its aftermath. Alun Karas's innocent mistake. The thousands who had become infected, and would have died. I took her back to the groves, made her watch the exudation, made her see the dying as they recovered.* The colony lives. The Core lives. Your gift to them.

I brought her into my own memories, made her see the Core attack as I had experienced it. How it felt to be unable to stop them. How we had both been raped. How I had nearly died in the darkness that had followed. How she had saved me despite what I had done. I live. Your gift to me.

I made her see Kao Torin, dying on the ward where she had left him. Then further back in time, to the moment just before she had injected him with her own blood. He had died. She had brought him back to life. Kao Torin lives. He has the time to bid farewell to those he honors. To you. Your gift to him.

I can't bear it. *All the rage left her, leaving only grief and self-loathing.* Oh, God, Duncan, I can't. I can't.

I ended the link, and held her until she stopped shaking. Then I helped her to her feet.

"Duncan." *She tried to touch my face, then snatched her hand back.* "Oh, no, what have I done?"

"I will recover." *I wiped some blood from my nose and mouth with the back of my sleeve.* "Be at peace, Cherijo. Be at peace with yourself." *I let her go, and moved away.*

"Duncan."

I stopped.

"I'm . . . I'm sorry."

So was I.

I was weeping as we both emerged from the link, and Reever kissed away each tear. I took a moment to steady myself, and then I looked into his eyes. They were wet. He was waiting for my permission to go into the last, worst memory. "I'm ready."

I was not prepared to see the Jorenian as he was. His body looked wasted, his face gray with pain and fatigue. Yet when I drew a chair up beside his berth, he opened his eyes and made a gesture of welcome.

"I thank you for coming." He studied my face. "You are injured?"

"A small accident. It's nothing." Hopefully my eyes would not swell shut from the beating Cherijo had given me in her grief before we were finished, or I would need assistance returning to my quarters. "Are you sure you want to do this now?"

"I am dying." He smiled. "When my House is before you, will you Speak for me?"

"Yes."

He drew in a shallow breath, then made his formal requests. When he had finished, he asked, "Do you still have the dagger?"

I produced the blade, and handed it to him.

He turned it slowly in his hand. "This is not part of my Speaking, but I must also ask this of you." He gazed at me. "After I embrace the stars, I would ask that you Choose Cherijo."

"I will look after her—"

"No. That is not enough. You must Choose her."

I wanted to bury the blade in my own chest this time. "I can't. You don't know . . . you don't know what I am. What I have done."

"There is no one for her but you. No one else is strong enough to protect her. No one else honors her more. This is all that matters to me." His hand shook as he drew the blade down the center of his palm, making a shallow cut. Green blood oozed from the gash. "Warriors of different Houses seal their vows with blood." He handed me the blade. "Once made, they cannot be broken."

Slowly I made the same cut in my own palm, and we clasped our hands together.

"I entrust you with my Chosen, Duncan Reever."

"I will Choose her," I told him as I watched our blood

mingle and fall in red-and-green-streaked droplets to the linens on his berth. "And I will protect her with my life."

"My thanks." He closed his eyes, and slipped into unconsciousness.

"The Jorenians came for him that day," Reever told me as I opened my eyes. "I helped them smuggle him out of the FreeClinic and to their ship. I asked for a position on the crew so that I could be close to you."

"So that you could keep your promise to Kao," I said, feeling wretched. "You never told her."

"No. I never did."

How much of this man's life had Cherijo inadvertently ruined, all for that promise he made to her dying lover? "I understand."

"No, you do not," Reever said. "I did not follow you to Varallan to keep my oath. It was not merely to fulfill the vow I made to Kao Torin. I wished to be near you. You were the other half of me. I could feel it in the balance of everything when we were together. I wanted to be near you always. I knew that being near might be all we would ever have together, but I thought it would be enough."

"Do you believe that Cherijo loved you, Duncan?"

He nodded. "In her way. She loved medicine, and devoting herself to her calling. I did not mind. I only wanted to share part of her life."

"Well, I hope you have some happy memories of that love, for it is over." Before his eyes could grow cold, I wrapped myself around him. "My love cannot be a thing of convenience, to be indulged in when I am not busy. I want you too much for that.

Yes, I can love you, Duncan Reever, but you had better think on what that means. Nothing will come between us. Not my work, not the Hsktskt, not the Jorenians, nothing. I will love you with all that I am, and all that I will be. More than anything. More than my life."

"How can you feel that way?" He didn't believe me.

"You were not her first love, but you are mine, and I have chosen you." I smiled slowly. "Will it be enough for you?"

"Jarn," he said just before he kissed me, "that is more than I ever dreamed."

TWENTY

I spent the night with the man I loved, and for the first time since I had agreed to become his woman, we truly explored that love. We talked and we laughed and we gave each other pleasure. We shared memories and fears. We slept as if welded together. Not once in all those long hours did I feel guilt or shame for being with him when I could have been in Medical. I needed this time for us, to prove to my husband that he was the center of my life, and to prove to myself that I was his.

No more was I to be Cherijo's ghost.

I left Reever sleeping when I rose early the next morning to report for duty. As I walked alone to the lift outside our quarters, I felt a strange tingling sensation in my head.

"That would be my fault," Maggie said. *"I have to leave you now."*

I stopped and braced myself against one wall. *Why?*

"Duncan's memories of you two lovebirds and all I have stored won't fit in the one functioning implant you have left," she told me. *"One of us has to stop imprinting you, and I figure you need him right now more than you need me."*

I didn't like the red-haired woman, so I felt little regret at the thought of her disappearing. *Where will you go? Will you be contacting me again?*

"*I go to merge with what is left of the Jxin. We keep each other company in the void. By the time you need me again, Jarn, you'll know how to make the connection.*"

The tingling sensation disappeared, and after a moment I sighed and continued on to Medical.

ChoVa remained closeted in the lab, and Squilyp was busy performing rounds. I apologized to the Senior Healer for my absence, but did not bother to make excuses.

"I will relieve ChoVa once I have checked PyrsVar's vitals," I promised as I picked up the renegade Jorenian's chart. I looked over at the view panel into his isolation room, saw his form huddled under the berth linens, and frowned. "He has not yet risen this morning?"

"No, I told the nurses to keep him sedated." He looked around. "The night shift charge nurse didn't leave a report for me before she went off duty."

"Perhaps she left it in his room." I went back and unlocked the door. The room was a disordered mess, and I sighed as I reached to draw back the berth linens covering the outlaw's head—and uncovered the head of the unconscious, gagged charge nurse instead. "Squilyp," I called, dropping down to look under the berth. "Squilyp, PyrsVar has escaped."

The Senior Healer hopped over, took in the scene with a single glance, and went to the nearest console to signal the captain. Xonea replied with the news that the launch bay crew had been found gagged, bound, and drugged a few minutes ago, and that a launch was missing.

I scanned the nurse, who had been given a massive dose of sedative, and released her bonds before the ward nurses came to transfer her out of the isolation room. ChoVa had not yet emerged from the lab, so I went to tell her what had happened, and found the lab in worse condition than PyrsVar's room.

An infuser that had been used to administer a sedative for a large female Hsktskt lay on the deck next to ChoVa's empty seat. Subsequent signals to her quarters and the captain revealed that the female Hsktskt was no longer on the ship.

"He must have abducted her and taken her with him," I told Squilyp as we searched the lab.

He went to the analyzer that had been left running and pulled up the last of ChoVa's tests. "Jarn, come here."

I went to look at the data. Beneath the long list of tests on the bone dust and PyrsVar's biopsy tissue were the same results: *positive*.

"She found the cure." I checked the components of the compound that had been used for the test. "We have everything we need to synthesize a countermeasure. Enough for the entire population of Vtaga." I looked up at him. "Do you think she tested it on PyrsVar?"

"We cannot know. I will have the nurses begin processing," the Omorr said. "You and I have been ordered to report to command."

We left the staff busily producing the necessary

medicine and hurried to command for an emergency meeting with the captain and his officers.

"How much worse were PyrsVar's symptoms last night?" I asked Squilyp.

"He threatened to blow up the ship and everyone on it if we did not release him," the Omorr told me, and then lifted a hand. "I have already signaled engineering and environmental services. As far as we can tell, he did not have the opportunity or the means to plant any explosive device or sabotage the star drive or the power systems. I do not believe in his state that he could have done much damage. He was too unsteady."

"That may have changed." I could not believe ChoVa would wait to administer the compound. "If she tested him with the successful enzyme, and he reverted to what he was before being exposed to the bone dust . . ."

"Let us deal with facts," the Senior Healer suggested. "Of which we have few."

Reever met us at the command center. After he gave me a brief, warm embrace, he nodded toward the helm. "We have located the launch. PyrsVar left it in the desert. We think he may have taken ChoVa with him to his final destination."

Perhaps she had not given him the compound. "Why would he take her? And where?"

"ChoVa understands this epidemic as well as Jarn does," Reever said. "She is also the daughter of the ruling Akade. There was no one more valuable on this ship to him than her, except perhaps you."

We went in and briefed the captain and his officers with what we knew. They in turn filled in some of the gaps.

"Before he left the upper atmosphere, PyrsVar sent a signal to this location in the mountains," Salo said, pointing out one of the tallest peaks in the range being holoprojected over the conference table. "This is approximately three hours due north of the desert."

"SrrokVar's stronghold," I said. "That must be where he was taking her." I shuddered to think of my friend at the mercy of that madman. Would he expose her to more of the dust? "Have we informed the Akade of what has happened?"

"TssVar acknowledged our signal, but did not respond," Salo said. "The rioters are massing around the Palace. He believes his security grid will be overwhelmed sometime today, unless help from Tingal arrives."

"Will the Tingaleans arrive in time?" I asked the captain.

"We do not know," Xonea admitted. "The last signal they sent indicated they would send assistance, but with their usual reticence, they did not specify when, or how much."

"Then the responsibility rests on us." I looked at my husband. "We must go to the planet and find ChoVa, and do what we can to help TssVar until reinforcements arrive."

"We cannot fight an entire population of Hsktskt gone insane," Xonea said, very gently.

"I am not proposing that we do." I turned to Naln, the chief of engineering, who sat beside me. "I can synthesize a large amount of the enzyme that will end this epidemic, but it will be impossible to administer it in the traditional fashion. Is there some way we can put it into the water or food supply?"

"Not without great difficulty, and there is no guarantee all those infected would ingest it." The engineer considered my question. "There are atmospheric drones we use to test alien air quality and content. I may be able to modify them to fly low and release the substance in a mist over large masses." She grinned at me. "Every Hsktskt on the planet may not eat or drink, but they must all breathe."

The Adan were happy to have something to do, and armed themselves for battle as we prepared a rescue team to jaunt to the surface.

"There will be wounded to deal with," the Omorr said. "I will begin assembling medical teams to go in once the population is under control. Our first priority will be to assure that all medical facilities are open and fully functional."

Naln made a discovery with a trial run of the modified atmospheric drones that she reported to me at once.

"I know how this dust is being delivered to the inhabitants," she said over her relay to me. "Very small drones, not dissimilar to the ones I have made to disperse the countermeasure, are being sent into the populated areas in the midst of each night. They have been releasing tiny amounts of the dust into the mist-venting systems of every building during the time when most of the occupants are sleeping. They return to their point of origin immediately after, so they have not been discovered. We have the entire process captured on vid now."

"Can you tell from where the dust drones are originating?" I was almost afraid she might tell me the desert, but she gave me surface coordinates that matched those of SrrokVar's stronghold.

"The Hsktskt will need to do much to prevent future outbreaks once they have been dosed with the countermeasure," Naln warned me. "Given the rate of dust dispersal, by now every edifice in the city will be contaminated."

It seemed ironic that the Hsktskt had been living with and willingly breathing in the very thing that was driving them insane.

Reever did not wish me to go on the rescue mission, and spent some moments trying to persuade me to remain on the ship and wait for him.

I waited until he paused for breath, and then I kissed him in front of the captain and most of the officers on the ship. "Nothing comes between us. Not the Hsktskt, not Vtaga, not this mission. Wherever you walk, Husband, shall I follow."

There were some tense moments in the launch bay when Qonja and Hawk showed up to join the sojourn team. The Adan were clearly unhappy at being in the presence of the ClanSon they had just repudiated, but the ClanLeader made a point of showing willing if somewhat distant courtesy to the two men.

On the way down to the surface we reviewed the tentative plans we had made to approach SrrokVar's stronghold.

"I can fly reconnaissance over the structure

before we bring in the ship," Hawk suggested. "I am accustomed to heights and the low temperatures, and I am able to evade weapons fire more easily than the launch."

Reever nodded. "What we are interested in knowing is what manner of defenses the stronghold has. Jarn was not able to see much of the outside of the structure when PyrsVar took her there. Whatever is there, it will likely be well disguised."

"I do not think he will have much in the way of weaponry," I said. "The low temperature is his main defense against any Hsktskt, and he will not be expecting humanoids to attack to save ChoVa or the Hsktskt."

We saw columns of smoke rising from the city as we descended to cruise level and changed direction for the mountains. I stared at them, wondering if UgessVa and her household had gone with TssVar to the Palace.

"They are one of the strongest and most dominant of the Hsktskt lines," Reever murmured to me, folding his hand over mine. "If anyone survives this, it will be TssVar's blood."

Salo, who was piloting the launch, spoke over the audio com. "I have just received a message from the *Sunlace*. The Tingaleans have sent five battalions and most of their fleet, which have just arrived and are moving into orbit. They have brought cryoweapons with which to subdue the rioters."

"That should be effective," the Adan ClanLeader said. "Pilot, how long before they begin landing their forces?"

"The captain said the first troop shuttles have already launched for the surface," Salo answered.

"This madman may wish to send out his drones to dose the Tingaleans with this fear dust," the Adan said. "Hawk, while you are scouting, see if you can determine from where they are being launched. It should be our first target when we strike."

Salo flew over the stronghold, using a neighboring mountain as cover while he put the launch into a hover and opened the hull access doors to permit Hawk to fly out into the icy winds.

"Come back to me," Qonja said, clasping his lover's hands in his briefly.

"I will, *evlanar*." With a grin Hawk jumped out of the launch and spread his wings, sailing up and away from us.

I had observed most of the Adan looking away from the show of affection between the two men, and clamped down on a surge of anger. Now was not the time to address the ridiculous prejudice of the Jorenians. I would attend to it once this epidemic was over and we had saved the Hsktskt from mass suicide and murder.

Salo reversed the engines and landed on an outcropping, and the men began to prepare their supply packs, body armor, and weapons. Reever made me wear one of the lightweight vests designed to protect the vital organs of the chest, and placed a too-large battle helmet on my head.

"I cannot see." I pushed up the edge of the helmet, which had sunk down over my eyes. "I might as well blunder into a weapon."

"You will stay behind me," Reever said. "I will be your body shield."

"I make a better shield than you do," I reminded him.

"I am quicker and more agile." He adjusted the fit of the helmet. "Indulge me on this."

Hawk returned a short time later, his immense brown wings filled with snow, which he shook off before reentering the launch.

"I have located SrrokVar's drone launchers, and what I think is the main staging area. A few pulse grenades should destroy both." He glanced at me. "Healer, I saw no signs of life, but the stronghold is heavily barricaded and all of the viewers blacked out. This SrrokVar does not intend to come out, or let anyone so much as look inside."

"Did you see how we can best enter the structure?" the Adan asked him.

Hawk nodded, and went to the console to pull up a schematic of the mountain and the stronghold. "There are air and water conduits here and here." He pointed to the spots at the very top of the structure. "Several vent panels at the base also looked promising, but they are more likely to be mined, or otherwise fortified and defended."

"We will create two diversions," the Adan decided. "One by firing into the snow on the ridge above the structure, which should fall and knock out any surveillance drones SrrokVar is employing to monitor his perimeter on the main entry level. The second will be smoke charges, fired into the flanking vents here. If they are mined, we will know." He turned to my husband. "You and your team will go down through the air conduit. Send a probe first to ensure there are no traps waiting for you."

"Salo, drop us there," Reever said, pointing to a ledge just above the air conduits. "We will wait until we hear the first charge go off below, and then we will move in." To the Adan, he said, "Maintain contact beacons so that we know where you are."

The launch made a wide sweep around the mountain before coming up from behind the stronghold. Salo hovered above the wide ledge only long enough for us to jump down to it before taking off. Hawk also disembarked, but he did not stay on the ground. His task was to observe from above and report to Salo what progress we made.

The outside air was so cold that it hurt to breathe. I covered my face with my thermal mask and followed Reever to the edge to look below. The air conduits were only two feet down, close enough to lean over and touch.

"Launch the probe," Reever told Qonja, who switched on the small surveillance unit and dropped it over the side. It transmitted an image signal as it descended, showing the conduit open and clear of devices. Nothing emerged to prevent or impede its progress.

"It should not be so simple," I murmured to Qonja and my husband as we watched the drone travel the length of the passage. "Why would he go to so much trouble to conceal the stronghold and yet leave this access unguarded? It is as if he wishes us to use these conduits."

"I agree. It is probably a trap," Reever said as

soon as the drone emerged. "We are taking the water conduit."

"How do you know this?" Qonja asked.

"I know the Hsktskt. No centuron would swim through water when he could climb through an air duct, and SrrokVar knows this as well. As Jarn said, he is not expecting humanoids." He took breathers out of a supply pack and handed them to us. "Be prepared, for the water will likely be cold."

Even with the breathers and our heavy garments, the plunge into the frigid water conduit took my breath away. Reever went first, with Qonja and me following. Tethers attached to our belts kept us from being separated once inside.

The conduit and gravity made our swim a rapid one, and once we were down into the structure the conduit separated into three horizontal supply pipes. Reever took the smallest one, which led out to spill into a wide, deep collection unit. Reever dove down into it, and then swam to the side and gestured for us to do the same. We were all soaked and shivering as we climbed out of the reservoir and stood in what appeared to be a central equipment room.

Reever took off his breather and pointed to a secured door. "That one," he told Qonja, who set a small decoder unit on the locking mechanism and released the door. My husband drew his blade and pistol as he looked around the corner before moving through.

Qonja offered me a pistol, but I showed him my Iisleg blades. "I did not think you would bring them," he said to me as we followed Reever into a dark corridor.

"I hope I do not have to use them," I said, wincing as I heard a muffled but massive explosion detonate somewhere outside. "I think the Adan have found SrrokVar's primary fortifications."

"You are in error," someone said. Out of the shadows emerged a pleasant-looking service drone armed with two rifles and a transmitter. "SrrokVar, I have encountered three intruders in the service quadrant. Two Terrans and a Jorenian."

Reever shot the drone's control case, which caused it to explode. I covered my face with my arms to protect it from the sparks and shrapnel, so I did not see from where the other drones that surrounded us came.

"Too many," Qonja said as Reever dodged out of sight and one of the drones sped after him.

"You will lower your weapons," another drone said. When Qonja and I did so, it turned and indicated a hall to the left. "This way."

Our dripping garments left a wide, wet trail behind us, one I hoped would not dry before Reever found it. Qonja and I were led into SrrokVar's lab from a back access panel, and for a moment the brightness of the lights blinded us.

My eyes adjusted, and I saw ChoVa, bound to a punishment post, her bare back scored with several lash marks. She sagged, apparently unconscious, from the manacles around her wrists. Beside her stood PyrsVar, in chains that had been passed through a wide alloy ring bolted to the floor.

SrrokVar had placed him close enough to watch ChoVa being whipped, but not to stop it.

"Turn up the emitters," SrrokVar said as he walked toward us. "Some of our guests have arrived."

TWENTY-ONE

"There will do," SrrokVar told the drone.

I had been dragged over to the punishment post, stripped of my coat and tunic, and hung by my wrists next to ChoVa. Qonja had resisted briefly, and had been knocked unconscious by a bioelectric charge emitted by one of the service drones. He had been placed on a table by a rack of surgical instruments and strapped down.

Another explosion from outside the stronghold distracted SrrokVar. "Excuse me. I believe I must start executing the other half of your pathetic attack team." He wandered off with two drones trailing after him.

I turned my head to see PyrsVar staring with undisguised hatred at SrrokVar's back. "Did ChoVa give you the countermeasure?" I asked him. I had to know if he was sane enough to help us.

"She did." He looked at her, and then me. "As soon as I came to my senses, I knocked her out and took her from the ship."

I tested the fit of the manacles, which were strong and uncomfortably tight. "Why?"

"I needed her help to stop my sire, and she would

not have agreed to come with me on her own." He nodded toward Qonja. "Why do they come here?"

"To rescue you, and save the people." The unnatural position of my arms made them ache, and shifting my weight only created more strain on my joints. "PyrsVar, if you had asked, we would have helped you. Next time, don't assume we wouldn't."

He nodded. "Can you help me now?"

"Now he asks." I sighed. "The Adan will be here soon, as will Reever. We only have to be patient and try to keep your sire from killing us before they breach the stronghold." More explosions rocked the structure, and I heard the ominous sound of stone cracking and rumbling. "Or send it tumbling down the side of the mountain."

The sound of our voices made ChoVa stir, and her eyelids lifted to reveal bloodshot eyes. "Jarn." She groaned before she straightened, supporting her weight with her feet. "Someone was beating me."

"It is my fault," PyrsVar said to her. "I should not have brought you back to Vtaga. I should have left you in safety with the warm-bloods."

The hissing sound that escaped her sounded more exasperated than angry. "You are warm-blooded too, outlaw. And, I think, just as impulsive as they." She tested the chains binding her to the post. "This is not favorable." She saw Qonja on the exam table. "Did anyone escape the guard drones?"

I nodded. "My husband. He will be here soon."

SrrokVar returned carrying a number of cases and equipment, which he placed on the floor in front of us. "I think I shall record this punishment for posterity. It may be the only time in history that a humanoid and a Hsktskt are beaten to death simultaneously." He removed a large, ugly-looking blade with a serrated edge. "I wonder how long you both would live without your limbs attached."

"Let them go, sire," PyrsVar said in a surprisingly meek voice. "I am the one who has betrayed you to your enemies, not them. It is I who deserve your punishment."

"You see what happens when my kind spends too much time around the warm-blooded? They develop a conscience. No, the blade will not do." SrrokVar shook his head and extracted a familiar-looking device from one of the cases and held it out for me to see. "Do you remember your fondness for being burned, Dr. Grey Veil?"

"I do," I said, feeling my skin crawl as a memory of Catopsa returned to me. "It almost drove me out of my mind."

"Yes, well, that is rather the point of my not killing you." His artificial mouth turned down at the corners. "So sad, really. I am as I am, and the rest of my people are well on their way to losing their minds. Why should you be spared your fair share of the horror?"

"I did nothing to deserve it."

"Neither did I, my dear. I was only doing my work when you inflicted this misery upon me." He came close to me. "Despite the delights of your enhanced cerebral capabilities, I never regarded your mind as particularly special, you know. You are quite pedestrian in your patterns of emotion over logic, but it does make you much more amusing to torture." He switched on the instrument, the branding plates of which began to turn dark red, and then orange as they heated.

"If you touch her with that, Doctor," I heard my husband say from somewhere above us, "I will fire at your head."

"You do that, Terran." SrrokVar tested the surface of the branding instrument. "My cranial case is specially reinforced to protect my brain. You'd need a small bomb to sever my spinal cord—it has also been reinforced and shielded—and to separate the head unit from the rest of me."

Reever took careful aim. "Your cardiac organ is not shielded. Assuming you have one."

"That is where you are wrong, HalaVar. While I was repairing the wreck your wife made of my head, I also had my torso and most of my organs replaced. There was some immediacy involved, as well. Cryostasis, you see, does such terrible damage to the Hsktskt physiology."

"No Hsktskt would lower himself to become a reconstruct," ChoVa said. "Except you."

"That is where you are correct, Doctor. A reconstruct is a drone with the brain of a living thing—completely unacceptable for my purposes. The body I took is all natural flesh." He dropped his cloak to display a powerful physique. "Perhaps you recognize the scale pattern, PyrsVar." He pulled open the tunic he wore to bare his chest. "He was your biological parent before I had him killed and his head removed."

PyrsVar screamed his rage, his Jorenian claws fully extended as he fought the chains.

"Move away from the women," Reever called, "or I will shoot you until you fall."

"Lights." The lab was plunged into darkness, with only a glow of orange-white coming from the glowing brand plate SrrokVar held. "There, now if you shoot you'll only hit one of the women." SrrokVar peered down at me. "Where shall I start, Doctor? Where did that sadistic guard on Catopsa repeatedly burn an identification brand on you? Down the length of the forearm, wasn't it?"

Something flew into the lab—Hawk, I realized a moment later—and between me and SrrokVar. The madman staggered back as the winged Terran fired at his face. Through the darkness I saw Reever run over to a control panel and begin opening the access doors.

"Kill the Terran," SrrokVar shouted.

SrrokVar's drones tried to shoot Hawk, but the winged Terran flew out through one of the doors as quickly as he had entered the lab. The lights began to come back on one by one.

"I don't need emitters," SrrokVar said as he lumbered toward me and ChoVa. Hawk's face shot had struck the madman's artificial features, which were melting and sliding away from his braincase. "I can burn her without seeing her."

Reever reached me before the madman did, and tried to release the manacles holding me and ChoVa to the post.

"Behind you," ChoVa said.

I saw SrrokVar looming behind my husband even as the Adan and PyrsVar's outlaws poured into the lab through the doors he had opened. "Duncan."

"I love you." He turned and lunged at SrrokVar, knocking him over.

The two rolled across the floor of the lab as they wrestled with the branding instrument between them. SrrokVar was almost successful in driving it into Reever's face, but then my husband flipped to one side and drove his daggers into the Hsktskt's chest.

I heard chains snap, and PyrsVar rushed over to drag SrrokVar off Reever. What my husband had started he finished with his claws, eviscerating the madman.

Reever struggled to his feet and turned to look at me. "PyrsVar, help me free the women and then—" He stopped, and a strange look passed over his face before he dropped to his knees. Blood blossomed on the front of his tunic. Behind him stood one of SrrokVar's service drones. In his back was Srrok-Var's serrated sword.

"Kill the Terran," the drone repeated SrrokVar's command as it backed away. "Kill the Terran."

One of the Adan shot it, and someone released me from the chains. I rushed over to my husband, who remained upright despite the sword that had been driven through his body.

"Duncan." I saw the position of the blade. "Hawk, Qonja, help us." I lowered my voice. "I can operate," I assured him. "SrrokVar has everything I need here. I will repair the damage and you will be fine."

"Not this time, Wife." He touched my face with a bloodied hand. "You saved me when I needed to be saved. Remember that, beloved."

"No." I felt the life spilling from him. "I need you to live. I need you with me. Duncan."

"I will always be with you," he promised, and then he rested against me, his cheek on my shoulder. *Here is all that I am, Jarn. All that I was, and all that I know. Remember me until we are together again.*

His memories poured into me.

As Hawk and the others helped me carry him to a table, the link wavered and dwindled. I did not bother to strip out of my garments as I seized a laboratory shroud large enough for six of me and draped myself as best I could.

"Qonja, ChoVa, assist me," I said as I quickly checked the surgical instruments SrrokVar had prepared. They could repair as much damage as they could inflict. He also had equipment designed to keep badly wounded beings alive for as long as possible. "See if there is something I can use to establish a sterile field. ClanLeader Adan, signal the Torin and tell them to send Squilyp down here. I will need him to bring everything necessary for a Terran in critical care post-op. Do it now."

"We should move him to the ship, Jarn," ChoVa said as she limped over to my side.

"No time." As Reever's respiration began to falter, I dragged over an oxygen rig. "Qonja, we will intubate him now. ChoVa, if you can remain on your feet, scrub."

I operated for seventeen hours to repair Duncan Reever's injuries. As soon as we opened his torso I saw that the sword had pierced both his liver and heart, and the damage inflicted by the jagged blade had virtually destroyed both organs. In ordinary circumstances, I would have attempted a double transplant, but there were no Terran organs to be had on Vtaga or the Jorenians' ship. It would take many weeks to grow new, bioartificial replicants from Reever's own cells.

With ChoVa's help, I repaired what I could, and took him off the heart-lung machines long enough to ascertain that his heart would not beat on its own. Then I restored life support and spoke to the Omorr, who had arrived on-planet halfway through the operation and had used the time to set up an intensive-care area in the least-damaged section of SrrokVar's facility.

"How long to retrieve replacement Terran organs?" I asked him as we watched the machines keeping my husband alive clean and pump his blood. My body drooped with exhaustion and vibrated with nerves. I felt like a frayed cord, about to snap.

Squilyp adjusted the drip on Reever's intravenous line. "Months. Terra keeps live donor organs quarantined on their homeworld, and refuses to have them transplanted into any being unless they prove their genetic purity. Jarn." He turned me toward him so that I would look into his face. "Duncan will not last more than a week on life support. He is too badly injured to place in stasis."

I glanced down at the Hsktskt shroud I had wound around myself. Reever's blood stained it here and there. "I know."

"You cannot save him."

I refused to admit defeat. There had to be a way;

I only had to think it through. "This is not the first time I operated on my husband. He was stabbed on Terra." Ruthlessly I dragged up the memories of that time. "Cherijo's sire repaired his kidney by impregnating the damaged one with special cells. Hypercells. They were programmed to regenerate the organ."

The Omorr's gildrells went stiff. "You remember that."

"I have all of Duncan's memories of it." Which were less technical than I cared for. "You and I discussed a method of duplicating the chameleon cells."

"It was only a discussion. You understood your father's theory, and had ideas on how to replicate the equipment and hypercells. We had planned to conduct research and tests on them after we finished our work on Oenrall," Squilyp said. "The League took you shortly after that, during the Jado Massacre."

I, too, understood the theory, but I did not have memories of Cherijo's findings, or what she had observed during her sire's original surgery. "There was nothing in Cherijo's journals. Did I write anything in Duncan's chart about it?"

The Omorr shook his head.

"I will take a sample of his kidney tissue," I said, turning back to the berth. "We will begin from there."

"You told me that your father wished to design the chameleon cells to degrade over time, as a type of self-building scaffolding that could be replaced by natural organ cells. Reever's last physical showed only normal kidney tissue," Squilyp said. "They are no longer present in his body."

I had to remember. "Leave me alone with him."

The Omorr hesitated, and then nodded and hopped away.

I sat down and took my husband's hand in mine, careful not to dislodge any of the lines and tubes keeping him alive. I did not weep, nor did I feel sorrow. Instead I concentrated on the memories Reever had poured into me, going over each one moment by moment.

For days I worked. I did not sleep or eat unless coerced. And I failed, time and again, to find a way to save Duncan Reever's life.

All I had to console myself were his memories.

She will wake soon, and return to her duty. She will think of Kao with sadness and grief, but she has already made many new friends among this crew. The Jorenians have adopted her, and very shortly she will be made a citizen of Joren. They will do everything they can to protect her, and if anyone attempts to harm her, they will hunt them down and kill them slowly.

If I do not get there first.

Cherijo is young, and has a long life ahead of her. I know she will devote herself to healing the sick and the injured, and she will fight her father and the League for her freedom.

She may never care for me, but that does not matter. I have made my Choice. For as long as I live, I will stay with her. I will watch over her, and I will protect her. If necessary, I will die for her.

I do this not for balance, nor for the blood vow I made

to Kao Torin. I do this because I discovered I do have emotions—or at least, one emotion.

I love her.

"You don't have to die for me," I whispered.

The Hanar's Palace had not been destroyed by the plague riots, but like much of Vtaga it bore new scars. I would not have come here, would not have risked moving Reever, but the damage to SrrokVar's stronghold had resulted in buckling walls and ceilings, making it unsafe to occupy. The Akade had sent a glidecraft used for medical rescues and transport, and with it Squilyp, ChoVa, and I were able to transfer my husband without disrupting life support.

Reever could not live without the machines. Soon even they would not prevent his death.

The private chambers we had been assigned still smelled of smoke, and impact marks left by displacer rounds fired from below pocked most of the view panels. As ugly as the confrontation with SrrokVar had been, I felt glad I had been spared witnessing the fighting in the city. I had seen enough of war, and violence, and men dying for no sane reason.

"Jarn." Alunthri, who had come down from the ship with Squilyp, brought in a tray with steaming servers. "I thought you might like to have some tea before the ceremony begins."

The Chakacat, as I had learned over the past week, had a soothing way about it that seemed to intensify under crisis. It had practically made itself my servant, gently bullying me into eating and resting while the nurses attended Reever.

I did not want the tea, but I could not remember when last I ate or drank, so I went to accept it. "You should go back to the ship, Alunthri. There is not much more to do here." Except end my husband's life for good.

"Once I needed sanctuary, and Cherijo provided it for me. She spoke for me, and when I was denied the dignity of sentient rights, pretended to be my owner so that I could have a semblance of freedom." Its bullet-shaped head titled forward. "I am only returning that care and love."

"Mama." Marel came to me and hugged my legs as she had once done with Reever. She looked up at me. "Can't you make Daddy wake up now?"

Alunthri's eyes glittered, perhaps with tears, before it silently retreated, leaving me alone with my child.

My husband's impending death had shaken everyone, but over the last two days the sharp despair and self-hatred I felt over being unable to save him had begun to ease. I was almost ready to let him go. He had given me his memories of me, as well as the rest of his life, and in them I could be with him whenever I wished.

Marel refused to believe her father was dying. She ignored the machines performing his life functions for him, and spoke to him as if he were only ill. No matter how carefully I explained the matter to her, she still insisted he was only sleeping.

"He can't wake up, baby." I picked up Marel and held her close before turning back to the view panel overlooking the city. "Look at all the people. They came here to see Hanar TssVar honor your Daddy."

Hsktskt from all over Vtaga had traveled to the capital, and were massing in the streets beneath the Hanar's Palace. Much of the city still lay in ruins after the plague riots, and it would take some time for the inhabitants to rebuild, but calm prevailed. ChoVa's enzyme had neutralized the bone dust, and once the city's structures were fully decontaminated, the citizens could return to living in them and begin the process of recovery.

"Healer."

I turned to see the Hanar and his son standing behind us. "Is it time?" TssVar nodded, and I put down Marel and drew on her cloak before shrugging into my own outer robe. I looked through the open doorway to the adjoining chamber, where two nurses kept watch over Reever. Seeing a Jorenian and a Hsktskt no longer seemed strange, but I could not look upon my husband's inert form for long. It tore at me.

"Healer."

I pulled my thoughts into order and turned to the Hanar. CaurVar took Marel by the hand, while TssVar offered me his arm in Terran fashion. "Thank you."

We went out to the reception area, where the Hanar's guards stood waiting to escort us to the ceremony.

"Your daughter and my son have formed a close friendship," the Hanar said as we watched them walk ahead of us. "I could not have imagined such a thing even a year ago, but now it seems promising."

"They are the first generation who will grow up

in this time of peace," I said. "They will need that friendship. We all will."

"I would like nothing more than for you and Marel to make Vtaga your home, if you wish to change your mind," he reminded me.

The Hsktskt offer of sanctuary had startled and touched me, for I had not expected it. But as much as I cared for TssVar and his people, Marel and I needed to make our own place. Then, too, I did not know where or with whom that would be.

I did not wish to face choosing a new direction for my life any more than I wanted to turn off Duncan's life support. The Jorenians had already expressed their wish for me to return with them to their homeworld, and take up my responsibilities as a member of the Jorenian Ruling Council. Maggie's story about the threat of the black crystal, and the promise I had made to her, still haunted me. SrrokVar was not the only person who had wished revenge on me, or desired the secrets of immortality.

My daughter and I would always be targets.

Xonea had suggested gathering ships and crews from Joren to mount an expedition to find the surviving members of the Odnallak race, who might be persuaded to help us investigate the spread of the black crystal through our galaxy. I could not discuss it at the time, or even think about it for too long. It seemed obscene to make plans that would only initiate after the man I loved died.

Xonea and most of the crew from the *Sunlace* joined us out in the corridor, where a detachment of Jorenian warriors joined ranks with the Hsktskt guards.

The captain came to stand beside me. "You have not slept, have you?"

I shook my head. "Has there been any word from Kevarzangia Two?" I had asked Xonea to contact Cherijo's friends there and request their assistance in finding replacement organs for Reever.

"Dr. Mayer signaled just before we came down to the planet. He has contacted every medical facility with transplant capabilities within one hundred light-years of Vtaga. No one can provide a tissue match." He rested his six-fingered hand on my shoulder. "I think you must release him to the embrace of the stars."

Salo and Darea had come to the planet to pay their respects, like most of the crew, and had told me about the Jorenian funerary custom of sending the body of the deceased into space where it would be pulled into a star's corona; a strong symbolic expression of their belief that the dead embraced the stars. But as much as I respect my adopted people's beautiful customs, I thought of the salvagers SrrokVar had told me of, and their practice of body-snatching in space, and knew I would not be abandoning Reever to the whim of the stars. I also knew that my husband preferred the Hsktskt tradition. I knew because I knew everything about Duncan now.

The honor guard escorted us out to the ceremonial platform that had been constructed above the streets, where we stood beside an enormous unlit pyre, upon which rested the draped body of the former Hanar.

PyrsVar came to stand with me and Xonea. The

Hanar had exonerated him of his crimes against the people, but he still looked a little lost.

"We gather here to pay tribute to those who were taken from us," TssVar said, his voice ringing out in the absolute stillness as he addressed the people. "No one on Vtaga has been left untouched by the madness, not even those who came to help us overcome it. In the Palace, the Terran male known as HalaVar lies dying. HalaVar entered my life by saving it. His blood name, Duncan Reever, will be added to our lines, and his story will be told, so that we never forget what he, his mate, and those who came with them have sacrificed for us." He looked out over the mass of silent citizens. "As your chosen Hanar, I will work to show Reever and his people that the Faction can be the sort of allies that they have been to us."

Many in the crowd were not Hsktskt. There were several humanoids; the slaves whom TssVar had freed in the aftermath of the plague. Here and there I saw Tingalean peacekeeping troops, who had landed and controlled the rioters while we had gone to rescue ChoVa and PyrsVar from SrrokVar's stronghold. On the very fringe of the crowd stood the desert outlaws who had helped the Adan at the stronghold. For their efforts, they had been pardoned and invited to rejoin Hsktskt society.

"We honor the Hanar before me," TssVar said, lighting a torch from the flames of an immense brazier. "As we honor all those who have gone to the life after, or who will soon depart."

Marel suddenly darted around me and ran into the Palace. I gave the Hanar an apologetic look before I hurried after her. I should have known that the Hanar's funeral would prove too much for her.

I found my daughter in the chamber with her father. She had climbed onto his berth and was clutching his hand between hers. The two attending nurses hovered close by but did not interfere. I gestured for them to leave us, and waited until they withdrew before I spoke to the child Duncan had given me.

I approached the berth, hating myself more than at any other moment since my husband had been injured. "Marel."

"Daddy won't die," she said. "He promised me he wouldn't leave me anymore." She leaned in over her father's face. "Wake up now, Daddy. Mama doesn't know you're just sleeping. Please wake up."

"He can't, Marel," I said, putting my arms around her. "He would come back to us if he could, but his body is too badly injured."

Her eyes turned from green to gray as she glared at me. "You fixed him. CaurVar said you did. At the bad man's place. You operated on Daddy."

"I did." I felt the crushing weight of my failure. "I have tried everything I know to repair his wounds, but it is not enough. I can't heal him."

"You don't have to, Mama." My daughter reached down and jerked one of the tubes out of her father's chest before I could stop her. "He's not going to die anymore." She struggled wildly as I lifted her away. "Daddy, please, you have to wake up *now*."

Marel managed to squirm out of my hold and ran away from me to the other side of Duncan's berth. She dislodged one of the power supply units and the heart-lung machine keeping my husband alive ceased operating.

I shouted for the nurses as I went to enable the backup power system, leaning over Duncan to reach the berth console. That was when I heard a choking sound, and looked down.

"Duncan?" I whispered.

A long-fingered, scarred hand reached up and touched my wet cheek before it fell back.

"Duncan."

My hands shook as I removed his breathing tube, and clenched as he took a ragged, voluntary breath. By then the nurses were beside me. I pressed my fingers to his throat, and felt a slow, sluggish pulse beat where none should have been. "Dævena yepa. It cannot be."

Duncan's eyelids open to slits, and his lips moved. I bent down to hear the faintest whisper of my name before the crowds in the street below began shouting.

"I need transport," I said, ripping off my funeral robe and handing it to one of the nurses. "Where is ChoVa?"

The female Hsktskt stood behind us. "I've already signaled for medevac." She nodded toward a scout ship docking just outside the chamber balcony. "Surgery is standing by."

Marel climbed onto the berth and cuddled next to her father. "I told you, Mama," she said, smiling at me. "He was just asleep."

At the medical facility, which seemed empty now that all of its dust-crazed patients had been released, ChoVa, Squilyp, and I placed my husband in a critical-care unit and examined him for the next two hours. Duncan came in and out of consciousness, and only spoke a few words, but they were coherent.

"His vitals are very low," ChoVa said after we had finished a complete imaging scan of Duncan's torso, "but the damaged organs appear to be functioning as normal. I think he will live."

Squilyp turned to me. "What did you do to him?"

"Nothing." I shook my head, completely bewildered.

ChoVa transferred the results of our scans onto the screens at the nurses' station. The three of us left my husband with his Jorenian and Hsktskt nurses to view the results.

"The sword cut his liver and heart in two," I said as I pulled up the thoracic scan. "My surgical repairs were not enough to enable them to function as they are now. How can this be happening?"

"Your repairs have vanished." ChoVa stepped forward and pointed to the areas where I had operated. "There is no scar tissue present in either organ. No lascalpel marks. Nothing."

I stared at the scans until I thought my eyes would go blind. "I scanned him myself. He was . . ." Duncan's memories of being stabbed, and the surgery I and my father performed on him, came back to me. "The chameleon hypercells Joseph Grey Veil put inside Reever. They have to be responsible for this."

"They did repair the kidney damage, but they degraded quickly and disappeared more than a year ago." Squilyp retrieved the hematology report and results from the tissue scans. "The test results show abnormal cells permeating the heart and liver, the same way the hypercells were present in his kidney when you returned from Terra. Which is unlikely, if not impossible."

"They must have been dormant somewhere in his body," I murmured, glancing back at the critical-care unit. "Perhaps the damage to the organs triggered them." I recalled something Cherijo had once said to Reever about her ability to heal. "Or they have altered his immune system to be like mine."

"I do not understand," ChoVa said. "What is this chameleon? How can cells that have died show up in a patient's body again? An immune system that repairs organ damage this severe?"

Squilyp began telling her about his observations of the hypercells in my husband's kidney, but I slipped away and went back to the critical-care berth.

Reever opened his eyes while I scanned him again, just to be sure nothing was failing. "You look beautiful, beloved."

"So do you, Husband." The internal damage from the sword had vanished, and I detected no residual brain damage. "How do you feel?"

"Disoriented. I couldn't see you, but I could feel some things. I heard your voice, and Marel's." His gaze never left my face. "Is she all right?"

"She will be now." I threw aside the scanner and took his hand in mine. "You've ruined the Jorenians' party, you know. As well as the Hanar's."

"Have I?"

"There were going to be ten thousand people here to watch your funeral pyre burn tomorrow. Then we were to go to the ship and celebrate in some Jorenian fashion." I smiled through my tears. "We'll have to tell everyone to go home now."

He smiled a little. "Send my regrets."